A Beggar's Art

A Beggar's Art

SCRIPTING MODERNITY IN JAPANESE DRAMA, 1900–1930

M. Cody Poulton

UNIVERSITY *of*
HAWAI'I PRESS

HONOLULU

15 14 13 12 11 10   6 5 4 3 2 1

Library of Congress Cataloging-in-Publication Data
Poulton, M. Cody.
A beggar's art : scripting modernity in Japanese drama, 1900–1930 / M. Cody Poulton.
p. cm.
Includes bibliographical references and index.
ISBN: 978-0-8248-3341-1 (hardcover : alk. paper)
ISBN: 978-0-8248-3452-4 (pbk. : alk. paper)
1. Japanese drama—20th century—History and criticism.   2. One-act plays, Japanese—
Translations into English.   I. Title.   II. Title: Scripting modernity in Japanese drama, 1900–1930.
PL739.6P68 2010
895.6'2409—dc22

                                                              2009042765

Designed by Julie Matsuo-Chun
Printed by The Maple-Vail Book Manufacturing Group

Contents

Preface

Forget *kabuki*. Ignore tradition. Move, don't dance! Talk, don't sing!

—OSANAI KAORU, *admonishing the actors during*
rehearsals for Tsubouchi Shōyō's En the Ascetic

For a couple of decades in the early twentieth century, straddling the Taishō era (1912–1926), drama enjoyed something of a heyday in Japanese literature. Almost every writer of the day at least dabbled in this form, and many—including Tanizaki Jun'ichirō, Yamamoto Yūzō, Kikuchi Kan, Kume Masao, Arishima Takeo, Mushanokōji Saneatsu, Nogami Yaeko, and Ueda (Enchi) Fumiko, to name just a few—established themselves as playwrights before or while still settling into fiction as their dominant medium of expression. Some, like Yoshii Isamu and Kinoshita Mokutarō, were poets who caught the drama bug. Many more—men and women like Suzuki Senzaburō, Okada Yachiyo, Hasegawa Shigure, Kubota Mantarō, Kishida Kunio, and Akita Ujaku—devoted themselves almost exclusively to writing for the stage. One of the first scholars to write a major study of modern drama in Japan, Ōyama Isao, lists some eighty professional playwrights active in Japan between about 1900 and 1940; the volume of work that they produced is immense.[1] Some of the earliest modern Japanese literature to be translated into European languages was of drama by Shōyō, Tanizaki, Yamamoto, Mushanokōji, Kikuchi, and Kishida (among others). Kōri Torahiko even wrote drama in English, and at least one of his plays, *The Death of Yoritomo*, was performed on the London stage.

Many of these writers, particularly those who were almost exclusively playwrights, are practically forgotten today, and the ones we remember are often remembered for other things. In fact, drama is a subject that has been given remarkably short shrift in Japanese literary studies over the past century or so.

Tsubouchi Shōyō's *Essence of the Novel* (*Shōsetsu shinzui*, 1887), for example, has amassed a significant body of criticism in English, to say nothing of Japanese, but this work was really a footnote to a life devoted to theatre and drama, and few since Shōyō's death in 1935 have bothered to study the playwright's works in any great detail.[2] The only prewar Japanese playwright whose work is still read, discussed, and performed with any regularity is Kishida Kunio, and his reputation has been tarnished in Japan by his collaboration with the militarists in the early 1940s. By the 1930s, something happened to drama and theatre in Japan, such that the so-called "age of Taishō drama" seemed in retrospect like a flash in the pan. True, many of the plays (especially the translations available from the 1920s and early '30s) are rather dated now. But a major chapter in the study of modern Japanese literature and theatre would be missing if we neglected these works, and, in fact, there are some fascinating gems still to be found there. While the rise of the so-called New Theatre (*shingeki*) movement in Japan in the early twentieth century has been fairly well documented, considerably less attention has been focused on the role that drama played in the modernization of Japanese literature and theatre during this time.[3]

Japan has one of the greatest theatre traditions in the world, and drama has played no small part in this. The country has produced unique forms like *nō*, the puppet theatre, and *kabuki;* the latter two in particular played a crucial role in the rise of early modern Japanese culture. It would be no exaggeration to say that during the Edo era, *kabuki* was the dominant form of cultural expression for the Japanese. The theatre spawned a huge industry of related artistic media, including *ukiyoe* (pictures of the floating world), fan magazines, and illustrated playbooks. Fans vied to imitate their favorite actors in such amateur theatricals as *chaban kyōgen*. References to popular *kabuki* actors and plays were also used as marketing ploys to sell new stories and commercial products. Family feuds; hidden, mistaken, and revealed identities; the quest for a fetish, like a family sword or scroll (a device called a "weenie" by early silent movie actress Pearl White and a "McGuffin" by Alfred Hitchcock); true crimes like extortion, murder, larceny, adultery, double suicides, and vendettas—all were stock plot devices that were first exploited in the puppet and *kabuki* theatres. These "theatrical" devices found their way not only into Edo pulp fiction but also into such storytelling arts as *kōshaku* and *rakugo*.[4] The enormous casts and convoluted plots in, say, Kyokutei Bakin (1767–1848) or *kabuki* history plays (*jidaimono*) demonstrate not only a love of the performative, but also a veritable narratomania prevalent in Edo culture, a tendency that on stage is necessarily translated into spectacular physical action: theatre is plot made flesh.

Playwrights like Chikamatsu Monzaemon and Kawatake Mokuami made a significant contribution to the creation of this popular culture, but for centuries drama had remained essentially a pretext for performance, and it is not until the introduction of Western dramatic theory in the nineteenth century that the Japanese themselves began to pay much attention to drama as a literary genre.

By the first decade of the twentieth century, the staging of Ibsen, Gorki, Chekhov, and Shakespeare by *shingeki* theatre companies like Osanai Kaoru's Free Theatre and Tsubouchi Shōyō's Literary Society ignited an interest in literary circles in the possibilities of drama both as a literary form and as a way of disseminating new ideas. But events took place in Japanese literary and theatre circles earlier in the Meiji era (1868–1912) that paved the way to what was called the "age of Taishō drama." The first chapter of this study traces the emerging recognition of drama as a literary genre in the context of attempts to reform *kabuki* and make it a performing art that could address the challenges of the modern world. Theatre, however, had to undergo a revolution before it could make a place for modern drama in Japan. From the Taishō era onward, efforts to accommodate the new dramaturgy to traditional stagecraft were increasingly abandoned. Osanai's injunctions to his actors on opening night for *En the Ascetic* at the Tsukiji Little Theatre (Tsukiji Shōgekijō) in 1926 to "forget tradition" signaled the rejection of the native and a virtually wholesale acceptance of what was foreign. And so during the Taishō era, we see drama's rise but also its demise in Japan, at a point when it had just begun to find itself in the works of dramatists like Kishida Kunio and Kubota Mantarō. I use the word "demise" guardedly because excellent work has continued to be produced well into the present, by writers like Abe Kōbō and Mishima Yukio, not to mention others who have been above all playwrights, like Betsuyaku Minoru. What has fallen, rather, is the estimation of drama as an art form among many in both the theatre and literary worlds in Japan.

A number of reasons can be offered for this decline. First, as Kishida Kunio himself admitted, drama is "a beggar's art" (*kojiki geijutsu*), something that can be artistically complete only if it serves the theatre, where on stage the lines of a text can be fleshed out by living actors before a live audience.[5] The rise of performance studies since the 1960s has come about in recognition, after decades of slavish attention to the text, of what is essentially nonliterary about the performing arts. Osanai himself was well aware that theatre was more than simply drama. No playwright can enjoy artistic autonomy like novelists or poets; no matter how satisfactory as literature, there is always something lacking in a play if we only read it. Yet at the same time, it is prey to the whims and vagaries of others who may or may not choose to realize it on stage. As anyone knows, bad direction or acting can destroy the pleasure of a great play. Whether good or bad, productions are in any case an expensive proposition. Indeed, the vicissitudes of funding and fashion often conspire to neglect the work of writers who are not living. With very few exceptions—especially in Japan, where a chasm still yawns between classical and modern performing arts—the theatre world seems to lack a historic consciousness. Many contemporary playwrights, to say nothing of actors and directors, simply do not know the work of their forebears, even if their top award, the Kishida Drama Prize, is named after one of them.

Kishida's own case is emblematic of the dubious role playwrights had in the creation of modern theatre in early-twentieth-century Japan. Political events, particularly the rise of fascism and its stranglehold over all forms of expression in the 1930s and '40s, played an important role in drama's demise as a respected form of literature. *Shingeki* had been politically active from as early as the 1920s, and through the 1930s many playwrights, directors, and actors in Japan would resist authority in a manner far more courageous and concerted than novelists or poets ever did. The collaborative nature of theatrical work quite likely gave *shingeki* artists a solidarity and strength in numbers that isolated poets and novelists did not feel in the face of political oppression. But by the same token, the theatre world was politicized in ways that limited the scope of artistic expression, and those who did not believe that it was their task to promote overtly leftist political ideals found themselves increasingly estranged from the theatre world and thus easily co-opted by the rightists. Well into the 1960s, *shingeki* retained its reputation as a center for increasingly doctrinaire leftist political expression, which alienated many intellectuals who did not share the same views. The critic Kobayashi Hideo was typical of those who came to distain *shingeki* when he wrote in 1960 that "ever since the Tsukiji Little Theatre, the real purpose of what they call *shingeki* hasn't been to put on a play so much as to gather together a group of like-minded comrades [*dōshi*] called '*shingeki* fans.'"[6]

It should be stressed here that modern drama in Japan is *not* synonymous with *shingeki;* rather, the latter played a somewhat adversarial role in the rise of modern drama. A seminal figure in the modernization of Japanese theatre, Osanai Kaoru must take a lot of the blame here, for in two crucial moments in *shingeki*'s development—the founding of Osanai's Free Theatre in 1909 and of the Tsukiji Little Theatre in 1924—he would make a point of privileging foreign over domestic drama. New Theatre essentially became synonymous with the importation of *Western* drama and theatre to Japan, to a great extent at the expense of the nurturing of a native Japanese dramatic art. In the early years of the last century, most playwrights had to content themselves with productions, if at all, of their plays by artists trained in *kabuki* or its offshoot, the *shinpa* theatre, and not by those schooled in the methods of modern stage art. Certainly drama took longer than fiction to evolve as a modern form of literary expression in Japan, and the challenges of developing a contemporary vernacular dialogue also had something to do with this. Contemporary critics and historians of the genre in Japan tend to use such terms as *kindaigeki* or *kindai gikyoku* (both meaning "modern drama") to describe this form.

I will argue here that there was also an essentially *anti-theatrical* element to the modernization of Japanese culture during this period. Despite *kabuki*'s dominance over popular culture, aesthetic standards began to shift radically during the Meiji era. The rise of the notion that all literary forms should be devoted to the portrayal of a modern, privatized self played a large part in this transition. A time came when a literate, rather than an oral and performative, culture invaded all the arts. Rhetorically speaking, modernity found expression in Japanese literature through the devices of confession and dialogue; the former gave rise to personal fiction, the latter to the language of modern drama. The eventual victory of monologic expression over the dialogic imagination is an important reason for the literary precedence of fiction over drama in early-twentieth-century Japan. As a consequence, fiction (*shōsetsu*) began to replace the play (*shibai*) as the paradigm of cultural expression. By the same token, there was a narrowing of subject matter and attenuation of plot, with an often claustrophobic focus on modern subjectivity creating by the 1920s the "plotless fiction" that novelist Akutagawa Ryūnosuke would praise as the sign of "pure literature." Modern Japanese cultural expression thus moved from a polyphonic or dialogic mode of narrative to something closer to internal monologue; at its most extreme, plot is abandoned for a lyrical exploration of consciousness in the "I-novel."

Something of this anti-theatrical quality can even be detected in the contours of modern drama itself. Modern drama had several common features (or at least ideals), including the following: coherent and rationally constructed plots; realistic, psychologically delineated and fully individuated characters struggling for self-determination in a harsh and antagonistic society; colloquial, matter-of-fact dialogue; and a minimum or complete lack of musical, choreographic, or spectacular effects. A remark by Osanai Kaoru about Gerhart Hauptmann's *Lonely Lives*—a work to which the protagonist of Tayama Katai's *The Quilt* (*Futon*, 1906) turns obsessively for inspiration—pretty much sums up the new anti-theatrical dramaturgy. Osanai said of this signature work of German naturalism that it was "a play that is not a play, in the sense that there are no occasions for acting."[7] At the same time, theatre was pressed into the service of conveying a "message" that was ultimately more intellectual, even ideological, than sensual; indeed, the theatre became, to an extent to which it had never been before in Japan, a forum for the illustration of social problems and the exploration of ideas and possible solutions. Modern dialogue drama, like fiction, became a medium for the personal expression, above all, of its author. Accordingly, the status of the playwright rose over that of the actor, who increasingly was called upon to deliver faithfully the words as they had been written (and frequently printed) down. By the same token, however, much of the fun of theatergoing was lost, and increasingly the experience of seeing a play was like being taught sometimes harsh and frequently boring lessons in modern life. A number of the dramatists themselves were not entirely happy with this turn of events. Tanizaki Jun'ichirō, for one, professed that he preferred an "art rich in sensual pleasures over that with deep intellectual content." Hence, he favored *kabuki* over Ibsen, whose impact on modern Japanese audiences had been profound but was "liable to give them bad dreams." The experience of going to the modern theatre—being forced to sit still quietly and listen without the accompanying pleasures of food, tobacco, or alcohol and no music or dance but just a lot of talking—was too much like school. So Tanizaki claimed, "If I want to see a play these days, I still run to *kabuki,* even though I'm not entirely satisfied with it. In any case, there I can see richer colors, more beautiful physical action than I can on the modern or *shinpa* stages."[8]

The didactic tendency in modern drama became even greater as theatre became politicized in the 1920s and '30s, as if to regain by ideological means the sociality theatre had naturally lost in its march to modernization. During this time, however, the New Theatre movement was never able to achieve either the popularity or the cultural importance hitherto enjoyed by *kabuki*. Its artistic aspirations, conflictingly highbrow and populist, left much of its potential audience bemused; people turned to *kabuki* or *shinpa*, or to more contemporary pleasures like the cinema or the Asakusa opera, for their entertainment.

Such were the challenges facing a Japanese playwright in the first half of the last century. Yet despite all these, some excellent work was achieved, and this book attempts to redress the neglect into which many playwrights have fallen and demonstrate that, in fact, modern drama flourished in the first decades of the twentieth century. Introductory chapters outline the development of drama from the 1880s until the 1930s, but the bulk of this book is given over to translations, with introductions, of nine one-act plays by nine different playwrights. These plays will give the reader a sense of the development of modern drama in Japan, often at great odds, from early experiments in the form to works that, in the opinion of this author, stand head to head with the best of twentieth-century drama anywhere. While multi-act plays were also written and produced, the one-act provides an opportunity to present a broad cross-section of works by many of the best dramatists of their time. There are also important historical and formal reasons for my having selected only short plays from this period. I go into further detail on these in chapter 2, but suffice it to say here that like the short story was for fiction, the one-act play was the definitive form for drama during the Taishō and early Shōwa (1926–1989) eras; it was the offspring and expression of a quintessentially modern sensibility. By the same token, I have selected only plays set in modern times; there are none here that could be loosely described as *shin-* (new) *kabuki*, though *kabuki* artists staged a number of these works and some playwrights, like Suzuki Senzaburō and Hasegawa Shigure, frequently wrote historical plays.

Space limitations have necessarily made my choice even more selective. Seminal earlier playwrights like Kinoshita Mokutarō and Yamamoto Yūzō have been left out, but their legacy is seen in some of the work of others presented here. This book leaves off in the early 1930s, and because of my study's interest in the development of a colloquial dialogue (a central feature of modern drama), its focus has been on the so-called "literary" school of dramatists, culminating in the playwrights of the magazine *Playwriting* (*Gekisaku*): Kishida Kunio, Kubota Mantarō, and Tanaka Chikao. Another book is needed to do justice to the work of leftist playwrights during the 1920s and '30s, but I have included Akita Ujaku's *The Skeletons' Dance* (*Gaikotsu no buchō*) as one of the finest examples of politically engaged drama in this period.

The selection here presents a good sampling of what current criticism has identified as the most representative drama of this period. I have been guided in my selection by the work of many Japanese scholars who, in the past decades, have been working diligently to reclaim modern drama's status as a literary genre; some are members of an earlier generation, like Nagahira Kazuo, Ochi Haruo, and Ōyama Isao; more recent ones include Inoue Yoshie, Nishimura Hiroko, Hayashi Hirochika, and other contemporary scholars belonging to the Modern Theatre History Study Circle (Kindai Engekishi

Kenkyūkai). Four of the plays translated here—Okada Yachiyo's *The Boxwood Comb* (*Tsuge no kushi*), Kikuchi Kan's *Father Returns* (*Chichi kaeru*), Suzuki Senzaburō's *The Valley Deep* (*Tanizoko*), and Akita Ujaku's *The Skeletons' Dance* (*Gaikotsu no bucho*)—I first encountered in an anthology put together by this group.[9] Earlier, I lamented the general ignorance of early-twentieth-century drama among contemporary Japanese theatre practitioners, but there have been some notable exceptions: at Theatre X in Tokyo, Kawawa Takashi, a veteran *shingeki* director, has been active for several years now staging modern "classics," drama from the late Meiji, Taishō, and Shōwa eras. There have also been revivals of several modern classics at the New National Theatre in Tokyo. Another group of contemporary directors and actors associated with Art Space (Geijutsu Sōzōkan) in Osaka has staged a series called Classic Renaissance. Productions I saw there of Izumi Kyōka's *The Ruby* (*Kōgyoku*), Hasegawa Shigure's *Rain of Ice* (*Kōri no ame*), and Kishida Kunio's *Two Men at Play with Life* (*Inochi wo moteasobu otoko futari*) inspired me to translate these plays. Japanese women's literature is still underrepresented in translation, and drama hardly appears at all; with the inclusion of two plays here by women, I hope in part to redress that lack. To this list I have added two prewar classics, Kubota Mantarō's *Brief Night* (*Mijikayo*) and Tanaka Chikao's *Mama* (*Ofukuro*). The introductions provide biographical information on the playwrights and the context of their work, but readers may wish to read the plays first lest what I have to say about them spoil their first impressions.

The subject matter is that of modern drama everywhere: adultery and marital discord, family crack-ups, children pitted against their parents. Both the bourgeoisie and the proletariat are represented here, and modern pretensions are lampooned as much as modern predicaments are lamented. Akita Ujaku's play addresses a specific historical moment, presenting a startling indictment of the persecution and massacre of innocent Korean residents in the days following the Great Earthquake of 1923. Each of these plays is written in the modern vernacular and explores and exploits the possibilities of dramatic language in Japanese. In all, I have opted for a variety of styles—realism prevails, as it does in modern drama everywhere, but there are examples of symbolism and expressionism too. Though best known for his distinctively lyrical realism, the play by Kishida that I have translated here is a radical work, a black comedy anticipating the Theatre of the Absurd.

I would like to thank a number of people who have read drafts of this work and offered useful corrections and suggestions: Matsuda Hiroko, Tachibana

Rumiko, Tamagawa Hiroko, Toyoshi Yoshihara, Ueno Sonoe, Mari Boyd, Brian Powell, Tom Rimer, and my anonymous readers. My thanks too to Hanako Masutani's excellent indexing. Research funding was provided by a generous grant from the Social Sciences and Humanities Research Council of Canada and assistance from the Dean of Humanities at the University of Victoria. I was also able to use on more than one occasion the fine facilities at the International Research Center for Japanese Studies in Kyoto. My thanks too to the brilliant team of editors at the University of Hawai'i Press: Patricia Crosby and Cheri Dunn; and to my copy editor, Bojana Ristich. They have turned the sow's ear of my manuscript into a silk purse. As always, any mistakes that remain are my own. Finally, I would like to express my gratitude to my wife, Mitsuko, for her love, support, and patience. This work is for her.

A Note on Names

Japanese names are presented in the customary manner, with surnames first, followed by personal names. Standard practice is to refer to an author by surname, but there are exceptions, such as when an author is best known by a pen name; also, when a surname may confuse a reader with that of another author, the author in question is often referred to by personal name.

1

Meiji Drama Theory before Ibsen

As with so many other aspects of life in Meiji Japan, theatre also went through the convulsions of modernization, and theatre "reform" (as it was called) was part and parcel of a public effort to create a modern, "civilized" nation. These were, in the first place, top-down efforts by the government to clean up *kabuki*'s unsavory reputation as a vulgar entertainment for the masses and make it presentable to both foreigners and the gentry, the former samurai class. From the very first decade of the Meiji era, the theatre was identified as an important site for promoting the government's official program of "civilization and enlightenment" (*bunmei kaika*), but *kabuki* was also by its disposition a deeply conservative institution and suspicious of government meddling. This is not altogether surprising: both as an art and as a business, *kabuki* had evolved in reaction to official restrictions, and by the 1870s it was one of the few vestiges of Edo culture that did not seem threatened with extinction.

Kabuki's relationship with authority had always been complex. The Edo shogunate (*bakufu*) considered it a necessary evil to be tolerated but strictly regulated, just like prostitution, and throughout the Edo era the *bakufu* frequently stepped in to ban plays of a politically sensitive nature, punish actors for pretensions beyond their station, and (on one occasion) even close down a theatre completely (the Yamamura-za in 1714). In turn, the theatre was careful to pay lip service to government moral and sumptuary edicts, all the while attempting, within these narrow confines, to provide the public with a world of thrilling action, glamorous actors, and the larger-than-life characters they played. Along with the licensed quarters with which the theatre remained associated both geographically and socially, *kabuki*'s reputation as a place of not only sexual fantasy but also sexual practice ensured, on the one hand, its central role in the popular culture of the Edo era and, on the other, its notoriety as a place beyond the pale of polite culture.

Neither *kabuki*'s popularity nor its dubious reputation changed substantially during the first years of the Meiji era. If anything, the new Meiji government viewed it as an even greater embarrassment and impediment to calls for "civilization and enlightenment." Official legations to the West, as well as accounts by those who traveled and studied there in the 1860s and '70s, portrayed the theatre as an entertainment for high society, a place for the cultivation of finer sensibilities and moral principles. The *nō* theatre had served a similar but limited purpose for the ruling class of the Edo era, but it endured great hardship for several years after the dissolution of the old regime before, in the late 1870s, regaining a modicum of official patronage.[1]

At the same time, the new Meiji government began to take a proactive role in *kabuki* reform as well. As early as April 1872, the Tokyo municipal government issued a directive to the three major theatres, the Ichimura-za, Nakamura-za, and Morita-za: "With respect to the fact that in recent times both nobility and foreigners are increasingly going to the theatre, portrayal is hereby forbidden of any lewd acts that adults would be ashamed to see in the company of their children. Furthermore, plots for the edification of audiences should be introduced."[2] This was followed up in June by a similar directive from the newly established Ministry of Instruction (Kyōbushō). As Fujiki Hiroyuki notes, this "top-down reform" focused on four specific areas to do with the dramatic text:

(1) Theatre should be a didactic tool for edifying the masses;
(2) Plays should therefore have a moral message, promoting virtue and castigating vice;
(3) The subject matter should be refined, and vulgar and lewd elements expunged;
(4) Plays should faithfully portray historical facts as they occurred.[3]

Further measures were implemented a decade later, in 1882, with "regulations for playhouses" issued by the Tokyo police department mandating a license system for theatres; limiting their number, seating capacity, and hours of performance; and establishing a reporting and censorship system for the performance of plays, as well as reserved seating for police watchdogs. Government censorship of the theatre would become in many respects tighter than it had been even under the Tokugawa shogunate.[4]

Artful accommodation to authority had always been *kabuki*'s modus vivendi. When Morita Kan'ya XII (1846–1897) opened his Shintomi-za in 1878, the theatre's lead actor, Ichikawa Danjūrō IX (1838–1903), read a speech decrying the salacious ways of traditional *kabuki* and vowing to "clean away the filth."[5] The speech had been written for him by the journalist and publisher Fukuchi Ōchi (1841–1906), a man closely connected to the government and one of the spearheads of *kabuki* reform. Danjūrō's speech is illustrative of the extent to which the theatre at least paid lip service to government directives.

During the first two decades of the Meiji era, *kabuki*'s response to official pressure to clean up its act was most evident in its pursuit of greater topicality and historical verisimilitude, particularly in playwright Kawatake Mokuami's (1816–1893) "crop-haired plays" (*zangirimono*) and "living history" (*katsureki*) plays for the actors Onoe Kikugorō V (1844–1903) and Danjūrō. But the essential features of *kabuki* acting and dramaturgy had not changed, and the introduction of new subject matter or historically accurate details in costume and nomenclature were fairly superficial and ultimately satisfied neither the government nor the public. Calls for more substantial reform came, leading to the establishment of the Society for Theatre Reform (Engeki Kairyōkai) in 1886. Organized by a number of Japan's leading political figures, including Prime Minister Itō Hirobumi, Foreign Minister Inoue Kaoru, and Minister of Education Mori Arinori, the Society's de facto chairman was Itō's son-in-law, Suematsu Kenchō (1855–1920), a man who had spent nine years abroad, two of them at Cambridge University. Financier Shibusawa Eiichi, politician and educator Toyama Masakazu (1848–1900), scholar Yoda Gakkai (1833–1909), and Fukuchi Ōchi were also prominent members. In its constitution, the Society identified three major goals for reform: do away with *kabuki*'s tradition of vice and produce a theatre that encouraged virtue; promote the importance of new drama; and construct modern theatre buildings.

This was an era in which reform (*kairyō*) was the buzzword for many enterprises (including language, dress, education, religion, fiction, and prostitution, among others); what lay behind many of these were efforts by the government to persuade the world that Japan had become a modern, civilized nation and was thereby able (it was hoped) to do away with the unequal trade treaties foisted on the country by foreign powers after its "opening" to the West in the 1850s. The overall aim of the Society was to transform *kabuki*

3

from a popular into a highbrow art form, analogous to the theatre and grand opera Suematsu and many of his colleagues in the Society had seen performed in the West. Opinion on how this was to be accomplished widely varied from member to member, however, from those who advocated the eradication of practically all elements that define *kabuki*—the *hanamichi* runway, the *onnagata* (male actors of female roles), the *geza* incidental music, the *chobo* (narrator and *shamisen* accompaniment, a device inherited from the puppet theatre), *kuroko* stage hands, and so on—to those who believed traditional *kabuki* could be rehabilitated with some scrupulous trimming.[6] Suematsu Kenchō, for one, reflected the latter view. In a speech entitled "Opinions on Theatre Reform," he noted that reform should not entail simply donning Western dress and imitating what was done on the European stage, but rather keeping what worked while changing what was no longer appropriate. Much of his criticism was targeted at the traditional repertory of plays and the role of the playwright. In the past, the playwright had been no more than "a slave to the actors." While acknowledging that the likes of a Shakespeare (to say nothing of a Chikamatsu Monzaemon or Takeda Izumo) did not appear every day, Suematsu stressed that substantial reform to *kabuki* would come only when the theatre attracted first-rate writers, and he proposed a prize for the best plays, which would then be published and produced with government support. The publication of drama and not just its staging, he added, would serve to promote reasoned criticism and raise the literary standards of plays.[7]

Much of the problem with *kabuki* drama, Suematsu asserted, lay in its impurity as a literary genre. The West had comedy and tragedy, with tragedy held up as the nobler form, but these distinctions were blurred in *kabuki,* such that most plays were "neither truly sad nor truly amusing."[8] Moreover, *kabuki* showed no regard for the Three Unities of time, place, and action extolled (but seldom practiced) in classical European theatre. *Kabuki* plays were too long and convoluted, and their casts were too large. With regard to acting, Suematsu insisted that "without female actors real theatre cannot be created," but he expressed doubts as to how female actors could be included under present conditions. He proposed the establishment of a joint-stock company to raise funds for a new theatre and the training of new actors and dramatists.[9]

Suematsu decried the old moralism of promoting virtue and castigating vice (*kanzen chōaku*) that was pushed on *kabuki* during both the Edo era and the early years of Meiji, but he did view the theatre as a place where the sensibilities of all classes (and not just the gentry) could be refined. Theatre was therefore useful inasmuch as it could play a role in nation building. Nonetheless, for many of the Society's critics, this view smacked of more government inter-ference. While in agreement with many of Suematsu's main points, Tsubouchi Shōyō (1859–1935) took issue with his covert didacticism, arguing, as he had done in his 1885 *Essence of the Novel* (*Shōsetsu shinzui*), for the independence of aesthetic criteria over moral principles. "Immoral" characters like Iago and Shylock were frequently subjects for great art, he stressed.[10] Shōyō followed this argument up with a more concerted critique of the Society's proposals in an essay entitled "Expressing my modest opinions upon hearing of the estab-lishment of the Society for Theatre Reform": "The reform of playscripts is the essential basis of any theatre reform, and unless this is carried out, all other reform measures will be of no avail. . . . Since, fundamentally, the main pur-pose of the theatre, as of the novel, is to portray the truth (the truth of human emotions, the truth of social conditions), to be so concerned with extraneous matters as to kill this truth is a dangerous priority."[11]

Shōyō felt that both the Society for Theatre Reform and Danjūrō's "liv-ing history" plays were predicated on a superficial reform of *kabuki*, focusing on matters to do with costume, makeup, scenery, and stage properties. The essence of historical drama, Shōyō asserted, lay not in faithfulness to histori-cal facts, but in the portrayal of truths that only drama could express. *Kabuki* characters were stereotypes, and dramatists were needed who could create flesh and blood human beings. Similar criticism came from Takada Sanae, an educator who, like Shōyō, played a key role in the establishment of Waseda University. Like many others, Takada stressed the importance of cultivating new drama written by playwrights who were independent from the old system of the *zatsuki sakusha*, or stable of writers employed by theatres to write works at the request of actors and managers.

Given that the Society for Theatre Reform represented overwhelm-ingly government interests and had very little input from either theatre or intellectual circles, it was met with resounding criticism and accordingly had little power to effect any change. Both Morita Kan'ya and Ichikawa Danjūrō rejected its proposals for reform, and the Society came under attack from prominent intellectuals. The reform movement reorganized itself twice, first into the even more conservative Society for the Betterment of Entertainment (Engei Kyōfūkai) in 1888, then the following year into the more inclusive Ja-pan Entertainment Society (Nihon Engei Kyōkai), which enlisted as members a number of intellectuals like Takada Sanae, Shōyō, Mori Ōgai (1862–1922), art historian Okakura Kakuzō, and journalist and translator Morita Shiken, as well as *kabuki* actors like Danjūrō. Hijikata Hisamoto (1833–1918), minister of the Imperial Household Agency and grandfather of Hijikata Yoshi (1898–1959), one of the founders of the Tsukiji Little Theatre, was its chair. The chief results of these official efforts to reform theatre were, first, a command performance of *kabuki* before Emperor Meiji in 1887 and, second, the opening in Tsukiji of the Kabuki-za, Tokyo's largest theatre for that time, in 1889.

From *Kyakuhon* to *Gikyoku*: The Birth of Drama as a Literary Genre

The Meiji era was an age when the very terminology for theatre and literature was being invented, most often as translations of Western ideas that bore little relationship to the traditional forms that had hitherto been defined by such words as *engeki* (theatre) or *bungaku* (literature), themselves Japanese transliterations of Chinese terms. Indeed, although Japan could boast a plethora of theatrical forms, no umbrella term existed to encompass them all. The lack of agreed basic terms for such concepts as theatre and drama muddled the debate, as did efforts for reform in the Meiji era, Mōri Mitsuya notes. The graphs for *engeki* (演劇), for example, were frequently glossed as *shibai* (play); the term was generally regarded as synonymous with *kabuki*.[12] From 1877 to 1890 "drama" (*gikyoku*) was not even listed as a literary genre in the *Statistical Yearbook of Japan* (*Nihon tōkei nenkan*).[13]

As we have seen, much of the debate surrounding theatre reform in the 1880s revolved around efforts to recognize the artistic value of the dramatic text and to reform *kabuki* playscripts (*kyakuhon*) in accordance with newly imported Western ideals of dramatic form. In addition to the high social status accorded to theatre in nineteenth-century Europe and America, the importance accorded there to drama as a literary genre exercised some of the best minds of the Meiji era. As has been noted, the significance of drama as a literary genre in the West is exceptional and is surely based on the contingent fact of the central role it plays in classical Greek culture and Aristotle's *Poetics*.[14] Nishi Amane (1826–1894), Mori Ōgai's mentor, was instrumental in introducing Aristotle and Western drama theory to the Japanese. His *Hyakugaku renkan* (1870–1872) identified a variety of poetic forms, including epic, lyric, ballad, and drama. Drama was further distinguished into comedic and tragic forms; these forms were more refined than those seen in Japanese theatre, which was "a medium for the lewd and base," Nishi asserted.[15] Numerous other Meiji intellectuals, from liberal politician Nakae Chōmin and critic Ishibashi Ningetsu (1865–1926) to novelist Futabatei Shimei (1864–1909) and

Dostoyevsky translator Uchida Roan (1868–1929), served as conduits of Aristotelian drama theory, via nineteenth-century aestheticians like Hegel, Lessing, and Belinsky. Many recognized that while Japan had a rich and venerable theatrical culture and even a number of illustrious playwrights, nonetheless the dramatic text had counted for little or nothing of literary value.

Meiji was thus a period that saw the emergence of drama as a literary genre in contrast to the *kabuki* playscript, which had served to feature the actors' skills. In *Acting like a Woman in Meiji Japan,* Ayako Kano describes how theatre in Meiji Japan came under the influence of a new, Western-inspired logocentrism that privileged the written—and particularly the printed—text over any other form of artistic expression. Such privileging would have a crucial impact on efforts to "reform" theatre and, in the first instance, reflected in an emerging consensus that the dramatic text would have to play a key role in this reform. Suematsu Kenchō bemoaned the fact that *kabuki* playwrights were slaves to the actors, but the "New Theatre" (*shingeki*)[16] would create a new hierarchy of creativity, transforming actors into "interpretive slaves" of a godlike author, whose written words must be faithfully given voice on stage without change, unlike the typical practice of *kabuki* actors, who would ad lib when they forgot their lines or felt the language simply didn't suit them.[17] In large part, this move reflected a power struggle between the traditional *kabuki,* where actors were king, and the rising Meiji intelligentsia, who felt increasingly that external control of the theatre was needed to elevate it into a more respectable art form. Kawatake Mokuami, *kabuki's* preeminent playwright of the nineteenth century, would signal a major change when he published a play, *Shimoyo no kane jūji no tsujitsura* (Crossroads at ten bells on a frosty night), in the pages of *Kabuki shinpō* (Kabuki news) prior to staging it at the Shintomiza in 1880. It was thought, however, that professional writers independent of the traditional theatre world were needed to assert drama's new status as a literary genre. Both Yoda Gakkai and Fukuchi Ōchi, fellow members of the Society for Theatre Reform, would be among the first playwrights for *kabuki* who were not "stable" writers. (There were some exceptional cases during the Edo era of independent writers, like Kaibara Ekiken [1630–1714], who wrote *kabuki* plays.)

In theatre particularly, but also in many of the other popular storytelling arts of Edo and Meiji Japan—*kōdan* and *naniwabushi* (military tales) and *rakugo* (comic monologue), to name a few—the distinction between author and performer was often fuzzy. The story was not primarily a text to be read but a script for performance, to be heard with the ear and seen physically acted

out. The Meiji era was a crossroads of experimentation, where the public, theatrical, and performative culture of Edo was eventually exchanged for a literary
culture of private reading and appreciation of written texts. In his introduction
to a seminal essay by Maeda Ai on the transformation of reading practices in
the Meiji era, James Fujii notes that the second decade of Meiji (roughly the
1880s) opened "the nation to modernity as a moment of failed community
where solitary reading and privatization echo the silencing of not just reading,
but of the sociality that found brief expression in the Freedom and Popular
Rights Movement" of Nakae Chōmin.[18] Maeda describes how the spread of
publications in movable type and the rise in literacy levels revolutionized the
practice of writing and its reception in the Meiji era. "Interest in the literary arts had been nurtured by oral literary traditions," including *kabuki,* he
writes, describing how such oral forms of recitation as *rōshō* (sonorous reading)
and *sodoku* (reading literary Chinese not so much for the meaning as for the
sound) emphasized the performative, rhythmic, and material qualities of language over its semantic or mimetic value.[19] Writing in 1932, the ethnologist
Yanagita Kunio could still claim that Japanese literature "has not yet crossed
the bridge from an oral to a literary art."[20] Though this process was protracted
in Japan as it underwent modernization, evidence of substantial change could
already be seen in the 1880s and early '90s. Shōyō remarked in 1891 that "the
ancients 'read' the works of others with their ears, while people today enjoy
the benefit of reading with their eyes," adding that the new practice of private reading "must follow the principle of excavating the deep significance of
the text."[21] Literary and artistic practices increasingly emphasized language's
function as a medium for representation, where the aim of artistic expression
was not so much to portray appealing patterns or colorful surfaces but rather
to lay bare the interiors of the human soul. Accordingly, literary efforts moved
away from highly figurative lyric or prose, classical diction, and musical or
rhythmic effects toward prosaic locutions and plain speech—in short, toward
the creation of a modern vernacular literature: *genbun itchi,* literally the "uni-
fication of the vernacular and literary."[22] Thus there was a shift away from
the voice of the actor, reciter, or storyteller to the authorial "voice" of the text
itself. Increasingly, then, the purpose of a literary work, whether fiction, poetry,
or drama, would be to articulate what Shōyō called the author's "true intent"
(*hon'i*), or subjectivity.

Professional storytellers like San'yūtei Enchō (1839–1900) nonetheless
played a significant role in the construction of a modern literary idiom. Many
critics have noted that his performances (and the dictated texts that were

popular spinoffs of Enchō's work) impressed writers like Futabatei Shimei, who, with his *A Drifting Cloud* (*Ukigumo*, 1887), would forge a new vernacular idiom for fiction in Japan. Shimei's translations of Turgenev also provided a stylebook for modern fiction, but (Maeda tellingly notes) he was equally impressed by dramatic recitations of Russian literature given by Nicholas Gray, his teacher at the Tokyo University of Foreign Studies. (This was an age when Charles Dickens's highly theatrical recitations of his own novels were powerful generators of book sales.)[23] If it seems paradoxical that the old oral arts (*wagei*) pointed to a modern idiom of expression, it must be remembered that *kabuki* and storytelling provided the first inkling of modern vernacular expression in Japanese culture. Even Edo pulp fiction was heavily dialogue-driven.

One other feature of Meiji culture was its quest for artistic and generic purity, and many critics would take traditional Japanese plays to task for their "impure," hybrid form. As noted, drawing on Aristotle and other Western theorists, Nishi Amane and other critics in his wake divided literature into three major genres: epic or narrative, lyric, and drama. Discussing the characteristics of these genres, Hisamatsu Sadahiro, in his *Doitsu gikyoku tai'i* (An outline of German drama, 1887), wrote that "drama harmoniously combines the two forms of epos and lyric into one genre," and "it would not be wrong to say that it is the most refined and elegant of all the arts," encompassing the purest elements of such various forms as choral and instrumental music, architecture, painting, dance, and so on—essentially a reiteration of Richard Wagner's idea of a "total art." Indeed, Hisamatsu concludes, "Drama is the most artistic of all the arts."[24]

Like Hisamatsu, Mori Ōgai too asserted that the dramatic text was the most important element in a theatrical work. Decrying "our long established habit of disregarding the element of poetry in a play," he argued for "first the drama, then the performance. The drama is primary, the performance secondary."[25] In Japan, however, Ōgai continued, "the ideal of performance has degenerated into a set of rules for promoting familiar ways of thinking and doing—rules that do not clarify the Society's ultimate goals."[26] In his criticism of the Society for Theatre Reform's program, Ōgai would argue for a narrower definition of drama than Hisamatsu's notion of a total art, however, making a clear distinction between what he called "straight drama" (*seigeki*) and "opera" (*gakugeki*), with the latter "falling somewhere between a *jidaimono* in *kabuki* and a *jōruri* puppet play." He complained of "distracting 'operatic elements' in our national practice." In opera, the stage business (*Händlung*) is slower and more elaborate, but "a play should be given life through its text: it should

9

present poetic nuances in dialogue form, with the actor bringing the script to life. . . . If the audience needs a good deal of stage business to hold its attention, this can only mean that the play is not a good one or it is not being well performed."[27] He argued for a "simpler and more truly artistic theatre" that did not try to "distract the audience with specious shows of 'real' stage effects."[28] In other essays, he called for "backstage poets" and "a theatre that makes dialogue the master."[29]

Ishibashi Ningetsu's *Gikyokuron* (Drama theory, 1893) would echo and expand upon many of Ōgai's opinions. Opening his essay with the statement that "I hold that drama is the most important genre in poetics," Ningetsu calls for Meiji "to become an age in which drama flourishes."[30] He laments that the Edo era slighted drama and that contemporary criticism has privileged fiction. Outlining the characteristics of epic, lyric, and dramatic literature, Ningetsu stresses that drama "must not be confused with epic."[31] He defines drama as "something that manifests the actions (including suffering) of men from the past and renders them artistically, relying on the language of the dramatis personae."[32] He approvingly cites Chikamatsu's definition of language in *jōruri* [puppet theatre] as "a living thing essential to the action . . . portraying reality as it is, while also showing by means of art what is not real."[33]

Ningetsu would not be the first or the last critic to hold up Chikamatsu as a standard-bearer for dramatic literature. Noted as being the first dramatist credited as "author" (*sakusha*) of his own plays, it is said that Chikamatsu switched from writing *kabuki* to *jōruri* because the puppets couldn't change his lines the way *kabuki* actors did.[34] William Lee has pointed out that the rise of Chikamatsu scholarship in the 1880s was linked to the "discovery" of drama as a literary genre.[35]

The most important critic to write on Chikamatsu was Tsubouchi Shōyō, whose formidable energies turned away from fiction to drama after the mid-1880s. The comparison between the two great dramatists of Japan and England, Chikamatsu and Shakespeare, nonetheless highlighted for Shōyō what the new drama in his country desperately required. In what is a seminal text of Meiji drama criticism, "Our Nation's Historical Drama" (Wagakuni no shigeki, 1893–1894), Shōyō would write that traditional Japanese drama (particularly Chikamatsu's and Mokuami's history plays) could be characterized as "dream-fantasy plays" (*mugen-geki*):

> In what respect do they resemble dreams and fantasies? It is in their ridiculous scripts, the farfetched events they portray, their unnatural characters,

their desultory relationships, their absurd plots, their plethora of *metamor-phoses* and *inconsistencies*, their lack of *unity of interest*, their shocking incidents, their exaggerated acts—in all these respects they are fantasies that exist only in dreams. [Italicized words here and below are given in Chinese characters but provided with English glosses.][36]

Japanese drama, in short, exhibits a dreamlike view of life, where fantasy is not distinguished from reality and it is impossible to reason why events happen or characters act the way they do. Life may seem like a dream, Shōyō continued, but we need to make sense of it, and so too with drama. Only fools and madmen would take pleasure in the purely irrational. Shakespeare's plays, he goes on, are "tragedies of *character*," whereas Japanese history plays are typically "dramas of *intrigue*" or of *fate*. In such plays, "Events have no causal relationship and characters have no *individuality*. In Shakespeare's masterpieces, at the same time that there is interest (*umami*) in each and every act, there is an overlying idea (*honshi*) running through the entire work which gives rise to a kind of microcosm, but the ingenuity of our drama, while rich in interest particular to each act, completely lacks any overlying idea."[37] The beauty of such dramaturgy is manifest in the part but not the whole. Shōyō stressed what had been noted earlier by Suematsu, that puppet plays and *kabuki* made a travesty of the Three Unities of time, place, and action. The pleasure afforded by traditional Japanese theatre, Shōyō acknowledged, lay in its "remarkable variety, not only of *appearance*, but also of *tone*," its ability within the course of an entire play or program to run the gamut of human emotions, with "sudden swings from the severe to the salacious, from the refined and elegant to the ludicrous, now virtuous, now violent, now awesome, now weird, never just one thing or another."[38]

This paratactic instinct, a taste for variety over cohesion, was underscored in late Edo culture by two dramaturgical trends in *kabuki*. One was *naimaze*, the technique of "twisting together" separate narrative strands, often discrete plot lines with quite independent casts of characters that would be familiar to audiences from other plays.[39] The other trend militating against structural, stylistic, or thematic unity was called *midori:* breaking up multi-act history plays, dramas that we have seen were already loosely structured, then shuffling them together in a kind of "best of" program with isolated acts from *sewamono* (domestic plays) and dance plays. For Edo more than for Kamigata (Osaka and Kyoto) audiences, performance of favorite actors trumped plot. The *midori* program is still typically the way a *kabuki* production is put together. Presenting multi-act dramas in their entirety (*tōshi-kyōgen*) is still rather exceptional, often reserved for such plays as *Chūshingura*, and it is a relatively recent phenomenon of somewhat antiquarian instincts.[40]

Earlier efforts to reform drama, such as those of the Society for Theatre Reform, were inconsistent and contradictory, Shōyō asserted. He proposed three major items for a more substantial reform of Japanese drama:

(1) A clear distinction between dramatic and narrative modes. (This is essentially the same advice that other critics like Hisamatsu, Ōgai, and Ningetsu had given, as well as Shōyō in his own "Bijiron-kō" [Essays in rhetoric, 1892].)

(2) Greater structural consistency: a "unity of *interest*" that is equivalent to the theme or action of the drama;

(3) Character as the mainspring and rationale for all actions and events of the drama.[41]

Danjūrō's "living history" plays or the roughhouse political *sōshi* (hooligan) and *shosei* (student) plays of people like Sudo Sadanori (1867–1907) and Kawakami Otojirō (1864–1911), Shōyō claimed, managed to be innovative in only superficial effects, such as costuming and makeup, setting, subject matter, or declamation, but the dramaturgy had not substantially changed, and that was precisely where reform was required.

What we see, in short, in Shōyō's critique is an attempt to create a discrete literary genre for drama predicated on a more individuated portrayal of human character, where the self is constructed out of conflict with other emerging selves.[42] Moreover, he advocates a strong, cohesive, and rational structure in which a logical cause-and-effect sequence of events is constructed out of the actions of individual characters. Such a structure creates an aesthetic of unity and purity, in contrast to the hybrid, episodic, and discursive beauty of *kabuki* and puppet plays. At the same time, in contrast to *kabuki*'s aesthetics of surfaces, Shōyō points toward a dramaturgy of interiors that attempts to anatomize the human soul.

In contrast to Shōyō, who believed that a modern theatre could be created by reforming *kabuki*, the romantic poet and critic Kitamura Tōkoku (1868–1894) doubted whether *kabuki* could ever incorporate the new dramaturgy of Western theatre. Inspired by Shōyō's essay on historical drama, which was then still being serialized in the pages of *Waseda Literature* (*Waseda bungaku*), Tōkoku published an essay entitled "What Lies Ahead for Drama?"

(Gekishi no zento ikaga) in the December 1893 issue of his journal *Bungaku-kai* (Literary world). Asserting that "a revolution in the theatre must come through a revolution in the drama," Tōkoku believed *kabuki*'s conventions were a great stumbling block to reform. Where Shōyō saw a lack of overall coherence to the structure of a *kabuki* play, however, Tōkoku praised what he called its "*symmetrical harmony*" (*seigōteki chōwa;* here too English glosses are given for the Chinese characters), a harmony achieved by a highly refined synthesis of movement (dance), music (*narimono*), gesture, dialogue, narrative accompaniment, and so on.[43] Japanese dramaturgy was, nonetheless, a slave to such harmony of rhythmic and choreographic form. Tōkoku praised *kabuki* dance but noted that it was designed to highlight the art of the actor, and in performance one forgot all about the character the actor was playing and even the plot, becoming enthralled in, as it were, a "moving painting." Subordinating the actions of the dramatis personae to choreographed movement and instrumental accompaniment destroyed any attempt at realistic identification of the actor in the role; hence action was predicated on aesthetic principles quite alien to how drama was understood in the West. (*Drama*, after all, means "action" in Greek, but in Aristotle the term refers chiefly to the plot). *Kabuki* dance, which exemplified the aesthetic of this theatre, in short, was scenic, but it was not dramatic.[44] The spirit of Japanese theatre, Tōkoku stressed, was to highlight theatrical events, not the actions of the stage characters. The knot tying movement to music must be disentangled before real reform could be seen. If the new drama was to become a "mimetic art" (*mokeiteki bijutsu*), then it would require the concerted work of two kinds of playwrights: those independent of *kabuki* and its conventions and those who could interpret the new aesthetic to dramaturges skilled in the old forms.[45]

Tōkoku put his finger on the problem of how, in practical terms, *kabuki* could ever be transformed into a modern dramatic art, but his proposed solution was weak and undeveloped. Matsumoto Shinko notes that Tōkoku's theatre criticism reflects his keenly felt sense of the disjunction between tradition and modernity, the nigh impossibility of marrying the new to the old.[46]

Putting Theory into Practice: *Genbun Itchi* and the Problem of Dramatic Dialogue

Tōkoku's interest in dramatic form dates back to some of his earliest writings. After Tōkoku's death (by his own hand, at the age of twenty-seven in 1894), the poet and later novelist Shimazaki Tōson (1872–1943) would write volubly of his friend's love of drama.[47] Like many of his generation, the theatre reform movement of the 1880s had awakened Tōkoku to drama's importance as a literary genre. His most important play, *Hōraikyoku* (Song of Penglai, 1891)—clearly written under the influence of Shakespeare's *Hamlet,* Goethe's *Faust,* and above all Byron's *Manfred*—portrays a poet grown sick of the world who climbs Penglai, the mountain of Daoist legend, to commune with the immortal spirits there. Lured by a mountain nymph who resembles his dead wife, he disappears into a cave, never to return to the world below.[48] Written in classical Japanese in the five-seven syllable prosody of traditional verse, *Hōraikyoku* baffled Tōkoku's contemporaries, who could not decide what sort of creature it was: poetry or play? Tōkoku himself expressed in the preface to the play his doubts as to whether the contemporary theatre could stage it. Akiba Tarō writes the following:

> Though structurally it is a drama, [Tōkoku's play] is too poetic and too subjective, such that his wild, vehement, complex, and delicate ideas and sensibilities could not find adequate expression in our theatre as it was, so he had to resort to borrowing from the models he had of Western dramatic verse. Skepticism, suffering, pessimism, idealism, romanticism, rebellion, destruction: there was simply no way all these sentiments, which Tōkoku attempted to portray in his dramatic world, could be given expression within the conventions of traditional Japanese drama.[49]

Hōraikyoku nonetheless paved the way for drama as a literary form to express the thoughts and emotions of its author, and though no theatre yet existed that could stage such work, it inspired similar attempts by other writers associated with the literary world (*bundan*) and not theatre circles. The 1890s marked the emergence of drama as a literary genre, with works published in the burgeoning literary magazines of the day, journals like *Literary World* (*Bungakukai*), *Waseda Literature,* and *The Weir* (*Shigarami zōshi*). (One of the first drama collections for reading, however, was of *kabuki* plays, mostly by Mokuami: *Kyōgen hyakushu* [A hundred plays], published by Shun'yōdō in eight volumes in 1892–1893.) Tōkoku's friend Tōson wrote a play called *Hikyoku biwa hōshi* (The biwa priest: A tragic lyric, 1893), and Kōda Rohan (1867–1947) penned *Yūfuku shijin* (The happy poet, 1894), but both works were clearly exercises in literary form and neither writer had much interest or hope in seeing them staged.

Following "Our Nation's Historical Drama," Shōyō also wrote several history plays, the first of which was *Kiri hitoha* (A paulownia leaf, 1894–1895), about the fall of the Toyotomi family in the late sixteenth century, as well as a sequel to this play, *Hototogisu kojō rakugetsu* (A sinking moon over the lonely castle where the cuckoo cries, 1897). Clearly his model was Shakespeare, whose history plays and tragedies presented a dramaturgy and language that could, he felt, make *kabuki* drama a literature and not simply a pretext for stage art.[50]

In the introduction to his translation of *A Sinking Moon*, J. Thomas Rimer notes that "writing after his enthusiastic immersion in Shakespeare's historical dramas, Shōyō created a spoken language for the play that is elevated, resonant and complex. It closely resembles neither traditional *kabuki* dialogue nor modern speech but represents, rather, an experiment at creating a kind of 'Shakespearean' analogue in the Japanese language."[51] Though not immediately staged (*A Paulownia Leaf* was first produced in 1904 and *A Sinking Moon* in 1905), both works achieved some theatrical success and are still occasionally performed.

Both Tōkoku and Shōyō would make considerable advances in dramatic structure and characterization, as well as in the introduction of themes that were alien to the traditional theatre, but dramatic language remained resistant to change. The language of drama is by nature that of dialogue, but as we have seen, traditional Japanese drama contained within it considerable elements of both the epic and the lyric. Over the course of centuries, Japan's traditional performing arts had developed rhetorical styles that were radically different from the dialogue of modern Western drama. In the first place, classical Japanese diction does not make a clear distinction between indirect and direct speech. Ayako Kano notes that in traditional Japanese theatre—*nō* and puppet theatre and to some extent *kabuki* as well—"there is no clear distinction between dialogue and narration," between direct, first-person speech and indirect, third-person narration. This is most obvious in the *nō*, where the chorus may speak on behalf of the *shite* (protagonist), or alternatively the protagonist may refer to the character he or she plays in the third person. Though jarring in English, this shift of grammatical person, between direct and indirect speech, is seamless in Japanese. Indirect rather than direct speech governs all the traditional performing arts. Kano adds that in the puppet theatre all speech, whether construed as "dialogue" or "narration," issues from the mouth of the chanter. Even *kabuki* dialogue—or, for that matter, any speech in the theatre—is indirect and mediated simply by virtue of the fact that theatrical language is not spontaneous: the actor is a mouthpiece reiterating words provided by someone else.[52]

Kabuki sutezerifu (ad libbed dialogue), if anything, only highlights the artificiality of stage speech by calling attention to the actor's versatility, his ability as an actor rather than a character in a play, to intensify the pleasure of performance. Kano goes on to characterize *kabuki*'s nonverbal elements, notably song and dance, as forms of "indirect speech."[53]

Thus, neither *kabuki* nor puppet theatre was, strictly speaking, dialogue drama. Traditional drama, including *kyōgen*, is predominantly in verse or patterned dialogue (versified or rhythmically delivered), often combined with long passages of monologue and narrative. The language of the Japanese theatre until quite recent times was typically regarded as something larger than life, to be delivered in a higher register than ordinary spoken language. Stage dialogue and social discourse—conversation—were fundamentally different creatures. Certain practical considerations, such as the need for an actor to project his voice so as to be heard by all members of the audience in a theatre, helped create a uniquely theatrical style of declamation. In time, this style acquired its own aesthetic in *kabuki*, giving rise to patterned speech such as *watarizerifu*, a rhythmic device whereby dialogue is shared among stage characters. Rhetorical patterns in *kabuki* reached their apogee with Mokuami's distinctive seven-five prosodic speeches and dialogue or his bravura *yakuharai* monologues, in which a hero harangues his adversaries.

The closest thing to "dialogue" in traditional Japanese drama is *mondō*, literally "question and answer," a word employed in *nō* to describe what is ultimately a rather minor function of this genre—that is, a verbal exchange between stage characters. This term originally referred to philosophical debates as practiced by Confucianists and Zen Buddhists. Something of this didactical function can still be detected in *nō*, but *mondō* never quite had the connotation of communication or debate that "dialogue" has had in the Western tradition. Instead, the form typically conveyed the imparting of knowledge from master to disciple, rather than shared discovery of the truth through dialectical reasoning. In short, the Western notion of dialogue was predicated on a more horizontal, egalitarian set of social relations than that which existed in traditional Japanese society. The language of modern drama, which posits highly individuated characters struggling for self-realization in conflict with their peers, was alien to the Japanese social sphere. Traditional Japanese drama would typically resolve any potential conflict in a transcending of the self through identification with nature or higher spiritual and social ideals such as nirvana or fealty.[54] The standard term used today for stage dialogue is *serifu;* in other contexts, the word *taiwa* is also used for dialogue. Dialogue essentially involves an exchange between individuals where the unspoken subject, the point of talking, is to explore and establish the terms of the relationship between the speakers. Contemporary playwright Hirata Oriza contrasts *taiwa* with *kaiwa* (conversation) as follows: *taiwa* is "the exchange of new information between strangers," whereas *kaiwa* is "pleasant speech between people who already know each other." Japanese, he claims, are notoriously poor at dialogue.[55] In a world in which relationships are not problematized, conversation can reign freely, but dialogue is difficult.

One of the cardinal aspects of modernity in any art is its attempt to conceal the devices of its mediation, to present directly an illusion of reality "as it is." In linguistic terms, for the theatre this involved a transformation of stage art from indirect to direct speech. This project of making language more immediate and transparent worked at cross-purposes to the rhetorical function of speech in, for example, *kabuki*. There was a populist, if not democratic, reason behind this effort. The shift from a classical to a "colloquial" language in written documents and spoken utterances was indicative of the project of modernization in virtually all elements of Japanese culture. As Karatani Kōjin has pointed out, the vernacularization of modern literature was in fact an artificial and literary creation; at the same time, Meiji nation-building efforts to forge a standardized spoken Japanese created a language that was equally synthetic. Moreover, class lines divided the language of the theatre from that of polite society, and language reform reflected the implementation of new schema of social stratification. "Standard Japanese" (*hyōjungo*) was closer to the dialect spoken by Tokyo's ruling *shizoku* class, men and women who were typically the offspring of samurai, whereas *kabuki* dialogue was typically the language spoken by the working-class Edo townsperson.

In fiction, critics identify the beginning of vernacularization in Futabatei Shimei and Oguri Fūyō's literary experiments in the 1880s, a task that did not achieve fruition perhaps until the 1920s, with the first installments of Shiga Naoya's *A Dark Night's Passing* (*An'ya kōro*). In the realm of public documents, it can be argued that a truly vernacular language was not in place until after 1945. Vernacularization in Japanese drama lagged behind that of fiction by more than a decade and some, like Hirata Oriza, claim it is still an unfinished project.[56]

Playwright Kinoshita Junji (1914–2006), one of the few others who has written on vernacularization in the theatre, has argued that the irrational elements of traditional Japanese drama are intrinsic to the classical language. Unlike modern adaptations of classical Western drama, traditional Japanese drama is resistant to translation into a modern vernacular. Kinoshita points out that, unlike the West, Japan had to grapple with the creation of modern dramatic dialogue in modernizing its theatre.[57] It is not really until the Taishō era that dramatists came close to writing dialogue in a modern vernacular. Those who wished to write drama had to struggle not only with *kabuki* conventions, but also a choice of what register of language to exploit. In the absence of a common spoken language, "reformist" *kabuki* playwrights like Fukuchi Ōchi and Yoda Gakkai resorted to classical Chinese and Japanese locutions, as if in an attempt to shake off the yoke of *kabuki* diction. Vernacular speech eluded the Meiji playwrights, especially those with literary pretensions, and the drama written in the 1890s by people like Tōkoku, Tōson, and Rohan was predominantly in the seven-five prosody of classical Japanese poetry. Ironically, as drama evolved as a literary form, it initially estranged itself even further from colloquial expression, the lifeblood of modern stage dialogue.

Kinoshita has noted how the drama and translations of Shōyō and Ōgai, Meiji Japan's most indefatigable exponents for the modernization of theatre, reprised the history of the Japanese language. I will have cause to examine Ōgai's plays in further detail in chapter 2 and so will restrict my discussion here to Shōyō's work. Plays like *A Paulownia Leaf* or *Urashima Tarō: A New Lyric* (*Shinkyoku Urashima Tarō*, 1904)—a work in which Shōyō would try to put into practice his theories of lyric drama—never broke new ground stylistically, however.[58] As noted above, Rimer calls Shōyō's style "elevated, resonant and complex," but these attributes did not necessarily make it an easy language for stage delivery. Hirata Oriza counters that "were one to read it in print, one could make out what he means, but there are many passages that, were one to hear them only, one really would have no idea what was being said."[59] Hirata deems that it was impossible for actors untrained in this strange amalgam of "translatese" (*hon'yakuchō*) and pseudo-classical diction to make such dialogue intelligible. Nor did the diction of Shōyō's *En the Ascetic* (*En no gyōja*, 1917), the first Japanese play to be performed at the Tsukiji Little Theatre, in 1926, mark a radical departure from that employed in *A Paulownia Leaf* or *A Sinking Moon*. Shōyō's lifelong quest to create a modern theatre out of the flesh and bones of *kabuki* would remain quixotic; it would seem its theatrical conventions stymied his creativity as a dramatist. On the other hand, his greatest experiments in the modernization of dramatic language would take place in his translations of Shakespeare. Over the course of fifty years, from 1884 to 1934 (just one year before his death), he translated Shakespeare's entire oeuvre, not only some thirty-seven plays but also his narrative verse and sonnets.

Though he is not consistent or thorough in his analysis, Kinoshita identifies five stages in the development of Shōyō's Japanese translations over this time: from versified puppet theatre or *kabuki* diction, through experiments with *nō* and *kyōgen* and the classical, literary idiom of the Heian romance (*monogatari*), to a mixture of the literary and colloquial, finally, quite late in his career, to a more or less modern colloquial language.[60]

In his own drama, Shōyō managed to achieve a greater synthesis of modern and traditional forms, yet he did so not by tackling modern subject matter but by re-envisioning how the past was to be portrayed. Neither he nor Tōkoku crafted dramatic dialogue in a vernacular tongue about matters close to the daily lives of their contemporaries, however. The language of Japanese drama until the twentieth century essentially remained in a classical, literary idiom, increasingly divorced from the language spoken on the streets, one that itself was undergoing a revolution.

Shinpa Adaptations and the Melodramatic Imagination

Shōyō's history plays marked the beginning of the new genre called *shin-* (new) *kabuki*, and in the ensuing years, many playwrights such as Okamoto Kidō (1872–1939), Matsui Shōyō (1870–1933), Mayama Seika (1878–1948), and Hasegawa Shin (1884–1963) would ensure that the repertoire of *kabuki* drama was being refreshed by excellent new work.[61] With Mokuami's death in 1893, the position of the traditional house dramaturge was in peril, but even so, many of the independent and more educated playwrights still found that writing for the stage was sometimes a thankless task. Little honor or remuneration came from it; actors and managers changed what had been written at will, and the "stable" playwrights, already insecure, especially gave these new dramatists a hard time. Okamoto Kidō recalled how he and another *shin-kabuki* playwright, Oka Onitarō (1872–1943), were constantly bullied by jealous and insecure dramaturges requesting constant rewrites and even complaining in one case that an actor could not dance to the trash they had written.[62] An attitude prevailed that theatrically satisfying drama could not be written by "amateurs."

By the 1890s, however, *kabuki* had become almost by definition a thing of the past. Shōyō's *kabuki* plays were a considerable advance over "living history" plays, but it was increasingly apparent that for the portrayal of modern life, *kabuki* was limited as a theatrical form. Nor were the "crop-haired" plays much more successful at this task. "Can traditional acting techniques properly express modern Japanese lifestyles?" ask Brandon and Leiter in the introduction to their volume of translations of *kabuki* plays from the mid-to-late nineteenth century. "One unintended consequence . . . is that *kabuki* increasingly became identified with its pre-Meiji, traditional—that is feudal—repertory."[63] In contrast, by the 1880s, "Change had become the norm. . . . Surface reality could not mask the lack of connection between the daily lives of the audience and the inner life of the dramatic action, even if that action was set in the present day. One could easily accept stylized acting in plays set in pre-modern times. Such acting and dramaturgy that supported it, however, may have seemed alien to dramatic characters dressed in raincoats and bowler hats."[64] In the meantime, another type of theatre was emerging that seemed to catch the tenor of the times better than *kabuki:* the politically engaged but amateurish productions being staged by Sudō Sadanori and Kawakami Otojirō that would later become known as *shinpa,* or "new school."[65]

As it wrestled with a new way of portraying the modern age theatrically, *shinpa* reflected the kind of debate that was going on in Meiji criticism on the proper function of drama and fiction in contemporary society, a debate that essentially revolved around what kind of theatrical realism would prevail. Traces of a nascent realism can be seen in Japanese literature and drama as far back as *The Tale of Genji* and Zeami's theories of imitation (*monomane*) in the *nō.* To be sure, however, it is not until the Edo period that we see the establishment of certain social conditions—the rise of the middle classes and a consumerist popular culture that catered to their tastes—essential to the creation of a home-grown version of realism. The term *sewamono,* literally "gossip plays," suggests a more colloquial, dialogic style, as well as the topicality of the subject matter of domestic drama. Actor Sakata Tōjūrō (1647–1709) predicated his art on realistic acting, but he noted that because *kabuki* was a popular entertainment, it was necessary to make life look more beautiful than it really was.[66] Though *kabuki* acting could be at times startlingly realistic, its dramaturgy was not, and verisimilitude alone was never the ideal.[67]

In many respects, *kabuki* could be more accurately characterized as a melodramatic theatre. It shared all or some of the following elements common to melodrama: a stress on musical accompaniment for emotional effect, sensationalism and extreme emotional displays, stereotyped characters presenting moral polarities, a narrative structure that featured outrageous coincidence and convoluted plotting, and *deus ex machina* resolutions (among others).[68] Its heroes, heroines, and villains were presented scenically, as surfaces in a pictorial composition, as if painted in primary colors emphasizing their function as types. There is thus a focus on simplicity rather than complexity in character-ization, a metaphysical or semiotic, not psychological or humanistic, portrayal of people. In this respect, melodrama has been described as "monopathic," as opposed to the "polypathic" nature of tragedy.[69]

As an expressive mode in both literature and theatre, melodrama both reflected and made intelligible (which is also to say inoculated people from) the shock of modernity. In his book *Melodrama and Modernity*, Ben Singer identifies two kinds of realism that were operative in the arts of the nineteenth century: "absorptive realism" and "apperceptive realism." The former is a natu-ralist version of realism, an attempt to create a transparent and quasi-docu-mentary mode of verisimilitude. The latter is a kind of verisimilitude that "does not create a strong feeling of diegetic immersion in the represented space."[70] Displaying a kind of apperceptive realism, melodrama thus occupied a middle ground between the romantic and the realistic modes—in Nicholas Vardac's turn of phrase, a "romantic realism."[71] Its romantic element—a predilection for spectacle and strong emotional effects, its larger-than-life characters and its coincidences, its dreamlike plots of virtue vindicated after extreme suffering—was treated with all the realism modern stagecraft could muster. In both the West and Japan during the nineteenth century, the greatest efforts at producing realism were expended not on dialogue, dramaturgy, or acting but on the spec-tacle: staging, lighting, and sound effects. Whereas in Shakespeare and other playwrights of the past, highly figurative language was employed to conjure images in the mind's eye, nineteenth-century melodrama employed technology to achieve the same visual effects. As Singer puts it, "Incredible sights were pre-sented with credible diegetic realism."[72] Cinema, Vardac pointed out, grew out of a demand for such a "romantic realism." In both the West and Japan, theatri-cal melodrama gave birth to, and was eventually upstaged by, early cinema.

In much the same way, *shinpa* melodrama provided the theatrical bridge between tradition and modernity in Meiji theatre. The instinct toward a more realistic art was reflected in both the topicality of the new plays and their focus on action and dialogue over dance and music. Borrowing the term from Ōgai, Kawakami Otojirō characterized his style of theatre after his company's tours of Europe in 1900–1901 as *seigeki*, "straight drama," focusing on dialogue, a less episodic dramaturgy, and actresses to play women's roles.[73] A more tradi-tionalist camp would succeed, however, in defining the *shinpa* style as a kind of musical or lyric theatre (*gakugeki* or *shigeki*) that employed *kabuki* presen-tational techniques such as *geza* incidental music, the *hanamichi*, and, most important, the *onnagata*.

The transitional, hybrid nature of *shinpa* was literally embodied in the *onnagata*, who represented *shinpa*'s ambivalent stance between the stylization of traditional theatre and the "absorptive" mimetic mode of modernity. The *shinpa onnagata* Hanayagi Shōtarō commented that "80 percent of *kabuki*'s essence lies in the *onnagata*'s art," which was devoted to the creation of a "weird beauty," a consciously artificial image of femininity that had a homoerotic charge. In *shinpa*, the *onnagata*'s eroticism was downplayed, and its portrayal of women tended to be more naturalistic than *kabuki*'s. But realism was not the ultimate goal of *onnagata* acting for *shinpa* any more than it was for *kabuki*. Hanayagi used the metaphor of painting versus photography to compare the way an *onnagata* (as opposed to an actress) would play Otsuta in the "Yushima no keidai" scene in Izumi Kyōka's *Onna keizu*. Hanayagi wrote that actresses were simply too realistic for the *shinpa* stage, "lacking the chiaroscuro of the *onnagata* portrayal. There is something unsettlingly carnal about an actress's performance—one can practically smell her—as she exposes only what is real: her body." Women are equated with realism; then both are rejected here. Ultimately what is most important is not the performer's sex, Hanayagi claims, but the performance of femininity. Strict training (likened to that of the *ningyōzukai*, or puppeteers, in puppet theatre) is necessary to capture the "weird beauty" of *kabuki* heroines like Agemaki, Yatsuhashi, or Princess Taema. The art of the *shinpa onnagata*, Hanayagi stressed, was essential in the classical portrayals of prewar women, who were almost necessarily associated with the kimono. By the same token, actresses could not play geisha until they learned how to "play *onnagata*." In this respect, *shinpa* would remain the "moving painting" of *kabuki*, rejecting both the heightened realism of *shingeki* and the "moving photographs" (*katsudō shashin*) of cinema.[74]

Initially, *shinpa* plays were composed by the actors themselves, in much the same manner as in early *kabuki*, hastily improvised (*kuchidate*) out of rough plans sketched together before a production began but subject to constant change depending on expedience and audience approval. In its development out of a form of agitprop in the 1880s into a full-fledged art form, this theatre drew heavily for its material on contemporary news items and, later, novels, moving from the sensationalism of Kawakami's earlier productions—titles like *Shock!* (*Igai*) and *Shock Again!* (*Mata igai*) speak volumes—to the sentimentalism of mature *shinpa* drama, much of it adapted from the popular fiction of the day. Hanabusa Ryūgai (1872–1906), who scripted many of the early *shinpa* adaptations, came from the traditional circles of *kabuki* stable writers, having apprenticed under the playwright Kawatake Shinshichi III (1842–1901).

Those who were most active writing plays or adaptations (*hon'an*) of other works directly for the *shinpa* stage came from a school of writers, the Friends of the Ink Stone (Ken'yūsha), associated with Ozaki Kōyō (1867–1903). The Ink Stone writers had a special knack for writing vivid dialogue. During the 1890s and the early 1900s, fiction by Kōyō, his associates, and his students— men like Yamada Bimyō (1868–1910) and Izumi Kyōka (1873–1939)—was readily dramatized, often by other Ink Stone members, like Oguri Fūyō (1875–1926), Satō Kōroku (1874–1949), Hirotsu Ryūrō (1861–1928), and Yanagawa Shun'yō (1877–1918). The popularity of such fiction, which typically was serialized in the newspapers and magazines of the day, inspired stage versions, which in turn generated more sales of the novels in book form. Such a system pleased audiences and readers and to some extent provided royalties for the novelists, but—as was the case with the *shin-kabuki* playwrights— adapting the work of others only to see one's script further adulterated by the actors was scarcely satisfactory from an artistic standpoint.

The *shinpa* adaptations of Izumi Kyōka's fiction were brilliant examples of this stage art; many are still performed today.[75] Kyōka's fiction was exemplary of a style of literature popular before the rise of naturalism in the first decade of the twentieth century, with thrilling, highly melodramatic plots and language richly figurative and pleasing to the ears. Thus, in both narrative and stylistic terms, such literature harked back to an earlier time, one already on the way out by the 1900s, where the consumption of literature was still to some extent a public or communal event, where the pleasure of reading could best be captured by oral recitation and not by silent reading alone. In an essay entitled "The Rhythm of Sentences," for example, Kyōka wrote the following: "I believe that literature should appeal not to the eye but to the ear, which is to say that I write prose that even an illiterate person could understand were it read out to him."[76] Kyōka continued, well into the Taishō era, to write works that in a sense memorialized this earlier stage of Meiji popular culture. The *shinpa* adaptation of his 1914 novel *Nihonbashi* is a case in point. Writing of the relationship between this novel and its adaptation for the stage (Kyōka later published his own dramatization in 1917), Saeki Junko has rightly pointed-ed out that "dialogue from the novel has been transposed verbatim to his dramatic text, and narrative parts are lifted whole from the novel for the stage notes."[77] Passages of the novel were written to order for the *shinpa onnagata* Kitamura Rokurō, who would play Okō for the first stage production in 1914. (Kitamura also had a hand in adapting the novel for that production.) Kyōka, and *shinpa*, excelled in speeches like Okō's address to Katsuragi on Ichikoku

Bridge: "It was the night after the Doll Festival, it was spring, and the moon was shrouded in clouds; there on the bridge we both set free our whelks and clams; and the policeman recorded our names, side by side, in his little notebook. He called me your 'wife.' We were both on our way to pay our respects to Jizō, who ties two lovers together, there on the West Bank; and if he can't do that, the world's a dark, dark place!"[78]

Such bravura performances, akin to a *kabuki tsurane* (tirade), became *meizerifu* (literally "famous speeches"), showstoppers that simultaneously summed up the character, the play, and the whole genre of theatre in a few emotionally charged lines. The rhetoric of *shinpa* dialogue—highly rhythmic, sonorous, and figurative—remained close to the aesthetic of *kabuki*. Dramatists, actors, and audiences took pleasure in language for its theatrical effects as much as for its ability to delineate a character or advance the plot. Theatre scholar Dōmoto Masaki has remarked that the essence of theatre resides in moments when a character says or does something that defies our expectation and, hence, interpretation; the tirades and *coups de théâtre* of *kabuki* or *shinpa* epitomize this feature, but they are notably lacking in the modern theatre. The realistic, rational, and prosaic language of modern drama, which had fallen under the "sin of interpretability," spelled the death of the *meizerifu*, he notes.[79]

By the first decade of the twentieth century, *shinpa* was staging adaptations of Western drama too. After their American and European tours at the turn of the nineteenth and twentieth centuries, Kawakami Otojirō and his wife Sadayakko would produce some of the first Japanese versions of Shakespeare, Victorien Sardou, Alexandre Dumas *fils*, Maurice Maeterlinck, and many other European playwrights.[80] Many of these adaptations would play fast and loose with the originals, often changing the setting of the dramas and names of the characters to make them more "Japanese." Kōyō himself had adapted Molière's *L'avare* and *Le médecin malgré lui* (*Natsu kosode* and *Koi no yamai*); the latter, Kinoshita argues, is one of the few plays prior to 1900 that was written in anything close to the vernacular. "Had he lived any longer," Uchida Roan commented, Kōyō "would no doubt have distinguished himself more as a playwright than a novelist."[81] These experiments to naturalize European theatre by accommodating it to existing Japanese forms and conventions were the theatrical version of *wakon yōsai* (Japanese spirit, Western means). *Shinpa* therefore did not predicate its identity on a clean break with tradition but attempted to assimilate Western cultural products within the context of existent Japanese expressive forms. The cultural paradigms for Western influence, at least in the theatre, remained those of the *hon'an* and *kyakushoku:* dramatic adaptations. In the first decade of the twentieth century, however, *hon'yaku* (translation) would become the greater force for change.

By then, a new drama instigated by playwrights like Henrik Ibsen was making its presence felt in Japan. Its radically modern and foreign dramaturgy could not be accommodated so easily into the traditional forms of *kabuki* or even *shinpa*. New ideas required a new language, new actors, and a new theatre. The status of drama in Japan by the first decade of the twentieth century thus represented something of an impasse. Producing new drama was not so straightforward as creating new fiction because its life was not meant to end on the page. To realize it on stage required an expensive outlay of financial and artistic resources not yet available in Japan: new playhouses and modern techniques of direction, acting, lighting, and stagecraft. Even more important, it needed a public who understood and appreciated it. New work was being written, often directly or indirectly under the influence of Western models of dramatic literature, but a theatre had not yet been created to produce much of it without resorting to various unsatisfactory expedients and compromises.

PART
I

2

The Rise of Modern Drama, 1909–1924

"The opening of the Free Theatre is nothing other than the expression of our desire to live," proclaimed Osanai Kaoru at the premiere of Ibsen's *John Gabriel Borkman* on November 27, 1909. Novelist and playwright Tanizaki Jun'ichirō (1886–1965) was at the premiere and recalled of Osanai that "such glory comes perhaps but once in a lifetime for a man."[1] It was not only a defining moment in Osanai's career as the most charismatic force for the *shingeki* movement, but it also captured a time in which the theatre served for a generation of younger writers and intellectuals as a focus for the aspirations of the age. For Tanizaki, Osanai was a mentor and sponsor for his earliest published works, of both fiction and drama. Kikuchi Kan (1888–1948) likewise recalled that he and many other young writers saw in Osanai a model for the new intellectual. Kume Masao (1891–1952) attested that the Free Theatre had inspired him to start writing plays.[2] Mori Ōgai, who translated *Borkman* for the Free Theatre production, has the hero of his novel *Youth* (*Seinen*, 1910–1911) reflect on its significance:

> Since Junichi felt that this was an important event from the viewpoint of contemporary thought, he became a member of the Free Theater immediately after the play's announcement as if he had been waiting impatiently for just this moment. Earlier, when he was still at home, one of Shakespeare's plays had been performed. When it came to performances of Shakespeare or Goethe, no matter how good the acting, and there could

be no doubt about the quality of the plays, they would have had difficulty in making a profound impression on today's youth. Not only would these plays not affect young men, but the majority of our youth could not possibly appreciate such classical works. . . . To put this in a more extreme fashion, if a new Shakespeare-like play were to be published now, young Japanese would probably not even call it drama but would dub it theater. They might say its poetry was too wordy. And they would probably say the same about Goethe's works. . . . And the reason for this reaction might have been that the tongues of these men, accustomed to the strong stimulus of realism in the modern world, would find it difficult to appreciate the deep calm tastes of a century or more ago.[3]

For his part, Tsubouchi Shōyō felt that Japanese theatre wasn't quite ready for Ibsen, still insisting that Shakespeare was the necessary bridge for the Japanese to theatrical modernity.[4] Note, however, the distinction made above between "theatre" and "drama": one represented the past, the other the future. Ōgai was right: Ibsen marked the birth of modern drama in Japan. It was also the birth of the *shingeki* movement, a fact that was borne out by another Ibsen production, that of *A Doll House,* by Tsubouchi Shōyō's Literary Society in 1911. (We shall see that it was Shōyō's student Shimamura Hōgetsu [1871–1918] who was the driving force behind that production.) It was not only "young men" who were affected by Ibsen's plays. Almost single-handedly, the plays were responsible for the "new woman" (*atarashii onna*) phenomenon.[5]

The following decade saw the flourishing of literally dozens of little theatre companies bent on staging new drama, both foreign and Japanese, including Kamiyama Sōjin's Modern Drama Society (Kindaigeki Kyōkai, 1912);[6] Sawada Sōjūrō's Creative Experiment Company (Sōsaku Shienkai, 1913) and New National Theatre (Shin-kokugeki, 1916); Aoyama Sugisaku's Fort Theatre (Toride-za, 1918); and Hijikata Yoshi's Friends' Theatre (Tomodachi-za, 1919), to name just a few. The breakup of Shōyō's Literary Society in 1913 saw the establishment of two important companies by alumni from that theatre: Shimamura Hōgetsu's Art Theatre (Geijutsu-za, 1913) and Ikeda Daigo, Tōgi Tetteki, and Doi Shunshō's Anonymous Company (Mumeikai, 1914). (The Art Theatre staged what was that generation's biggest hit, an adaptation of Tolstoy's *Resurrection,* starring Matsui Sumako [1886–1919], in 1914.) The Takarazuka women's musical troupe was founded the same year.

Kabuki actors also established companies dedicated to the production of new drama; these included Onoe Kikugorō VI's Kyōgen-za in 1914; Morita Kan'ya XIII's Literary Arts Theatre (Bungei-za, 1915); the Five Voice Company (Goseikai, 1913) and Annals Theatre (Shunjū-za, 1920) of Ichikawa Ennosuke II (1888–1963); and Matsumoto Kōshirō VII's New Kabuki Society (Shin-kabuki Kyōkai, 1919). Nor were *shinpa* actors remiss in founding new troupes, including the following: Kawai Takeo's Public Theatre (Kōshū Gekidan, 1913); Inoue Masao's New Historical Drama Society (Shin-jidaige-ki Kyōkai, 1914); and the New Theatre Company (Shingeki-za, 1919), established by Hanayagi Shōtarō and Yanagi Eijirō.

It was a time when modern theatre and drama became major players in the rising bourgeois culture. Such a plethora of new theatre companies could not have arisen were there not also plays to be produced and a public interested in coming to see them. There was hardly a writer during the Taishō era who was not also a playwright. To list them all here would be tedious, but the exceptions (Natsume Sōseki and Shiga Naoya spring to mind) could be listed on the fingers of one hand. Print media supplied a venue for the publications of new plays and criticism about them. Spearheading such interest was *New Tides in Thought* (*Shinshichō*), a journal founded in 1908 by Osanai Kaoru. (Kikuchi Kan and Tanizaki Jun'ichirō were also on the editorial board.) Most of the mainstream literary journals, including *The Pleiades* (*Subaru*), *Central Review* (*Chūō kōron*), *Literary Annals* (*Bungei shunjū*), and *New Fiction* (*Shin-shōsetsu*), published new plays as well as theatre criticism; many of the members of *White Birch* (*Shirakaba*), including Arishima Takeo (1878–1923), Mushanokōji Saneatsu (1885–1976), Nagayo Yoshirō (1888–1981), and Satomi Ton (1888–1983), also wrote drama. Other late-Meiji theatre journals included *Kabuki* (established by Mori Ōgai's brother Miki Takeji in 1900); *Entertainment Illustrated* (*Engei gahō*, 1907); *Entertainment Club* (*Engei kurabbu*, 1914); *New Entertainment* (*Shin-engei*, 1916); *Theatre and Criticism* (*Geki to hyōron*, 1922); and, last but not least, *New Tides in Theatre* (*Engeki shinchō*, 1924). By the 1920s, several important drama anthologies came out, including the *Overview of Contemporary Drama* (*Gendai gikyoku taikan*, 1922); the *Anthology of Contemporary Playscripts* (*Gendai kyakuhon sōsho*, 1923); and the massive fifty-volume *Collection of Japanese Drama* (*Nihon gikyoku zenshū*, 1928–1930), of which some twenty volumes were devoted to modern plays. Dramatists were quicker to organize themselves than novelists (though many were the same individual): the Japan Playwrights Association was established in 1920 by Yamamoto Yūzō (1887–1974), Kikuchi Kan, and Nagata Hideo (1885–1949), one year before a similar guild was founded to protect the interests of novelists. In certain years, writers like Tanizaki spent more time writing plays than fiction.

In short, Taishō was an era when theatre became a key forum for the exchange of artistic, social, and political ideas in Japan and drama came into its own as a literary form. Critic Endō Tasuke remarks that drama was a youthful literary form that expressed the energy, idealism, and "histrionic" character of the writers who came of age during this period.[7] Many have noted that while the title character of *John Gabriel Borkman* is an old man, the Free Theatre's production focused on the son, Erhart.[8] Erhart's "I want to live!" became a rallying cry for the new generation of Japanese rebelling against their fathers.

We have seen that by the 1880s Japanese intellectuals were well aware of the high status of drama as a literary genre and the social importance accorded to theatre in the West. But the drama that men like Fukuchi Ōchi, Suematsu Kenchō, and Mori Ōgai saw on European stages in the 1870s and 1880s for the most part remained well within the realm of the melodramatic "well-made plays" of Sardou and Dumas *fils*. These were not so far removed from the aesthetic of *shinpa* or even *kabuki*. Rather, it was the work of Ibsen and his contemporaries that brought about a revolution in Japanese theatre—and, in a broader sense, letters—during the first decade of the twentieth century.

Ibsen's impact on late-Meiji Japan was profound and inspired both imitators and reactions against the social drama that the Norwegian epitomized. Recognition of his importance was rather slow to come to Japanese intellectual circles, however. Though plays like *A Doll House* (1879), *Ghosts* (1881), and *An Enemy of the People* (1882) were being staged throughout the 1880s in Germany and beyond, there is no evidence that Mori Ōgai, the chief exponent for modern European drama at this time in Japan, was familiar with his work until after his return to his homeland in 1888. (There was, of course, a time lag from the production of these plays in Norway to their reception elsewhere.)[9] The first reference to Ibsen—notably it is by Ōgai—is in 1889, but here (as well as in a review of contemporary literature by Shōyō in 1892) there is no evidence that Ōgai had actually read anything by this playwright. Neither Ōgai nor Shōyō knew what to make of him, being unsure of whether he was a naturalist or a symbolist.[10] (Ibsen wrote plays in both styles over the course of his career, and these concepts were still hard to grasp for contemporary Japanese critics.) Though some, mostly partial and inaccurate, translations were published in the 1890s, it is not until almost the turn of the century that Japanese critics took real notice of the playwright.[11] In 1901, Takayasu Gekkō (1869–1944) published *Social Dramas by Ibsen* (*Ipusen-saku shakaigeki*), containing complete translations of *An Enemy of the People* and *A Doll House*. Playwright Naka-mura Kichizō (1877–1941) read Gekkō's translations and recalled that he had initially been rather put off by Ibsen's rationalism, but he (like his contempo-raries) was still not used to reading drama.[12] Growing interest in Ibsen's work can be seen, however, in 1902 in the attempt at a translation (from English) of *John Gabriel Borkman* by the poet Ishikawa Takuboku (1886–1912). The first stage production of an Ibsen play was an adaptation of *An Enemy of the People* by Hanabusa Ryūgai and his Western-style Theatre Company (Yōshiki Engekisha) in 1902. Both Ryūgai and Gekkō demonstrated an awareness of Ibsen's significance for modern drama in Japan. In particular, Ibsen provided a model for how to portray inner character and motivation through dialogue and gesture without a resort to, for example, the style of narration or long monologues that had been employed in the *kabuki* and puppet theatres.[13]

Ibsen's most ardent proponent was Shōyō's disciple, Shimamura Hōgetsu, who returned to Japan in 1905 from a three-and-a-half-year stint in Europe, where he had seen many of the Norwegian's plays performed. In the January 1906 issue of *Waseda Literature,* Hōgetsu proclaimed "an age of Ibsen." The playwright's death less than six months later coincided with a burst of home-grown naturalist literature in Japan that was in large part inspired by Ibsen's work. Memorials and accolades filled the Japanese press. *Waseda Literature* devoted a special issue to Ibsen in July 1906, featuring essays by Hasegawa Tenkei (1876–1940), Tayama Katai (1871–1930), Ueda Bin (1874–1916), and other late-Meiji luminaries. Yanagita Kunio, who would later become the fa-ther of Japanese folklore studies, described the galvanizing effect of reading Ibsen's plays:

> One is not so much moved as shocked by these ordinary characters, whose tempests, stirred up around the table of a conventional drawing room, seem not concocted out of an imagination divorced from reality, but natural and convincing, as if they had been witnessed and recorded just as they had happened. They did not seem in any way strange or exotic to us who are, after all, foreigners to the customs of Norway. The way the writer expresses all this so boldly and precisely seems almost supernatural.[14]

In 1903, Yanagita established the Ibsen Society for the study of Ibsen's plays, the Ipusen-kai, whose members read like an honor roll of early twentieth-century literati: Tayama Katai, Hasegawa Tenkei, Iwano Hōmei, Tokuda Shūsei, Kanbara Ariake, Masamune Hakuchō, Osanai Kaoru, and Akita

Ujaku (1883–1962), to name a few. Missing from this list were Shōyō, Ōgai, and Hōgetsu, who yet had important roles to play in the promotion of Ibsen's work.[15] Hōgetsu would translate *A Doll House* (from an English translation) for the 1911 Literary Society productions, including the one at the Imperial Theatre that catapulted Matsui Sumako into stardom. (Ōgai supplied another translation of *A Doll House* [dubbed *Nora*] from a German translation, for Kamiyama Sōjin's Modern Drama Society production in 1913.)

Through the efforts of the Ibsen Society and Hōgetsu's criticism, the Norwegian's plays inspired a generation of Japanese naturalist writers. Iwano Hōmei, Nagata Hideo, Nakamura Kichizō, Sano Tensei (1877–1945), and Mayama Seika are a few of the playwrights who wrote what were called "social dramas" (*shakaigeki*) or "problem plays" (*mondai-geki*) patterned after Ibsen. For all the excitement that his work aroused in Japan in the last years of Meiji, however, Ibsen seems to have had a greater impact on fiction. His influence was less as a dramatist than as a social critic, Mōri Mitsuya writes.[16] Ibsen's ideas are debated in two definitive Japanese coming-of-age novels at that time, Natsume Sōseki's *Sanshirō* (1908) and Mori Ōgai's *Youth*; Japanese versions of Ibsen's men and women begin to crop up in the pages of other novels, like Arishima Takeo's *A Certain Woman* (*Aru onna*, 1919).

The Problem of How to Dramatize Modern Life

What were some of the main features of the new drama introduced by Ibsen and his contemporaries? The meaning of "drama," as we have seen, is action, and its chief medium of expression is dialogue. Thus, in its purest form drama is rooted in people, events, and actions presented concretely, in the here-and-now, before an audience of spectators. It is by its nature resolutely concrete, behavioristic in its presentation of people and their relationships, acted out on stage for all to see. The essence, in short, of pure drama is the ability of a stage character to take action.

Györgi Lukacs is a good guide on the rise of modern drama. "Man grows dramatic by virtue of the intensity of his will, by the outpouring of his essence in his deeds, by becoming wholly identical with them," he writes.[17] "In Shakespeare's time, the decisive conflicts still occur in a form which worked strongly upon the senses."[18] Lukacs's remarks here are addressed specifically to Renaissance Western drama, yet he could be talking about *kabuki*. Traditional European drama "rested on solid metaphysical foundations," a sense of ethical values and a way of understanding the world shared by both the stage characters and the audience.[19] Human relations were still defined according to a feudal worldview, one of organic unity to which all individuals were subject. Though relationships could be problematized, the system that defined them was ultimately beyond question. The conflict that was an essential element of all drama was therefore presented as conflict between powerful individuals and not that of an individual against an entire order represented by society, nature, or God.

The new drama reflected the destabilization of relations, values, ways of being, and means of production inaugurated during the Enlightenment and brought to fruition under industrialization during the nineteenth century: "New conflicts result from the new patterning of sensibility, and this at precisely the juncture where, in the old order of society, the relation of higher to lower rank (master to servant, husband to wife, parents to children, etc.) found stability. . . . What kind of man does this life produce, and how can he be depicted dramatically? What is his destiny, what typical events will reveal it, how can these events be given adequate expression?" Lukacs asks.[20] Modern dramaturgy was, above all, a dramaturgy of consciousness, of self-awareness. The force of awakening individual identity began to replace the role of destiny or God in determining personal agency. We have seen how for Shōyō character supplanted destiny or "intrigue" as the engine of drama.

In the new drama, self-realization became a personal goal but also a problem, however. The strong individuals of Shakespearean drama ironically give way in the modern drama to an individualism of powerless people. The lack of a common mythology thrusts the stage hero back upon himself to question every event that happens, every act he must take. The introspection of the first "modern" stage character, Hamlet, thus stands in high relief to the instinctive action of Renaissance revenge plays or, for that matter, the hyperbolic emotions and energies of *kabuki* or *shinpa* stage characters. As the modern world rationalized human relations, however, individual identity became abstracted, and relationships between people became more impersonal. Family and other social ties become insuperable constraints for the heroes and heroines of the new drama. In a world with no longer any enduring mythology, it is the individual who becomes problematized. How is drama possible in a world in which true free action becomes increasingly difficult?

> Every suffering is really an action directed within, and every action which
> is directed against destiny assumes the form of suffering. . . . The heroes of
> the new drama—in comparison to the old—are more passive than active;

they are acted upon more than they act for themselves; they defend rather than attack; their heroism is mostly a heroism of anguish, of despair, not one of bold aggressiveness. Since so much of the inner man has fallen prey to destiny, the last battle is to be enacted within.[21]

"Survival as an individual, the integrity of individuality, becomes the vital centre of drama. Indeed, the bare fact of Being begins to turn tragic," Lukacs adds.[22] The passivity of the modern hero presented a substantial problem for the dramaturgy of Ibsen and his contemporaries, however. In a shift of focus from outward, aggressive action to inward, passive suffering, the appropriate medium of artistic expression became less dramatic and more epic or lyrical. The new drama took on more the qualities of the modern novel, with its focus on the inner thought processes of its protagonists, or of poetry, where subjectivity overcomes third-person objective description.

Developing on Lukacs's theories, Peter Szondi has analyzed how modern European dramatists attempted to negotiate this inherent dramaturgical problem.[23] In Ibsen and Chekhov, the events of the past dominate, determine, and limit the actions of the present, and characters slip into reminiscent monologues to add temporal and psychological depth to the present action (or lack thereof) portrayed on stage. Hauptmann's naturalist drama subjected action and character to a ruthless determinism. August Strindberg wrote, "I believe that the complete portrayal of an individual life is truer and more meaningful than that of a family";[24] his expressionism postulated a radically personal "I dramaturgy" that shifted the focus from the social or family unit, from history to autobiography, to the individual ego as the center of dramatic action. In such drama, individual character was increasingly smashed into fragments of a disintegrated self. Maeterlinck's symbolist *drames statiques* seemed to deny the very underpinnings of dramatic form, attenuating action and interpersonal relationships; similarly Hugo von Hofmannsthal's lyric drama eschewed action for the creation of a mood.

Through their dramaturgy modern playwrights tackled the problem of how to stage modern life. Though their solutions were various, they had one thing in common—namely, an estrangement from what had typically been regarded as "dramatic": the sphere of interpersonal relationships, the here-and-now, public action. Of all the forms modern drama took, naturalist dramaturgy was closest to the novel; this similarity may explain why ultimately it was the least stable, quickly giving birth to its successors, symbolist and expressionist drama, and also perhaps accounting for why Ibsen's social dramas had a more profound influence on early-twentieth-century fiction than they ultimately had over work for the stage.

The One-Act Play and Mori Ōgai

One solution for the dramaturgical challenges of staging modern life for European playwrights in the 1880s and '90s was the one-act play. "A Scene, a 'Quart d'heure,' seems to be the type of theatre piece for people today," wrote Strindberg in 1889.[25] It was also an immensely popular form for Taishō playwrights. The one-act stood in relation to the more traditional multi-act play in the same way as the short story did to the novel. Kikuchi Kan assessed the advantages of one-act dramaturgy in a 1924 essay:

> Truly dramatic events do not occur so often in the life of a certain individual or group of people. If one thinks about it, such events have occurred perhaps only once in our life to date and perhaps will occur not more than two or three times in our entire life. In that sense, a dramatic event occurs very seldom and within a very brief span of time.
>
> It therefore follows that even if one writes a play in five or even four acts with a certain protagonist, not every act will contain something dramatic in it. The dramatic event will occur in the fourth or fifth act, and the rest of the play will be there to lay down the plot or set up the character. In short, the play will be filled with anti-dramatic (*higikyokuteki*) elements. Of course, in order to write of intricate dramatic events, there is no doubt that it is interesting to incorporate preparatory scenes, scenes like black storm clouds roiling over a peaceful sea. But the essence of drama is not to be found in character portrayal or circumstantial exposition. So since it is enough to write only what is dramatic, whatever conflict may exist requires no more time than is afforded by a single act. . . . I have a sense that for a dramatist the one-act play is the most direct and honest form. . . .
>
> From the standpoint of audience appeal, the one-act will in due course surely come to dominate all other forms of drama. Just as the short story is the natural offspring of modern literature during the second half of the nineteenth century, so too is the one-act play the last-born child of the modern drama movement; thus, it should assume its destined place as inheritor of the stage. After all, the frenetic pace of modern life renders it impossible for audiences to spend long hours at the theatre, making it all the more essential that the playwright gets his point across in as little time as he can.[26]

As we see, Kikuchi (who had learned his dramaturgy well at the feet of George Bernard Shaw and J. M. Synge) used brevity and economy as arguments for the one-act play. His critique of the multi-act perhaps also hints at a recognition of the increasingly anti-dramatic nature of modern dramaturgy. Thus, the one-act is seen as a way to recover the dramatic by its intense focus on a single, isolated event. Peter Szondi, however, notes the following:

> The modern one-act is not a Drama in miniature but a part of the Drama elevated to the whole. . . . Because the one-act no longer draws on inter-personal events for its tension, this tension must already be anchored in the situation. . . . If it is to maintain a semblance of tension, it must elect a borderline situation, a situation verging on catastrophe—catastrophe that is imminent when the curtain goes up and that later becomes ineluctable. Catastrophe is a given, lurking in the future: gone is the tragic, personal struggle with a destiny whose objectivity humans could . . . resist through their subjective freedom. What separates the individual from destruction is empty time, time that can no longer be filled by an action. . . . Thus, even on the level of form, the one-act proves to be the Drama of the unfree.[27]

It is unlikely, however, that contemporary Japanese writers had this insight; many were attracted to the form's potential to isolate and highlight moments of intense emotion and conflict.

By the Taishō era, the one-act had become one of the most popular literary forms, and most of the credit for introducing it rests with Mori Ōgai, both for his translations of Western drama and for a significant number of one-act plays he wrote in the first decade of the 1900s. We have already seen that his criticism, especially his advocacy of "straight drama" shorn of spectacle and driven by dialogue, had a profound influence on the development of drama as a literary genre in the 1890s. Had Ōgai done no more than translate from European literature, his reputation as a central figure in modern Japanese intellectual life would have been assured. Much of what he translated was drama, published in the pages of *The Pleiades* and his brother Miki Takeji's journal, *Kabuki*.[28] Of Ibsen's plays alone, he translated *Brand* (1902), *John Gabriel Borkman* (1909), *A Doll House* (1913), and *Ghosts* (1914). In 1909 and 1910, Ōgai published two collections of one-act plays in translation (over a dozen in total) by Gabriele d'Annunzio, August Strindberg, Gerhart Hauptmann, Frank Wedekind, Maurice Maeterlinck, Arthur Schnitzler, Hugo von

Hofmannsthal, Rainer Maria Rilke, Oscar Wilde, Hermann Sudermann, and others. Kaneko Sachiyo calls these anthologies "indispensable guides for young literati who wanted to write drama." Mafune Yutaka (1902–1977), a major playwright of the 1930s and '40s, called Ōgai's translations a bible for young dramatists.[29] Ōgai completed the cycle with a collection of a dozen of his own one-act plays, *My One-Acts* (*Waga hitomakumono*), published in 1912.

As with Shōyō's translations of Shakespeare, something of the history of the Japanese language can be traced in the development of Ōgai's own dramatic style, from the measured, classical, but very rational seven-five syllable prosody of his earliest play, *The Jeweled Comb Box and the Two Urashima Tarōs* (*Tamakushige futari Urashima Tarō*, 1902, commissioned by the *shinpa* actor Ii Yōhō), to later plays like *Shizuka* (1909) and *The Ikuta River* (*Ikutagawa*, 1910), which were written in unadorned, contemporary colloquial dialogue.[30] Form follows content to some extent here: Ōgai's earlier plays, which are set either in the historical past—*Urashima* and *Nichiren's Sermon at the Crossroads* (*Nichiren tsuji seppō*, 1904)—or somewhere exotic, like India—*Purumula*, 1909—use versions of the classical idiom as a kind of alienation effect. For *Nichiren's Sermon*, Ōgai employed a kind of *kyōgen* style. *Purumula* presented problems: "I tried out various styles, but nowadays there's no set way to write historical plays. A Western play, if lyrical, might be written in free verse, or in prose form, but since we don't have rules about such things, it was a real chore, and an even greater one since I was writing of matters long ago in a foreign land."[31] Like Shōyō earlier on in his career as a translator, Ōgai settled on a modified puppet theatre style. *Shizuka* and *The Ikuta River*, on the other hand, though set in the distant past, are both close to the modern colloquial. In his last play, *The Soga Brothers* (*Soga kyōdai*, 1914), Ōgai reverted to literary Japanese. Kinoshita Junji claims Ōgai was one of the few playwrights of his generation who gave serious thought to the problem of language, yet his experiments are not altogether successful.[32] The dialogue in even his modern colloquial plays seems wooden, artificial, and argumentative, as if Ōgai were using his characters to push an idea and not reflecting on how his people actually conversed. For his experiments with dramatic language and his use of the one-act play as a medium for the exploration of ideas, Ōgai had a profound influence on a future generation of playwrights. But his plays remain corseted by the influence of Western drama.

Translating the West

Translated drama had a profound impact on the production of domestic plays, both sparking and inhibiting Japanese creativity. The role of translation (as opposed to adaptation) of Western drama during the first decade or so of the twentieth century has been neatly summarized by Ayako Kano:

> As Westernization fades from foregrounded theme to backdrop, free-wheeling adaptation (*hon'an*) gives way to straight translation (*hon'yaku*). The connecting thread is a new, or heightened respect for the original: a sense that the original Western text must be taken seriously, treated with reverence, transplanted carefully to Japanese soil, with as little disturbance as possible. Whereas Westernization in the early years of Meiji was characterized by a pragmatic attitude of borrowing whatever seemed useful from the sources and adapting it to the Japanese environment, even when the result was a haphazard mishmash, Westernization in the late Meiji and early Taishō years was both more careful and more wholehearted. Whereas in the 1870s and 1880s, Western institutions were imported because they were useful and functioned better, in the 1900s and 1910s, Western ideas were imported because they were thought to be universal and make you a better person. Whereas straightening theater meant borrowing useful plots from Western plays and adapting them into Japanese theater; New Theater meant making Japanese theater as Western as possible.[33]

This shift in sensibility by the first decade of the twentieth century is captured in Ōgai's *Youth:* "How had classical Shakespeare been performed in Japan up to now? According to today's newspapers and magazines, Venice had become the town of Yashiki-machi in Surugadai, and the actor playing Othello appeared on stage in the braided uniform of a Japanese army general wearing the Third Order of Merit for his role in the Sino-Japanese War. Just to imagine such a setting and costume would certainly have caused today's youth to feel as if they had been insulted."[34]

The new taste for authenticity presented Japanese writers in the first decades of the twentieth century with a dilemma, however: how might writers liberate their own voice without having that voice preempted by the alien forms and ideals they attempted to emulate? Could foreign ways of thinking, being, and acting ever be assimilated? Should they? Ōgai had a keen understanding of what happened to Western culture when it was introduced to

Japan. Noting that "the Japanese people import all kinds of systems, all kinds of *isms*," a character called Fuseki (a stand-in for Natsume Sōseki) remarks in *Youth* that "At first, Ibsen was Norway's little Ibsen, but after turning to social drama, he became Europe's big Ibsen. When he was introduced to Japan, however, he again reverted to the small Ibsen. No matter what comes to Japan, it turns into something small."[35]

The problem of how to "translate" the West was a dilemma felt more keenly in the *shingeki* movement than in perhaps any other area of contemporary Japanese culture.[36] *Shingeki* was faced with what Gioia Ottaviani has called a "twofold learning process," in which it had to learn the codes of not only a new theatrical model, but also the "unfamiliar cultural reality" reflected in that form.[37] Before modern theatre as an artistic form could be born, it had to undergo a revolution in thinking, in the discovery of the individual self, in human relationships, and in attitudes toward society. Nor was it enough to put such new ideas on paper; they had to achieve concrete form on stage, with living characters faced with realistic human problems with which Japanese audiences could identify. Inasmuch as translated drama was the model— indeed provided the majority of the repertoire—for the New Theatre, actors had somehow also to transform themselves into Europeans. Kishida Kunio (1890–1954), who would become a key *shingeki* figure, would in the 1920s sum up the problem of doing Western drama in Japan: "To transpose the words themselves from one language to another is one thing. When it comes to the various problems in staging a foreign play, the most important element remains the impersonation of the characters by the actors. No matter how a Japanese will disguise himself, he will not look like a Westerner. . . . To a certain extent, unless the actor's appearance, movements, and expression are 'translated' into Japanese terms, their original meanings will be lost to us."[38]

The tensions raised by the attempt to reconcile foreign models with personal expression played out as a debate over the relative virtues of translated drama and original work written by Japanese. It was a debate that exercised the energies of dramatists and theatre practitioners for the better part of two decades. Osanai threw down the gauntlet the year he inaugurated the Free Theatre, proclaiming "an age of true translation for both playscripts and directing methods."[39] The same year, 1909, in the pages of *Entertainment Illustrated*, Osanai got into a debate with the playwright Mayama Seika over the merits of staging translated over domestic drama. In an open letter to the *kabuki* actor Ichikawa Danshi (who played Erhart in the Free Theatre production of Ibsen's *Borkman*), Osanai wrote that "I hope to bring about in the Japanese theatrical world a real 'epoch of the foreign play in translation,' both in the matter of the plays themselves and the acting technique; modern Japanese plays will come later."[40] He qualified this remark immediately by noting that he planned to stage modern adaptations of the works of Chikamatsu and Ihara Saikaku. (Indeed, in the late 1920s, Osanai would direct versions of Chikamatsu at the Tsukiji Little Theatre.) He added that he was also interested in "new Japanese social dramas" but that there were "really very few of these. And among these few are not many good ones. We probably will not have this type of play in our repertory for the time being."[41] In a rebuttal entitled "Sow New Seeds," Mayama Seika expressed doubts as to whether Japanese audiences were ready for Osanai's radical ideas. He also asserted the importance of the playwright in guiding theatre reform.[42] Countering this, Osanai struck a chord that would remain a leitmotif throughout his career as a theatre director: "How much of a contribution have literary men made in the past to the progress of theatrical art? I have real doubts about this. My opinion is that while harm has certainly been done, no good has been contributed at all."[43]

As we have seen, since the 1880s, the general drift had been toward the elevation of drama to literary status and, by the same token, the rise in the importance of the dramatic text and the playwright. This movement helped spark the boom in playwriting during the Taishō era, but it was not a trend Osanai fully supported. The Free Theatre would stage several modern Japanese plays—Mori Ōgai's *The Ikuta River;* Nagata Hideo's *A Fiend for Pleasure* (*Kanraku no oni,* 1911); Akita Ujaku's *First Dawn* (*Daiichi no akebono,* 1911); and two plays by the poet Yoshii Isamu (1886–1960), *Yumesuke and the Monk* (*Yumesuke to sō to,* 1910) and *Kawachiya Yohei* (1911)—but Osanai clearly saw that his mission was to produce plays by Ibsen, Chekhov, Gorky, Maeterlinck, and other Europeans. This impetus to produce Western drama grew even stronger after his first trip to Europe in 1912–1913.

The major *shingeki* troupes focused their efforts on the production of foreign drama, not domestic. Some two-thirds of the plays staged by Shōyō's Literary Society and Osanai's Free Theatre were European. Already by 1913, the plethora of translated plays was identified as a major problem. Hasegawa Tenkei took Osanai to task for his neglect of domestic drama, declaring the preference for staging foreign plays "superstitious" and calling for its eradication. The bodies of Japanese actors are simply not suited to the playing of Europeans, he said.[44] (We shall see below that others take the same tack.) In 1915, another critic, Masumoto Kiyoshi, would similarly lament the "decline of *shingeki*" due to its overemphasis on translated drama. It had become harder and harder to stage good Japanese plays in a style that matched their content.[45] But others like Honma Hisao would argue that Japanese theatre was still in a state of transition. Drama had not yet reached appropriate artistic standards, and it was necessary to stage translations of European plays.[46] The end result was that *shingeki* essentially became synonymous with not only Western stagecraft and acting technique but also Western drama. The vast majority of domestic drama, if staged at all, was produced by *kabuki* and *shinpa* troupes, new wine in old bottles.

The argument has been made that much of the drama written and published during the Taishō era was never meant for the stage anyway. Many writers seemed content in using the form as a literary experiment, producing *lesedrama*, work written less for the stage than for the page, or armchair theatre. Though Osanai and others would stage a number of his plays, Tanizaki for one admitted that "I wrote plays as a form of fiction. I cannot entirely abandon the notion of 'drama for the sake of reading,' I suppose. It would be enough if the reader were able to construct and illuminate in his mind a stage where he freely manipulates his actors, thereby enjoying the illusion of the drama."[47] Such remarks do not speak well for the art of drama, however. Though in his later novels Tanizaki would demonstrate a flair for dialogue and dramatic pacing, his plays are discursive, static, and filled with long expository speeches. A closer professional association with the theatre might have given Tanizaki and many of his contemporaries more opportunity to hone their skills at writing good stage dialogue.[48] Pointing out that "too many novelistic elements had crept into" Tanizaki's plays, Osanai would take an axe to Tanizaki's script for his production of *The Age of Terror* (*Kyōfu jidai*, 1916) at the Tsukiji Little Theatre in 1927.[49] Though he was a prolific dramatist and his plays were frequently staged in the 1910s and '20s, the work of Mushanokōji Saneatsu likewise betrays a discursive sensibility that is singularly undramatic, with characters more like puppets expounding the ideas of their maker. As exercises in literary form or the use of dialogue to advance an idea, these works may have some appeal, but they are not *drama*, something that can hold our interest when performed by live actors on stage. For that, dialogue must be an integral part of the action.

From the second decade of the twentieth century, playwrights became increasingly estranged from direct involvement in the theatre world. At the same time, their model—foreign drama—also tended to inhibit personal expression. Kishida Kunio had doubts that the performance of translated drama alone could be a sufficient medium for the expression of what was relevant to contemporary Japanese. He would write in 1923 that Japanese playwrights "were able to acquire almost nothing of substance from the influence of foreign drama. It would not be an exaggeration to say that Japanese drama remains in the Stone Age as far as literature is concerned."[50] Some of the challenges faced by dramatists in assimilating Western ways can be seen in the work of Ibsen's epigones in Japan. Playwrights found it a hard task to make Japanese characters speak and act like a Nora or an Erhart. Writing of works like Mayama Seika's *First Person* (*Daiichi ninsha*, 1907) and Nagata Hideo's *A Fiend for Pleasure*, Akemi Horie-Webber comments that "some of these plays show a curious poetic conflict: while they adopt the ideas of their original models, the actions of the Japanese heroes seem to be frustrated. Their natural impulses as characters and their thematic ideals seem to be in conflict."[51] A similar tension can be found on a linguistic level. The Japanese dialogue attempts to replicate the style and syntax of the original plays that served as its models, often resulting in strained and exotic metaphors and locutions that seem anything but what a Japanese person would actually say.[52] The Japanese language literally strained under the weight of new ideas.

In a more substantial sense, the new drama epitomized by Ibsen may have been ultimately uncongenial to the Japanese, who, though excited by the ideas in his plays, typically try to avoid conflict and argumentation in their social dealings. The artificiality of so many of the social dramas written in Japan in the early 1900s can be attributed to a large extent to a failure to transform their stage characters into Japanese versions of Europeans. Many critics, like Nagahira Kazuo and Ōzasa Yoshio, have suggested that Maeterlinck, whose plays were more congenial to Japanese social tastes, had a greater impact on modern Japanese drama than Ibsen ever had. Certainly Maeterlinck's influence can be detected in the still, even static, nature of many of Ōgai's plays and, through Ōgai, the work of his student Kinoshita Mokutarō (1885–1945) and that of Yoshii Isamu, Kubota Mantarō (1889–1963), and others. A dramaturgy and dialogic rhetoric of Japanese social interaction could not be invented overnight, but the themes that Ibsen and his contemporaries would introduce to the vernacular of modern drama—the growing self-awareness of men and women; domestic, class, and intergenerational tensions; all the fault lines that began to appear in any society faced with the challenges of becoming "modern"—demanded a voice. Dramatists of the Taishō and early Shōwa eras would experiment with every mode available to them—chiefly naturalism, symbolism, and expressionism—to articulate the concerns of their generation.

In the following pages, we shall look at four one-act plays from a dozen years leading up to the Great Earthquake of 1923. These works represent what I consider are fairly successful attempts to assimilate European ideas, stagecraft, and style into an idiom congenial to contemporary Japanese audiences and readers. In short, they present modern Japanese people (bourgeois, urban, working class, and provincial) and their concerns in language that is for the most part close to how ordinary people indeed spoke. Given the narrow focus on the one-act on isolated situations, subject matter centers on the modern family, especially on marital relations, and (with the exception of Izumi Kyōka's symbolist tribute to Maeterlinck) the works are strongly realist in style, though at times, because of the implication of catastrophe that hovers over the form, these plays are not without a certain melodramatic flourish.

OKADA YACHIYO

....

THE BOXWOOD COMB

INTRODUCTION

As we have seen, the Japanese premiere of Henrik Ibsen's *A Doll House* by
Tsubouchi Shōyō's Literary Theatre in 1911 had an electric effect on Japan's
intelligentsia. Nora's character sparked intense debate, not least in the pages
of *The Blue Stocking* (*Seitō*), the feminist magazine established by Hiratsuka
Raichō. Okada Yachiyo (1883–1962) recalled that on the night she went to
see *A Doll House*, she was so excited she couldn't sleep.[1] Yachiyo was already
a well-established novelist and playwright whose reputation had, at least until the establishment of the Free Theatre in 1909, eclipsed that of her older
brother, Osanai Kaoru. Considered as good a writer as poet Yosano Akiko
and novelist Higuchi Ichiyō, she had published her first work, a brief sketch
called *Encounter* (*Meguriai*), in 1902, in the literary magazine that Akiko and
her husband, Yosano Tekkan, had founded, *Morning Star* (*Myōjō*). This was
followed by a succession of short stories and novels that were published in the
leading literary magazines of the day. At the same time, Mori Ōgai's brother,
Miki Takeji, had hired her as a theatre critic for his journal, *Kabuki,* and in
1905 she published a dramatization of Tokutomi Roka's *Ashes* (*Haijin*), still

---

Photo of Okada Yachiyo (1922) courtesy of the Museum of Modern Japanese Literature, Tokyo.

regarded as one of the finest stage adaptations of a Meiji-era novel.² Scholar Akiba Tarō has praised the work for its strong dramatic tension. The play faithfully captures the novel's lyricism without lapsing into the sentimental-ism typical of so many of the *shinpa* adaptations.³ The same year Yachiyo published her first original play, *Wasteland* (*Yomogiu*), in *Morning Star.* She was poised to play an important role at the beginning of a new age of drama inspired by the founding of the Literary and Free Theatres.

Family connections played a not insignificant role in Yachiyo's life. Her father, a military doctor, was a close friend of Mori Ōgai, and it was Ōgai's formidable mother who introduced Yachiyo to the painter Okada Saburōsuke, recently returned from studies in France.⁴ (Another famous artist, Foujita Tsuguharu, was a cousin.) She and Okada were married in 1906; it would be a stormy relationship, marked by several periods of separation. Yachiyo ex-pressed at one point a preference for young and attractive actors (her husband was her senior by some thirteen years); for a while she took the brilliant *shinpa* actor Yanagi Eijirō as a lover. She and Saburōsuke separated, first in 1925 and for the second time during a trip they made to France in 1930; her husband returned early to Japan while Yachiyo lingered on in Europe until 1934. She remained estranged from her husband until his death in 1939.

All the while, Yachiyo was active as a playwright and novelist, serving on the editorial board of *The Blue Stocking* and in 1922 founding the magazine *Women's Art* (*Nyonin geijutsu*) with Hasegawa Shigure. Throughout her life she was also active in promoting children's theatre, and in 1948 she established the Japan Women Playwrights' Association (Nihon Joryū Gekisakkakai). Her memoir of her brother, *Osanai Kaoru's Young Days* (*Wakaki hi no Osanai Kaoru*), published in 1940, is still considered a classic. Akiba Tarō remarks that Yachi-yo's dramatic output was small compared to her fiction, but her plays are, with few exceptions, first-rate.⁵ Nobel Prize–winning novelist Kawabata Yasunari compared her work favorably to that of Izumi Kyōka, Nagai Kafū, Tanizaki Jun'ichirō, and Kubota Mantarō: elegant, urbane, a bit cynical, with a whiff of vulgarity, "too strong to fall into the trap of sentimentalism and too ironic and rebellious to lapse into received opinion."⁶

An expression of Yachiyo's own reservations regarding the institution of marriage, *The Boxwood Comb* was undoubtedly written as a kind of response to *A Doll House,* but it is no pale imitation of Ibsen's work, as so many of the social dramas written in Japan during this period were. True enough, Yachiyo's heroine, Otsuna, is not afraid to speak her mind or kick against the constraints of her marriage, but in fact the vector of the play is diametrically opposed to

Ibsen's play. Where Nora balks at her suffocating bourgeois life with Torvald, Otsuna has already been cast out but is desperate to return to her husband, expressing at one point the old-fashioned longing to feel what it is like, even for one day, to sit in the family shop, managing the household accounts. For this reason, although Akiba Tarō and others have called Otsuna an Ibsenesque "new woman," Inoue Yoshie has called the play "a tragedy of . . . a woman who cannot become a 'new woman.'"[7] Indeed, it is her ambivalence that gives Otsuna's character psychological depth and raises the play above that of a merely ideological statement. Otsuna's predicament is not actually a lack of love in the marriage—it would seem that she and her husband, Toyonosuke, still feel strongly for each other; rather, Otsuna deeply resents the presence of Toyonosuke's father, Tōhei, in the house. Although Tōhei is portrayed as a meek and reasonable man, Toyonosuke's older brother and sister have already turned the old man out, hinting that he is more trouble than he appears. Otsuna's hard-bitten upbringing has taught her how to put up with domestic suffering, but the bliss of the first few years of her marital life alone with Toyonosuke have been snuffed out by the meddlesome Tōhei, and she wants her husband back. For his part, Toyonosuke calls on his responsibility as a son to care for his aged father, insisting that Otsuna has been bitter and violent toward the old man. (An outburst in which she pushes Tōhei over, cutting him on a knife, precipitates her third and last expulsion from the house.) Many critics have echoed critic Ōe Ryōtarō's remark that the play highlights "the spite and rebelliousness of Japanese women repressed under the old family system," in which the woman was little better than a servant to her husband's parents, but the situation is topical for anyone who has had to deal with in-laws, and Toyonosuke's protestations of Confucian filial piety ring a bit false.[8] Toyonosuke was under no legal obligation to take in his father, and he seems more concerned about his own reputation—what his siblings will think—than about his wife's plight. In this respect, his fixation on respectability resembles that of Torvald in *A Doll House*, notes Inoue.[9]

The Boxwood Comb may also have been written as a response to Mori Ōgai's short story "Half a Day" (Hannichi, 1909), which reflects the author's own wife's resentment against his strong-willed mother. The protagonist wonders:

> Was there any other woman in the world like his wife? How was it possible, in a country where rigid concepts like filial piety existed, to have a woman so unfeeling as to speak about her mother-in-law like that in front of her

husband? Even in Western thought, a person's mother was sacred—there wasn't a woman alive who believed it was all right to slur her mother-in-law in front of her husband. . . . He wondered about this special product of the present age, which was changing each and every one of its values.[10]

Ōgai's protagonist clinically (and chauvinistically) concludes that his wife's jealousy is "perverse" but that the winds of ideological change, especially regarding women's rights, sparked her "perversity." Otsuna too claims that her own predicament had driven her into a kind of madness. Indeed, her problem is that unlike Nora, she has nowhere to turn: both her husband and her parents have rejected her. A woman's lack of independence is echoed in the words of the more naïve Osode, who expresses reluctance to ever get married even as she is being dragged into an *omiai*, a meeting with her prospective husband. *The Boxwood Comb* is thus a tragedy of a woman's place, her limited options, in Meiji society. Cornered lovers choose death in traditional Japanese drama, but this work, like Higuchi Ichiyō's *Nigorie* (Troubled waters, 1895), presents the disturbingly modern solution of murder-suicide.

The Boxwood Comb was not staged until 1921, in a *shinpa* production at the Yokohama Theatre. Kitamura Rokurō's *shinpa* theatre company Seibidan staged the play two years later, in Asakusa Park in Tokyo; Kitamura would regularly produce the play during his long career. *Shinpa, shingeki,* and even *kabuki* have since the war frequently staged the play; a 1962 Literary Theatre (Bungaku-za) production starred Sugimura Haruko (1909–1997). The latest production for which I have a record is one by the Progressive Theatre (Zenshin-za) in 2004. The translation here is based on the texts in Okada Yachiyo: *"Tsuge no kushi,"* in *Nihon gikyoku zenshū* 36 (Shun'yōdō, 1929), and *"Tsuge no kushi,"* in Nihon kindai engekishi kenkyūkai, *Nihon no kindai gikyoku,* 63–77.

Nakamura Tsuruzō as Toyonosuke and Kawai Takeo as Otsuna in Asakusa Shōchiku-za production of *The Boxwood Comb*. Photo in May 1927 issue of *Engei Gahō*. Photo courtesy of Hibino Kei.

OKADA YACHIYO

THE BOXWOOD COMB

FIRST PUBLISHED:
Entertainment Club, September 1912

FIRST PERFORMANCE:
Yokohama Theatre, 1921

CHARACTERS

....

TOYONOSUKE, *husband, 25 years old*
OTSUNA, *his estranged wife, 25 years old*
TŌHEI, *his father, 52 years old*
OSATSU, *an old woman sent by* OTSUNA, *50 years old*
OSODE, *a local girl, 17 years old*
TAMEKICHI, *a shop boy, 14 or 15 years old*

TIME: *Summer*
PLACE: *Tokyo*

(A side street off a major thoroughfare. At stage right, the rear of a storehouse, sur-rounded by an earthen wall, and an alleyway leading off it. At stage left, another alleyway bordered similarly by another earthen wall. At center is the storefront of a comb shop with its noren *curtain hanging down. On either side, to right and left, are shelves for storing boxes of combs and blocks of wood for making them. There is a window at stage left, underneath which is a cushion and table where tools for comb making are laid out. The storefront where the shelves are has a wooden floor; glass doors divide it from the private quarters, which have* tatami *mats and what look like a sitting room and a kitchen beyond. Under the shop eaves hang festival lanterns.*

TOYONOSUKE *sits off to one side in a stylish cotton kimono, by an ashtray, smoking a pipe. He is a handsome but haggard-looking man. The distant sound of festival drums. The curtain opens.)*

TAMEKICHI: *(Standing there.)* So, Toyo-san, you've got till the day after tomorrow to finish that comb for the bangs. I'm sorry for making you work on a holiday like this, but it's the Master's orders. I hope it's all right. And are you all right with the marriage proposal? They're expecting you both tonight. Don't forget.

TOYONOSUKE: *(Lost in thought.)* Yes, yes, all right.

TAMEKICHI: Day after tomorrow, right? Now, why would a man like Toyo-san make a comb with thirty-three teeth?—Mistress said so too. Why'd you do it, Toyo-san?

TOYONOSUKE: *(Taking out a comb wrapped in paper and looking at it.)* It ain't like I made it that way on purpose.

TAMEKICHI: So how come having thirty-three is such bad luck?

TOYONOSUKE: Damned if I know. Some story that if you stand at a crossroads at nightfall and stroke the teeth of the comb and curse somebody, your curse will come true. An old superstition, that's all.

TAMEKICHI: No kidding! So if it was me did the cursing and I cursed you and said, "Tonight you will die," then you'd die, would you, Toyo-san?

TOYONOSUKE: *(Stroking the comb, then suddenly stopping.)* Watch what you wish for, there! Go on, get home with you! The Master will bawl you out for goofing off.

TAMEKICHI: All right, all right. Don't forget tonight. Or the day after tomorrow. *(He quickly leaves by the alley at stage left.)*

TOYONOSUKE: *(Deep in thought, he counts the teeth on the comb and clicks his tongue.)* How come there were thirty-three? I've never made such a fine comb as this one. *(The sound of someone knocking out the ash from a pipe upstairs. Clicks his tongue again.)* They're still at it. *(He wraps the comb back in the paper and puts it inside his kimono, then opens the glass doors and makes to call upstairs.)* Hey, Dad! *(Pause.)* Dad!

TŌHEI: *(Offstage.)* Yeah!

TOYONOSUKE: You can talk all night, but it won't change anything. Give it a break and come down.

TŌHEI: We were just finishing.

TOYONOSUKE: *(Returning to the storefront.)* And in this heat. How long are you going to be up there? Why'd she have to send that bitch?

TŌHEI: *(Enters from back. He has a gentle face.)* Osatsu says she's leaving.

OSATSU: *(A vulgar-looking woman, cheaply dressed. Enters behind TŌHEI.)* So, whatever happens, you're through with Otsuna?

TŌHEI: I've said it already, but I'll say it again—the two of us fellows can manage quite well on our own.

OSATSU: *(Glancing sharply at* TOYONOSUKE.*)* You're such a coward, Toyo-san. Have you forgotten what you promised Otsuna?

TŌHEI: *(Seeing that* TOYONOSUKE *is offended, interrupts what he is about to say.)* This one *(points at* TOYONOSUKE*)* said it before, but I'll say it again—we might have told her we'd call for her once we had our store, but that was, after all, just to get rid of her. Even if we do have a store again—and it's a store in name only—it's all thanks to the Master, and we have to go along with his advice on the marriage proposal too. The Master doesn't take kindly to Otsuna, you know. Please tell her, no hard feelings.

OSATSU: In other words, you're telling me you won't take her back because the Master won't go for it? Right, now I understand you. So what you're saying is Toyo-san's getting himself a new wife to look after the shop. Hah, hah!

TOYONOSUKE: *(Unable to keep his tongue.)* Wise up, Osatsu! Who said I was taking a wife?!

OSATSU: Don't play the fool with me! Weren't you and Tame-don, the Master's boy, just talking about a marriage proposal? I may be old, but there ain't nothing wrong with my ears!

TŌHEI: Wait a second there—

TOYONOSUKE: *(Cutting in.)* If you don't watch what you say to this woman, you'll just make more trouble for the Master. Leave it be.

TŌHEI: I guess you're right.

OSATSU: Anyway, I'm just the messenger, here to pass on what I was told to say. But what are you two going to do with Otsuna?

TŌHEI: Well, I'll discuss it with my boy.

TOYONOSUKE: No discussion necessary. I'm not going to have a wife who raises her hand against my dad.

TŌHEI: Now, that ain't no skin off my nose. But I can't stand idly by and watch my own son so put out all the time. Besides, it's hardly fair to the Master either. So, sorry, but the answer's no.

OSATSU: But Otsuna feels bad about it too. She blames herself something awful for hitting you, Pop. That's why she wants to—

TOYONOSUKE: *(Shaking his head.)* I won't listen, I won't! No excuses, thanks. Even if my dad asked me to call her back, I wouldn't. I can't forgive Otsuna when I think of how she was so mean to my father.

OSATSU: Why, Otsuna feels awful about it too. Don't you think, Toyo-san, after all the girl's been through, that it's too much to tell her now you're calling it quits? Look—you've finally got yourself a decent place close to the Master, and you could send her home anytime you want. The poor girl says all she wants is to sit there in the shop, even a day would do, and see what it feels like to be the lady of the house. I can tell you, if there's any more trouble, I won't side with her. I'll give the girl hell, I will.

TOYONOSUKE: *(Refusing to give her any quarter.)* No deal! I don't know and I don't care how many times you've vouched for her. It's because she's not here that I've managed to get this place. No way am I having a wife who gives my dad grief.

OSATSU: So if your dad doesn't care for the girl you've picked, you'll throw her out till you get one he likes?

TOYONOSUKE: What business is it of yours?

OSATSU: That's right, I'm just a nosy old bag. Maybe so, but who for, eh? Weren't you in love with Otsuna?

TOYONOSUKE: *(Starting to stand.)* Now—

OSATSU: No need getting all hot and bothered about it! Hah, hah. Why don't you cut her a bit of slack? How about it, Pop?

TOYONOSUKE: No way. I put up with it twice—no—three times already. I even had her apologize to my dad and come back to live with us. After all, without a wife around I had to put my dad to work, make him fix dinner when I'm too busy and all that. I felt sorry for my old man; that's why I agreed to let her come back, but only if she apologized to him. But I'll tell you this for starts that woman's temper is something wicked. Just because my dad and me were whispering to each other—or so she says—she suddenly lashes out at him. See for yourself. *(Rolls up* TŌHEI's *sleeve and shows off his bandaged elbow.)* It ain't even healed yet. Hitting an old man, for God's sake! Knocked him back so he fell and cut his elbow on a kitchen knife lying there. Call it an accident if you want, but if she had half a care for her husband's old man, it wouldn't have happened in the first place. No way I'm going to take in a woman who'd hurt my own dad. Uh, uh!

OSATSU: So you're saying it's out of the question, are you?

TOYONOSUKE: Enough already! Shut the hell up and leave.

TŌHEI: Now, now, mind your tongue, boy. Don't get mad, Osatsu—just go home. I ain't going to let a little scratch bother me if my boy loves the girl. He's got other problems to deal with, so why don't you come back some other day when you feel like talking?

OSATSU: So you've made up your mind not to take her back, have you, Toyo-san?

TOYONOSUKE: That's right. My mind's made up.

OSATSU: Right, then. That's what I'll tell her.

TŌHEI: Mind what you say, though, Osatsu. We don't want her playing around with knives like that again.

OSATSU: Aren't you the brave one, though, Toyo-san! I wouldn't give her back even if you begged me.

TOYONOSUKE: *(Bitterly.)* Thanks for nothing. She ain't even your own kid. Go on, get out! The holiday's a waste, and all 'cause of you.

OSATSU: Why, sorry to trouble you. Don't forget, mind you. *(Spitting out these words, she begins to leave by the alley at stage left.)* So I'll tell Otsuna you boys have already settled on another bride.

TŌHEI: You can't say that, Osatsu!

TOYONOSUKE: Forget it, Dad. Let her go.

OSATSU: You're a big boy now, aren't you, Toyo-san! *(Leaves by the alleyway.)*

TOYONOSUKE: She gave you a hard time, Dad. Why don't you go have a nice hot bath? *(He himself looks wan and exhausted.)*

TŌHEI: Hell, I went last night. You go. It's a holiday after all. I'll go lie down instead.

TOYONOSUKE: *(Puts on a brave face to hide how bad he feels.)* Really? I'll go have a bath, then.

TŌHEI: *(Noticing his complexion.)* You don't look so well. Is there anything wrong?

TOYONOSUKE: Nah, just a stiff neck, that's all. I'll go, then. *(Stands, then sits down again.)* Hey, Dad.

TŌHEI: What?

TOYONOSUKE: I know what we said, but being the way she is, she's not above coming herself to complain about it. If she comes when I ain't here, don't look weak at all. You tell her what-for and send her packing, 'cause if you don't it'll be me who leaves next time. Understand? There's no way I'm going to let her hurt you again. I'd never be able to face big brother or sister if I did.

TŌHEI: Don't you worry; I can't just stand there and act like a coward when I've seen how much you've suffered. But Toyo, I don't want you to feel bad either. If you love the woman, then go on, take her back. She'd listen to reason if you spelled it out for her. Why, I'm an old man, Toyo—I figure I'd better get used to being a nuisance. I already exhausted my welcome with your brother and sister. You're the youngest—you've done more than your share to look after me. I don't mind if that wife of yours gave me a bit of trouble. If you feel even a wee bit sorry for that woman, have her come back, and if it doesn't work out for me, I'll go live someplace by myself.

TOYONOSUKE: For heaven's sake, Dad, I beg you, don't talk like that! If ever I made you leave, then the rest of them would start saying stuff like, look at him, talking like he's better than us, taking Dad in but all gaga over a woman who cuts the old geezer! How could I ever face them again after I made such a to-do out of taking you in? Please, Dad, stay put and don't talk like that anymore. I beg you. Why would I feel anything for Otsuna? If you ever let her back, why, I'd be the one to leave.

TŌHEI: Right, then. I may be a nuisance for you, but I'd die happy if you read me my last rites.

TOYONOSUKE: Don't talk like that, please! You're only asking for trouble. I'm going now, so you watch out for her. I doubt if she'll come, but if she does—she's done it before—mind you don't give her any slack.

TŌHEI: Don't worry. I'll be fine.

TOYONOSUKE: I won't be long. *(Begins to go inside, then stops.)* Oh, and Osode might come with her mother, so make sure you have them wait. I'm supposed to take her to the Master's place tonight.

TŌHEI: *(Happily.)* So, finally, it looks like it'll all work out?

TOYONOSUKE: Uh huh. It's pretty much settled. Madam says she wants to see the girl for herself, but I'm not supposed to tell her that. The idea is we're going to see a show they're putting on at the Master's place 'cause of the festival.

TŌHEI: That was smart. After all, the young master fell for her when he saw her at the *kiyomoto* teacher's.[11] No money, but her mother's clever and her brother's respectable. Good match for the lad.

TOYONOSUKE: That's right. He's no slouch himself when it comes to a modern education or how to make a living. Osode's a lucky girl. I'll be off then. I'll lock the back door on the way out. You mind the store.

TŌHEI: Right. Take your time.

*(*TOYONOSUKE *goes inside. Presently there is the sound of a door closing. Enter* OSODE *from the alley at stage left. She is a well-bred-looking girl, with her hair up in a* shimada. *She is dressed for an outing and carrying a cashmere* furoshiki.*)*[12]

OSODE: *(Peering in the store.)* Grandpa! Grandpa!

TŌHEI: *(He is lying down but rises when called.)* Is that you, Osode? My, but aren't you pretty!

OSODE: Now, don't be naughty.

TŌHEI: Come on in. Where's your mother?

OSODE: *(Sitting on the veranda in front of the store.)* A customer arrived just before we left, so she told me to go on ahead.

TŌHEI: Is that so now? Well, come on in.

OSODE: This is just fine. I ran into Toyo-san just now. *(Points at the alley.)*

TŌHEI: Yes, he headed off for the bathhouse.

OSODE: *(Plaintively.)* What sort of place is this house that Toyo-san's talking about, Grandpa? Is his store a big one?

TŌHEI: It's not that large, really. There's a garden. Quite a nice one too.

OSODE: Is that so? I suppose there's a master and a madam and a young master, a chief clerk—lots of people.

TŌHEI: To be sure. They're receiving guests today.

OSODE: But I'm not really one for going to other people's houses. I much prefer being on my own, I do.

TŌHEI: Hah, hah. . . . The guests won't care for that.

OSODE: I don't mind.

TŌHEI: Hah, hah.

OSODE: But they said they're going to put on a play. The chief clerk and the shop boy.

TŌHEI: Is that so? I don't know anything about that. You like plays, Osode?

OSODE: I do, but I've hardly ever had a chance to see one, except the odd one at the Kabuki-za. Everybody says Toyo-san's wife looks just like Kawai, but I don't know any Kawai. Calling him by his surname makes him sound like a businessman, though.[13]

TŌHEI: Hah, hah. I guess it does. But I heard you play a mean *kiyomoto*. Why don't you play for me sometime?

OSODE: I'm not good at all. But the younger master's brilliant!

TŌHEI: Then you ought to accompany him on the *shamisen* while he sings.

OSODE: But I'd sound awful on the *shamisen*. He's too good.

TŌHEI: I've never met him before. What sort of fellow is he?

OSODE: What sort of fellow? A man, of course.

TŌHEI: Ever heard of a "young master" who was a woman?

OSODE: You're just making fun of me, Grandpa!

TŌHEI: If you're going to get in a huff like that, nobody will marry you.

OSODE: Who needs a husband?

TŌHEI: So you're going to be a burden on your brother for the rest of your life?

OSODE: I wouldn't be a burden on him, even if I lived with him for two lifetimes.

TŌHEI: Maybe not on him, but if he got himself a wife, you'd find out soon enough how much of a pest you were.

OSODE: But he's still at school, for heaven's sake! Take a wife? Don't make me laugh.

(Enter OTSUNA *from the narrow alleyway at stage right. Her hair is in the "gingko leaf" style.[14] She is wearing a fashionable summer cotton kimono with a black satin obi, into which she has hidden a razor wrapped in scarlet silk. She snoops around* TOYONOSUKE's *shop.)*

TŌHEI: Hah, hah, hah. Maybe not now, but soon!

OSODE: I doubt it.

TŌHEI: Not yet, you may think, but before you know it, you'll be somebody's wife yourself.

(Blanching, OTSUNA *listens carefully.)*

OSODE: I'm just not going to get married, that's all.

TŌHEI: Hah, hah, hah. . . . Come on in. Toyo will be back any time now, and so will your mother. Let's go upstairs and have a cup of tea. The weather's gotten rather sticky. Come on upstairs. It'll be a bit cooler there.

OSODE: What's happened to my mother?

TŌHEI: She'll be here soon. Come on in now.

(Holding her furoshiki, OSODE *enters and makes to go upstairs.* OTSUNA *slips out of the alley and jealously peers inside. Footsteps from stage left.* OTSUNA *hides in the alley at stage right. Enter* TOYONOSUKE *from the alley at stage left, holding a towel and some soap, looking fresh from the bath.)*

TOYONOSUKE: *(Looking at the shop.)* Hey, Dad! I'm back. *(Seeing* OSODE's *sandals.)* Is Osode here, then?

(There is no answer. TOYONOSUKE *sits down on the veranda.* OTSUNA *enters from the alley.)*

OTSUNA: *(Lowering her voice.)* Toyo-san. *(*TOYONOSUKE *turns around, gasps, and stands up.)* Don't you love me anymore?

TOYONOSUKE: *(Looks back at the store, then turns toward* OTSUNA.*)* Just you wait there. *(Begins to go inside.)*

OTSUNA: *(Stopping him from entering.)* Are you going to run away on me?

TOYONOSUKE: *(Forcefully.)* Of course not. *(*OTSUNA *lets go of his hand. Again he peers inside and prepares to go in.)* My dad's upstairs.

OTSUNA: Say the two of them are upstairs. Your dad's got himself a new daughter-in-law, eh? Congratulations! *(Bitterly wipes away her tears.)*

TOYONOSUKE: Don't talk nonsense! Since when did I get a new wife?

OTSUNA: Quit hiding things from me! She's younger than me and prettier too.

TOYONOSUKE: Keep your voice down! You're talking rubbish. She's marrying the young master, she is.

OTSUNA: Don't take me for a fool. Do you really think somebody like the Master would take in a girl like that?

TOYONOSUKE: It don't matter what kind of girl she is. If the young master takes a liking to her, there's no reason why he wouldn't marry her. You've no reason to be jealous.

OTSUNA: But it's my nature. You can't try to fool me with a story like that. You're taking Osode to the Master's place tonight, aren't you? I know everything. They sent someone over to tell you to bring her, didn't they?

TOYONOSUKE: You're taking it all wrong.

OTSUNA: Wrong? If you heard what I heard your dad say about this "bride" a moment ago . . . it burns me up! Do you really mean to get rid of me?

TOYONOSUKE: Surely you ought to know how I feel, don't you?

OTSUNA: Didn't you tell Auntie to tell me you wouldn't let me back, not for anything?

TOYONOSUKE: But you had to go and use that old bag again. You want to get it over with and settle matters once and for all, do you?

OTSUNA: *(Beginning to feel somewhat relieved.)* No, not really. You're too patient. A man like you has to be shown something to remind you of his woman. I was beside myself with worry. Last time I went home only because you said you'd make sure you'd do something to make it right. That was half a year ago, and still no word from you. And then on the sly you pulled up stakes and moved house on me.

TOYONOSUKE: But I couldn't help that. The Master told me to move someplace closer to them, and my dad said he wanted to move too.

OTSUNA: So it's all right so long as the Master and your father tell you so, eh?

TOYONOSUKE: Not exactly, but surely I'd be a bad son if I let my dad live someplace he didn't like, even for a little while.

OTSUNA: So it would have been fine if I'd never found this place, I guess.

TOYONOSUKE: No, that's not true. But it ain't like I moved abroad—it's still the same neighborhood, surely.

OTSUNA: But there's no way I'd have been able to find you if luck wasn't on my side. *(Weeps.)*

TOYONOSUKE: But, my dad—

OTSUNA: My dad, my dad; every other word you say is "my dad." You love him so much, do you? You love him so much you're prepared to throw your own wife out on the street?

TOYONOSUKE: Yes, I love him. Love him so much I'd throw my own life away. It burns me up wondering why on earth you can't even try to find a place in your heart for the old man, even a smidgen of what I feel for him. *(His eyes filled with tears, gazes at* OTSUNA.*)*

OTSUNA: Why is it? Why can't I be as gentle-hearted as you? Surely it wouldn't be so hard, would it? If only I could be as good as that Osode.

TOYONOSUKE: That's right. That's all you got to do.

OTSUNA: *(As if imagining something.)* Asking me to cover my ears and hold my nose, no matter what's said or done, even if it makes me crazy. . . . No, I won't! I hate it! Hate it!

TOYONOSUKE: You don't want to; that's why you can't. Why, if you were as gentle as Osode, I'd never have told you that you and I were through. You think I like saying that?

OTSUNA: So you don't hate me?

TOYONOSUKE: Of course I don't hate you.

OTSUNA: I'm so happy to hear that. So you told Auntie what you told her just because your dad was there.

TOYONOSUKE: Of course.

OTSUNA: Then let's run away together.

TOYONOSUKE: *(Shocked.)* Don't talk rubbish. Who'd dump his own dad and elope with his wife? Think about it.

OTSUNA: But won't your dad tell you you've got to marry Osode?

TOYONOSUKE: What are you talking about? I told you, she's the young master's—

OTSUNA: That's a lie. Such a nice girl, your dad thought. He must hate me.

TOYONOSUKE: She's not as nice as you make her out to be. You could be as nice as her if you listened to a bit of reason.

OTSUNA: And how many times have I come back because I meant to listen to reason? Why is some other woman nicer than me? Even I've run out of patience with myself. But I'm so lonely without you—so lonely I don't know how I can go on! I beg you. I'd do anything to see that your dad's looked after if a little cash could settle matters. Come on, let's run away together.

TOYONOSUKE: That's impossible.

OTSUNA: So what am I to do?

TOYONOSUKE: We can't stay together if you don't become a woman who'll do whatever she needs to please my dad.

OTSUNA: And what about you?

(She stares hard at TOYONOSUKE. OSODE'*s voice is heard upstairs.* TOYONO-SUKE *drags* OTSUNA *to the alley at stage left.)*

OSODE: *(Entering from inside, followed by* TŌHEI.*)* I'll go look. What happened to my mom, I wonder?

TŌHEI: I wonder. And what's happened to Toyo? I thought I heard voices just now. . . . Toyo! . . . Maybe he ran into her. Everybody's gone to the festival. . . . Toyo! Are you there?

OSODE: There's his soap and towel. That's odd.

*(*TOYONOSUKE *enters from the alleyway.* OTSUNA *hides.)*

TŌHEI: Is that where you were! What were you up to?

TOYONOSUKE: Why, the ditch cover came loose. Can't have somebody falling in, can we?

TŌHEI: That so? *(Gazing at* TOYONOSUKE'*s face.)* But you sure look awful. Did something happen?

TOYONOSUKE: Nah, nothing. Nothing at all. Just that stiff neck of mine that's bothering me.

TŌHEI: That ain't good. If you're feeling so bad, maybe you shouldn't be going to the Master's place.

OSODE: Shall we cancel?

TOYONOSUKE: We can't do that. This has all been arranged for you, girl. How 'bout this? Can't you go for me instead, Dad? What do you say, Sode-chan?

OSODE: But surely we'd be imposing on your father?

TŌHEI: No skin off my nose.

TOYONOSUKE: Thanks, Pop. It's easy—all you have to do is say something came up. Of course I mean to go. As soon as I'm ready, I'll close up shop, but you go pick up Sode-chan's mom first. I'll see you later.

TŌHEI: Right, then. You'll be all right on your own, will you?

TOYONOSUKE: Sure. It's nothing.

TŌHEI: Then I'll go throw on a jacket. *(He goes inside.)*

TOYONOSUKE: Give my respects to Madam for me, will you, Sode-chan? You never know who's going to be there. Don't laugh too much, okay?

OSODE: Really? . . . What'll I do if I laugh?

TOYONOSUKE: It don't matter if you laugh a little.

*(*OTSUNA *spies on them.* TŌHEI *comes back out, bringing a pair of clogs.* OTSUNA *hides again.* TOYONOSUKE *takes the clogs from his father and lays them out for him to put on.)*

TŌHEI: Much obliged. Shall we go then, Sode-chan? Why don't you lie down for a bit? Get a bit of rest before you come.

TOYONOSUKE: Go ahead; don't worry about me. I'll be there soon. The streets are crowded, so mind how you go. Those floats are dangerous, you know.[15]

TŌHEI: Right, then. We'll take the side streets.

TOYONOSUKE: Uh, uh. It's safer in the main streets. Make sure you pay my respects to your mother, Sode-chan. I'll be there soon.

OSODE: We'll see you soon then.

TŌHEI: Go lie down now.

(The two leave by the alley at stage right.)

OTSUNA: *(Entering from the alley at stage left.)* How come those two get along so well? I hate them! I feel like throwing rocks at them.

TOYONOSUKE: Don't do anything so stupid. What would you do if you hurt the girl?

OTSUNA: Damn them!

TOYONOSUKE: Damn them? It's you who's damned. What was it made you such a bitch, anyway?

OTSUNA: You're to blame if I've become a bitch.

TOYONOSUKE: What?! You saying I was the one who gave you such a wicked temper?

OTSUNA: Well, didn't you? You waited till now to criticize me, but why weren't you harder on me from the first? Surely you never said to my face I was a bitch or anything like that till your dad came to live with us. I never used to be such an irritable woman. You say I've got a bad temper, but you're the one who gave it to me. Until your dad showed up, I was free to think and do as I pleased without a care for what others thought. And you were happy too; you never ever yelled at me. But then your dad came to live with us, and you were the one who lost his temper, always telling me to do this or do that. It was daddy, daddy, from morn' till night, till I hardly knew whether I existed or not. Sometimes when I wanted to talk to you about something, your dad would give a little cough and you'd fly right to his side. Or there was someplace I wanted to go with you, but it always fell through because of your father. . . . Till your dad came you never put me down, but ever since he showed up, I haven't felt myself at all. You always made me feel so small that I wished if it was going to be like this, you'd put me in my place from the beginning. Before I came to live with you, I was stuck with a drunken mother and mean old stepmother and never had a day when I could take it easy, not even a minute. Between all their bickering and scolding I just got smaller and smaller. Then when I came to live with you, suddenly I felt myself getting bigger. It was just like I'd stepped out of a cold wasteland into warmer, greener pastures. Even if sometimes I was made to go back to that cold wasteland for a while, I figured that was fate—I wasn't one to resist. But I've spent so long in that warm, green place that I've forgotten all about what it was like to feel the cold, and I haven't got the strength to put up being sent back to that cold, cold wasteland anymore. Never once when I was stuck in that wasteland did I wonder what it was like to be anywhere better—well, maybe sometimes I did, but you showed up just when I'd resigned myself to my fate and dragged me off against my will to a better place. Didn't you? If you send me back to that place now, I'll freeze to death! The old me would have been able to put up with it, but not now. I can't. I tried everything to stay with you; I tried crying, tried to get you back from your dad, but it was no good. That's when I started acting up, but you always sided with your father and never once stood up for me. When I realized it was impossible so long as your dad was there, I wondered how I could get rid of him. That's when I really tried to bait him, but he'd never stand up to me. I was at my wit's end trying to think up some way of getting him to leave. I did it all so I could win you back. I don't think I did anything wrong. It was because I wanted to win you back that I started to hate him. But you never tried to understand how I felt, not even a little. You only blamed me. If you wanted to blame me so much, why didn't you do so from the start? . . . I thought, if only your father weren't around. I'd like to see your dad suffer, and I don't care who does it! I don't want anybody to treat him nice! *(Bursts into tears.)*

TOYONOSUKE: You've got a right to say what you do. But you only listen to yourself and never listen to what anybody else says. How did you get so twisted? You've never once tried to think about what sort of man my father is.

OTSUNA: That's right. Never. There's no way I'm going to like somebody who stole my husband.

TOYONOSUKE: You're still not making sense. So long as you feel the way you do, I'll never be able to be with you.

OTSUNA: Was it your father coming to live with us that made you so hard? There's no way I can feel that you love me like you used to.

TOYONOSUKE: You don't understand. You don't even try.

OTSUNA: I can't understand! I can't understand! There's no way. *(Shaking her head violently, weeps.)*

TOYONOSUKE: Hush! Somebody's coming. Come with me.

(The two hide again in the alley at stage left.)

TAMEKICHI: *(Entering from the alley at stage right, walks up to the shop.)* Hello? Toyo-san! Toyo-san! Madam's waiting for you. She says to hurry. Toyo-san!

(Leans over the veranda and peers inside, then picks up the comb wrapped in tissue.) It's the comb. Thirty-three teeth, eh? *(As if remembering.)* Toyo-san's not here. Maybe he's dead. Damn. Didn't she tell you to bring the girl? She's waiting for you. . . . *(Enters the shop and opens the glass doors.)* Nobody home. Then he must've left. What a pain! *(He tosses the comb into the shop and leaves at stage right.)*

(Presently TOYONOSUKE, *looking pale, comes out of the alley at stage left.* OT-SUNA *follows, clinging to his sleeve.)*

TOYONOSUKE: Let go of me! I have to go to the Master's place.

OTSUNA: No! I won't be made a fool of, especially by that Sode-chan!

TOYONOSUKE: Why don't you understand? Haven't I told you already that she's to become the young master's wife? Quit being so jealous. Let go! *(Tries to shake her loose.)*

OTSUNA: *(Tripping but not letting go.)* For heaven's sake, Toyo-san, forgive me, but don't go to the Master's place today. If you don't go today, I promise I'll be nice. . . . I'll be so nice it'll kill me.

TOYONOSUKE: Playing your trump card, eh? You've fooled me one time too many. I'm not falling for that again.

OTSUNA: Don't say that, please. I beg you! *(She falls on her hands and knees and pleads.)*

TOYONOSUKE: Please don't do that, Otsuna. There's nothing I can do. *(Exhausted, sits down on the veranda, then, noticing the comb, takes it.)* Here, comb your hair with this. Go home today, accept your fate, and if you still love me, wait till I come for you again. . . . Why, this is the best comb I've made in ages. A bit of me went into making it. It's yours, so look after it for me. Come on, Otsuna. *(He puts the comb in* OTSUNA's *hair.)*

OTSUNA: *(Weeping.)* I'm not going home! Not even if I die here.

TOYONOSUKE: Die?

OTSUNA: Yes! I came prepared.

TOYONOSUKE: *(Thinking for a while.)* It's no good. I can see through your tricks. Go home today. The time will come, so wait. I won't ask you anymore to do what's not in you and look after my dad. I was wrong to try and force you. Just wait till I come for you. I won't even insist that you be nice to the old man's memorial tablet.[16]

OTSUNA: Don't say that, Toyo-san. I won't lay a hand on him. Never again. If ever I did, you could divorce me for an eternity and still I wouldn't complain. If my right hand touched him, I'd use my left to kill myself. I won't lie to you. Please, Toyo-san.

TOYONOSUKE: No. It's no good. If you feel this way now, why didn't you apologize then? Even though I wept and begged you, you wouldn't apologize for hitting my dad, not from your heart. That's okay. I accept that. I know you know you did something wrong, so it's all right. But how do you expect me to keep a woman who hurt my own dad, no matter how much I love her? Imagine what would happen if my eagle-eyed brother and sister got wind of that? How could I ever face them again after I made such a show of taking the old man in?

OTSUNA: No! I apologize! See? I'm begging you on my hands and knees! *(Grudgingly, she kneels on the ground and bows.)*

TOYONOSUKE: It's too late. You're sorry now, but why weren't you then?

OTSUNA: *(Clinging to* TOYONOSUKE, *who attempts to leave.)* Toyo-san! How did you become so hard? *(Weeps.)*

TOYONOSUKE: Guess why. You fooled me time and time again, and every time I let you, I made my dad suffer and I was the butt of my brother's jokes. But I put up with it. My brother and sister too put my dad through hell. Still, they never laid a hand on him, not once. I took my old man in, promised to do my best and look after him, but then you go and cut him. I don't care how much I love you—how can I face the world with you still at home? I want to be strong. And you need to be put in your place. If I was the one who gave you your wicked temper, you were the one who made me so hard. We both became what we didn't want to be. So long as I can't safely send my father on his way, I can't see how I can ever be with you.

*(*OTSUNA *suddenly looks up and, clutching the razor blade in her obi, makes to run off.)*

TOYONOSUKE: Why are you looking like that? Where the hell do you think you're going with that razor?

OTSUNA: If your dad's gone, the two of us can be together.

TOYONOSUKE: *(Holding her back tightly.)* Have you gone mad?

OTSUNA: Yes, I'm mad! I'm a demon! What was it? Three times you threw me out? Didn't I get an earful every time that happened from my own mom and dad? But I put up with it. What I couldn't put up with, though, was having to face your father's ugly mug every day. And the third time, they couldn't care less. There was no way I could stay there. I'd be better off dead if you won't take me back. I don't care if I do kill your dad, all I want is just one more day, even another hour with you, just the two of us alone. I don't want to die like some wretched woman thrown away by her man.

TOYONOSUKE: You think people would give you even a minute's peace if you killed somebody? Even if nobody found out about it, you think I'd give a woman who killed my dad even a second of my time?

OTSUNA: Ah!

TOYONOSUKE: Let go! If anybody saw us like this. . . . Let go! *(He tries to wrest away the razor, but* OTSUNA *clings to it desperately, staring hard at him.)* What's the matter? Calm yourself! I'll think of something. Please, Otsuna! I hear voices. Let go! *(The sound of festival floats slowly approaching.)* Hey. The floats are coming. If you don't let go, somebody's going to get hurt. Somebody might see us.

OTSUNA: *(Gazing at him without even blinking.)* Toyo-san.

TOYONOSUKE: What?

OTSUNA: Let's go someplace. Somewhere your dad can't find us.

TOYONOSUKE: Huh?

*(*OTSUNA *suddenly clings to* TOYONOSUKE *and stabs him in the side. They fall, one top of the other. The cries of the floats swell, then begin to fade. They both struggle to get up.)*

OTSUNA: Forgive me, Toyo-san.

(Still clinging to TOYONOSUKE, *she stabs herself below the breast. The cries of the floats fade away.)*

—The curtain closes quietly.—

THE RUBY

Introduction

By the beginning of the Taishō era, Izumi Kyōka was already a well-established novelist. He had made a name for himself in the 1890s, while still in his early twenties, as a writer of sensational stories noted for their action, ornate language, and biting social criticism. The rising *shinpa* star Kawakami Otojirō staged a bowdlerized version of one of Kyōka's first successful novels, *Loyal Blood, Valiant Blood* (*Giketsu kyōketsu*), as *Taki no shiraito* (named after the novel's heroine) within months of the novel's publication in 1894. The play, about a circus entertainer forced to commit murder in order to raise money for her lover's school tuition fees, was a hit; indeed, it sparked a theatrical genre. Such dramatizations of contemporary fiction—the precursors, in a sense, of the soap opera—ensured the development of *shinpa* into a mature stage art. Both the reading and the theatergoing public had an enormous appetite for sentimental and melodramatic tragedies. Kyōka's fiction in particular featured the rising class of young professionals in love with "professional women": entertainers, geishas, prostitutes.

Many of Kyōka's plays continue to be performed. Of all the Meiji novels

Photo of Izumi Kyōka (ca. 1900) courtesy of the Museum of Modern Japanese Literature, Tokyo.

that *shinpa* staged, Kyōka's have had the longest shelf life. Several other Kyōka novels, including *A Woman's Pedigree* (*Onna keizu*, 1908), *A Vigil's Tale* (*Tsūya monogatari*, 1909), *The White Heron* (*Shirasagi*, 1910), and *Nihonbashi* (1914), became standard *shinpa* repertoire, and in so doing, they also helped ensure the writer's lasting popularity. "*Shinpa* would never have been born," actor Kawai Takeo remarked, "had it not been for the influence of the "Kyōka plays. . . . If one counted not just the novels, but also the plots we borrowed from them, why, it would amount to an incredible number of plays. As you know, the master's prose and dialogue are difficult; the masses' ears are not attuned to it. So the novels were staged one after the other, in a thoroughly plagiarized form."[1]

Kyōka maintained an association with the *shinpa* theatre and lifelong friendships with two of its star *onnagata*, Kitamura Rokurō and Hanayagi Shōtarō, but by the first decade of the 1900s he was increasingly dissatisfied with the liberties *shinpa* companies were taking with his novels. At the same time, he had taken a beating from the rising camp of naturalist literature in the decade since the death of his mentor, Ozaki Kōyō, in 1903. Much of his fiction had in fact taken a considerable departure from the familiar world of the novels that *shinpa* adapted. The new trend in his work was not, however, toward greater realism but rather in the direction of unbridled fantasy. Kyōka delved into the world of dreams, myth, symbol, and the occult in such novels as *The Kōya Saint* (*Kōya hijiri*, 1900) and *Grass Labyrinth* (*Kusa meikyū*, 1908), breaking new ground in the emerging genre of fantastic literature.

By the end of the Meiji era, Kyōka had begun to write stage adaptations of his own work and, subsequently, original plays. Practically all of Kyōka's plays, works like *The Sea God's Villa* (*Kaijin bessō*, 1913) and *The Castle Tower* (*Tenshu monogatari*, 1917), were written in the Taishō era. *Shinpa* would stage only two of his original plays, *The Ruby* (*Kōgyoku*, 1913) and *Demon Pond* (*Yashagaike*, 1913), and most of Kyōka's drama would have to wait until the 1950s, or later, to be staged. *The Castle Tower* had its first production in 1951, *The Sea God's Villa* in 1955; *Kerria Japonica* (*Yamabuki*, 1923) was not staged until 1977, and other works, like the fascinating *Polytheism* (*Tashinkyō*, 1927; it is based on the *nō* play *Kanawa*), have still not had professional productions. It was the post-1960s generation of the experimental *angura* theatre that would champion Kyōka's original plays. Directors like Ninagawa Yukio, Miyagi Satoshi of Ku Na'uka, and Kanō Yukikazu of the contemporary neo-*kabuki* troupe Hanagumi Shibai have presented Kyōka as a herald of the avant-garde. Indeed, with its disorienting amalgam of nostalgia, horror, and surrealistic comedy, much of the Taishō playwright's drama anticipates the work of Kara Jūrō and Terayama Shūji, who also staged versions of Kyōka's plays and fiction.

The Ruby was the first of Kyōka's original plays to be staged and, incidentally, had the distinction of being the first public open-air production of a modern play in Japan. Directed by novelist and playwright Yamamoto Yūzō and starring Inoue Masao (an enterprising *shinpa* actor noted for staging unusual new drama), the work was performed on the grounds of the former Satake estate in Tabata, Tokyo, a fitting place for the play's setting.

The Ruby is one of Kyōka's most daringly poetic and symbolist works. The theme of a woman's adultery is told almost entirely in a chain of connected images, many of them (as is typical in Kyōka) color-coded: flowers and rainbows, a ruby ring, crows, pampas grass, autumn wind, and swirling leaves. As in the *nō* drama, Kyōka's ornate language conjures up a world, and much of what occurs is related to us rather than enacted. A maid in the service of a wealthy couple confesses to the jealous husband how a crow has stolen a ruby from the ring on her mistress's finger, a gem that is then found by a stranger who agrees to return it only on condition that the mistress dress as a crow to retrieve it; he soon becomes her lover. Even the crow has a part to play here, for she and two of her avian companions devote much time (as is typical in much of Kyōka) to, first, making fun of humans, then to discussing when and how to make a meal of them. The adulterous couple is illuminated in a spotlight, only to be plunged into darkness again, hinting at their death at the hands of the jealous husband. Fraught with an overripe eroticism and shot through with flashes of black humor, the story of an unfaithful wife is quite literally framed by an artist who seems in his drunken stupor to have dreamed up the whole tale. The work's symbolist treatment of adultery is reminiscent of Maurice Maeterlinck's *Pelléas et Mélisande* (1892), but it also stylistically owes much to *nō*. (Kyōka's mother came from a long line of *nō* musicians and actors who were in service to the Maeda clan in Kanazawa during Edo times.) Indeed, the drunken artist is much like the *waki* of *nō* theatre, a passive spectator to an event largely told, not enacted, one concerning people who are little more than shadows and memories.

But perhaps the work was too ahead of its time after all because it baffled many contemporaries. Writing in *Imperial Literature* (*Teikoku bungaku*), Sangu Makoto, a student of English literature and later translator of Yeats, remarked:

> I could not avoid feeling that as rich as *The Ruby* is in Kyōka's uniquely beautiful and symbolic language, it was nonetheless too fantastic. A work of

this sort needs to be grounded in a firmer sense of reality, something that is lacking here. It distresses me to say this because I have so much respect for the genius of this gentleman. Of course, he is a romantic, but I couldn't help but think that the work would have been that much better had he drawn upon myth and legend, in the way that Yeats does.[2]

Reading this play some years ago, I felt I agreed with Sangu. *The Ruby* struck me as an interesting but not altogether successful experiment. My opinion changed after seeing a production of the play (quite possibly the first since its 1913 premiere) in 2002. Simple but effective lighting and staging were used to present images suggested in Kyōka's hypnotic dialogue, thus underscoring the passage from this world into another and making sense, without being too explicit, of much of what seemed obscure on the page. Here theatre demonstrated that it was more capable than literature in treating metamorphosis, a strong motif in Kyōka's work: the painter, with his canvas on his back, looks like a monstrous kite; the three crows in black boots, dresses, and gloves are sexy women, while the maidservant in her disguise is a poor excuse for a crow, and yet there is enough of the other in each for us to wonder which is human and which supernatural.[3] The original Japanese text can be found in Izumi, *Kyōka zenshū*, 26:1–27.

Performance of *The Ruby* at the Satake Estate in Nippori. Photo in December 1913 issue of *Engei Kurabbu*. Photo courtesy of the Shōchiku Otani Library, Tokyo.

Okuma Neko, Koyama Ai, and Seiho as the three Crows in Yūgekitai production of *The Ruby*, December 2002, Art Space, Osaka. Dir. Kitamoto Masaya. Photo by Miyauchi Hiroshi, courtesy of Yūgekitai.

Izumi Kyōka

THE RUBY

FIRST PUBLISHED:
New Fiction, July 1913

FIRST PERFORMANCE:
November 1913,
dir. Yamamoto Yūzō

Characters

The ARTIST
The MISTRESS
The CHAMBERMAID *(disguised as a crow)*
The HUSBAND
The LOVER
Five CHILDREN
Three CROWS *(dressed like the Chambermaid)*

TIME: *The present; early winter*
PLACE: *A moor on the outskirts of town*

CHILD 1: It's coming! From far away, from over there, where the station is!
CHILD 2: What? What?
CHILD 3: It's staggering this way and that. There's something big on its back.
CHILD 4: Even its shadow is tipsy.
CHILD 5: It must be heavy.
CHILD 1: Somebody moving in, do you think?
CHILD 2: Who cares?
CHILD 3: Look! It's like it was carrying an enormous shoji screen on its back. It's like a kite on legs!
CHILD 4: Let's put a string on it and see if it flies!
CHILD 5: Yes, yes! Sounds fun!
(Those with kites play with their kites and those with spinning tops play with their tops. One who has no toy to play with pretends to reel in a string.)

ARTIST: *(Wearing a soiled jacket and staggering drunkenly. Tied to his back by cords is a silk painting stretched on a wooden frame. In the light of the setting sun on this withered moor in early winter, his face looks flushed, lonely.)* I failed. Failed! Failed gloriously! *(Totters unsteadily on a cane. He looks like an exhausted woodcutter. Pause, then shouting.)* To hell with them! I'll show the bastards.

(Surprised by the voice and seeing the approach of the living toy that he is reeling in, the CHILD *holding the string abruptly gives the line some slack and feigns indifference.*

Unaware, the ARTIST *stops and watches the children at their play.)*

ARTIST: Hard at play. I'm jealous. Hey, kids, you having fun there?

(Seeing how he looks, the CHILDREN *chuckle.)*

CHILD 3: *(The one who reeled him in.)* Yes, we were having fun.

ARTIST: *(Ranting drunkenly.)* What did you say? *Were* having fun? I won't let you say "were"—you're too young for that. . . . "*Too* young"—why, that's an odd thing to say to a bunch of kids. *(Laughs.)* Hah, hah, hah. "*Were* having fun." Now, that sounds too sad, just too damn miserable, as if it's all game over, boys. Say, "We *are* having fun." Have fun, kids! Have fun! Don't be stingy with it! Hm? How about it?

CHILD 3: But you're angry with us, aren't you?

ARTIST: *(Not understanding.)* Me angry? At what? . . . What would I be angry at? I nearly killed myself doing some paintings for the Ministry of Education's art show; I bowed and scraped and begged the gatekeeper for the selection committee to accept them, but he made a fool of me, pelted me with platitudes till I had no choice but to back out. But did I lose my temper? No, I skulked away, leaning on my walking stick, artwork on my back and tail between my legs! Had I a stronger gut, I'd fill my belly with horsemeat and *sake* and dance and rave for you, but I'm beat and I haven't had a stitch to eat. Too sick for *soba*, so back at the station I made do with a bowl of *udon* instead. I'm a spineless, poor excuse for an Edo boy, with worms for guts, so how could I get mad at a bunch of kids like you? I'm hardly a man.

(The children all gaze at him, wide-eyed.)

CHILD 3: When I saw you coming, sir, I just got it into my head to stick a string on you and reel you in.

ARTIST: Stick a string on me? . . . Reel me in? Why, I'm not angry! What kind of game is that?

CHILD 1: Sir, it was the way you were staggering this way and that.

CHILD 2: From a distance, it was just like you was a kite.

ARTIST: A kite, you say? *(Looks at the painting he is carrying.)* Aha. So *(imitating a kite)* that was your game, was it? But when I got closer, you figured I'd get mad at you and so you quit, did you? ... Don't say you *were* having fun, though! That's too dreary! Too sad. Courage, boys! Have your fun, why don't you? Reel me in, come on, pull! I'll be your kite, I'll fly for you. High in the sky, I'll spy on the Ueno art show. Why, I'll even spy on Osaka! Kyoto too. I'll take a gander at all Japan—no, the whole damn world! ... Come, boy, raise me up! That's right! You, give me a pull. Go, boys! Go! *(Laughs.)* Hah, hah, hah.

(The CHILDREN *momentarily hesitate. One* CHILD, *figuring that the* ARTIST *is in a good mood, hugs his back and pretends to raise the kite.)*

CHILD 3: *(Runs back, pretending to pay out the string,)* This kite's too big. I can't raise it all by myself.

CHILD 4: I'll help! *(Puts his spinning top in his pocket and stands beside him. With the other* CHILDREN *in unison.)* Blow, wind! Blow! Blow from the mountains!

ARTIST: *(As the children let go, he spreads his arms wide.)* Look at me! I'm a kite! I'm the king of the castle, and you're a dirty rascal! I can do anything! *(Makes a face.)*

(As the CHILDREN *pull the string, he sails back and forth around the stage until he trips over the roots of a tree and stumbles flat on his backside. He heaves a sad sigh. Dusk falls.)*

CHILD 3: We've lost our kite.

CHILD 1: It's dark now. ... Just right.

CHILD 2: So ... shall we do it again?

THE OTHERS: Yes, let's! Let's! *(They all let go of the kite strings and spread out slightly so as to make a circle. They sing, circling, repeating.)*

CHILDREN: God of the pot,
Now here's your lot,
Speak not of now or long ago—
Set the scene
In the mountains green
And crow your way to Haguro![4]

ARTIST: *(He is silent, lost in thought, then with a deep sigh, he stands and watches them.)* Hey, there! What song is that?

CHILD 1: What song? We don't know, but if you sing it like this, then somebody will start to dance.

ARTIST: Dance? Who?

CHILD 2: Who? Somebody in the circle, somebody crouched down here, will dance, they say.

ARTIST: But there's nobody there.

CHILD 3: It's very creepy.

ARTIST: Creepy? What is?

CHILD 4: You see, it's not like you decide you're going to dance. Rather, you just start dancing all by yourself. Despite yourself. That's why it's creepy.

ARTIST: Let's try! Let me in!

ALL: Are you sure, sir?

ARTIST: Of course! Hang on. *(Takes off his painting and leans it against the tree.)* Right! Are you ready?

CHILD 3: You close your eyes.

artist: Okay. To drunkenly dance my way through life—what more could I ask for?

ALL: Set the scene

In the mountains green

And crow your way to Haguro!

(As they sing, the CHILDREN *begin to circle around the* ARTIST. *In time to the rhythm, they close the circle, then make it wider. The* ARTIST *falls into a trance, as if unconscious, and one arm, then a leg, begins to jerk weirdly. The singing voices become clearer; it grows darker.*

At that moment, from behind the tree something strange appears. Its face and beak are black; its head is like a crow's, and it is shrouded in a long black robe like a cape. It is the CHAMBERMAID. *She takes her place among the* CHILDREN *and moves around with them.*

Crouched on the ground, the ARTIST *raises himself halfway up and, swaying his upper body left and right, pretends to dance.*

Then three figures, dressed as CROWS *like the first one, appear from behind the tree, take their places among the* CHILDREN, *and circle around the* ARTIST *with them.*

The CHILDREN *continue to sing. None of them appears to notice the presence of their strange visitors. When the other three* CROWS *have joined the* CHILDREN, *the* ARTIST *rises to his full height and begins to dance as if completely in a trance. Taking their cue from the* CHAMBERMAID, *the three* CROWS *begin to leap around as if their feet have left the ground. As they begin to dance madly, the* CHILDREN *stop singing.)*

CHILDREN: *(Taking in their hands two stones, they strike one against the other and intone four or five times.)* Something evil this way comes, something shady casts its spell.

CHILD: *(Shouting; it makes no difference which one.)* Look! It's really come!
(All the CHILDREN *scatter and run away.*

Leaves fall.

In the swirling leaves, the ARTIST *and the* CHAMBERMAID *and the three* CROWS *dance like fiends. The artist is wearing shoes. The* CHAMBERMAID's *skirt has a scarlet lining, and her feet are white. The three* CROWS *are black from head to toe.)*

ARTIST: *(Exhausted, collapses flat on his back.)* Water! Give me some water!
(They all stop dancing. The three CROWS *spread their arms, and, as if interlocking wings, they stand arm in arm, watching over him.)*

CHAMBERMAID: *(With the voice of a very young woman.)* He's fallen asleep. . . .
My, what a good-for-nothing he is! A poor excuse for a man. . . . Well, I guess he'll wake and leave, all in good course—I don't expect he'll get in the way of our little party. . . . Now!
(The CHAMBERMAID *goes to the tree, and from a thicket of pampas grass growing there, she takes out three bamboo poles that have been tied together. She stands them, crisscrossed, and lays a round board on top to make a table.*

The other three CROWS *silently approach and set out two canvas folding chairs on either side.*

The CHAMBERMAID *takes a bottle of wine from a carpetbag and lays it on the table. The* CROWS *put out green and red bottles of wine together with some glasses.*

Presently, The CHAMBERMAID *brings out a candle and lights it. The stage turns bright.)*

CHAMBERMAID: *(As if just thinking of it, she pours out some wine into a glass and holds it to the light.)* How beautiful! The way the light shines clear through! It's just like that other time, when, in the dappled light of the setting sun, my mistress held up her hand and, gazing at the jewel in the ring on her slim white finger, said, "See the rainbow in the sky, yonder to the east—this stone could be the rainbow's eye." *(The* CROWS *cock their heads and listen.)* Ah, if I could drink a wine that was like distilled jewels, what would it taste like? *(She lifts the cloth draped around her throat to expose the face of a woman and makes to drink but then hesitates.)* This is my mouth, but if I were a crow, it'd be my neck right here. Ew! It's like my throat was slit. On second thought, I'd better not. . . . Listen to me! Prattling away to myself as if there were anybody here listening! . . . *(Looks around.)* Madam always said, "If you want to tell someone a secret but you're with somebody else, you can send coded messages by jiggling the legs of the table you're sitting at." Hey, Mr. Table! With your three legs, you're the perfect prop for a séance.[5]—That was wrong of me. I shouldn't talk like it was alive. Never give your secrets away. Hey, you! Keep what you heard to yourself. Don't tell anyone. Oh, what to do with the wine I poured? Ah, I've got an idea! *(Approaches the drunken* ARTIST. *One of the* CROWS *approaches and cradles his head in her lap.)* Hey, Mr. Drunkard! Here's your water.

ARTIST: *(Drinks. Coming to.)* Ah, the sun's risen! But I live in darkness. *(Falls asleep again.)*

CHAMBERMAID: The sun's risen? Did he see my crow-form through the red wine? He must be dreaming of the sun he painted. He's speaking riddles. Ah! I know, let's make a bed for him.

(She returns to her original place and, from the thicket of pampas grass, takes out a tent, which she pitches over the table. To her left and right, the CROWS *help out. The audience can see through the backdrop of the tent.)*

CHAMBERMAID: This'll be fun. *(Stands downstage center in front of the tent. The* CROWS *stand on either side.)* Ah, the sun's completely set now.

(She realizes for the first time that there are other figures in the shape of crows around her, but she seems to doubt her own eyes. Increasingly suspicious, she slowly starts to move back and forth. The crow-shaped figures follow her movements. She raises her hand, the CROWS *raise their hands; she waves her sleeve, the* CROWS *wave their sleeves, imitating her every movement. She stands on tiptoe, they stand on tiptoe; she crouches down, then watches as they crouch down. Overcome with panic, she finally runs away.*

Enter the HUSBAND. *He is wearing a gray overcoat and carrying a thick walking stick; his face is concealed by the heavy brim of his hat. He is a heavy and foreboding presence.*

The CHAMBERMAID *runs into him and, shocked, spreads wide her arms. The* HUSBAND *grabs hold of one of her sleeves. In an attempt to escape him, the* CHAMBERMAID *makes to threaten him. She caws at him like a crow, but her cries sound like a woman.)*

HUSBAND: What's this? You mean to fly away on me? You with the gates of hell for wings? *(Grabs her in his fists and knocks her over. The* CHAMBERMAID *falls onto the ground. The other three* CROWS *feign surprise.)* You're grounded, whore. Your kind doesn't cry like that. Come on, what kind of cry does a crow with clipped wings make?[6] Show me.

CHAMBERMAID: Forgive me, sir. Forgive me!

HUSBAND: Aha! "Forgive me, sir." Is that your cry? "Forgive me, sir?"

CHAMBERMAID: Yes, sir.

HUSBAND: Uh huh. *(Nods heavily.)* I hear you, I hear you. But tell me, what about my voice? You know it?

CHAMBERMAID: Yes, sir.

HUSBAND: You say you know my voice. So, look up—what do you see?

CHAMBERMAID: Master, I—

HUSBAND: *(Pinning down her skirt with his cane.)* Stop fidgeting! I haven't impaled you and strung you up in that tree, not yet anyway, so stop that flapping around, you whore! Kneel! Now out with it!

CHAMBERMAID: Please, Master, I'm awfully sorry. I've been terribly naughty.... The other day, when Madam was holding one of her fancy-dress parties out in the garden, everybody told me how good I looked in this costume. That's when I started getting the wrong ideas. It was ... after that, when Master went off on his trip and there wasn't much for me to do around the house. I asked Madam for leave—I'd say I was going shopping—then come out here and amuse myself scaring passersby like this. Well, it's gotten to be a habit. That's why, tonight.... I'm awfully sorry. I've been terribly naughty. Please, Master, forgive me.

HUSBAND: Is that all you have to say?

CHAMBERMAID: Excuse me?

HUSBAND: Is that all you have to say for yourself, woman?

CHAMBERMAID: Uh *(her voice lowers)*, you're asking me what I was doing here tonight? ... The way I look—well, I could see my shadow so clearly out here in the dark of the moor. That alone would have been scary enough, but then I noticed there were two, three more figures moving around with me. *(The three CROWS, each standing off to one side, nod again.)* I was frightened out of my wits, so I bolted and ran right into ... into you, sir. But, Master, when did you get back?

HUSBAND: From my trip? Hm. *(Sneering.)* So, you all think I went on a journey, do you?

CHAMBERMAID: Yes, the day before yesterday, to Hokkaido.

HUSBAND: My Hokkaido's out there, just beyond the walls of my estate.

CHAMBERMAID: *(Shocked.)* What?

HUSBAND: I've been to hell and back, you might say. After all, it's a journey we've all got to make one of these days, like it or not. Anybody would have done what I did, if they were in my shoes. It's an old, old trick, but I had no choice. You ought to know; when matters took a turn for the worse, the master of the house—yours truly—had to do something. Like pretend to take a trip. You might not have figured it out, but *he* did. I bet you had a pretty good idea, though—that's why you leapt at the chance. The Master's gone—so you can work your mischief and to hell what anybody thinks. You're like a thief who steals a bell, then covers his ears in the hope nobody will hear it ring. And one of these days it *will* ring. That's fate for you— people hear things. So out with it. Don't try to hide from me! When? When did all this start?

CHAMBERMAID: When, you ask? You mean those shadows I saw? Why, just now—

HUSBAND: Shut up. Don't talk to me about shadows. When did you three start dressing up as black as your black hearts and skulk around my estate?

CHAMBERMAID: I'm sorry, Master, but I don't know what you mean.

HUSBAND: There's a pistol in my pocket. You don't think I'll use it?

CHAMBERMAID: What?

HUSBAND: So tell me.

CHAMBERMAID: Forgive me, Master. It was around the end of spring. A beautiful rainbow was reflected in the garden pond, in among the wisterias and azaleas, and there, where the rainbow fell to earth, was a huge bird. Her head was pale purple, her breast feathers like an azalea ablaze in scarlet. That rainbow was her trailing tail, and she seemed to gaze up at us on the second floor. It was a day Master was away, and Madam sat at the railing watching this scene. "How lovely! Look at that bird, so big she fills the sky—I could make a hairpin from the feathers of her head and a sash from her tail. Doesn't she look like a bold general facing off against her foes, with her crested helmet and a fine tunic for a tail!" she said. "But the rainbow has no eyes and can't see, and so, poor thing, she falls headlong into the water. Here, I'll give you an eye." And as she spoke, she raised her right hand: on the finger was a ring, and in the ring was a ruby. But aloft it was no rainbow, and lowered, it didn't look like my mistress's eye. So she took it off.

HUSBAND: She took it off, did she? She removed it.

CHAMBERMAID: Then she took it in her snow-white fingers, held it high, high above the green leaves, and pretended to thread it through the rainbow. The sky glowed through her slender fingers, and the ruby shone in the light of the setting sun and turned into a dazzling rainbow's eye. It was then, I think. The garden, the pond, all went dark, and even the rainbow disappeared. Something black swooped down and spread its wings as if to blind us, then stole that ring from my mistress's hand and flew away. It was a crow and must have mistaken the ruby for the fruit of a tree, glistening with dew. It didn't fly far, only to the pine on the little hill in the garden, a black thing there against the big, round, scarlet sun setting over the wall. In my bare feet I ran down into the garden. I shouted at it, and the crow flew off over the wall, there, just by the back gate. It's been some five years since I began my service here, but never once has that gate been opened.

HUSBAND: That's right. That gate wasn't to be opened. We only opened it twice because there was a death in the family, bad luck to purge. But never before has bad luck come in that way.... And you were the one to open it?

CHAMBERMAID: Yes, the key was rusted firm in the lock and wouldn't turn, but when I pushed, it opened. The key rusted through and fell off. Outside the wall was someone—he'd been strolling by, it seemed. He stood there, staring at Madam's ring. It had fallen from the crow's beak into his outstretched hand.

HUSBAND: The bastard. He was the one, was he?

CHAMBERMAID: Yes.

HUSBAND: So it was him.

CHAMBERMAID: I explained our, er, predicament and asked him to return the ring, but he said as if to joke with me, "No, I can't give this back to you because though it may have come from a human hand, I got it from the beak of a crow. I'll return it, anytime, but only to a crow." He laughed and refused to give it back. Then he said, "Don't worry, I'll look after it. You can trust me," and from his pocket he produced a business card. "Interesting," Madam said. So a day was arranged, and around dusk—the same time of day as before—she invited him to come wait outside the back gate. Meanwhile, Madam had this, uh, crow costume made up. I was supposed to put it on and go get the ring from the man, but the mistress said "Let's have a little fun with him," and she dressed up in it and went to meet him outside the garden wall. But she was concerned she might give the children playing out in the fields a scare by the weird way she was dressed, so she invited him into our garden pavilion.

HUSBAND: So he came in by that gate, did he? He used the gate.

CHAMBERMAID: "Look, we've surprised him!" Madam whispered to me. Then she said, "Crows don't take things with their claws." So she raised this *(points to where the hood over her head opens at the throat)* and took the ring— the ring the man held in the palm of his hand—took it in her mouth.

HUSBAND: Her mouth, you say. She certainly wasted no time. The viper! Why, I'd like to grab hold of her jaws and rip them apart with my bare hands. The slut! *(Raises his foot and stamps on the withered grasses.)*

ARTIST: Ah, ah. *(He makes only two sounds, as if having a nightmare.)*

HUSBAND: *(Noticing him for the first time.)* Get over here, whore. *(Points with his stick.)*

CHAMBERMAID: *(Trembling.)* Yes.

HUSBAND: Put on that head and dance for me, dance like a crow. I need to know exactly how it looks—the black thing that has infested my garden. Dance! I've got a pistol in my pocket, remember.

(The CHAMBERMAID waves her black sleeves like a crow. She tries to dance, but it looks more like trembling. She and the HUSBAND, following behind, exit.)

THREE CROWS: *(Calling in unison.)* Don't blame us!

CROW 1: *(Cackling.)* Hah, hah, hah, hah. What should we say, then?

CROW 2: There's nothing we can say. Obviously, they'll have to blame it on the crows.

CROW 3: So what these humans have done is our fault then?

CROW 2: Blame? Fault? What humans have done only humans can fix—let them balance their own books, settle their own accounts. It's nothing to do with us.

CROW 3: True, let humans shoulder their own sins and retributions. Let them argue over it. After all, the one who started this mischief was Madam O-Ichi there. Better we find us a seat up high somewhere to watch the action. We're not much fun standing here, watching and worrying and flapping and clapping our beaks, are we?

CROW 1: No, we haven't done anything wrong. What humans call good and evil doesn't mean anything to us. All I did was perch on the rooftop there, looking for supper. And that's when the thing that lovely lady called "a rainbow's eye" got caught here *(points at her beak),* in this black proboscis of mine. Lately I haven't had the pleasure of indulging in any meat, no blood either, to say nothing of those exquisite eyeballs. I've heard say that some of the choicest delicacies in this world are phoenix marrow and griffon jaws. But a rainbow's eye . . . well! The roof was as precipitous as the bluffs over Kobe.[7] You'd risk your neck on the descent even if you could live for eight thousand years, let me tell you. If I were a hawk and it was fried tofu, it'd be, er, a piece of cake. Picking something out of a human's hand is a neat trick, but it's hardly one of our strong points, for us crows. To catch it in your beak, then swoop down into the courtyard with it would be one thing, but tell me, how to carry off the eye of a rainbow? All I had to do was scare her and fly off with it, but you can't bite down and get a good purchase on the thing—it's too damn hard, so hard my tongue went numb.

My ancestors taught me little more than how to pick off mud snails, so I have to admit I threw in the towel. Boy, was I mad! That's why I couldn't give a damn what humans said or did.

CROW 2: Ain't that the holy truth? Lord Sakyamuni himself couldn't have said it better. If it was wrong to pinch O-Ichi's ring, then you'd have to say the sun after a shower would be a mistake, so too a warm spring day or a rainbow. If perchance you see a lovely rainbow in the sky, then pretty flowers will also bloom on earth, mysterious flowers you'd never see in any nursery, no peonies or chrysanthemums, no, nor anything a monkey might pluck and festoon his raincoat with. Nameless flowers. Flowers like rainbows, in other words. A flower like that in a human's house would be like the fabled blossoms of an *udumbara* blooming on somebody's wall.[8] For us, in this benighted world of men, to gaze on such a flower exploding in bloom would be dazzling, like a brilliant rainbow. Don't you think? There's nothing so fine as to gaze on a flower so strange it'd make you forget your family, your life and limb—everything. And of all the flowers, this crimson gem that blossomed in O-Ichi's hand should be wrapped in tissue-thin Yoshino paper and put away in a case made of glass like crystallized dew! The black hands of humans may lust for it, but in the end they would pluck it and spill its petals. Humans seem to think it's something like a pair of kid gloves or a silver bracelet. Each looks pitch black to the other, just as we look as black as night to humans. Why, take that old man who came just now, with his pistol, spouting flames curling around his arm—he'd tear that mysterious flower I mentioned to shreds. Barbarian! If it's beautiful just to gaze upon, then let the flower bloom, though it bear no fruit.

CROW 3: Yeah, yeah. Flowery words, Number Two—morning for the cherry blossoms, morning for the dew, and morning for the breeze, but you're still an old crow in mourning dress and in a hurry for her breakfast. "Let the flower bloom, though it bear no fruit"—what rubbish is that? Hah, hah, hah. Don't make me cackle. Just what're we doing here? Waiting for the rainbow to scatter, and then we'll eat, we'll pick, we'll lick and suck. . . . All day, all night, all night these days, we wait our turn at the trough, clearing our throats, noisily smacking and clapping our beaks.

CROW 2: Indeed, that's why I'm waiting. A bug would spill more petals lighting on a cherry branch than us creatures. How could we lay our claws on such a flower, its ruby stamen blossoming in the calyx that is the great ring of that mysterious rainbow? We watch for the breeze to come in the evening and scatter the petals of the little poppies. But for those two flowers whose love has blossomed, all other humans are pretty much as wind when it comes to passion or desire. Yes, and what of the master here? Her husband. Like those who lord over the depths or the peaks, he's a storm, a whirlwind. Cruel master! He would scatter them all, to the last petal.

CROW 1: Who is it, flapping his beak like that, who lies in wait for the wind to scatter them?

CROW 2: Hah, hah, hah, hah! It is us! Hah, hah, hah! We spin fine and flowery words, but in fact we bide our time for prey. Besides, this flower with its ruby stamen may have blossomed from a rainbow, but when it scatters, its petals will turn into flesh and blood and florid guts. And, presto! an oily monkfish's mantle, such a morsel! Yum! Oh, let us prey!

CROW 3: When? When? I can't bear to listen! *(Flaps her wings.)*

CROW 2: No rush. Whichever way, she's ours. Those soft white limbs will lose their resilience and turn into some fine sweetmeat for a lacquer bowl fashioned from the root of a tree or a delicate little saucer made out of leaves—it's the fate of all flowers—but till then, we can do no more than keep watch on our prey. We'll have to amuse her till she leaps and dances like a fool for us. Don't they say a sea bream caught on a hook tastes better than one scooped up in a net? We mustn't torment her or make her suffer, mind you. Let her swim in the wine-dark sea.

CROW 1: So we've set the scene, pitching the tent, laying out the chairs and table.

CROW 3: With our black wings we shielded their human eyes from all we've done *(points at the tent)*. How naïve they were to think they could hide their patio furniture from us in that thicket of pampas grass! Still, stepping back and looking at our handiwork, I have to say this is really a job for lowly maids and servants. We may be crows after all, but we could do with a bit more respect than that!

CROW 2: Lions, tigers, leopards—beasts that course the earth. And our comrades of the skies: eagles, hawks, and ospreys, those charming creatures that hunt for prey. . . . And what of bears? They look like the acorns they go foraging for. And cranes? The sight of them, wagging their tails chasing after little loaches, is not so fine that it warrants any applause from us! Know that anything and anyone, when it comes to eating, loses all delicacy and decorum. So much more the case with going for the kill. One doesn't stand on formalities when pigging out. And such bones to gnaw on! Ah, a victim's wretched fate! But those bones would make a tasty sop indeed. *(Trembles with pleasure.)*

CROW 1: *(Listening and staring at the prostrate figure of the drunken* ARTIST.*)* Number Two. Hey, Number Two.

CROW 2: Aye!

CROW 3: "Aye!" she says. You're a saucy one for a ghoul, aren't you.

CROW 2: Ask me and I'll cry, "'Cor, ain't you cute?"

CROW 1: Now, jokes aside, I've been thinking here—we can wait for the *entrée*, but what about this dish laid out for us here?

CROW 3: Surely before we get drunk on his wine-soaked blood, we'd be well advised to line our stomachs with something. Not on an empty tummy, please.

crow 2: Indeed, it's almost suppertime. It's just occurred to me, but I daresay this fellow isn't quite ready for eating. Let's have a look at his face, just to be sure.

(The three CROWS *flutter over and sniff at the* ARTIST's *head, hands, and legs.)*

CROW 1: 'Cor, what a pong!

CROW 3: Yummy.

CROW 2: Not yet, surely. Look how he clenches his teeth. Generally speaking, a man who puts a cork on it even when asleep is like a clam. Try and pry your beak inside and if you're not careful, he'll have you by that eloquent tongue of yours. Next thing you know, you'll be dinner for any nasty little cur that comes along. Let some quadruped like that come taste the merchandise first, and if it's safe, we'll swoop down on it. Besides, he looks like slim pickings. There's barely any fat on him at all.

CROW 1: At a time like this, I'd be happy if he was jerky.

CROW 2: You think there's honor in risking your life for a bit of man-leather? Wait for the caviar!

CROW 3: Wait you say, but, my, what a ripe odor is wafting my way!

CROW 1: The reek of humans. The smell of a woman.

CROW 2: Watch your tongue, bitch. Better say this, that the mysterious flower makes the air smell sweet.

CROW 3: Oh, incense most rare, of aloes and orchids.

CROW 1: A scent smelled but twice or thrice in a hundred years of slaughter at Suzugamori.[9]

CROW 2: Old words from a strange bird.

CROW 3: And she tries to look so young, too. Hah, hah, hah!

CROW 1: My cackling in the dark like this gives even me the creeps.

CROW 3: What would a human say if he heard us?

CROW 2: He'd say only, "The crows are cawing."

CROW 1: Clueless, eh?

CROW 3: Wretched creatures!

CROW 2: *(Taking them under her wings.)* Look! Look! Go to them like chambermaids, greet them! *(Takes out a lit candle from inside the tent, stands blackly in the field and raises her arm aloft.* CROW 1 *and* CROW 3 *crouch beside her trailing skirts.)*

(Well upstage, beyond the pampas grass and slightly off center, beyond the tent, the silhouettes of a man and woman appear. One is the LOVER, *the other is the* MISTRESS, *beautifully illuminated.)*

CROW 2: *(Chanting in a weird voice.)* Love is wind—evanescence, wind. To leave is to cleave—grass in the wind; and meeting, too, is grass in the wind. Passion? Nothing more than dew. Life, too, is dew. What cries are insects; what sings, insects too. All that's left is the moor. Let it be, leave it alone!

(As CROW 2 *intones her spell,* CROWS 1 *and* 3 *kneel and pray. A burst of wind blows out the light. The stage goes pitch black.*

At first, there is no moon, but presently it appears, bathing the stage in its wan light. The MISTRESS *and her* LOVER, *as well as the three* CROWS *have disappeared. Only the tent remains.*

The ARTIST *wakes violently. He looks around defensively, then hurriedly opens the wrapper covering his painting. He fumbles in his pockets for a match and lights some dry grass.*

A small blaze starts. On the silk surface of his painting there are the forms of three crows.

The ARTIST *stares, transfixed. He raises his arm, as if to fend off enemies, and glares.)*

ARTIST: Behold my painting!—But wait! Is it a picture, or are they real?

—Curtain—

KIKUCHI KAN

....

FATHER RETURNS

INTRODUCTION

A 1920 production of *Father Returns* by *kabuki* actor Ichikawa Ennosuke II's company Shunjū-za at the Shintomi-za created a sensation. The playwright himself recalled the event some years later:

> I'll never forget that night on October 25, 1920, when *Father Returns* made its debut. I went to see it with several friends and acquaintances, including Akutagawa [Ryūnosuke], Kume [Masao], Satomi [Ton], Yamamoto [Yūzō], and Eguchi [Kan]. As the play progressed, I couldn't hold back my tears. When I thought it was just me who was crying, I saw even Akutagawa, beside me, weeping. When the curtain closed, I was bathed in the praises of my friends. Knowing that these were fellows who wouldn't simply resort to flattery, I was beside myself with joy. In all my life as a writer I have never yet experienced such sheer pleasure, such emotion, as I felt that evening.[1]

In fact, this was not the premiere of the play—its first production was in August 1919—but Ennosuke's production impressed everyone who saw it.

He would continue to stage *Father Returns* throughout his long career as one of *kabuki*'s leading actors, and Kikuchi's play became standard fare for numerous companies, including amateur theatre groups. No other Japanese play of the twentieth century has enjoyed such popularity or been staged so many times.

Kikuchi wrote a number of chiefly one-act plays from 1914 to 1924, a decade that, together with his editorship of the coterie magazine *New Tides in Thought*, helped spark the boom in what came to be called "Taishō drama." His undergraduate thesis at Kyoto University in 1916 was on Irish drama, and he later claimed that Shaw was one of his most abiding influences as a writer. In 1914 he had already written *Heroes of the Sea* (*Umi no yūsha*), a play inspired by J. M. Synge's *Riders to the Sea*. The first successful stage production of any of his plays was in 1919, by Nakamura Ganjirō I (1860–1935), of *The Loves of Tōjūrō* (*Tōjūrō no koi*), about the late-seventeenth-century *kabuki* actor Sakata Tōjūrō, who created the romantic hero (*wagoto*) role for which Ganjirō was so famous. Ennosuke's production of *Father Returns* secured Kikuchi's reputation, and by the opening of Osanai Kaoru's Tsukiji Little Theatre in June 1924, Kikuchi was Japan's most celebrated playwright. As editor also of *Central Review,* a general interest magazine that became the flagship for a publishing empire, he was one of the most powerful figures in Japanese letters and would remain so until Japan's defeat in 1945, when the Americans forced him out of public life because of his collaboration with the militarists during the war.

Until *Father Returns,* much of Taishō drama had been a pale imitation— if not of Ibsen, then of Maeterlinck—and most of it would be accused of being *lesedrama.* Kikuchi for one would accuse another highly successful writer of this time, Mushanokōji Saneatsu, of using drama as a pulpit for expounding his ideas and treating his characters like puppets.[2] A diligent student of the form (he carefully read William Archer's *Playmaking,* which Osanai Kaoru would later translate), he had a better sense of stagecraft than most other writers of drama at that time, most of whom were less playwrights than novelists experimenting in another literary form.

Kikuchi was a master of the one-act play, focusing intensely on a single dramatic event and the characters embroiled in it, portraying it with utmost economy and tension. Critic Kobayashi Hideo praised Kikuchi's style for its "highly logical structure, economical action and dialogue, a penetratingly psychological portrayal of his characters, and healthy moral vision."[3] A strong thematic, indeed moral, vision, combined with a strong logicality and realism, underscores all his work for the stage. "The spirit of modern theatre, regardless of where it is from," Kikuchi wrote, "is a reaction against and an attack upon existing customs and morals. Here in a country like Japan, customs and morals have latched like a scab onto our social lives. The work of a modern dramatist must be to peel off this scab."[4] In this sense, much of Kikuchi's work resembles that of his friend Yamamoto Yūzō, who also wrote drama to expose particular social or moral problems.

For critic Oyama Isao, *Father Returns* was a "textbook"; for playwright Yashiro Seiichi, "the archetype" for one-act plays.[5] Certainly Kikuchi's sure sense of dramatic form helped place this work in the canon of modern Japanese drama, but this alone does not explain the profound emotional impact the play had on contemporary audiences. Why did *Father Returns* leave its audience, even a confirmed cynic like Akutagawa Ryūnosuke, in tears?

This brief play—it is less than thirty minutes long in performance—focuses on what happens to a family when the father, Sōtarō, a man who had abandoned the family some twenty years before, suddenly appears on the doorstep. The oldest son, Ken'ichirō, had assumed the father's role in his absence, and he is the one most upset by his return. Ken'ichirō is old enough to remember how his father squandered the family fortune and then ran off with another woman.

In short, *Father Returns* portrays an almost Oedipal struggle between a father and son. Sōtarō's wayward past and wretched present are humiliating to a young man who has desperately tried to hold the family together. Ken'ichirō deeply resents the way Sōtarō had treated his mother. This father-son conflict illustrates an underlying intergenerational tension at the heart of Japanese society at the end of the Meiji era. Much of the literature of the Taishō era pitted sons against fathers or father surrogates, as in such novels as Natsume Sōseki's *And Then* (*Sore kara*, 1909) and *Kokoro* (1914) and Shiga Naoya's autobiographical *Reconciliation* (*Wakai*, 1917). Much writing was therefore devoted to the decline of the old Meiji patriarchy and its replacement by a less confident, more conflicted generation of modern men. Indeed, the decline of the family system has been a theme at the forefront of Japanese literature and film for the past century. Ueno Chizuko has made the interesting observation that there is a common tendency for Japanese families faced with a crisis to expel the individual member thought responsible, rather than band together to support that member.[6] In *Father Returns*, it is the erstwhile patriarch Sōtarō whose profligate actions are seen as a threat to family solidarity. Ken'ichirō, who has become the de facto patriarch, is most in favor of rejecting the man

who had earlier abandoned them. His stance flies in the face of the old Confucian ideal of filial piety (we are told that the family had traditionally served as
teachers of Confucian philosophy to the local daimyo), but as far as Ken'ichirō
is concerned, his father has revoked his right as *paterfamilias*. The overriding
myth of the Meiji era was that of *risshin shusse*, the dream of success through
dint of education and hard work. But as Inoue Yoshie notes, in contrast to the
typical pattern of family sacrifice (particularly the mother's) for the eldest son's
future, in this play it is the eldest son who sacrifices himself for the survival
of his mother and siblings, all because the father had abandoned them.[7] "The
reason I studied so hard," Ken'ichirō claims, "was so I could show that bastard.
I wanted to get back at the man who abandoned us. I wanted to prove to him
that I could lose a father and still grow up to be a man."

The implicit message of this play would therefore seem to be "father
returns but is rejected." Still, the outcome of the play is not determined solely
by Ken'ichirō's attitude. In fact, the ending is effectively ambiguous. Sōtarō
leaves the house, despite the efforts particularly by his wife, Otaka, and second
son, Shinjirō, to take him in. Then, Ken'ichirō experiences a sudden change
of heart, ordering Shinjirō to go find him and bring the old man back, but
the curtain closes before Sōtarō has been found. There is some evidence that
the earliest productions by Takeda and Ennosuke had attempted to close the
open-endedness of the play. It would seem that Takeda's version had the old
man found, followed by a happy family reconciliation.[8] For his part, Ennosuke,
according to Eguchi Kan, had a neighbor announce that Sōtarō had drowned
himself, thus making explicit a tragic ending that was only hinted at in the text
itself.[9] What is more problematic perhaps is the matter of Ken'ichirō's sudden
change of heart. This *peripeteia* may have a good dramatic pedigree, but it
threatens to defuse the critical message of the play in a display of sentiment.
Writing of a revival by Ennosuke that he saw in 1924, Kishida Kunio wrote:

> *Father Returns* would seem to be Mr. Kikuchi's masterpiece. There are even
> those who say that it is a classic that modern Japan has given to the world.
> ... I was deeply impressed. I couldn't suppress my tears.... It was, however,
> a regrettable artistic flaw of the play that it made the audience weep so
> much.... If I may be allowed to say so, it is a perversion of art to expect
> artistic effect through the production of commonsensical sentiment.... I
> do not mean to say that Kikuchi Kan's *Father Returns* is devoid of any ef-
> fect but the commonsensical. For one thing, the play is distinguished by a
> vivid sense of realism, and he uses deft strokes to imply without explaining

outright the development of a character's psychology. It was marvelously effective as a work of drama, but does this alone qualify it as a masterpiece of modern Japan?[10]

Similar criticism was leveled by *kabuki* critic and director Takechi Tetsuji at a postwar production by Ennosuke: "This change of heart at the end fell for an old *kabuki* cliché—to wit, the notion that 'cut as one may, one can never sever the ties of parent and child,' thus betraying the feudalistic character of Ennnosuke's *kabuki* acting."[11] Ennosuke's interpretation of the role, which had seemed so realistic and radically modern in 1920, had by the 1950s acquired the air of an old *kabuki* warhorse extolling outmoded family values. If indeed the aim of modern drama was to make its audience think more and feel less, then Kikuchi's play harked back to an earlier, more sentimental and melodramatic mode of theatre, but the changing reception of this play is indicative not only of changing aesthetic standards, but also of changing attitudes toward the family system and the individual's place inside it. In this sense, Kishida demonstrates that he was a more modern (but no doubt less popular) dramatist than Kikuchi.

This translation is based on the text in Sofue and Asada, *Nihon kindai bungaku taikei*, vol. 49: *Kindai gikyokushū*, 127–141.

Ichikawa Ennosuke II in the title role of *Father Returns*, Shintomi-za, October 1920. Photo courtesy of the Tsubouchi Memorial Theatre Museum, Waseda University, Tokyo.

KIKUCHI KAN

FATHER RETURNS

FIRST PUBLISHED:
New Tides in Thought, January 1917

FIRST PERFORMANCE:
Akasaka Royarukan, August 1919,
dir. Takeda Masanori

CHARACTERS

KURODA KEN'ICHIRŌ, *twenty-eight years old*
SHINJIRŌ, *his brother, twenty-three*
OTANE, *their sister, twenty*
OTAKA, *their mother, fifty-one*
SŌTARŌ, *their father, fifty-eight*

TIME: *ca. 1907*
PLACE: *A town on the coast of Shikoku*[12]

(A six-mat tatami room in a modest middle-class house. Upstage center is a chest on which sits an alarm clock, and downstage is a long wooden charcoal brazier where a kettle is steaming. A low dining table has been set out. KEN'ICHIRŌ has just returned from his work at City Hall; he has changed into a kimono and is relaxing, reading the newspaper. His mother, OTAKA, is sewing. It is early October, around seven in the evening, and already dark outside.)

KEN'ICHIRŌ: Where's Otane gone, Mum?
OTAKA: Off to deliver some sewing.
KEN'ICHIRŌ: Don't tell me she's still doing that. Surely she doesn't have to anymore.
OTAKA: Yes, but she'll need a decent kimono when she gets married.
KEN'ICHIRŌ: *(Turning over a page of the paper.)* What became of that offer you told me about?

OTAKA: They kept begging me to give her away, but it seems she didn't fancy the man at all.

KEN'ICHIRŌ: He had money. Would have made a fine match.

OTAKA: Maybe so, but one can have a small fortune and spend it all and, when all's said and done, still have nothing to show for it. Why, our house had some twenty, thirty thousand yen in bonds and real estate when I first came, but your dad blew it all away living high off the hog. He might just as well have fed it to the wind. (KEN'ICHIRŌ *says nothing, as if recalling unpleasant memories.*) I learned the hard way, so I'd rather Otane married for love than money. Even if her husband's poor, so long as he's got a good heart, life shouldn't be too hard on her.

KEN'ICHIRŌ: Ah, but how much better it'd be if he had both.

OTAKA: And if wishes were horses. . . . Otane may be pretty, but we're hardly well-to-do. . . . Besides, the smallest wedding outfit these days will easily cost you a couple of hundred yen.

KEN'ICHIRŌ: Otane's had a hard time of it ever since she was a kid, and all because of Dad. We ought to make sure at least she's married off properly. Once we've got a thousand saved up, I suggest we give her half of it.

OTAKA: That's hardly necessary—even three hundred would do. I'll feel even more relieved when you get yourself a wife. Everyone says I had bad luck with a husband but good luck with kids. I didn't know what I was going to do when your dad left us. . . .

KEN'ICHIRŌ: (*Changing the subject.*) Shin's late.

OTAKA: That's because he's on duty tonight. Shin said he's getting a raise this month.

KEN'ICHIRŌ: Is that so? He did so well in high school, I'd imagine he's not happy staying a primary school teacher. There's no telling how far he'll go if he sets his mind to it and studies some more.

OTAKA: I've had someone on the lookout for a wife for you too, but so far no luck. The Sonoda girl would be a good match, but her family's more respectable than ours, so they may not want us to have her.

KEN'ICHIRŌ: Surely we can wait a couple more years at least.

OTAKA: In any case, once Otane's married off, we really do have to get you a wife. That'd fix everything. When your dad ran off, I was left with three babes in arms, wondering what on earth I was going to do.

KEN'ICHIRŌ: There's no sense dwelling on the past. What's done is done.

(*The front door rattles open, and* SHINJIRŌ *returns. For a mere primary school teacher, he is an impressive-looking young man.*)

SHINJIRŌ: I'm back.

OTAKA: Welcome home.

KEN'ICHIRŌ: You're dreadfully late tonight.

SHINJIRŌ: I had so much to do I was at my wit's end. My shoulders ache something awful.

OTAKA: We've been holding supper for you.

KEN'ICHIRŌ: You can have a bath after you've eaten.

SHINJIRŌ: *(Changing into a kimono.)* Where's Otane, Mum?

OTAKA: Went to deliver some sewing.

SHINJIRŌ: Hey, Ken, I heard something interesting today. Principal Sugita told me that he'd seen somebody who looked like dad in Furushinmachi.

KEN'ICHIRŌ *and* OTAKA: Eh!?

SHINJIRŌ: Mr. Sugita was walking down the street in Furushinmachi—you know, where all the inns are—when he saw someone ahead, about sixty years old. The man looked vaguely familiar, so he caught up to him and had a good look at him from the side. He could almost swear it was Dad, Mr. Sugita said. If it's Sōtarō, then sure as you're born, he'll have a mole on his right cheek. If so, I'll hail him, he thought, but when he got closer, the man slunk off down that side street by the Water God's shrine.

OTAKA: Mr. Sugita was an old friend of your dad's—the two took lance lessons together in the old days—so if anybody ought to know him, it'd be him. Even so, it's been some twenty years now.

SHINJIRŌ: That's what Mr. Sugita said. It's been twenty-odd years since he's seen him, so he couldn't be sure, but then again, this was somebody he'd chummed around with since when they were kids, so he couldn't swear he was completely mistaken.

KEN'ICHIRŌ: *(An uneasy light in his eyes.)* So Mr. Sugita didn't call out to him then.

SHINJIRŌ: He said he was ready to say something if the man had a mole.

OTAKA: Well, I suppose Mr. Sugita was wrong after all. If your dad had come back to this town, then there's no way he wouldn't stop at the old homestead.

KEN'ICHIRŌ: He'd never dare set foot in this door again, let me tell you.

OTAKA: Anyway, as far as I'm concerned, he's dead. It's been twenty years.

SHINJIRŌ: Didn't you say somebody ran into him in Okayama? When was that?

OTAKA: Why, that was ten years ago already. That was when the Kubo boy, Chūta, made a trip to Okayama. Your dad had brought some lions and tigers to town for a show, he said. He treated Chūta to dinner and asked about us. Chūta said he wore a gold watch on his *obi* and was all decked out in silk—cut a real figure, he did. But that's the last we've heard of him. That was the year after the war, so I guess it must be twelve, thirteen years ago already.[13]

SHINJIRŌ: Dad was quite the dandy, wasn't he?

OTAKA: Ever since he was young, he had no taste for the family studies but preferred to spend his time prospecting for gold and whatnot.[14] So it wasn't just the high life that got him in debt. He lost a small fortune exporting patent medicines to China.

KEN'ICHIRŌ: *(Looking even more perturbed.)* Let's eat, Mum.

OTAKA: Yes, yes, let's eat. I clean forgot. *(Leaves for the kitchen. From offstage.)* Mr. Sugita must've been mistaken. If he was still alive, he'd be getting on. Surely he would've sent us a postcard at least.

KEN'ICHIRŌ: *(More seriously.)* When was it Mr. Sugita ran into that fellow?

SHINJIRŌ: Last night about nine, he said.

KEN'ICHIRŌ: How was he dressed?

SHINJIRŌ: Not very well, apparently. Didn't have a coat on.

KEN'ICHIRŌ: That so?

SHINJIRŌ: How do you remember him?

KEN'ICHIRŌ: I don't.

SHINJIRŌ: Surely you do. You were eight then. Even I have a foggy memory of him.

KEN'ICHIRŌ: I don't. I used to, but I made a point of forgetting.

SHINJIRŌ: Mr. Sugita talks about Dad a lot. Says he was quite good looking when he was young.

OTAKA: *(Bringing supper out of the kitchen.)* That's right. Your dad was very popular. When he was a page for his lordship, one of the ladies-in-waiting gave him a chopstick box with a love poem inside.

SHINJIRŌ: *(Laughing.)* Why the hell would she do that? Hah hah hah hah.

OTAKA: He was born in the Year of the Ox, so that'd make him fifty-eight now. If he'd stayed put here, he'd be enjoying his retirement now. *(Pause. The three begin to eat.)* Otane should be home soon. It's getting quite cold out, isn't it?

SHINJIRŌ: I heard a shrike today, Mum, in that big elm at Jōganji. It's autumn already. . . . Oh, I've got some news for you, Ken. I've decided to get my English certificate. There aren't any good math teachers, you know.

KEN'ICHIRŌ: Good idea. So you'll be going to the Ericsons'?

SHINJIRŌ: That's what I thought. They're missionaries, so I don't have to pay them anything.

KEN'ICHIRŌ: In any case, if you want to show the world you can stand on your own two feet, you know you can't rely on your dad's reputation. So hit the books. I was thinking of taking the senior civil service exam myself, but they've changed the rules, and now you have to be a high school graduate, so I've given up the idea. You graduated from high school, so you've got to give it your best shot.

(The front door opens, and OTANE *returns. She is a pale-complexioned young woman of above average good looks.)*

OTANE: I'm home.

OTAKA: You're late.

OTANE: They had more work for me. That's what held me up.

OTAKA: Have some supper.

OTANE: *(Sits, looking rather worried.)* When I got back to the house just now, Ken, there was this strange old man loitering across the road, just staring at our doorway. *(The other three start.)*

KEN'ICHIRŌ: Hm.

SHINJIRŌ: What did he look like?

OTANE: It was so dark I couldn't tell for sure, but he was tall.

*(*SHINJIRŌ *goes over to the window and looks outside.)*

KEN'ICHIRŌ: Anybody there?

SHINJIRŌ: Uh uh. Nobody. *(The three children are silent.)*

OTAKA: It was the third day after Obon when he left home.

KEN'ICHIRŌ: I'd rather you didn't bring up the past anymore, Mum.

OTAKA: I used to feel as bitter as you do, but as I get older, my heart's not as hard as it used to be.

(All four eat their supper in silence. Suddenly, there is a rattling at the front door. KEN'ICHIRŌ'*s and* OTAKA'*s faces register the greatest emotion, but the nature of that emotion differs radically.)*

MAN'S VOICE: Hello?

OTANE: Yes? *(She makes no move to rise, however.)*

MAN'S VOICE: I wonder—is Otaka there?

OTAKA: Yes! *(Goes toward the front door as if sucked toward it. Henceforth, we can only hear their voices.)*

MAN: *(Offstage.)* Otaka, is it you?

OTAKA: *(Offstage.)* It's you! My God. . . . How you've changed.

(Their voices are filled with tears.)

MAN: *(Offstage.)* Well . . . you look . . . well. The children must be all grown up by now.

OTAKA: *(Offstage.)* Indeed. They've turned into fine young grownups. Come see for yourself.

MAN: *(Offstage.)* Is it all right?

OTAKA: *(Offstage.)* Of course it is.

(Returning home for the first time in twenty years, the haggard father, SŌTARŌ, *is led into the living room by his old wife.* SHINJIRŌ *and* OTANE *stare at their father, blinking in disbelief.)*

SHINJIRŌ: Is this Father? I'm Shinjirō.

SŌTARŌ: Why, what a fine young man you've become! When I left, you were hardly a toddler.

OTANE: Father, I'm Otane.

SŌTARŌ: I'd heard there was a girl, but, my, you're a pretty one.

OTAKA: Well, my dear . . . where to begin? It's a fine thing the children have turned out so well, don't you think?

SŌTARŌ: They say kids'll grow up even without their parents' help, and I guess they're right, aren't they? Hah hah hah. *(Laughs.)*

(But no one joins him in his laughter. KEN'ICHIRŌ *remains silent, leaning on the table.)*

OTAKA: Dear. Ken and Shin have both turned into fine young men. Ken passed the regular civil service exam when he was only twenty, and Shin here never fell lower than third place in middle school. The two of them now pull in about sixty yen a month. And Otane, well, as you can see, she's a fine-looking girl. We've had proposals from some fine places, let me tell you.

SŌTARŌ: Why, that's a fine thing indeed. I myself was doing quite well till about four, five years back. Had myself a troupe of some two dozen, touring the country. Then, when we were in Kure, our show tent burned down and we lost everything. After that nothing went right, and before I knew it, I was an old man. I started to miss my old wife and kids, so that's why I crept back here. Be good to me 'cause I don't expect I'll have much longer to live. *(Looks at* KEN'ICHIRŌ.*)* What d'ye say, Ken'ichirō? Won't you pass the cup to me? Your dad's not much used to drinking the good stuff these days. Ah, but you'd be the only one to remember my face, wouldn't you? *(*KEN'ICHIRŌ *does not respond.)*

OTAKA: Come, Ken. Listen to your dad. It's been years since the two of you met, so you ought to celebrate.

SHINJIRŌ: *(Takes the* sake *cup and offers it to* SŌTARŌ.*)* There you go.

KEN'ICHIRŌ: *(Abruptly.)* Stop it! You've no right to give it to him.

OTAKA: What are you saying? Ken!

*(*SŌTARŌ *gives him a sharp look.* SHINJIRŌ *and* OTANE *hold down their heads and say nothing.)*

KEN'ICHIRŌ: *(Goading him.)* We have no father. How could *that* be our father?

SŌTARŌ: *(Barely restraining his rage.)* What did you say?!

KEN'ICHIRŌ: *(Coldly.)* If we had a father, then Mum wouldn't have led us all by the hand to the breakwater and made us jump in with her. I was eight then. Luckily, Mum picked a spot that was too shallow; otherwise we'd have all drowned. Had I had a father, I wouldn't have had to go work as an errand boy when I was ten years old. It's because we had no father our childhood was so miserable. Shinjirō, have you forgotten how, when you were in primary school, you cried because we couldn't afford to buy any ink and paper? Or how you cried when we couldn't buy the textbooks you needed and your classmates made fun of you because you'd brought handwritten copies to school? How could we have a father? A real father wouldn't have let us suffer like that!

*(*OTAKA *and* OTANE *weep;* SHINJIRŌ *fights back the tears. Even the old man begins to lose his rage and succumb to grief.)*

SHINJIRŌ: But, Ken, see how much our mum's willing to forgive. Surely you can find it in you to let bygones be bygones.

KEN'ICHIRŌ: *(Even more coldly.)* Mum's a woman, so I don't know what she thinks, but if her husband's my father, then he's my enemy. When we were kids and times were bad or we were hungry and complained to Mum, she'd say, "It's all your dad's fault. If you're looking for somebody to blame, then blame your dad." If that man's our father, he's the one who's given us nothing but grief since we were just kids. When I was ten and running errands for the prefectural office, our mum was at home making matchboxes to make ends meet. One month she didn't have any work, and the three of us had to go without lunches. Have you forgotten? The reason I studied so hard was so I could show that bastard. I wanted to get back at the man who abandoned us. I wanted to prove to him that I could lose a father and still grow up to be a man. Do I remember him ever loving me? I don't think so! Till I was eight, he spent all his time out drinking, thanks to which he got over his head in debt, then ran off with another woman. The love of a wife and three children still didn't amount to any more than that one woman.

And when he disappeared, so did the passbook with sixteen yen in it that Mum had put away for me.

SHINJIRŌ: *(Holding back his tears.)* But Brother! See how old Dad's become.

KEN'ICHIRŌ: It's easy enough for you to glibly call him "Dad"! Just because some stranger you've never seen before comes crawling into our house and says he's our father, you suddenly feel sorry for him?

SHINJIRŌ: But, Ken, we're his own flesh and blood. No matter what happens, our duty's—

KEN'ICHIRŌ: To look after him, you say? Off he went and had the time of his life. Now he's old and can't get by any longer, he says, so he comes home. I don't care what you say. I haven't got a dad.

SŌTARŌ: *(Indignantly; but his anger is entirely feigned and carries no power or conviction.)* Ken'ichirō! How dare you speak like that to your own father!

KEN'ICHIRŌ: You may be my father, but you sure didn't raise me! You threw away the right to be my father when your children died, there on the breakwater, twenty years ago. Whatever I am today, I made myself. I don't owe anybody anything.

(Everyone falls silent. Only OTAKA'*s and* OTANE'*s quiet sobbing can be heard.)*

SŌTARŌ: Right, then, I'll leave. I've been a man of some means, I'll have you know. I made a small fortune in the past, and no matter how far I've fallen, I'm still able to feed myself. Well, sorry for the trouble I've caused you all. *(Indignantly makes to leave.)*

SHINJIRŌ: Wait, please. I'll look after you, even if my brother won't. Ken's your own flesh and blood, so even he'll come 'round soon enough, I'm sure. Wait! I'll do whatever I can to look after you.

KEN'ICHIRŌ: Shinjirō! What has this man ever done for you? I still bear the scars of his beatings, but what have you got to show for him? Nothing. Who paid for your primary school? Have you forgotten it was your big brother who paid for your tuition out of the wretched salary I made as an errand boy? The only real father you ever had was me. All right, go ahead and help that man out, if that's what you want. But if you do, I'll never speak to you again.

SHINJIRŌ: But—

KEN'ICHIRŌ: If you don't like it, you can leave. And take that man with you.

(The women continue to cry. SHINJIRŌ *says nothing.)*

KEN'ICHIRŌ: Thanks to the fact we had no father, I scrimped and saved, working late into the night, just so my little brother and sister didn't have to suffer like I did. I put you both through middle school.

SŌTARŌ: *(Weakly.)* Say no more. I must've put you all out by coming back. I won't trouble you again. I've got enough wits about me to figure out how to fend for myself. I'll be off then. Otaka! Look after yourself. I guess it's a good thing I left you after all.

SHINJIRŌ: *(Following his father as he attempts to leave.)* Have you got enough cash on you, sir? Surely you haven't had supper yet.

SŌTARŌ: *(His eyes shining, as if appealing to him.)* No, no. Thanks anyway. *(He stumbles at the entranceway and collapses on the lower step.)*

OTAKA: Be careful!

SHINJIRŌ: *(Helping him up.)* Do you have some place to go?

SŌTARŌ: *(Remains seated, dejectedly.)* Who needs a home? I'll die on the road. . . . *(As if to himself.)* I'd no right to come beating on your door, but still, I got older and weaker and found my feet naturally wending their way back to where I was born. It's been three days since I came back to town, and every night I'd stand outside the door here, but I couldn't bring myself to cross this threshold. . . . All said and done, I'd have been better off if I hadn't come. Anybody would make a fool of a man who came home penniless. . . . When I turned fifty, I started to long for my old home again, and I figured I'd bring back a thousand or two at least and beg your forgiveness, but when you're older it's that much harder to make a living. . . . *(Stands up.)* No matter, I'll make do somehow. *(He weakly gets to his feet and, turning back, gazes at his old wife before opening the door and leaving. The other four family members remain silent for some time.)*

OTAKA: *(Appealingly.)* Ken'ichirō!

OTANE: Brother!

(There is a tense pause that lasts some time.)

KEN'ICHIRŌ: Shin! Go, find Dad and bring him back.

SHINJIRŌ: *(Flies out the door. The other three wait anxiously. He presently returns, his face pale.)* I took the street south and looked for him, but there was no sign of him. I'll go north this time. Come with me, Brother.

KEN'ICHIRŌ: *(Anxiously.)* How could you have lost him?! He can't be lost!

(The two brothers madly rush out the door.)

—Curtain—

....

THE VALLEY DEEP

INTRODUCTION

Aside from *Koheiji Lives* (*Ikiteiru Koheiji*, 1924), which Ōyama Isao considered one of the most important Japanese plays of the twentieth century, not much is known about Suzuki Senzaburō (1893–1924) and the almost two dozen plays he wrote during his short life. Few of his plays have been republished since they first appeared, mostly in the early 1920s, and the fame of *Koheiji Lives*, which continues to be staged regularly and has seen at least two film versions, as well as the equally accomplished *Confessions of Jirōkichi* (*Jirōkichi zange*, 1923), has given readers and audiences the impression that Suzuki was a *shin-kabuki* writer, though only five of his plays have premodern settings.[1] Very little has been written about this playwright.

Suzuki spent much of his adulthood bedridden with the tuberculosis that would take his life, and he died at the age of thirty-one, just as he was starting to make a name for himself. "When my body is at rest," Suzuki wrote in a diary he kept when ill, the *Byōchūki*, "my mind flies and leaps. . . . I am free to do as I please."[2] No doubt his physical condition gave rise to a morbid imagination because his plays are filled with characters who are the victims

---

Photo of Suzuki Senzaburō (1926) in *Gendai Gikyoku Zenshū*. Vol 19. Kokumin Tosho, 1926.

of extreme psychological stresses and the perpetrators of sometimes shocking crimes. (His diaries and scrapbooks were filled with lurid reports from the crime and gossip pages of the newspapers.)[3] Suzuki demonstrates in his plays a taste for the devious and the abnormal; adultery, murder, and suicide are his stock in trade. The decadent quality of his work caught the tenor of the times and in many respects resembles the drama and fiction that his contemporary, Tanizaki Jun'ichirō, was writing around this time.

Born in Tokyo, Suzuki studied haiku and *tanka* poetry and was an avid theatergoer as a teenager. In 1913, at the age of twenty, he won an award worth one hundred yen—a substantial sum in those days—for *Before the Doors* (*Tobira no mae nite*), a play he submitted to a literary contest mounted by the Mitsukoshi department store. The same year he began working as an editor for Genbunsha, a publishing house, writing reviews for such magazines as *Entertainment Illustrated* and *New Entertainment*. Suzuki would continue working for Genbunsha, honing his skills as a theatre critic, until the company folded in the aftermath of the Great Earthquake of 1923. After his debut work (which appears to be lost),[4] Suzuki did not return to writing plays until 1919; he wrote the remaining twenty-two in a burst of creative activity in the remaining six years of his life. His morbid fascination for the cruel and abnormal is exemplified in such works as *Auto da fé* (*Hiaburi*, 1921), about a sadistic artist who ties up his mistress hand and foot for a portrait he is painting; then, when he finds that she loves his student, he attempts to set fire to her but is himself killed in the process.[5] Critic Kōno Toshirō sums up Suzuki's style as follows: "In Suzuki Senzaburō's drama we find hardly any signs of lightheartedness, humor, or wordplay; instead, they burn with the flames of ruin and twisted love. His plays are sparked by the flickering doubts that pass between men and women and are founded on what can only be called obsession."[6] Heady stuff, perhaps, but in fact Suzuki was a subtler stylist than this characterization would give one to believe, and his best plays rely less on sensational acts than on the underlying psychology that motivates his characters. Suzuki was a dramatist of great economy, and there are no characters, dialogue, or actions that do not advance the dramatic effect in his best plays. Though his concerns differed, his mastery of dialogue anticipates the work of Kishida Kunio. One of his later works, *A Secret History of the Mountain Yam* (*Yamaimo hitan*, 1924), has been likened to Kishida's *Two Men at Play with Life* (translated here) as a kind of vaudeville.[7] Unlike many writers who were writing plays during the Taishō era, Suzuki did not do so simply as a literary exercise. "Theatre is theatre," he stated. "It is not a byproduct of literature."[8]

The staging of *Auto da fé* by Onoe Kikugorō VI was praised by Ihara Seiseien as a new [*kabuki*] *sewamono* rendered as "pure realism."[9] But Suzuki did not consider realism the be-all and end-all of drama, writing that "realism is, in any case, not the most important element of direction. Realism touches on reality, but if beauty is not its result, then realism can be no more than a cheap trick for the actor. Realism is but a means to an end."[10] For this reason perhaps, Suzuki expressed a preference for *kabuki* over *shingeki*, which he claimed would "never be mainstream."[11] To his mind, *kabuki* still maintained the greatest integrity as a theatre art. Although he had been impressed with the Free Theatre's inaugural production of Ibsen's *John Gabriel Borkman* in November 1909, his favorite actors remained those from *kabuki* and *shinpa*, actors like Onoe Kikugorō VI and Ichikawa Sadanji II, from *kabuki*, and Kitamura Rokurō and Inoue Masao, from *shinpa*. Whether because of his own tastes or the lack of talent in *shingeki* troupes at the time, his plays were staged almost exclusively by *kabuki* and *shinpa* companies: *Father of the Foreigner's Whore* (*Rashamen no chichi*, 1919) by Inoue Masao, *The Valley Deep* by Hanayagi Shōtarō, and *Takahashi Oden* (1924) by Kawai Takeo and Kitamura Rokurō. Suzuki excelled at imparting a degree of psychological realism hitherto unseen in *kabuki*. In such *shin-kabuki* plays as *Confessions of Jirokichi* and *Koheiji Lives,* Suzuki refined the historical drama to new heights by his intense focus on character portrayal, strong theme, and logical plot.

The Valley Deep is an example of one of Suzuki's modern plays—that is, dramas set in the Taishō era. It is a tightly constructed exposition of the desperate action a woman, Toshiyo, takes when she realizes that her husband is having an affair. She has accompanied her husband, a professor at a university in Tokyo, and brother-in-law to a hot spring in the mountains, where her husband's lover is also staying. The scene the playwright sets up is almost novelistic in its conjuring of a particularly ominous atmosphere. All the action in this brief drama occurs in one room and on the adjoining veranda, and the play of light and shadow underscores the shifting emotions boiling beneath the surface of the protagonist.

The play is structured into fourteen very brief scenes—more vignettes, really—based on who is on stage at any given time. Accordingly, the dynamic of the play shifts constantly, depending on the exits and entrances of certain characters. The entire focus of the play, however, is on Toshiyo, who is in eleven of the fourteen scenes. Her murder of her husband's mistress and subsequent suicide are shocking and impulsive acts, and yet, given the skill with which the playwright has crafted the dialogue and interaction of his characters, they seem both natural and inevitable. The focus of the play is less on what is done than on why it's done. As Hanibuchi Yasuko notes, *The Valley Deep* is "a drama of a woman's self-discovery" as Toshiyo swiftly grows out of her happy naïveté, through jealousy, madness, and remorse, into a woman with no illusions about herself or others.[12] Doubt, she realizes, is something that turns people into adults. Her faith in her marriage, in her husband, had been like the ground beneath her feet. Thus, her choice of death, by throwing herself off the railing, is a fitting metaphor for her radical sense of spiritual displacement. Suzuki manages to impart to such homely acts as paring one's fingernails a degree of dramatic tension that reveals the inner apprehension and turmoil of his characters. His economical dialogue and intense focus on psychological motivation help reign in the melodramatic tendencies in this play.

The translation is based on the Japanese texts in Suzuki Senzaburō: *"Tanizoko," Jirōkichi zange hoka 4-hen: Gendai kyakuhon sōsho* 11, 69–106, and *"Tanizoko,"* in Nihon kindai engekishi kenkyūkai, *Nihon no kindai gikyoku,* 105–118.

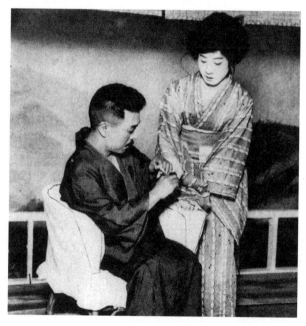

Fujimura Hideo as Kisaburō and Hanayagi Shōtarō as Toshiyo in Hongō-za production of *The Valley Deep*. Photo in July 1925 issue of *Eiga to engei*. Photo courtesy of the Shōchiku Otani Library, Tokyo.

SUZUKI SENZABURŌ

THE VALLEY DEEP

FIRST PUBLISHED:
New Entertainment, November 1921

FIRST PERFORMANCE:
Shōchikuza, June 1925,
dir. Hanayagi Shōtarō

CHARACTERS

....

KOJIMA KISABURŌ: *Thirty-five, a professor at a private university*
KOJIMA TOSHIYO: *Twenty-three,* KISABURŌ's *wife*
KOJIMA EISHIRŌ: *Twenty-six,* KISABURŌ's *younger brother*
WAKAMATSU ASAKO: *Twenty-seven,* KISABURŌ's *lover*
WAKAMATSU HATSUE: *Nine,* ASAKO's *daughter*
A hotel MAID

(A hotel room at a hot spring in the mountains. The room is in Japanese style, but it has a large bay window looking out onto a veranda over a deep valley. The hotel sits on the edge of the valley, beyond which is a line of steep, looming mountains. The deep pleats of the mountains' folds are hidden in clouds that obscure the sunlight, sometimes casting a gloomy pall over the interior. At stage left is a wide, Western-style corridor, along which there is a glass window with a white lace curtain.

Close to the window is a rattan chair upholstered in cloth and a low table on which stands a vase filled with mountain flowers. It is a quiet afternoon in early September. A swiftly running stream can be heard in the distance.)

1. KISABURŌ, TOSHIYO, AND EISHIRŌ

(The three have just finished a game of cards. TOSHIYO *is shuffling them.)*
KISABURŌ: No more for me.
EISHIRŌ: Count me out too.
TOSHIYO: Lose and you two get cold feet. Cowards.

EISHIRŌ: Don't brag, Toshiyo. It's a fluke that you should win like this.

TOSHIYO: What do you want me to do about it? This is the second round in a row I've won.

KISABURŌ: But you're not really winning, you know. It's not that you're actually good at this game.

EISHIRŌ: Yeah, the way you play is nuts. You're all hit and miss, like a blind snake lashing out at anything around it.

TOSHIYO: You say that just because you're a sore loser. Haven't you forgotten? A general who's lost the battle has no right to go blaming the troops. What a joke!

KISABURŌ: The joke is you winning—you're the weakest of the lot of us. Here I am, the strongest, losing.

EISHIRŌ: I'll grant you Toshiyo is the weakest, but I'm not convinced you're the strongest.

TOSHIYO: How dare you call me the weakest! Let's have another round then. I'll show you.

KISABURŌ: No way! Somebody save me. I've had enough of your babysitting.

TOSHIYO: You're really mean! You're the one who started this!

KISABURŌ: I think I'll go take a dip. Want to join me, Ei-chan?

EISHIRŌ: I just went. Why don't you go, Toshiyo?

TOSHIYO: No thanks! *(Takes out a towel and hands it to him.)*

KISABURŌ: *(On the way out.)* We'll be here for only another two or three days, so best make the most of it. *(Exits stage left.)*

2. TOSHIYO AND EISHIRŌ

EISHIRŌ: Will you be leaving the day after tomorrow?

TOSHIYO: The day after tomorrow or the day after that. It hasn't been decided yet.

EISHIRŌ: School starts back on the eleventh, so you'd be better off leaving the day after tomorrow.

TOSHIYO: We were going to leave before September, but your brother's gotten too comfortable here. . . . Including us, there are three parties who've been staying on at this hotel since the middle of July.

EISHIRŌ: That stylish young lady who's in that room at the end of the corridor —has her escort been here all this time?

TOSHIYO: No, he came the day Mrs. Wakamatsu arrived, I think. It's been about ten days now. This place really does get quite lonely come September, doesn't it?

EISHIRŌ: It'll still be baking in Tokyo. . . . The day I came it was as bad as it ever was in August.

TOSHIYO: I suppose so.

3. Toshiyo, Eishirō, and the Maid

MAID: *(Entering.)* Oh excuse me! I thought the madam from upstairs was here.

TOSHIYO: No, I haven't seen her all day. Is there something the matter?

MAID: A telegram came for her.

EISHIRŌ: She may be in the bath.

MAID: I see. Please excuse me. *(Leaves.)*

4. Toshiyo and Eishirō

TOSHIYO: A telegram? I suppose she's being called home too.

EISHIRŌ: Well, I doubt very much she'll go.

TOSHIYO: Aren't breakups awful?

EISHIRŌ: You haven't noticed anything, have you, Toshiyo?

TOSHIYO: What?

EISHIRŌ: About Mrs. Wakamatsu. Asako.

TOSHIYO: Has something happened to her?

EISHIRŌ: This time it was Asako who left him.

TOSHIYO: I heard that.

EISHIRŌ: And no sooner had she left him than she came here.

TOSHIYO: Quite the coincidence, wasn't it? I'd heard her name before but had never met her. It was a good chance to make myself a new friend.

EISHIRŌ: Heaven protects fools!

TOSHIYO: *(Brightly.)* Yes. But why do you say so?

EISHIRŌ: Well, you haven't asked what sort of relationship she and my brother have? I guess not. Toshiyo!

TOSHIYO: Relationship?

EISHIRŌ: An intimate one.

TOSHIYO: *(Laughs.)* Surely not! But, you know, I had this dream. It was the night she came to the inn. She and your brother went striding off up the mountain together. I couldn't keep up with them, but they didn't even look back, and holding each other's hands like they were the best of friends, they left me there stranded and all alone. What a nightmare! I told Kisaburō, and he laughed at me.

EISHIRŌ: That dream was telling you the truth.

TOSHIYO: *(Laughs.)* How embarrassing! Never in a million years would I have thought it possible, but I'm shamed I ever had such a dream. I've always believed it's better not to think such things, but then I realized that somehow, before I was even aware of it, jealousy had wormed its way into my unconscious. Don't dreams make you think the most outrageous nonsense!

EISHIRŌ: Toshiyo, is that all you think it is?

TOSHIYO: Why, of course I do!

EISHIRŌ: You have no suspicions about Asako and my brother?

TOSHIYO: *(Laughs.)* No! How could I imagine such a thing?

EISHIRŌ: Of course, you don't know anything about what he was like before you were married.

TOSHIYO: Sure I do. I know a lot.

EISHIRŌ: You know?

TOSHIYO: It's nothing to me. If there was anything wrong, I'd be better of if I didn't know. Besides, that's all history now.

EISHIRŌ: My brother has a lot to do with Asako leaving her husband.

TOSHIYO: They're old acquaintances, so I imagine he offered her advice.

EISHIRŌ: He could hardly offer her advice. He's the one in trouble here!

TOSHIYO: I haven't the faintest idea what you're talking about, Ei-san. . . . What I do know is that your brother is not that sort of person. *(Laughs.)* It's okay! Everything will be fine.

EISHIRŌ: As I say, heaven protects fools. Either that, or you're a real hypocrite.

TOSHIYO: The former. I'm no hypocrite. But I'm no fool, really. Rather, something much more than that. I can assure you, your brother's not the kind of person who'd do something immoral. *(Firmly.)* He's my husband, Ei-san!

EISHIRŌ: *(Smiles wryly.)* Hm. I fear something terrible will happen to you, Toshiyo.

TOSHIYO: Don't be silly! Want to bet on it?

EISHIRŌ: Do you really think this is something you can gamble on? . . . I'm not telling you this because I resent him, you know.

TOSHIYO: I know that. You're telling me because you feel sorry for me. And I appreciate it, I really do. Just leave your brother to me to deal with. Please.

EISHIRŌ: You're sure about this?

TOSHIYO: It's hardly prudent for me to say I'm sure.

EISHIRŌ: Asako's rented herself a private bath with a lock, hasn't she?

TOSHIYO: Uh huh. *(Laughs.)* You really are a busybody, aren't you, Ei-san? How petty!

EISHIRŌ: I'm telling you this because I've got my reasons.

TOSHIYO: But your reasons are lies, so forget it! You're just saying these things to make fun of me. *(Changing her tone.)* Shall we go for a walk?

EISHIRŌ: Have it your way! I'll go by myself.

TOSHIYO: *(Smiles.)* Oh, what to do with you! Well then, see you later.

EISHIRŌ: *(Takes his hat.)* Yes, see you later.

TOSHIYO: Go by the post office, would you?

EISHIRŌ: I can. You've got a letter?

TOSHIYO: Please send it for me. Thanks.

EISHIRŌ: Certainly! *(Takes the letter.)* To my mother, I see. You write her every day?

TOSHIYO: Yes, some interesting news too. I was complaining about you.

EISHIRŌ: Maybe you're not so dumb after all. Maybe that's why the family likes you so much.

TOSHIYO: *(Her face darkening slightly.)* That's not why I do it, though. I lost my own mother when I was young and don't have any brothers and sisters of my own, so that's why I guess I tend to think of you all as my own family. . . . You're all such fine people.

EISHIRŌ: I'll say it again: heaven protects fools; either that, or you're a hypocrite. *(Angrily.)* I've had enough. *(Leaves.)*

TOSHIYO: *(Seeing him out.)* What's with him?

5. TOSHIYO

(She sits deep in thought for some time. A cloud passes over, and the light in the room fades. TOSHIYO sits, pensively biting on the nail of her little finger; then, as if remembering, she looks at her finger and goes to get a small pair of manicure scissors. She steps out onto the veranda and, sitting up on the railing, begins to pare her fingernails.

Clouds roil around the mountain directly on the other side of the valley. A ray of sun obliquely breaks through and beautifully illuminates her profile. By the time she has finished paring the nails on her left hand, KISABURŌ has returned from the bath.)

6. TOSHIYO AND KISABURŌ

KISABURŌ: What are you doing, perched on the railing like that? . . . Be careful. If you fell, you'd die, you know.

TOSHIYO: *(Smiling cheerfully, stands up.)* You're right, if I fell from here, I'd be a goner. I don't want to die just yet. . . .

KISABURŌ: Ei-chan's gone someplace?

TOSHIYO: Yes! He went for a walk.

KISABURŌ: Shall I do your right hand?

TOSHIYO: Yes! Please. *(Hands him the scissors.)*

KISABURŌ: You've done the left hand already, have you?

TOSHIYO: Yes, there's just the right now.

KISABURŌ: *(Paring her nails.)* Why bother cutting them when they're as short as this? You could just file them instead.

TOSHIYO: I lost the nail file.

KISABURŌ: You could use some emery grass instead.[13]

TOSHIYO: You know what? Ei-chan was just complaining about me—he called me a hypocrite.

KISABURŌ: A hypocrite. Hm.

TOSHIYO: If not a hypocrite, then I'm a fool, he said!

KISABURŌ: *(Frowns slightly.)* You a fool? Why?

TOSHIYO: He didn't say. . . . When I gave him my letter to your mother to deliver, that's what he said. Ouch!

KISABURŌ: Sorry. It's 'cause you won't stay still.

TOSHIYO: You've really cut into the flesh. This is bad!

7. TOSHIYO, KISABURŌ, AND THE MAID

MAID: *(Entering hurriedly.)* It's a call from Tokyo. Shall I connect it through to the room here?

TOSHIYO: That's all right. It'd be faster if I took it downstairs. . . . By the front desk?

MAID: No, under the stairs.

KISABURŌ: If it's home, tell them we'll be back the day after tomorrow.

TOSHIYO: Yes. *(Leaves with the MAID.)*

8. KISABURŌ

*(*KISABURŌ *sits down in the rattan chair and smokes a cigarette. He begins to read the paper but immediately puts it down and looks outside.* WAKAMATSU ASAKO *enters.)*

9. KISABURŌ AND ASAKO

ASAKO: *(Furtively, from outside the room.)* Are you alone?

KISABURŌ: *(Turning around.)* Uh huh.

ASAKO: Can I come in?

KISABURŌ: Uh huh.

ASAKO: *(Appearing uneasy.)* My, but what a wonderful view you have from this room.

KISABURŌ: Sit down, why don't you?

ASAKO: *(Sits in the rattan chair facing* KISABURŌ*.)* I got a telegram from my brother. Telling me to come home right now!

KISABURŌ: *(Keeping an eye on the corridor.)* Ah. Well, I guess it's best you do go home.

ASAKO: Whatever happens, I'm not going back to Wakamatsu. I'll stay with my brother for a while, then I'll figure out something.

KISABURŌ: Figure out something? You can't live alone. What a nuisance.

ASAKO: A nuisance? A nuisance, you say? Do you realize how hard this is on me? . . . You're thinking it's high time to leave me, aren't you.

KISABURŌ: Of course not.

ASAKO: You still get along well with your wife, don't you? I must be like the devil for the two of you. You sure your wife has no idea?

KISABURŌ: I hardly think so.

ASAKO: She has no suspicions?

KISABURŌ: It seems not. You needn't worry. She's a total fool.

ASAKO: I pity her then. For trusting you. Your sins are doubled, aren't they?

KISABURŌ: Please don't hit me where it hurts. You think I enjoy this?

ASAKO: Sorry. *(A long pause.)* It's just that I can't bear to think about it. Because you don't belong to me. I left him and came here so I could be yours completely, and now you're driving me away.

KISABURŌ: I'm not saying anything of the sort. What I'm saying is, we're going back to Tokyo the day after tomorrow, so it's best you go back too.

ASAKO: I'm not just talking about being here in these mountains. If you're trying to be a part of my life, get out, my heart's no place for you to live, so go home—that's what the expression on your face is telling me. And I, I can't....

KISABURŌ: Are you having fun? Torturing me like this?

ASAKO: I'm the one who's being tortured. I can't go back to Wakamatsu and keep on spending my days like I have till now. I'm going to talk to your wife, tell her everything. And then ... and then....

KISABURŌ: Stop talking nonsense.

ASAKO: But I can't stand it any longer. It's too hard for me to bear. I want to be yours, that's all. And so I must have you. *(Suddenly reaches out and strokes his jaw.)*

KISABURŌ: Stop it. Somebody's coming.

(TOSHIYO enters the corridor and, seeing them, freezes. The two are unaware. She immediately withdraws.)

KISABURŌ: *(Forces her away.)* I thought I heard somebody. *(Stands and goes to the corridor.)* I'm sure I heard footsteps.... Didn't you notice?

ASAKO: You're hearing things. Your fear of your wife is playing on your imagination.

KISABURŌ: My imagination, was it? I'm sure there were footsteps.

ASAKO: But there's nobody there.

(KISABURŌ worriedly looks once again toward the corridor. TOSHIYO, deliberately making the sound of her footsteps heard, enters.)

10. KISABURŌ, ASAKO, AND TOSHIYO

TOSHIYO: *(To KISABURŌ.)* Are you leaving?

KISABURŌ: *(Awkwardly.)* Uh huh. Who was the call?

TOSHIYO: Somebody nice.

KISABURŌ: *(Dubiously.)* What's that you say?

TOSHIYO: Somebody nice!

KISABURŌ: Home, right?

TOSHIYO: No.

KISABURŌ: The call was for you?

TOSHIYO: Yes! Somebody who loves me. *(Laughs.)* Somebody I've been dreaming of for a long time. Hurry back to Tokyo, I'm so lonely I could die, he said! *(Laughs.)*

KISABURŌ: What sort of nonsense are you going on about? It had nothing to do with me?

TOSHIYO: That's right, nothing to do with you.

KISABURŌ: Mrs. Wakamatsu is here.

TOSHIYO: Is that so! *(Looks at* ASAKO.*)* Well, excuse me.

KISABURŌ: *(Begins to leave.)* Was it you who came a moment ago?

TOSHIYO: *(Earnestly.)* No, I just got here. Why?

KISABURŌ: Really! I'm going to go shoot some pool. I'll see you later, Asako.

ASAKO: Yes. Bye, then.

*(*KISABURŌ *leaves.)*

11. TOSHIYO AND ASAKO

(The two women are silent for some time. Then TOSHIYO *laughs in a cheerful voice.)*

TOSHIYO: Isn't that silly of me! Not saying anything. Please forgive me. I'm so inept.... *(Laughs.)*

ASAKO: No, it was me. I was thinking about something.... *(Forced laughter.)*

TOSHIYO: What's become of Hatsue?

ASAKO: Just before noon, the innkeeper said he was going to put out the boat and do some fishing, so he invited her out with him. They should be back anytime now.

TOSHIYO: She's so grown up. When I was her age, I'd never leave my mother's side. Especially when we were traveling.

ASAKO: She's a strange child. Warms to people in no time at all.

TOSHIYO: Just like her mother.

ASAKO: *(Glancing at her.)* Why, my husband always used to complain that I was so ill at ease with people!

TOSHIYO: But you go out to all sorts of parties and what have you.

ASAKO: Rather, I'm dragged out to them.

TOSHIYO: You're so beautiful, I'm sure the gentlemen fawn over you ever so much.

ASAKO: Dear me! *(Laughing.)* Now you're teasing me!

TOSHIYO: *(Not smiling.)* Why, my husband spoke ever so highly of you. "You ought to meet her," he said. "I want you two to be friends. Someone like you should spend more time with a person of her quality. I really must insist." *(Recalling that time, she forces back her bitterness as she utters each word deliberately.)*

ASAKO: *(Looking rather guilty, laughs.)* Rubbish! But, you know, I never would have thought I'd meet you here, in a hot spring resort like this. It made me very happy.

TOSHIYO: *(Her voice wavering slightly.)* Me too.... Nothing delights me more than to make a good friend like you.

ASAKO: Yes, let's be friends.

TOSHIYO: Yes! Yes!

ASAKO: Is there something the matter?

TOSHIYO: No. Why?

ASAKO: You were shaking just now. And your face....

TOSHIYO: Was pale? No, I'm always this way. I'm not very strong, you know.

ASAKO: Yes, I've heard you're rather frail.

TOSHIYO: My husband said so?

ASAKO: Yes! *(A long pause. She quietly goes and stands on the veranda.)* I was saying earlier that you have such a wonderful view from this room! Our room is so gloomy....

TOSHIYO: When we came here the other year, it was spring. It was even nicer then. Down below, all the mountain cherries were a mass of pale pink blossoms. *(Recalling that time.)* It's been four years now.

ASAKO: Your husband told me. *(Smiles.)* You were on your honeymoon, weren't you?

TOSHIYO: Yes! My, but you do seem to know a lot about me.

ASAKO: *(Looking over the railing.)* The valley's so deep, isn't it? It's scary.

TOSHIYO: You can faintly hear it—the rushing stream sounds so brave! ... *(Listening.)* Can you hear it? Hear how it roars!

ASAKO: You're right. Why, if you fell from here, you'd be a goner, wouldn't you? *(Sits down on the railing.)*

TOSHIYO: *(Also sits down.)* I heard someone sat here like us and actually did fall to his death.

ASAKO: How frightening!

TOSHIYO: Of course, he was drunk at the time.

ASAKO: It'd be no effort to die, would it? If you think of what it'd be like to suffer from a fatal illness, this would surely be a better way to go. Don't you think? *(*TOSHIYO *says nothing.)* Why, look! Over there, the sun's cast such a sad light.

*(*TOSHIYO *suddenly strikes* ASAKO *with all her force.* ASAKO *slips off the railing. Her body disappears over the other side, but she barely clings on by her hands.* TOSHIYO *attempts to pry her fingers away.* ASAKO *struggles violently, but* TOSHIYO *finally has her way.* ASAKO *plunges into the valley.* TOSHIYO *looks down at her. Then she falls to her haunches on the veranda, looking like she has lost her mind. A long pause.* KISABURŌ *returns.)*

12. TOSHIYO AND KISABURŌ

KISABURŌ: What's wrong? Why are you sitting there like that? *(TOSHIYO is silent.)* Has Mrs. Wakamatsu left?

TOSHIYO: Yes!

KISABURŌ: What are you doing there?

TOSHIYO: *(Stands.)* Nothing.

KISABURŌ: You look strange. Has something happened?

TOSHIYO: I was feeling sick to my stomach. Funny.

KISABURŌ: What's funny?

TOSHIYO: *(Her mouth smiles, but her eyes do not.)* What's funny? You didn't pick any flowers? Flowers for the dearly departed?

KISABURŌ: What an awful thing to say! I came back because I remembered something I had to do.

TOSHIYO: *(Sneering.)* For Asako?

KISABURŌ: Of course not. I remembered some urgent business for the principal's office. What did you and Asako talk about? Anything interesting?

TOSHIYO: Oh, yes. All sorts of things. *(Bites her fingernail.)*

KISABURŌ: You're biting your fingernails again. No matter how often I tell you, you still won't give up the habit. Did you clip them all?

TOSHIYO: No. That's right, I left a few unclipped. I forgot. I really must make sure I clip my fingernails at least.

KISABURŌ: Shall I? Where are the scissors? *(TOSHIYO looks around.)* Here they are. *(Begins paring her nails.)* They're hard to clip!

TOSHIYO: Take off more!

KISABURŌ: You shouldn't pare them too deeply. This'll do.

TOSHIYO: More!

KISABURŌ: If I cut you again, it'll hurt.

TOSHIYO: *(Suddenly withdrawing her hand.)* I'll pare them myself. *(Petulantly.)* If you don't have the stomach for it, I will. *(Takes the scissors and begins to clip her nails.)* Shall I snip off the tip of my finger? *(Takes a piece out of the tip of her ring finger.)*

KISABURŌ: Look, see what you've done now! Being so rough like that, it's no wonder you're bleeding.

TOSHIYO: You're right. I'm bleeding. It's still red! And I could've sworn all the blood in my body had turned as clear as water. . . . Why, look how red it is! Suck on my finger, would you, dear?

KISABURŌ: You silly thing. It must hurt. *(Sucks on her finger.)*

TOSHIYO: *(Laughs out loud.)* Doesn't this suit you, though! Why, you've sucked me dry, haven't you? Dear.

KISABURŌ: Stop kidding around.

TOSHIYO: Of all the things you've been to me, done to me, drinking my blood like this—that's the real you. You're a vampire!

KISABURŌ: Stop talking nonsense. Put a bandage on it.

TOSHIYO: I used to hate getting little cuts like this. But there's no sense hating a cut that can be fixed with a bit of sticking plaster, eh? It's cute, even. Never in my life have I ever thought a cut was cute. "A wounded heart"— isn't there an expression like that?

KISABURŌ: *(Lies back and begins reading a book.)* Uh huh.

TOSHIYO: There's something lovable about a wounded heart, don't you think? What bliss it must be to look at the scar and recall the wound! You know, my heart's never been wounded before. Not till now.

KISABURŌ: Hm. I guess not. *(Flips the page.)*

TOSHIYO: It was something flawless, smooth as lapis lazuli. A goldfish swam inside it. A beautiful goldfish. You. But then, the heart broke, all in the flash of a moment. I thought it lived inside, but the goldfish had already gone.

KISABURŌ: What are you rambling on about?

TOSHIYO: . . . Wounded in the heart—there's something pleasurable in it, you know? The sadness of being wounded is really a part of pleasure. Because it's not a real wound. Rather, it's like my heart's been smashed to smithereens.

KISABURŌ: *(Realizing.)* What was it Asako said to you?

TOSHIYO: Why, nothing. She said nothing, dear. Funny.

KISABURŌ: Funny, funny. That's the second time you've said that word.

TOSHIYO: But it is funny! It's so funny I want to laugh and laugh and joke around with you. Do you understand how I feel, dear?

KISABURŌ: Hm! *(Uneasily.)* No more than you understand how I feel.

TOSHIYO: That's right! That's what's so funny. But, you know, I belong to you. You may say you don't understand me, but I still remember things. The past, the fun we had. We spent our first night together in this room. Didn't sleep a wink, a night filled with fear, with joy. . . . I had a lonely childhood, but since I became your wife, it's as if I saw the world in a whole new light. Life became fun. My days were filled with pleasure. What I mean is, the world was you. Don't you see? You were everything to me. I forgot altogether that anything like doubt ever existed, even though it was something that nourished human beings, turned them into adults. Finally I was punished for scorning that little thing called doubt.

KISABURŌ: What the hell. . . ! *(TOSHIYO bursts into tears.)* Hey, hey! You silly little thing. Stop it now. What's got into you anyway? I love you, don't I?

TOSHIYO: That's not what's wrong.

KISABURŌ: What's the matter, then? Haven't you got the wrong idea about me?

TOSHIYO: No.

KISABURŌ: You're my wife. I'll never ever leave you, you know.

TOSHIYO: Oh, I've heard that before, plenty.

KISABURŌ: You telling me you're tired of hearing it?

TOSHIYO: No. There isn't a woman alive who'd tire of hearing those words. Especially a woman like me. One who's a fool for the men.

KISABURŌ: Cheer up, why don't you? And if there's something you want to ask me about, go ahead and ask.

TOSHIYO: Ask you about? I haven't the courage. I've never ever thought of doing any such thing. My suffering hasn't anything to do with what you've done.

KISABURŌ: Then what is it? What is this nonsense you're babbling on about?

TOSHIYO: It's not about you and her. It's about me. I feel sorry for myself, I'm angry at myself. . . . Why, I'm even laughing at myself.

KISABURŌ: *(Embraces her.)* Come on, now, cheer up. Go paint your face—you look strange. People will get the wrong idea.

TOSHIYO: I couldn't care less what other people think. *(Suddenly realizing she is in her husband's arms, in a panic she struggles to free herself.)* Stop it! Don't touch me!

KISABURŌ: Why?

TOSHIYO: Whatever!

KISABURŌ: You don't love me anymore?

TOSHIYO: No! I love you. More than ever before! I didn't know whether or not I loved or hated you. I became a part of you, so that everything—the mountains, the sky, your books, my scissors—they all looked like you. It was far more than a simple matter of love or hate. Now I know for sure that I love you. You were my guardian angel, but since today you've turned into a human being, one who's made me fall in love with you. Why can't I hate you?

KISABURŌ: I haven't done anything to make you hate me, have I? *(TOSHIYO is silent. KISABURŌ persists in trying to deceive her.)* In any case, there mustn't

be any misunderstandings between a man and his wife, don't you think?
They should say everything they want to say.

TOSHIYO: I haven't misunderstood anything. Would you please be quiet for a
minute? I'm trying to think.

(She sits in the rattan chair. KISABURŌ *returns to reading his book.* EISHIRŌ
enters with ASAKO's *daughter,* HATSUE. HATSUE's *thick hair is cut short to the
shoulders. She is wearing a dress.)*

13. Toshiyo, Kisaburō, Eishirō, and Hatsue

KISABURŌ: Where have you been, Hatsue?

HATSUE: On the lake!

EISHIRŌ: The owner here took the kids out on his boat!

HATSUE: Where's Mommy?

KISABURŌ: She went back to her room.

EISHIRŌ: Ah hah! The maid downstairs said she was in your room. That's why
we came here.

HATSUE: Bye! *(Starts to leave.)*

TOSHIYO: Hatsue! Come! Come over here! *(Stands and leads her back into the
room as if to embrace her.)* How was the lake? Catch any fish?

HATSUE: Yes, a few!

TOSHIYO: You caught a few, did you? Is that so? Was it fun?

HATSUE: Yes, very. Next time, let's all go together, Auntie.

TOSHIYO: Yes, let's do that. With Mommy and Auntie. *(*HATSUE *is squirming to
leave.)* Let's play a little, shall we? Your mommy will be coming back soon.

HATSUE: Really?

TOSHIYO: I promise. Now, what shall we play at together? Shall we put on
the gramophone? Or shall Auntie dance for you? *(*HATSUE *laughs.)* Do you
know how to dance? I bet you do. Your mommy dances, doesn't she?

HATSUE: Yes! A teacher comes to our house to teach her how. I can dance a
little too!

TOSHIYO: Is that so? Auntie can't.

HATSUE: Not at all?

TOSHIYO: That's right! Not at all. Can you teach me how, Hatsue? *(*HATSUE
laughs and looks down.) Oh, come on. Teach me.

HATSUE: But I don't know enough to be able to teach you.

TOSHIYO: Teach me as much as you know. So how does it go? Is this the way?
(Makes HATSUE *stand and rests her hand on her shoulder.)* One, two, three, four.

HATSUE: *(Bashfully.)* I don't want to. Besides, only men and women dance together. Have Mr. Kojima teach you. You can dance, can't you, Mr. Kojima?

KISABURŌ: Yes, I can.

EISHIRŌ: Dance with me, Hatsue!

HATSUE: No! I don't want to!

EISHIRŌ: Why?

HATSUE: I just don't!

TOSHIYO: Then let's play house together. You can be the husband, and I'll be the wife. The wife's a fool.

HATSUE: Why? Why is she a fool?

TOSHIYO: She just is. She was born that way. *(*HATSUE *laughs.* TOSHIYO *bursts into nervous laughter.)* Isn't that funny, now!

KISABURŌ: Hatsue, Auntie's not feeling very well right now. Toshiyo, why don't you give her a sweet?

HATSUE: I don't want a sweet.

TOSHIYO: I'll give you a ton of sweets. Will you wait for them? Till we have the wake.

EISHIRŌ: Wake?

KISABURŌ: *(Startled.)* What sort of nonsense is this now?!

TOSHIYO: Ah, hah hah hah hah! Yes, yes! Let's play a game, shall we? How about we play "funeral"? *(Lifts a rattan basket that had been set in the corner of the room onto her shoulder and walks around.)* You, Hatsue, come walk here. Right in front of the coffin.

HATSUE: I don't want to! Goodbye! I'm leaving.

TOSHIYO: But Mommy's not back yet. I'll show you something interesting. *(Thinks.)* I know, let's play tightrope. *(Goes out onto the veranda and mounts the railing.)* See? *(Walks.)*

EISHIRŌ: *(Shocked.)* Toshiyo! Please don't do anything stupid!

KISABURŌ: Be careful! *(Angrily.)* Stop it, for heaven's sake!

TOSHIYO: Dear . . . dear . . . it's all right. Watch me. The earth, so firm under her feet—suddenly no longer there. Have you ever seen a woman walk on thin air before? Have you ever seen such a thing?

KISABURŌ: *(An uneasy premonition.)* Hey. Quit joking around.

TOSHIYO: Like this, for example—a body floating on . . . nothing. Goodbye! *(She spreads her arms and falls back, toppling head over heels off the railing into the valley.)*

KISABURŌ: Ah!

14. Kisaburō, Eishirō, and Hatsue

EISHIRŌ: Toshiyo!

(He and KISABURŌ *rush to the railing and look down.)*

KISABURŌ: *(Screaming like a madman.)* Somebody come! Hurry! Hurry!

(Overcome with shock, HATSUE *is silent at first, then bursts into tears. The sad light of the setting sun falls obliquely across the room.)*

—Curtain—

PART
II

3

After the Quake

Shortly before noon on September 1, 1923, a major earthquake struck the Tokyo region. Cooking fires, wooden houses, and broken gas lines caused a conflagration that would not die down for days. Severed water mains prevented firemen from putting out the fires. Estimates vary, but almost 700,000 houses were either partially or totally destroyed.[1] Approximately 140,000 people perished, as many as 40,000 in a single place, the Military Clothing Depot in Ryōgoku, where people had fled to open ground to escape the flames. The city's entire infrastructure was destroyed.

The earthquake initiated the so-called "dark valley" of the Shōwa era, which lasted until yet another disaster struck, the firebombs of 1945. Nakajima Kenzō, author of *The Shōwa Era* (*Shōwa jidai*, 1957), remarked that one of the greatest tragedies of the earthquake was that it provided an excuse for the suspension of civil liberties and civil law.[2] All the major newspaper offices were razed in the earthquake and fires, cutting the flow of communication about the disaster and leading to the spread of wild rumors that Koreans were setting fires and poisoning wells. As many as six thousand innocent citizens of Korean descent were massacred by roving bands of soldiers and vigilantes. On September 4, soldiers murdered the proletarian playwright Hirasawa Keishichi and another prominent leftist, Kawai Yoshitora, in Kameido, a badly hit district near Ryōgoku on the east bank of the Sumida. The following day, the Japanese prime minister issued an announcement that Koreans were not responsible for the chaos, but the crackdown on various political and ethnic minorities continued. Martial law was declared on September 8. On September 16, the anarchist Osugi Sakae and his partner, Ito Noe, were killed by a secret police officer, Amakasu Masahiko, who was the only one ever held accountable for the wave of repression that followed the quake. The incident nonetheless politicized many, especially in the theatre world. Itō Kunio, a young actor at the time, was accused by vigilantes of being a Korean agent provocateur near the Sendagaya station in Tokyo. He denied it but subsequently changed his name to commemorate the moment of his political awakening, and, as Senda Koreya (1904–1996), he became twentieth-century Japan's most important stage director.

Many critics have noted that the Great Kantō Earthquake marked the end of the old feudal city of Edo and the birth of Tokyo as a modern metropolis. Tanizaki Jun'ichirō applauded the opportunity to rebuilt Tokyo into a cosmopolitan mecca along the lines of New York or Shanghai. The ruins provided a blank slate to create modernistic experiments in the arts and, eventually, a thriving mass culture of popular music, film, literature, and journalism. The Japanese would prove, as they would again after 1945, that they could rise like a phoenix from the ashes of destruction.

The year 1923 was a watershed for Japanese theatre as well. Practically every major theatre had been destroyed in the quake and fires. The relaxation of building codes for the post-disaster reconstruction made it possible to build on a shoestring the Tsukiji Little Theatre, which opened, less than a year after the disaster, on June 13, 1924. One of the theatre's founders, Hijikata Yoshi, had rushed home from Europe when he heard of the earthquake and enlisted Osanai Kaoru's support in building what Brian Powell has called "Japan's first modern stage."[3] Kishida Kunio had returned from France only a couple of months before, to attend to his family on the death of his father. He had spent the previous two years studying at Jacques Copeau's Le Vieux Colombier and hoped to make his mark in the Japanese theatre world.

The opening of this new theatre excited considerable interest among the Tokyo intelligentsia. A meeting was held at Keiō University on May 20, 1924, to discuss the event. Presentations were given by Tsukiji Little Theatre associates (dōjin) Wada Sei (who spoke on the theatre's stage and auditorium design), Hijikata, and playwright and Keiō lecturer Kubota Mantarō; another playwright, Mizuki Kyōta (1894–1948), acted as emcee. Osanai Kaoru spoke last. He began innocently enough, first addressing the building itself: "There are many theatres that can pack in the audiences, but not one that is worth accommodating theatre. Our Tsukiji Little Theatre is a crude sort of building, like a packing case, but it's a vessel that can take any sort of theatre without anything leaking out."[4] The Tsukiji Little Theatre was to be a "laboratory" for new theatre in Japan. In contrast to audiences of the past, who came to the theatre for a good time, "our audience must be students," Osanai asserted. He admitted that he himself was unsure what direction he wanted to take:

> I was twenty-nine years old in 1909 when I founded the Free Theatre . . . . and, fumbling around in the dark, I made a mess of things. Now, fifteen years later, I find myself with a group of people groping around in the dark again. Which is to say, I deny my past. In fact, I used to be proud of what I'd accomplished, but I discovered recently that none of it served me any good. Here I am, back to where I was when I was twenty-nine, groping around in the dark, throwing myself right into it. This may sound out of place, but one can't really say that the future of Japanese theatre looks very bright.[5]

Then Osanai dropped a veritable bombshell:

> Now, concerning the plays we'll put on: for the next couple of years anyway, we plan to stage only Western drama.
>
> Why won't we do Japanese plays? I have a simple answer. We directors have not been inspired to do anything by current Japanese playwrights— and I'd have to count my own works as well.[6] If there were a play we felt like directing, we'd certainly plan on doing it, no matter what country it came from. . . . We're not averse to Japanese plays, nor are we trying to ape the West. We're staging [Western drama] simply because there aren't any Japanese works that whet our desire to direct them.[7]

This in fact was news to Hijikata, who had been planning to stage a couple of Japanese plays himself.[8] Apparently Osanai had not consulted his colleagues. He concluded his speech with an admission that his remarks would no doubt alienate some old friends.

Indeed, his old friends on the board of the leading theatre magazine of the day, *New Tides in Theatre*, were stunned.[9] Kikuchi Kan, one of the board members, had reservations about a theatre that refused to get its hands dirty with popular drama, and in a roundtable published in *New Tides in Theatre*, called the Tsukiji Little Theatre, ironically enough, a "coterie magazine" and Osanai's decision to stage only Western drama "asinine." Translation is necessarily a transitional art, so it is stupid to insist on doing only Western plays; Kikuchi added: "Even if he said he wanted to do one of our plays, I'd tell him 'no.' My idea of theatre is completely opposed to Osanai's. . . . It's a waste of time having short-legged, yellow-faced Japanese trying to pass themselves off as Europeans." Doing Western drama was like eating the Japanese version of Western food: it may look European, but it doesn't taste European, Kikuchi concluded.[10] Kubota Mantarō was more conciliatory, chiding Osanai more on how he had phrased his remarks. One could take it wrong and think he meant there was no value in staging Japanese plays, he suggested. Nagata Hideo thought Osanai made too much of the role of director, and Yamamoto Yūzō expressed bemusement over the choice of programming.[11] There seemed no consistency in the selection of plays with which the theatre had opened: Chekhov's *Swan Song* and Émile Mazaud's *Holiday* (both directed by Osanai) and Reinhard Goering's expressionist *A Sea Battle* (directed by Hijikata).

Osanai's appearance before the editorial board for another roundtable discussion (published in the August 1924 issue of *New Tides in Theatre*) was rather like one's willingly showing up for one's own lynching, said Asano Tokiichirō.[12] Osanai tried to preempt the board's attack with a prepared address entitled "For What Does the Tsukiji Little Theatre Exist?" The theatre had three purposes, he stated: theatre itself; the future; and the people. The first was the most germane for what ensued:

> Tsukiji Shōgekijō, like all other theatres, exists for theatre (*engeki*). . . . It does not exist for drama (*gikyoku*).
>
> Drama is literature. Literature has its own organs—newspapers, magazines, books—things that are printed. . . .
>
> We'll leave the literary critics to determine what value Tsukiji Shōgekijō's drama will have.[13]

What follows is a digest of the main points of the ensuing debate:

> Kikuchi: It's odd that you'll rely on contemporary audiences but not on contemporary playwrights.
>
> Osanai: You can't do good theatre unless you lead the people into the future. *Kabuki* and *shinpa* are fine insofar as they are able to express the common tastes of people today, but that isn't the aim of the Tsukiji Little Theatre.
>
> Kikuchi: If the quality of drama selected is not an issue for the Tsukiji Little Theatre, does that mean it's all right to perform bad plays?

Osanai: The quality may not be up to scratch from a literary standpoint, but theatre is another matter.

Kikuchi: So what are the Tsukiji Little Theatre's standards?

Osanai: We have not yet established any particular artistic ideologies or beliefs at the Tsukiji Little Theatre.

Kikuchi But you can't do theatre without ideals or principles of some sort.

Osanai: It's wrong to be ideologically bound. I may have no abiding theories, but I do have an objective, and that is "First the performance, then the drama."[14]

In effect, Osanai was reversing the formula that his own mentor, Mori Ōgai, had put forth some twenty-five years before: "First the drama, then the performance." He wished to assert theatre's independence as an art form from literature—in itself a noble idea, but curiously, it would seem, a step back to the aesthetic principles of the traditional theatre, particularly *kabuki*. It was an idea that was worth defending, but Osanai was beginning to weaken from the attacks of his former friends:

Osanai: When I said we would do Western drama, I didn't mean we wouldn't do Japanese plays. It's not that I'm picky.

Kubota: But I really wish you had phrased your remarks a bit more generously.[15]

Kikuchi continued to attack Osanai, this time for directing a minor play by Chekhov. Osanai remarked that Hijikata would not do Chekhov because he thought the Russian playwright was old hat. The differences in Osanai's and Hijikata's tastes, as many have noted, reflected the times when they visited Europe: Osanai in 1912 and Hijikata after the 1917 Russian Revolution. Osanai's model was still Constantin Stanislavsky's Moscow Arts Theatre, while Hijikata had been impressed with the expressionism of Max Reinhardt and Vsevolod Meyerhold. Osanai himself seemed to be coming around to the opinion that Chekhov was passé. "But just because something belongs to the present day doesn't make it better than what came before. You're too tolerant of novelty," countered Kubota, who urged him to be a bit more consistent and suggested that a denial of the past—particularly one's own old ideals—was a kind of self-denial. "What do you rely on if not yourself?" asked Yamamoto. "I can't help it if I change," protested Osanai.[16]

The debate ended with Osanai finally incapable of defending himself with any consistent theory or ideological program for the Tsukiji Little

Theatre. In the end, it was the mild-mannered Kubota, and not the strident Kikuchi, who appeared to deal the *coup de grâce*. The chief problem with Osanai and the Tsukiji Little Theatre's programming was a lack of an abiding vision for the theatre. Osanai was a passionate and charismatic figure, but he was often tactless and dogmatic, and his dogmatism ran especially at odds with his tendency to change his opinions on fundamental artistic matters such as the style of theatre he wished to promote. There is a sense in reading his essays that Osanai's mind was in permanent revolution. His views were changing radically during this time, but what views he had, he tried to defend tenaciously. Yet was this how a modern man should live? Where was the bedrock of his identity? Perhaps part of his charisma lay in the way Osanai seemed to embody the unhinged nature of modernity itself. Perhaps, too, Osanai was attempting to defend not only his own principles but Hijikata's as well. The two had conflicting visions for their theatre, visions that would eventually split the Tsukiji Little Theatre into two ideological camps, one strongly leftist and the other professedly apolitical.

Osanai himself was sensitive to the shifting winds of ideological change that were blowing in from the West, especially in this volatile period after the Great War and the Russian Revolution. Violent riots had swept Japan in 1918 over inflated prices for rice, and the early 1920s had witnessed a rising labor movement and numerous strikes. The Japan Socialist League (Nihon Shakaishugi Renmei) was founded in 1920, followed in 1922 by the establishment of the Japan Agricultural Union and the Japan Communist Party (which remained an illegal organization until after 1945). The names for such magazines as *Reform* (*Kaizō*) and *Liberation* (*Kaihō*), both founded in 1919, catch the tenor of the times. Hirasawa Keishichi started his Workers' Troupe (Rōdō Gekidan) in 1920. The leftist literary magazine *The Sower* (*Tanemaku hito*) had been founded in 1921 (playwright Kaneko Yōbun [1894–1985] was on the editorial board); in 1924, the same year as the opening of the Tsukiji Little Theatre, another leftist magazine, *Literary Front* (*Bungei sensen*), was established. Osanai himself was becoming swept up in the political vision of the new theatre. The Tsukiji Little Theatre, Osanai said, would exist for the "future" and the "people." It was the latter concept especially that would distinguish Tsukiji from the elitism of the Free Theatre, which Osanai had founded some fifteen years before. He wanted, he said, to make theatre as necessary to the common people as bread or rice, but perhaps it was too much to expect them to enjoy a solid diet of Western food. Soon enough, people would long for the comfort of *kabuki* and other popular performance. Politically or otherwise, *shingeki* was becoming increasingly didactic: audiences were there to learn, not so much to be entertained. But this was not necessarily a good box-office formula.

It was Osanai's insistence on the stage as a testing ground for ideas that distinguished his vision most from the traditional theatre, but he shared with *kabuki* the notion that drama was no more or less than a pretext for the theatrical event. It was the latter notion especially that pitted him against a generation of writers who were trying to create new drama in Japan, men (for the most part) who were eager to see their work staged by the most modern of Tokyo theatres and then were bitterly disappointed by Osanai's insensitive remarks. Taishō writers had worked hard to establish drama as a literary genre, and while some might have been interested in the form on merely literary terms, many were eager to see their works staged—eager, in short, to play their part in the creation of a new theatre.

The *New Tides in Theatre* playwrights certainly had doubts about the criteria used to select drama at the Tsukiji Little Theatre. Much of it seemed hardly superior to what they were writing. During their first roundtable discussion in June 1924, Yamamoto Yūzō mentioned that "a friend who had spent quite some time in France" had remarked that one of the three plays presented at Tsukiji's premiere, Mazaud's *Holiday*, was a bad translation of a mediocre play. It had bombed in France, he said.[17] The friend was Kishida Kunio. Osanai had in fact sent someone to ask Kishida to check the translation. Osanai himself had translated the play from an English translation he had read in the magazine *Theatre Arts*, and prior to the production, he had tried to secure a copy of the original. Kishida did not have one and so was unable to check the translation for its accuracy. Subsequently, Kishida managed to lay his hands on a copy of the French text and, realizing Osanai's inaccuracies, mentioned them to Yamamoto, who used what he heard as ammunition for his attack on the Tsukiji director.[18] Kishida, who had made his debut as a playwright just months earlier with *Old Toys* (*Furui omocha*) in the March 1924 issue of *New Tides in Theatre*, had every reason to want to be on Osanai's good side, but he was already being cast as an antagonist.[19] In fact, he shared Osanai's low opinion of many Taishō plays and would write in the December 1924 issue of the journal that "the hundred flowers that were supposed to have blossomed in this so-called age of drama presented in fact a veritable parade of pandemonium in broad daylight." Taishō was "an age when pseudo-drama was rampant. Novels are hard to write, so everybody writes plays instead."[20] But he was squarely in the *New Tides* camp when it came to emphasizing the

importance of the text. The fourth play produced at the Tsukiji Little Theatre hardly inspired more confidence. Why had the theatre selected *Wolves,*
wondered Kishida. Romain Rolland's play was, in a negative sense, the more
"literary" and, by the same token, the most "anti-dramatic" of plays:

> What I mean when I say "anti-dramatic" may have nothing to do with what
> the Tsukiji Little Theatre considers the "theatrical." Not "may"—in fact,
> I'm sure it doesn't. A drama, no matter how dull it is, can be turned into
> superb theatre in the hands of a great director—it's not necessary to harp
> on this, really. Besides, the Tsukiji Little Theatre has taken greater pains in
> selecting its programming than other theatres. But if that's the case, how
> on earth can this be a drama that whets your desire to direct? How can it
> possibly live up to the "ideal theatre" that you are striving for?[21]

Ultimately, it seemed quixotic to try and make great theatre out of poor drama.
Far more to the point was picking good scripts because great drama would always inspire a great director, and, moreover, an important part of the director's
job was precisely in selecting such plays.

It seemed that ideological criteria trumped artistic ones (*Wolves* was about
the French Revolution). But the two were increasingly harder to distinguish
in the politically charged climate of the 1920s. Perhaps nothing indicated this
difficulty more than Osanai's changing views of realist theatre. He had been
one of the first to champion this style, and his directing was still patterned
after Stanislavsky, but when the Tsukiji Little Theatre opened, he was changing his tune. Kikuchi Kan, the king of realism, was still Japan's most successful
playwright, but in 1924, both he and his style of theatre seemed poised toward
decline. Ever alert to new trends, Osanai had already written an attack on realism and Kikuchi in 1922:

> From the standpoint of world art, realism is already finished. You won't find
> realism in any of the finest works of art now: not in painting or sculpture
> or literature or theatre. And this is, of course, true for music and dance as
> well. But Japanese playwrights still insist on realism and Kikuchi Kan, who
> unfortunately is still stuck in this style, continues to be held in high respect.
> Soon the winds of a new aesthetic, which began to brew before the Great
> War and then erupted all over Europe when it ended, cannot help but de-
> stroy our Japanese realism (which I believe is an element of our bourgeois
> literature).[22]

It is no wonder, then, that it was Kikuchi, more than any of the other *New Tides in Theatre* playwrights, who lashed out at Osanai. Both he and Yamamoto would increasingly devote their considerable literary energies to fiction and editorial activities. Their estrangement from drama was indicative of a trend.

As Brian Powell notes, the Tsukiji Little Theatre "prepared for the first production of a Japanese play . . . divided within and attacked from without."[23] By late 1925 the theatre was already casting around for Japanese plays to stage, and the December issue of the house newsletter, *Tsukiji Shōgekijō*, solicited ideas from its readers. At the top of the list, with thirty-eight votes, was the newcomer Kishida. Several of his plays, including *Old Toys, Autumn in Tyrol* (*Chiroru no aki*), *Paper Balloon* (*Kami fūsen*), and *The Swing* (*Buranko*), were suggested. The second most popular was Mushanokōji Saneatsu with thirty-four votes. Tanizaki Jun'ichirō was a distant third with twenty-two votes, followed closely by Yamamoto Yūzō with twenty. Further down, in fifth and sixth places were Arishima Takeo and Akita Ujaku. Kikuchi Kan matched Ujaku with thirteen votes, followed by Kubota Mantarō and Suzuki Senzaburō with twelve each. Osanai himself ranked lower, matching the eleven votes accorded to Fujii Masumi (1889–1962) and Kaneko Yōbun.[24] The list represented a cross-section of Taishō drama, by the very writers whose plays Osanai had shown little interest in producing. Though Akita Ujaku stood independent of the *New Tides* playwrights in style and politics, he had been writing plays for longer than many of them; his first play, *First Dawn*, had premiered at Osanai's Free Theatre in 1909. Several others made the list, including Masamune Hakuchō, Yoshii Isamu, and Nakamura Kichizō, one of Ibsen's epigones. Besides Kishida, the only other relatively new faces were leftists Fujii Masumi and Kaneko Yōbun.

Osanai's ultimate choice was a play no one had considered, Tsubouchi Shōyō's *En the Ascetic*, which in the ten years since its publication in 1917 had never been staged. Osanai's choice sparked another round of shock and intense debate. Many thought the subject matter about a semi-legendary seventh-century mountain ascetic was arcane and its *kabuki*esque style dated. Akita Ujaku thought the theme irrelevant to contemporary life.[25] Some considered the play a veiled allegory of Shōyō's own battle with his erstwhile disciple Shimamura Hōgetsu, who left the Literary Society with his mistress, Matsui Sumako, to establish the Art Theatre. Osanai saw *En the Ascetic* as a drama about humanity's struggle with nature and the supernatural. It was an odd choice for a director who had been Shōyō's chief rival at the end of the Meiji era, and some suggest that it was an overture of goodwill to the grand old man of modern Japanese theatre. But Osanai also considered the play a technical challenge for his actors: the tension of downplaying *En*'s *kabuki* tendencies would be theatrically interesting. Recall his instructions to the actors in rehearsal (as noted in the preface): "Forget *kabuki*. Ignore tradition. Move, don't dance! Talk, don't sing!"[26]

En the Ascetic was a great box-office success. The production pulled the Tsukiji Little Theatre out of the doldrums, drawing back audiences that had become bored with the solid diet of Western drama.[27] The theatre extended the run for another week and revived the production the following year, in November 1927, in a much larger venue, the Imperial Theatre. But critical reception was mixed. Critics were impressed with the special effects, but "the acting left much to be desired, and the grand scale of the play required a significantly larger stage than the Little Theatre had to offer," Linda Keenan notes.[28] *New Tides,* typically, was the harshest in its criticism: the play was "full of bluster" and "too preachy."[29] Worse, its own playwright, Shōyō, hated it. "First two acts generally good; third act no good, a complete misinterpretation," he wrote in his diary, and the Imperial Theatre production, which attempted to do the third act according to Shōyō's conception of it, "was worse than the first time."[30]

En the Ascetic was the forty-fifth production at the Tsukiji Little Theatre. Until Osanai's death in December 1928, the theatre staged twenty-seven Japanese plays by thirteen playwrights; only 20 percent of the plays staged by the Tsukiji Little theatre were not foreign, a record for producing domestic drama that was worse than the Free Theatre's.[31]

The only plays the Tsukiji Little Theatre chose to do that were recommended by the theatre's subscribers were by Akita Ujaku, Mushanokōji Saneatsu, and Osanai himself. The theatre staged as many as six plays by Osanai and four plays by Mushanokōji: *Desire (Aiyoku), King of Life (Seimei no ō), Two Hearts (Futatsu no kokoro),* and *Three Priests (San ōshō).* Fujiki Hiroyuki suggests that Ujaku was selected because he and Osanai had both been invited to the Soviet Union in 1927 for celebrations of the tenth anniversary of the Russian Revolution.[32] Fujimori Seikichi (who had not made the list of desired playwrights) made a successful debut with his sensational *What Made Her Do It? (Nani ga kanojo o sō saseta ka).*[33] Fujiki comments that the Tsukiji Little Theatre's selection of Japanese plays was inconsistent and arbitrary but could be divided into roughly three categories: "safe" works by well-established writers like Shōyō, Mushanokōji, Tanizaki, and Nakamura Kichizō; proletarian drama by people like Fujimori; and plays by Osanai's protégés, people like

Kitamura Komatsu and Ueda (Enchi) Fumiko, who debuted as a playwright with *Restless Night in Late Spring* (*Banshun sōya*).[34] Completely missing from the list of plays the Tsukiji Little Theatre staged were works by Kishida Kunio, Kikuchi Kan, and Yamamoto Yūzō, the three playwrights Osanai had greatest cause to snub. Some speculate that had Osanai lived longer, he would surely have staged one of Kishida's plays, but it is unlikely that he would have directed any of Kikuchi's or Yamamoto's; in any event, Hijikata Yoshi and Aoyama Sugisaku directed most of the Japanese drama.

Osanai's disparagement of drama, particularly from his old comrades at *New Tides,* succeeded in driving yet another wedge between the two worlds of page and stage (*bundan* and *gekidan*), and over the coming decades, drama would seem less and less important as an object of literary production or study for aspiring writers, critics, and scholars. The face the Tsukiji Little Theatre presented both to the world and to itself reflected yet another ground for contention, between those who saw drama as a medium for political discourse and others whose criteria for evaluating a work, they professed, were entirely artistic. After Osanai's rejection of Japanese plays in 1924, Kikuchi Kan led a campaign to stage domestic drama with a rival troupe, the New Theatre Society (Shingeki Kyōkai), which produced its work in a larger theatre just behind the Tsukiji Little Theatre. (The company would fold in 1927, after Kikuchi pulled out his financial backing over Hatanaka Ryōha's desire to stage Western plays as well as Japanese.) After Osanai's sudden death on Christmas Day, 1928, the Tsukiji Little Theatre split along ideological lines. Leftists like Senda Koreya, Yamamoto Yasue (1902–1993), Kubo Sakae (1900–1958), Murayama Tomoyoshi (1901–1977), and Miyoshi Jūrō (1902–1958) established politically committed companies like the New Cooperative Troupe (Shinkyō Gekidan) and the New Tsukiji Troupe (Shin-Tsukiji Gekidan).

Osanai was wrong, however, about the demise of realism. The first Soviet Writers' Union meeting held in Kharkov, Ukraine, in 1932, effectively ruled that the only acceptable artistic form to be pursued was socialist realism, and this decision profoundly affected the kind of leftist plays that would be staged in the 1930s. Thus, productions like Hisaita Eijirō's *Fault Line* (*Dansō,* 1935) and *The Northeast Wind* (*Hokutō no kaze,* 1937), adaptations of Shimazaki Tōson's historical novel *Before the Dawn* (*Yoake-mae,* fp. 1934), and Nagatsuka Takashi's *Earth* (*Tsuchi,* 1937), culminating in the New Cooperative Troupe's production of Kubo Sakae's *Land of Volcanic Ash* (*Kazan-baichi,* 1938), characterized the politically charged realism of leftist theatre in

1930s Japan. Bertolt Brecht, the heir of 1920s German expressionist theatre, would not make an impact in Japan until Senda Koreya was able to stage his plays after 1945.

At the same time, a more bourgeois style of psychological realism came to dominate the plays of the apolitical and "literary" school of dramatists in the late 1920s and '30s. Some Tsukiji Little Theatre alumni like the brilliant actor Tomoda Kyōsuke (1899–1937) and his wife, the equally talented Tamura Akiko (1905–1983), felt increasingly disenchanted by the encroachment of politics on artistic decisions; they would found companies like the Tsukiji-za. It was the latter company toward which Kishida and others would gravitate in the 1930s, and after Tomoda was killed in action in China in 1937, Kishida, together with the playwrights Kubota Mantarō and Iwata Toyoo (1893–1969) and the actress Sugimura Haruko, would establish the Literary Theatre (Bungaku-za), one of the only troupes allowed to perform after the government crackdown on leftist theatres in 1940.[35]

The venues for staging new plays by Japanese dramatists remained limited, however, and Osanai's decision initially to stage only Western plays at the Tsukiji Little Theatre effectively closed a chapter in which drama was an important genre for practically every Japanese writer; thereafter, only the very dedicated would devote themselves to writing for the stage.

Osanai stood squarely at the center of every key debate that raged in Japanese theatre circles in the early twentieth century. What was theatre's purpose in a modern world? Was it as an agent of social change or as a place to explore the human soul (whatever that might be)? Was it a venue for the introduction of Western ideas and ways of thought and action or for the production of new dramatic texts written by the Japanese themselves? In both cases, Osanai stood for the former and strenuously resisted the latter. As theatre scholar Sugai Yukio has pointed out, Osanai's legacy served to distort modern Japanese theatre by excluding from its active participation the very playwrights who could have contributed so much to its development.[36] Dramatists like Kishida had to go elsewhere to see their plays produced. At the same time, notes J. Thomas Rimer, *shingeki*'s emphasis on translated drama would ensure for decades to come that modern Japanese theatre "would remain an intellectual rather than an emotional experience."[37] Osanai and his colleagues wanted to reach the people, but the means they used appealed to a narrow audience of mostly leftist cognoscenti. The general public was increasingly presented with improbable and alien ideals of thought and comportment and was less able to see itself presented onstage as it really was. Paradoxically, then, the rise of modern drama coincided with the gradual decline of theatre as a popular art in early-twentieth-century Japan.

If, however, Osanai is cast as the villain in this play, we nonetheless need to give this devil his due. He himself was not responsible for the increasing ideological polarization that was occurring in Japanese culture, especially the theatre, during the 1920s and '30s; it was a global phenomenon in which, both as artist and arbiter of modern culture, he felt a duty to take a stand. And this political position was also related to a legitimate aesthetic concern: if, as Lukacs and Szondi have suggested, modern drama came more and more to emulate the novel in its probing of the inner soul of the individual at the expense of its portrayal of social dynamics, modern drama in Japan may have represented a betrayal of the native, sociable theatricality of traditional Japanese culture. In order to preserve what he considered the essence of the theatrical experience, Osanai felt a need to expunge from it anything that smacked of being too "literary," too bourgeois. If modern culture severed the word from the human body, Osanai reasoned that in order to reclaim physicality in its new, "modern" form, theatre had to distance itself from anything too resolutely textual. Hence his dictum: "First the performance, then the drama." The leftist theatre to which Osanai and his epigones increasingly aligned themselves arguably attempted to create a new image of community, one that they felt could compensate for a traditional sense of solidarity lost to the modern, alienated self. It is ironic, however, that the impetus for this was intellectual, and its effect remained cerebral and not sensual. In the politically charged ferment of 1930s Japan, it is also a bitter irony that the more "literary" dramatists, people like Kikuchi and Kishida, who had in turn felt alienated by Osanai and his comrades, later collaborated with the militarists. But that is another story.

AKITA UJAKU

....

THE SKELETONS' DANCE

INTRODUCTION

At the time of the Great Kantō Earthquake, Akita Ujaku was on a lecture tour of his native Tōhoku (northeast) region, meeting fellow Esperantists.[1] He returned briefly to his hometown, Kuroishi in Aomori, leaving on September 4 for Tokyo. An army officer's remark on the train outside Tokyo about the rumor that Koreans had been lighting fires after the earthquake had made the other passengers laugh. Akita recorded in his diary that he was "shocked at the [Japanese] citizens' thoughtlessness."[2] On September 6 he reached his home in Zōshigaya and was taken the following day by vigilantes to a police station for interrogation; later the same day he was threatened by another thug when he returned home. For the next few days he toured the city, particularly the hardest hit districts in Honjo and Fukagawa on the east of the Sumida River. Learning that the police were cracking down on socialists like himself and his friend, the children's writer Ogawa Mimei, Ujaku decided it was best to return to Aomori. He left Tokyo on September 16 and before the month was out learned of the murders of Osugi Sakae, Hirasawa Keishichi, and others. "The citizens' ignorance is truly to be feared," he wrote in his diary.[3] He did not return to Tokyo until late October of that year.

Photo of Akita Ujaku (ca. 1920) courtesy of the Tsubouchi Memorial Theatre Museum, Waseda University.

Ujaku entered the department of English literature at the Tokyo Senmon Gakkō (the precursor to Waseda University) in 1902; by 1904 he had already met his literary idol, Shimazaki Tōson, and published a volume of verse. At school he became acquainted with Shimamura Hōgetsu, one of the most influential critics of the day, and began publishing short stories in *Waseda Literature* in 1907, and the same year he became secretary for Osanai Kaoru's Ibsen Society. In 1909 he joined Osanai's Free Theatre and published his first play. In 1913 he became a director of Hōgetsu's Art Theatre, leaving that company the following year with actor Sawamura Sōjurō to found another troupe, the Bijutsu Gekijō, which staged his first successful play, *Buried Spring* (*Umoreta haru*). He returned to work for the Art Theatre in 1918.

Ujaku's early plays tended to be romantic, lyrical, and idealistic. He revealed a keen sympathy for the underdog and a rising political consciousness as early as 1903, when he heard a speech by the socialist Kōtoku Shūsui. (Shūsui would be executed for treason in 1911 on largely trumped-up charges. The so-called High Treason Incident of 1910 was a foretaste of the murder of Osugi Sakae and other leftists after the earthquake.) In 1921 Ujaku joined the Japan Socialist League and began writing for the preeminent leftist journal of the day, *The Sower*, publishing the same year another important play, *Night at the Frontier* (*Kokkyō no yoru*). In 1927, together with Osanai Kaoru, he was invited to the Soviet Union for tenth-anniversary celebrations of the Russian Revolution. Though his dramatic output fell off by the late 1920s, Ujaku continued his work for the theatre, becoming editor of *Teatoro* magazine, as well as secretary of the Shinkyō Gekidan, one of the leftist spin-offs from the Tsukiji Little Theatre, in 1934. In 1940, together with several hundred other *shingeki* artists, he was rounded up and imprisoned; he spent the last years of the war in his native Aomori. Like Ogawa Mimei, he was also a much-loved writer of children's fiction. After the war, he published an autobiography; his meticulously kept diaries were published posthumously.

Ujaku's diary shows that he was developing ideas for a play about the earthquake as early as November 1923. He had completed the play, as he notes in Esperanto on the published text, on "la 14an de Januaro, 1924." A number of plays had been inspired by the earthquake, and the March 1924 issue of *New Tides in Theatre* was in part devoted to a review of these works. Shibata Shōei noted that all these works attempted to portray the event itself, a task beyond the technical resources of the theatre. In the same issue, Ujaku argued that what should have been portrayed was not the event itself but its effect:

Japanese playwrights are too lacking in social consciousness. For example, any lack of shock at the horrific earthquake or rage they may express at society's inaction afterward proves that as citizens or human beings, they are devoid of faith or even healthy disbelief. Everyone seems to take up his brush as if the events of a decade were those of a single day. . . . This is a time to liberate our subjectivities. We must lift up our eyes and see broader vistas. It is an age to set free our thoughts, words, and actions. The road ahead looks dark, however.[4]

This mixture of hope and pessimism was undoubtedly an accurate augur of the political climate of the day.

The Skeletons' Dance was one of the first works to address the slaughter of Koreans after the earthquake, and it is a wonder that it ever got published in the first place.[5] It appeared in the April 1924 issue of New Tides, by some strange fluke escaping notice by the government censors completely. Censorship of the theatre before 1945 was even more stringent than that of literature; not only were playwrights obliged to have all manuscripts vetted by the police before they were published, but also a stage production could be stopped at any time if production diverged from the approved text or was considered in any way offensive. Censorship could take various forms, the mildest and most common being to blot out the offending passages with crosses, or fuseji. When the police got wind of the explosive contents of Ujaku's play, they promptly stopped publication of the April issue of New Tides and confiscated any remaining copies they could obtain. Ujaku nonetheless published the work again the following year, though much of the dialogue, including all mention of Koreans, was blotted out. In 1927 he published an Esperanto translation of the play, but it would seem the first unexpurgated version was not published until after the war.[6] Its first production was not until February 1983, by the Mingei Theatre Company (Gekidan Mingei), to commemorate the hundredth anniversary of Ujaku's birth.

True to Ujaku's plan, The Skeletons' Dance does not portray the earthquake itself; it is set some hundreds of miles away from Tokyo, in an evacuation tent at "M" (Morioka?) Station. He is less interested in a realistic rendering of the disaster than in capturing its political, social, and spiritual effect; hence his call for a "liberation of subjectivity." In his directions, Ujaku indicates that "Cubist staging could be employed here. It might be interesting to try the 'Mavo' style." "Mavo" refers to a constructivist movement initiated by Murayama Tomoyoshi, Ogata Kamenosuke, Yanase Masamu, and others. Their first exhibition was in Asakusa in July 1923 and was restricted to paintings, but the group was active in architectural, interior, and stage design, as well as book and poster illustrations. Mavo also launched a magazine under the same name. Yanase Masamu had designed the sets for Ujaku's *Hand Grenade* (*Tenagedan*), which was staged together with August Strindberg's *Playing with Fire* at the Senku-za in April 1923. What Ujaku no doubt had in mind especially was the set design for the classic 1919 German Expressionist film *The Cabinet of Dr. Caligari*, with its nasty angles manifesting the distorted mental state of its characters.[7] *Caligari* was also the inspiration for perhaps Japan's first Expressionist film, Mizoguchi Kenji's *Blood and Soul* (*Chi to rei*, 1923). In any event, *The Skeletons' Dance* is one of the first examples of avant-garde modernist theatre in Japan. It predates the stage designs both for the Tsukiji Little Theatre's debut production of Georg Kaiser's Expressionist *Sea Battle* (in June 1924) and for another Kaiser play at the Tsukiji, *From Morn' till Midnight* (*Asa kara yonaka made*, December 1924), by the Mavo artist Murayama Tomoyoshi (who would by the 1930s be one of Japan's leading leftist playwrights).[8]

Ujaku's play begins realistically enough, with the groans of the suffering evacuees and a midnight conversation between two of them, an old man and a young "student" (*shosei*). The old man mentions the rumor that Koreans had stirred up trouble after the quake (some accounts said that they had poisoned wells and started fires), which the youth flatly denies. The play proceeds to paint an ironic portrait of a hypocritical upper-class woman, the wife of the local mayor, who has come to give aid to the sick and injured, though their filth and poverty disgust her. The drama takes a radical turn in both tone and style with the entrance of the vigilantes, who are searching for a Korean fugitive. The vigilantes claim that in order to protect the state, they must follow dictates above the law, to which the youth replies that the state cannot exist without the rule of law. He attempts to protect the Korean and launches into a long passage in verse, in which he accuses the vigilantes of betraying their own humanity, of being nothing more than skeletons with neither flesh nor soul, dressed in the meaningless garb of their "official" positions. Calling for the dawn of a "new race" (a notable theme of Expressionist theatre), the youth, hitherto powerless, begins to manipulate the vigilantes as if they were puppets, or rather "hideous skeletons" animated by "dead, moldering morals" and "contemptible ancestor worship." Then he turns them into stone, their petrifaction signifying the inability of the Japanese citizenry to take autonomous political action. Holding up the Korean as a "true human being," the youth leads the vigilantes—indeed everyone else but himself, the Korean, the old man, and the nurse—in a *danse macabre* punctuated from the wings by the sharp laughter of those who had died in the past for "thought crimes." This utopian dream, however, evaporates at dawn, which rises on a scene of the nurse consoling a mother for the death of her child. Her words, "but it was meant to be," could also be taken to refer to the deaths of the youth and the Korean at the hands of the vigilantes. In a production I saw of the play, these characters lay prone under sheets when the lights came up at the end. The road ahead indeed looks dark.

Despite the return to reality at the end of the play, Ujaku clearly felt that realism was insufficient as a style to express the "subjective truth" he sought here. Its Expressionist style, with motifs inspired by both Strindberg's *Dance of Death* (1900) and Ernst Toller's 1919 play *Transfiguration,* attempted to portray the "spirit" of his characters—in the words of Inoue Yoshie, "their ideas, self-complacency, anger, desires, despair, and hope"[9]—through the media of dance and music. Three-dimensional psychological portraits of the characters would have been beside the point. The play is thus significant not only for Ujaku's courage in grappling with such dangerous political subject matter, but also for his employment of some of the most radical artistic devices at his disposal then.

Japanese sources for the text translated here are Akita Ujaku: *"Gaikotsu no buchō," Engeki shinchō* 1, no. 4 (April 1924): 28–49; *"Gaikotsu no buchō,"* in Akita, *Akita Ujaku gikyokushū,* 1–33; and *"Gaikotsu no buchō,"* in Nihon kindai engekishi kenkyūkai, *Nihon no kindai gikyoku,* 148–159.

The Skeletons' Dance, February 1983 production at Yakult Hall, Tokyo. Photograph courtesy of the Tsubouchi Memorial Theatre Museum, Waseda University.

AKITA UJAKU

THE SKELETONS' DANCE

FIRST PUBLISHED:
New Tides in Theatre, April 1924

FIRST PERFORMANCE:
Yakult Hall, Tokyo, February 1982,
dir. Uchiyama Uzura

CHARACTERS

....

A YOUTH

An OLD MAN

A NURSE

A DOCTOR

A KOREAN

VIGILANTES *(later* SKELETONS*)*

A LADY

Various EVACUEES

OTHERS

PLACE: *Inside the tent of a first-aid station. (Cubist staging could be employed here. It might be interesting to try the "Mavo" style.)*

OLD MAN: Excuse me. . . .

YOUTH: Are you talking to me?

OLD MAN: Sorry to disturb you at your sleep, but what is this place?

YOUTH: *(Raising his head and glancing at the* OLD MAN.*)* This is M Station. Where are you going?

OLD MAN: I was headed for Hokkaido, but it's M Station, you say? . . . What time is it?

YOUTH: It's past two already.

OLD MAN: Will it be dawn soon then?

YOUTH: Not for another couple of hours.

OLD MAN: Is that so? . . . What a disaster! . . . For this to happen, and at my age. . . . What was that sound?

YOUTH: Nothing, just a train. When did you get here?

OLD MAN: Last night. . . . Late last night. . . . Why did this have to happen? It's crazy.

YOUTH: You had a bad time of it then, in Tokyo, did you? We were both unlucky, I guess.

OLD MAN: "Bad time" hardly begins to describe it. . . . I lost my daughter and my grandchildren. . . . Besides, I was sick and hardly in any state to be making a trip anywhere.

YOUTH: Is that so? I'm sorry for you. . . . Where was it your daughter and grandkids died? Honjo?

OLD MAN: No, Mukōjima. . . . I've been living in Mukōjima for some thirty years now. . . . I heard from a neighbor that my daughter fled with my grandchildren to the embankment. They were pushed into the river by the crush of people.

YOUTH: That's terrible. I heard that happened to a lot of people there. But luckily you managed to get away.

OLD MAN: I'd have been better off dead. . . . What have I got to look forward to now, with my daughter and grandchildren gone?

YOUTH: You've a right to feel that way. . . . But in this world of ours, we've got to hang on. If we do, something will turn up. . . . Mind you, I can't see any light at the end of the tunnel myself . . . but so long as one's alive, one's got to live.

OLD MAN: Is there somebody sleeping next to me? It feels like somebody's lying on top of my right arm. . . . Sorry to bother you, but could you have a look for me?

YOUTH: Yes, there is. . . . You can't move your right arm?

OLD MAN: I haven't been able to for some three years now.

YOUTH: How did you ever manage to come this far? . . . You should've stayed in Tokyo. . . . Hello? Could you please move your head there? You're lying on top of a sick man's arm. Please move.

(A MAN raises his head, opens his eyes, and looks at the other two. He appears to want to say something but simply smiles sadly at them and shifts over, then falls asleep as before, lying face up. Two or three other MEN raise their heads and gaze at the YOUTH and OLD MAN.)

OLD MAN: *(Breathing deeply.)* Thank you. . . . That feels a lot better now. . . . You must be tired. . . . I think I'll try to catch some sleep myself before morning. . . . Hey, what is that racket? . . . Is there a fire someplace?

YOUTH: *(Laughing.)* That's no fire. It's a locomotive. We're five hundred miles away from Tokyo here. No earthquakes or fires are going to get you here.

OLD MAN: That so? ... But aren't they saying the Koreans are going around lighting fires? ... It's really frightening.

YOUTH: *(Firmly.)* You believe it too? We should have a bit more faith than that. I'm doing what I can to find out the truth.

OLD MAN: Really? But if it's a lie, it's a terrible one.... Is it true that because of the rumors a lot of Koreans have been killed along the railroad tracks?

YOUTH: It is. I've seen a lot since yesterday myself.... I'm sick to my stomach of the Japanese. I thought we were a people with a bit more sense than that, but I feel completely betrayed by what's happened. And deeply disappointed. *(During this speech, a* MAN *in back raises his head and looks at the two. His eyes shine strangely.)*

OLD MAN: I know nothing of what happened, but if the Koreans didn't do anything, I feel sorry for them.... Why did they have to take it out on them again?

YOUTH: Because people have no faith. All they do is go around smugly wearing somebody else's clothes. I'm disappointed in the Japanese as citizens, but I won't lose my faith in them as human beings. It doesn't matter where they're from—all humans are, deep down, good and innocent.

OLD MAN: That may be, but I'm Japanese, and I think the Japanese are fine people.

YOUTH: Yes. I too want to think that, but I saw what the Japanese did last night, and I didn't want to think that my own countrymen could do such a thing.... If you didn't see what I saw, there's no way you could understand how I feel.

OLD MAN: In any case, it's turned into a nasty world, that's for sure.... Where are you headed from here?

YOUTH: I'm going back to Aomori. I've got brothers there.

OLD MAN: Is that so? ... If you don't mind my asking, have you got a job?

YOUTH: *(Laughing.)* Me? ... Why, I'm still a student.

OLD MAN: Is that so? ... Still studying, are you? ... Good for you.

YOUTH: And what line of work were you in?

OLD MAN: Me? ... Nothing special.... I worked for a foundry.

YOUTH: A foundry? You mean, like casting sculptures?

OLD MAN: Well ... I was really just a tradesman.... Nothing to write home about.

YOUTH: I know quite a few sculptors myself. There was Y, a poor fellow who was eking out a living casting medals and statues of the god Daikoku. He was living in Mukōjima too, I think.

OLD MAN: Y. . . . I think I've heard that name before. . . . Hey, it sounds like there's some kind of noise. Ever since the fire, my hearing's not what it used to be.

YOUTH: *(Listening carefully.)* It's nothing. You're just upset. You should try to relax.

NURSE: *(To a first-aid station ATTENDANT.)* Nishimura-san, go to the head-quarters and get us some more cotton batting. *(ATTENDANT exits right without speaking.)* Is there anyone here who doesn't feel well?

EVACUEE: Nurse, call me a doctor. . . . My stomach hurts so bad I don't know what to do.

EVACUEE: Nurse, bring me a glass of water.

EVACUEE: Nurse, can I board the boat in my state?

EVACUEE: Nurse, will this ticket let me board the boat for free?

NURSE: Quiet, everybody, please! I can't do anything for you if you all talk at once. *(To the OLD MAN.)* Are you getting on the boat tonight?

OLD MAN: I wanted to ask you. . . . Would it be impossible for me to stay here a bit longer? . . . I hurt so bad, I'm not sure I can go anywhere.

NURSE: Is that so? The doctor will be coming tonight, so I'll have him take a look at you.

EVACUEE: I want a glass of water. My body feels like it's burning all over.

NURSE: *(Drawing a glass of boiled water from a large bucket and handing it to him.)* There you go. Drink.

EVACUEE: Nurse, me too.

EVACUEE: Me too.

EVACUEE: Me too.

NURSE: You'll just have to wait your turn.

EVACUEE: You're mean.

EVACUEE: A spiteful nurse. . . . Really stuck up.

EVACUEE: I should never have come here in the first place. . . . Never in my life have I been treated so badly before.

EVACUEE: Yeah, they were so ever much nicer at O Station. . . . They can't understand how we feel 'cause they didn't get burned.

EVACUEE: Nurse, could you take this bandage off? . . . Ever since you put it on, it's been hurting something awful. . . . Ow! . . . It hurts!

NURSE: That shouldn't be. It may hurt a bit now, but in no time you'll be feeling better.

EVACUEE: Ah, it hurts! . . . Ah, it hurts! . . . I'd sooner be dead than hang around in a place like this.

EVACUEE: Quiet there, you! . . . This child here is deathly ill.

NURSE: Now, please try to be quiet. . . . I'm afraid she hasn't long.

EVACUEE: *(To the other* EVACUEE*):* Shut up, you old bag! . . . We ought to kill you instead. . . . Can't you see this child's going to die? . . . We're all suffering here.

NURSE: Now, now. I know how you all feel, but try to quiet down now.

LADY: *(Enters tent carrying a basket filled with various things.)* Good evening, everyone. You must all be tired.

NURSE: Good evening, madam. Thanks for coming. But why at such an hour as this?

LADY: I was up all night last night at Headquarters with the bureau chief's wife. You know? Even the bureau chief's wife stayed up with us!

NURSE: Is that so? Well, we appreciate it.

LADY: *(Looking at the scene inside the tent.)* Quite a few have left already, it seems. These are gifts from Headquarters.

NURSE: Why, thank you very much. I'm sure they'll all be delighted.

YOUTH: Won't you try to sleep?

OLD MAN: How can I sleep with all this racket? . . . I don't need anything. . . . I just want to have a decent rest. . . . But when I think of my daughter and the grandkids. . . .

EVACUEE: Who is that woman?

EVACUEE: Her? She's brought something. . . . Get a load of the rock on the ring she's wearing! . . . Maybe I should ask her to give it to me.

EVACUEE: White collar, crested jacket. . . . A real looker. . . . What d'ya think? Used to be a professional woman?

LADY: You must all be very tired, surely. . . . Please tell me if there's anything you need. Don't be shy, now.

NURSE: This is the wife of the mayor, everybody. . . . She's been working very hard for us all since the fire.

LADY: *(Laughs youthfully.)* My, but you flatter me! It's such a poor town, I'm ashamed to say that it's more than I can manage. But if it's in my power, I'll do all I possibly can, so do please speak up and tell me.

EVACUEE: *(To himself.)* Speak up? Isn't it obvious without our telling you? We don't have anything.

LADY: Anyone hungry?

EVACUEE: I'm not hungry, but I'm dying of thirst here.

LADY: Is that so? Here's a soft drink for you.

EVACUEE: I'm thirsty too, ma'am! I'm thirsty too!

LADY: I've only five bottles of soft drinks here. You'll have to share them among yourselves.

(*The* EVACUEES *all swarm around the* LADY *like beggars, attempting to grab bottles of soft drinks. The* LADY *blushes and tries to prevent all the bottles from being taken. The* EVACUEES *press in on her from all sides.*)

NURSE: Let me handle this, madam. . . . It's dangerous for you. . . . Now, settle down everybody! If you don't settle down you'll have to give back what you've got. Are you listening?

EVACUEE: Quiet, everybody! . . . I've got no need for any soft drink. . . . Let's give them to the ladies.

EVACUEE: Yeah, give them to the ladies!

NURSE: (*Taking the basket from the* LADY.) Yes, why don't you do that? I'll give you men some apples instead. (*She gives the women the bottles of soft drinks and apples to the men. The* EVACUEES *stretch out their arms to receive the gifts.*)

LADY: It's quite a task, isn't it, handing out rations? I feel I understand for the first time how much you all have suffered.

NURSE: It's nothing once you get used to it, madam. Thank you so much. They're all just like children. But I suppose they have a right to be.

YOUTH: You're not hungry?

OLD MAN: No . . . not much. . . . I just don't feel like eating.

YOUTH: It's unpleasant having to receive things, but there's something even uglier about the spirit of those who are doing the giving.

LADY: Well, I'll be taking my leave of you all now. Please do look after them. Farewell.

NURSE: Are you going? Thank you so much, madam. Please give my regards to the people at Headquarters.

LADY: (*Heading out of the tent with her empty basket.*) It looks like tomorrow will be another fine day.

NURSE: Is that so? Goodbye, madam!

ATTENDANT: (*Enters the tent with a box of cotton batting.*) Terrible news, Miss Yamada! Some Koreans have been killed in front of Headquarters!

NURSE: Were they up to something, the Koreans?

ATTENDANT: They say the Koreans were launching an all-out attack on the home guard.

EVACUEES: (*Practically all the men stand up as one.*) Koreans!

EVACUEE: The Koreans are here. I might have known it!

EVACUEE: The Koreans are beasts!

NURSE: Now, try to settle down, all of you! . . . The doctor will be here soon. . . . It's nothing to worry about.

EVACUEE: Nothing to worry about? . . . The Koreans want to slaughter us all! . . . Kill the Koreans!

NURSE: Miss Nishimura, quickly call the doctor here. Everybody—I'm here to look after you, so settle down until the doctor gets here.

EVACUEE: Let's wait till the doctor gets here.

EVACUEE: Yeah, good idea! Good idea!

EVACUEE: What should we do, nurse? Will the Koreans kill me? . . . My house got burned down. . . . Never would I have imagined we'd run into trouble here too, of all places. . . . Ah, what should we do?

OLD MAN: Is it true the Koreans are going to attack us?

YOUTH: *(Laughing.)* Why do they think that? That's a pretty bizarre notion of them attacking the home guard, surely. The Koreans don't have any weapons. How can a people who have been given no weapons dare carry out such a thing? Yesterday I met a staff officer from U Division, and he told me none of the Koreans had any weapons or bombs or anything.

OLD MAN: Really? . . . But why, then, would such a rumor be spread?

YOUTH: Because the Japanese have no faith!

EVACUEE: Who is that guy?

EVACUEE: He's a Korean!

EVACUEE: A Korean! . . . A Korean!

EVACUEE: Get him! Get the bastard!

OLD MAN: *(Rising halfway up.)* Really, everyone! You're not making any sense. . . . This nonsense about Koreans is all a terrible mistake. . . . You have to tell them.

YOUTH: No, there's no point trying. . . . They'll all know soon enough.

EVACUEE: Know what? . . . What will we know?

NURSE: Now, settle down, everyone. The doctor's coming.

DOCTOR: *(Wearing the uniform of a military doctor.)* What's going on here?

NURSE: They're all upset over the rumors about the Koreans.

DOCTOR: Hm, what could the Koreans do? Gentlemen! Do you doubt the power of the heroic Imperial Army? Fear not, gentlemen! The home guard division in this city is awaiting its marching orders as we speak.

EVACUEE: A division! . . . A whole division!

EVACUEE: Awaiting marching orders as we speak!

DOCTOR: I understand all too well your selfless love for the state. . . . You yourselves have sent so many devoted soldiers to serve in our forces. . . .

But fear not, gentlemen! ... The Imperial Army would not let them lay a finger on you. ... So long as you're here and in my charge, gentlemen, you must follow my orders.

EVACUEE: That's right! The army's here! We've got the army!

DOCTOR: Good thinking, lads. *(To the* NURSE.*)* How are the patients?

NURSE: Well, that one says ever since we bandaged him up, he's been hurting terribly.

DOCTOR: Hm, so long as it hurts, he's fine. If the treatment doesn't hurt, then it's not working. ... And the others?

NURSE: Well, that child over there is not in very good shape at all.

DOCTOR: Hm, that won't do. ... We'll move her to Headquarters in the morning. ... She was a fool to board the train with a child in that condition.

NURSE: Is there anything we can do for her right now?

DOCTOR: It's too late. ... *(The cries of an* EVACUEE *can be heard.)* There's still time before morning. Don't worry, lads. Get some rest. ... You mustn't make a fuss.

NURSE: Relax, everyone, and get some rest. ... You mustn't cry there. ... Your child will be fine. ... We're taking her to the hospital first thing in the morning. ... So sleep till morning comes. ... The rest of you too; get some sleep.

(The EVACUEES *all return to their places and lie down. The sound of the wind whipping the tent can be heard, and far off the barking of a dog. Then, the sound of a marching line of soldiers.)*

DOCTOR: I'll be at Headquarters. Let me know if there's anything that needs doing. You mustn't give the patients anything to worry about. ... And don't let them have their way. ... Do you understand?

NURSE: Yes, sir. I understand.

(The DOCTOR *leaves the tent, his saber making a rattling noise. The* NURSE *silently makes her way among the lines of sleeping patients. At the back of the tent, an* ATTENDANT *begins to nod off. Two, three barks of a dog.*

—A longish pause. A group of VIGILANTES *enter the tent. They are dressed in a variety of costumes, some in the uniform of reservists, others in old-fashioned tabards, some wearing bandannas, and still others in school uniforms. The one in command is wearing armor and brandishing a sword. They all carry some kind of weapon: a spear or sword or saber.)*

ARMOR: *(Gazing around inside the tent.)* Here?

TABARD: Yeah, here. ... This was the place. ... Come on in, everyone.

ARMOR: Bring the lantern, bring the lantern.

BANDANNA: *(Enters the tent holding the lantern.)* Where is he?

STUDENT: Be careful. He might be carrying a bomb.

RESERVIST: You think a bomb or two is going to make me shit my pants?

ARMOR: Hush! . . . Nurse, good evening!

NURSE: What do you want? . . . You can't come in here. . . . What on earth is going on here?

ARMOR: Actually, Nurse, we're looking for somebody. If you'd be so kind, let us in the tent.

NURSE: I can't allow it. The patients are asleep.

BANDANNA: Surely you don't have to say no to everything we ask. . . . Come on, let's go in and have a look.

NURSE: *(Her lips trembling.)* You mustn't! . . . I forbid it!

ARMOR: The fact is, Nurse, there's a Korean bastard hiding out here. . . . Somebody saw him get off the train. . . . For the sake of the fatherland, we have to kill the Koreans.

TABARD: That's right! For the fatherland! . . . For the peace of our citizens!

RESERVIST: That's right! For the peace of our citizens!

BANDANNA: Quit your muttering and get in there; look for him! . . . Get the bastard!

(The VIGILANTES *barge in among the patients, shining the lantern in their faces. Ashen-faced, the* NURSE *follows after them, looking pale. One of the* VIGILANTES *stands over a man who is squatting like a puppy behind the* OLD MAN *and the* YOUTH.*)*

BANDANNA: Here he is! . . . We've got him! . . . Bring the lantern over! . . . Look at his face!

MAN: *(Apparently a laborer in his mid-twenties.)* I haven't done anything!

STUDENT: *(Imitating him.)* I haven't done anything!

TABARD: Get him!

ARMOR: Don't rough him up. . . . I'll interrogate him. . . . Hey, dog! You're a Korean, aren't you? Lying to us won't get you anywhere, you know.

MAN: I'm Japanese. . . . What are you doing?

STUDENT: "I'm Japanese!" . . . Would any Japanese ever say that?

ARMOR: Quiet! . . . What's your name?

MAN: Kitamura Yoshio.

(The VIGILANTES *laugh.)*

ARMOR: Hm! Kitamura Yoshio, eh? . . . How old are you?

MAN: Twenty-four.

ARMOR: So, in what year were you born?[10]

MAN: *(Nonplussed.)* I ... er ... I. ...

(The VIGILANTES *all laugh.)*

YOUTH: *(Suddenly standing.)* Stop this! On what authority are you asking these questions? Who gave you the authority to do this?

OLD MAN: *(Flustered.)* Stop this! ... Please, stop!

ARMOR: *(Looking at the* YOUTH.*)* Who the hell are you?

YOUTH: *(Quietly.)* I'm a human being.

ARMOR: Of course, you're human. ... I'm not asking whether you're man or beast. I'm asking you what kind of man you are.

(The VIGILANTES *thrust out their lanterns at the* YOUTH's *face and mutter among themselves.)*

YOUTH: I'm a student. ... And who are you, to come barging into a tent of evacuees and rough people up at this hour of the night?

ARMOR: Rough people up? Have we roughed anyone up?

YOUTH: If that isn't roughing people up, then what is? Barging into a tent where evacuees are being treated, disturbing their sleep, asking for identification. What right have you to ask where people are from?

TABARD: What right?

ARMOR: Yeah, we've got a right.

YOUTH: Who gave you the right to do this? ... As far as I'm aware, no one but the army and the police have such a right.

OLD MAN: For heaven's sake, be quiet, man! Talk it over later—I'm sure they'll understand.

RESERVIST: You've got a lot of nerve asking us. Our authority comes from the most reliable of sources. Why, even the prefectural police have given us their stamp of approval.

ARMOR: Besides, we're not going to let a few little laws get in our way. ... What I'm saying is, we operate under the higher dictates of our loyalty to the state.

YOUTH: *(Laughing.)* Ha! The state? The state exists somewhere outside the rule of law? ... Now, isn't that interesting! So what is this state you're talking about?

BANDANNA: Who is this upstart? ... You've got no business spouting off here, so shut your trap! ... We're not going to put up with any nonsense out of you! *(Thrusts his spear at him.)*

YOUTH: No business, you say? Oh, yes, I do,
     You're the ones who have no business here,
     We've got the army, we've got police.

Look at you all!
In your armor, tabards, *judō-gi*. . . .
Don't you have anything better to wear?
(The YOUTH *looks at the "*KOREAN.*")*
Come, stand up tall.
Stand up, my man,
Maybe you're right,
Maybe this man is Korean,
But the Koreans aren't your enemy.
Japanese, Japanese, Japanese,
What have the Japanese done to you?
Who have made the Japanese suffer?
Not the Koreans, but the Japanese themselves!
It's a simple fact—can't you fellows understand?
(The YOUTH *takes the* KOREAN's *hand and lays his arm on his shoulder as if to protect him.)*
Look at this man!
He's a human being.
Look at his face!
Could he have killed innocent people?
Or poisoned your wells?
This man has enemies too,
But he doesn't hate you.
You all understand nothing.
You know nothing,
Nor do you even try.
Your comrades took his friends,
Men without sin, who bore no arms,
Men as obedient and innocent as leaves,
Your comrades cut them down without reason, killed them!
Look at this man!
What this man now has,
The only thing nature ever gave him,
Is his life.
Here is your true human being!
And who the hell are you?
All you fellows have
Are dead, moldering morals.

Your armor, that tabard,
Might have had some value as antiques.
But what good are they for a living human being?
If there's any blood coursing in those hearts of yours,
Then you should be wearing your own clothing!
Take off that armor!
Take off that jacket!
You're all marionettes with no life of your own!
Bloated corpses!
Mummies!
Skeletons!

BANDANNA: Japanese traitor!

TABARD: Fanatic!

STUDENT: Enemy of the state!

ARMOR: Get them both!

OLD MAN: Stop it, please! I'll take responsibility for this. . . . Please, you really must apologize to them all. . . . This is outrageous.

(*The* EVACUEES *run around inside the tent. The* WOMEN EVACUEES *weep.*)

NURSE: (*To the* EVACUEES.) Everyone, please leave the tent this minute! You mustn't hurt anyone!

YOUTH: (*To the* KOREAN.)
Come, my friend, take my hand,
If you're to be killed, then I'll die too!
Oh, Death!
How many hundreds, how many thousands,
In hundreds and thousands of years,
Have been slaughtered for their beloved countrymen?
We weren't born to fawn and
Toady to our stupid compatriots;
We were born to struggle and to die!
For the sake of righteousness, for friendship,
We will die!

(*The* VIGILANTES *begin to move about violently. Brandishing their weapons, they press in on the two from both sides. Holding aloft his sword,* ARMOR *faces the* YOUTH; TABARD *faces the* KOREAN, *with the* OTHERS *closing in on either side.*)

YOUTH: (*Speaking quietly but with force; this must not be confused with the notion of heroism.*)

Behold a new mystery!
From strength and friendship
A new mystery gives birth
To the founding of a new race of men!
Rise up and wash away
The dead and ugly mold you hide!
Tear off your mask,
Your false, contemptible ancestor worship,
Your heroism,
Your racism,
And dance the dance of hideous skeletons!
Wait, orchestra!
You hideous skeletons,
Turn to stone!
Turn to stone,
You hideous skeletons!
Hideous skeletons,
Turn to stone!

(With his sword still held aloft, ARMOR *turns to stone.* TABARD *similarly freezes, sword held high.* BANDANNA *freezes with his spear thrust out.* STUDENT *freezes, holding his bamboo spear.* OTHER VIGILANTES *all turn to stone. The* DOCTOR, *just about to enter the tent, similarly turns to stone.)*

YOUTH: Dance, skeletons!

(A sudden blackout puts the tent into darkness. A phosphorescent light illuminates the inside of the tent, revealing ten SKELETONS *standing in the same attitude as the* VIGILANTES *previously. [Note: The* SKELETONS *may be played by the same actors, who can do a quick change of costumes.])*

YOUTH: Orchestra! Strike up a waltz for these skeletons!

(The ten SKELETONS *begin to dance. Together with the* OLD MAN *and the* KOREAN, *the* YOUTH *stands by, watching.)*

YOUTH: A "death fantasia" to comfort the blameless ones, those who died before us. . . .

(The ten SKELETONS *dance a fantasia. Two or three* SKELETONS *begin to weaken. . . . Suddenly, on either side of the* YOUTH *is heard sharp laughter.)*

YOUTH: Oh, dead ones,
How right it is for you to laugh!
Orchestra!
A round dance to bid farewell

To you hideous skeletons.

Dance and dance till you fade away!

(The SKELETONS *begin dancing in a circle faster and faster until the circle is broken and their limbs snap off and fall in pieces to the ground. Sharp laughter. Blackout. The lights slowly come up, vaguely illuminating the tent's interior. The sound of weeping* WOMEN EVACUEES.*)*

NURSE: *(Quietly lifting her head.)* Poor thing. . . . But it was meant to be.

—Curtain—

—La 14an de Januaro, 1924—

KUBOTA MANTARŌ

BRIEF NIGHT

INTRODUCTION

Over the course of his long career as a playwright, Kubota Mantarō produced over sixty plays (not including children's and radio drama) in the turbulent years between the tail end of the Meiji era and Japan's postwar reconstruction. An accomplished poet and novelist, he was also a brilliant director and dramaturge whose *shinpa* adaptations of fiction by Higuchi Ichiyō, Izumi Kyōka, and Tanizaki Jun'ichirō are still periodically staged. Together with Tomoda Kyōsuke and Tomoda's wife, Tamura Akiko, Kubota established the Tsukiji-za theatre company, and in 1937 (after Tomoda's untimely death on military service in China), he and Kishida Kunio (along with others noted in chapter 3) founded the Literary Theatre, still the leading *shingeki* theatre troupe. He directed two of the most important *shingeki* plays of the prewar era, Mafune Yutaka's *Weasels* (*Itachi*, 1934) and Morimoto Kaoru's *A Woman's Life* (*Onna no issho*, 1945).

Called "the poet of Asakusa" for his delicate portrayals of the common people of his native Tokyo neighborhood, Kubota's dramas are essentially elegies to a way of life that even in the Taishō era was on its way out. His

---

Photo of Kubota Mantarō courtesy of the Tsubouchi Memorial Theatre Museum, Waseda University.

heroes and heroines—typically artisans, schoolteachers, minor bureaucrats, wives, mothers, and geishas—are the working-class "children of Edo" (Edok-ko) and not the more progressive, upper-class and cosmopolitan people of Tokyo's "high city" (*yamanote*) districts. Indeed, Kubota's affectionate evocations of life as it was before the earthquake—*Brief Night* is notably set around 1919—challenge (as Nagahira Kazuo put it) the "emptiness of Taishō modernity."[1] But it is not in his subject matter so much as in his style that Kubota's work marks a significant development in modern Japanese drama.

Kishida Kunio singled out three Taishō playwrights for making the greatest contribution to modern Japanese drama: Kikuchi Kan for his stress on theme, Yamamoto Yūzō for his skill in plot structure, and Kubota Mantarō for his literary style.[2] Yet of the Japanese authors whose plays he read during his Paris sojourn, it was Kubota whom Kishida admired the most. Kubota's exquisite style is expressed not in gorgeous imagery or the eloquence of his characters, however. A master haiku poet, he believed that "style is thrift" and restraint was strength. Indeed, his characters' reticence and their avoidance of conflict seemed anathema to many of the pretexts of modern drama. His characters typically avoid saying what is on their minds, and as a consequence the plays seem distinctly anticlimactic.[3]

For a writer like Kikuchi Kan (perhaps the best proponent of the kind of thematically driven realism learned from Ibsen and Shaw), reading a play by Kubota was a frustrating experience: "For someone like me, who expects that it is in the nature of drama for something to *happen,* when I read Kubota Mantarō's *Fukō* [Misfortune] I thought that the *exposition* just went on and on. Even though I was close to the end, with only a couple of pages left, still nothing had happened, which made me anxious. . . . There wasn't the slightest trace of any kind of 'play' I was expecting. It's beautiful *exposition*, but it isn't a play."[4] Kikuchi's remarks clearly spoke of a very different idea of drama from Kubota's. Indeed, avoidance of (or the inability to engage in) direct conflict—typically expressed in modern drama on the verbal plane—is much the point of Kubota's dramaturgy. What conflict or tension exists in his plays lies not in what is said, but typically in the pauses and ellipses, the silence between and under the seemingly inconsequential words that are spoken. For this reason, playwright Tanaka Chikao has called Kubota a "poet of small talk" (*aisatsu no shijin*).[5] Kubota makes the desultory speech of everyday life support more meaning than the language itself could possibly seem to bear, a technique that is strikingly similar to the style of film director Ozu Yasujirō, many of whose actors—people like Higashiyama Chieko and Sugimura Haruko, alumni of the

Bungaku-za—had been directed by Kubota. Kubota's dialogue and dramaturgy also anticipate that of the contemporary realist playwright Hirata Oriza.

In fact, Kubota was one of the first playwrights to capture the way Japanese actually speak, and his works singularly lack the cut and thrust of ideological debate, for which the modern dramatic form seemed best suited. Kubota acknowledged that it was Kinoshita Mokutarō's groundbreaking play, *Izumiya Dye Shop* (*Izumiya somemonoten*, 1911), that inspired him to become a playwright.[6] It was the general mood and setting evoked in Kinoshita's play, however, and not its theme that caught Kubota's imagination. The play portrays a family of Tokyo artisans who, on a cold New Year's Eve, await the return of their son, who, it is hinted, has been implicated in the so-called High Treason Incident, which brought about the execution of Kōtoku Shūsui and several other socialists. Kinoshita's play in turn seems to have been inspired by *The Intruder*, by Maeterlinck, who had a strong influence on Kinoshita and his mentor, Mori Ōgai. Kubota seems not to have been interested in the work's implicitly political message, but the device of creating a drama not directly about a particular protagonist, but rather around the people whose lives he affects, was one he would employ in *Brief Night* and many other works. The dramatic moment is one that typically occurs offstage or before the curtain rises, and what the play is "about" comes to light only gradually, through the random conversations of the dramatis personae. Kubota learned from Mokutarō a dramaturgy of poetic realism that paid homage to delicate turns of phrase and common expressions of the people he knew and loved best—his fellow Tokyoites—and their emotional attachments and sense of values. He portrayed perfectly ordinary people engaged in perfectly ordinary conversation about commonplace events, and yet his people, setting, and language were specific to a particular place and time.

Such a radically attenuated notion of dialogue strained the idea of what conventionally constituted the "dramatic," though the precedent clearly lay in Maeterlinck's symbolism, a style that gave birth to what the Japanese would call *seigeki* or *jōchōgeki*, "still dramas" or "sentimental dramas." The emphasis was less on action, event, or a particular theme than on a general mood evoked in the play. Such a style of drama was perhaps more reflective of the Japanese ethos than the ideologically driven works of the "social dramatists," people like Kikuchi Kan, and later such socialist playwrights as Murayama Tomoyoshi or Kubo Sakae, but by the same token it was deeply conservative. Kawasaki Akira notes that the inarticulate nature of Kubota's characters is linked to their inability to act, their sense of powerlessness.[7] In Kubota's case, style was evidently the man. Opinions vary—some describe him as stubborn, others as timid—but Kon Hidemi seems to catch best his paradoxical character: "There is no sense of resolution in Kubota-san. Perhaps no one can ultimately experience resolution, but he never even tried to take a resolute stance. But such an attitude, of someone like Kubota—a man who was timid, weak, irresolute, who seemed to stand there blankly, bending but not breaking to whichever way the wind blew—may be the most proper one after all."[8] Kubota's own nature is reflected in his characters: an eloquent expression of the passive resistance of the disenfranchised.

But such an attitude also obscures the difference between resistance and acquiescence. Critic Dōmoto Masaki writes that the reticence of Kubota's dialogue is reflective of the communal nature of traditional Japanese society, where a kind of "magical pact" existed among people that transcended logic and precluded the necessity of too much explanation or debate.[9] As the Japanese proverb puts it, eloquence is silver but silence is gold. In Kubota's plays, Dōmoto continues, "Before a word's associations have been exhausted, the following word consumes them and then spits them out. Before an image can be born, certain emotions are animated, giving rise to dialogue that is quite independent from the movement engendered by such emotions. For that reason 'events' as such never occur."[10] In fact, by stressing less what is said or done than the underlying motives and reactions of his characters, Kubota demonstrated that he was indeed a singularly modern playwright. In short, Kubota used language—and, even more important, its limitations—to shed light on the inner life of his characters; it was not their actions, speech, or behavior so much as their consciousness, their soul, that he wished to portray. It is therefore appropriate that Kubota's masterpiece, *The Ōdera School* (*Ōdera gakkō*), which Aoyama Sugisaku directed at the Tsukiji Little Theatre in 1928 to great acclaim, has been compared to Chekhov's *Cherry Orchard*, and it is probably no accident that his characters also demonstrate the same curious immobility of Chekhov's heroes and heroines. The disjuncture between thought and action—the "shadow" in T. S. Eliot's *The Hollow Men*—is one of the cardinal features of the modern consciousness. Dōmoto notes that before there can be conflict between people, there must exist a confrontation between an individual speaker and his or her language.[11] Such a confrontation, of course, is one between language and silence itself. As George Steiner has pointed out, such a concern informs the work of many twentieth-century writers.[12] Kubota's attention to what might be called language's aporias designates him as a modernist, though he was a traditionalist in his concerns.

It is hard to say, then, what a Kubota play is "about"—or, rather, saying what it is about seems beside the point. *Brief Night* is typical. In a nutshell, it is the portrait of a pampered son (Isaburō) of a now deceased shopkeeper (what sort of business is unspecified); the young man's poor judgment and taste for the bottle bring about the ruin of his house. The drama focuses on the negotiated breakup of Isaburō's marriage to Ofusa. It is late at night and the couple—together with his uncle Senzō; Senzō's wife, Oyoshi; Ofusa's mother, Osawa; and a loyal clerk, Jūkichi—have been up drinking. Like the dregs of their food and *sake*, their conversation consists of the leftovers of an awkward end to a difficult relationship. Senzō does most of the talking, and he is harsh and judgmental of his feckless nephew. Though not without its bitter words and even slapstick, the play resolves itself—or rather dissolves—in tears, and even the gruff patriarch Senzō can scarcely control the urge to weep. Isaburō and Ofusa, who are the supposed protagonists here, have next to nothing to say throughout the play, but it is not clear that either of them would willingly acquiesce to a divorce any more than Senzō himself would ultimately, unbendingly resist any attempt at reconciliation. Their silence speaks volumes, but ambiguously. The reticence of Kubota's characters does not point toward any form of social critique, but rather in the manner of late Ozu films, it presents a worldview: a sweetly sentimental and even Buddhist appreciation for the effect of time on all living things. A sense of *mono no aware* (the pathos of life) is conjured by his deep and singular focus on the small matters of existence. Several critics have pointed out that the titles of Kubota's plays—*Eventide* (*Kuregata*, 1912), *Rainy Skies* (*Amazora*, 1920), *Winter* (*Fuyu*, 1923), *Fireflies* (*Hotaru*, 1935), to name a few—read like haiku *kigo* (seasonal words). Nature is the final context and resting place for any human discord. As Tanaka Chikao puts it, "What is pure [about Kubota's drama] is the way in which the rank odor of human emotions [*giri ninjō*] is filtered through natural phenomena like water, grass, earth, and clouds."[13] Too solid flesh resolved into a dew.

The Japanese text on which this translation is based is in Kubota, "*Mijikayo*," in *Kubota Mantarō zenshū* (Chūō kōronsha, 1967), 5:375–392.

KUBOTA MANTARŌ

BRIEF NIGHT

FIRST PUBLISHED:
Central Review, January 1925

FIRST PERFORMANCE:
Shingeki Kyōkai, April 1927,
dir. Kubota Mantarō

CHARACTERS

SENZŌ

ISABURŌ

JŪKICHI

OFUSA, ISABURŌ's *wife*

OSAWA, OFUSA's *mother*

OYOSHI, SENZŌ's *wife*

TIME: *Ca. 1919*

PLACE: SENZŌ's *house in Asakusa, Tokyo, a neighborhood
by the banks of the Komagata River*

*(*SENZŌ, ISABURŌ, JŪKICHI, *and* OSAWA *are sitting around a low dinner table. On
the table are a lonely row of empty flasks of* sake *and two or three dishes of Western
food [perfectly ordinary things like pork cutlets and salad], which they have been
picking at. It has been already some two hours since they started drinking. It is a
night in early July, late.*

*They have been sunk in silence since even before the curtain rises and continue
so, gloomily, for some time.* SENZŌ, ISABURŌ, JŪKICHI, *and* OSAWA—*all four say
not a word, each watching over their own private thoughts.)*

SENZŌ: *(Suddenly turning toward the room next door.)* Hey, isn't it ready yet?
OYOSHI: *(From next door.)* Yes, in a minute.
(Again, silence.

Outside, there is the call of a noodle vendor's charamela.[14] *The sound
gradually recedes into the distance.*

Pause.

OYOSHI *leaves her place in front of the long brazier and brings some freshly heated* sake *for* SENZŌ. SENZŌ *takes the flask.* OYOSHI *returns to the next room. She fusses with the brazier, stoking the fire and adding water to the bronze kettle.)*

SENZŌ: *(To* JŪKICHI.*)* Have some hot—

JŪKICHI: I've had enough. . . . Thanks—

SENZŌ: Come on—

JŪKICHI: All right, then. Thanks. *(Holds up the* sake *cup on the table in front of him.)*

SENZŌ: Finish what you got there—

JŪKICHI: This is plenty—*(Gulps down the remaining* sake *that has gone cold in his cup. He then holds up the cup again to* SENZŌ. SENZŌ *pours.)* Thanks. . . . That's plenty. *(Takes a sip, then lays down the cup.)*

SENZŌ: *(To* ISABURŌ, *quite coldly.)* Isa-san. . . . *(*ISABURŌ *raises his head when called.)* Have some hot. *(*ISABURŌ *looks down, saying nothing.* SENZŌ *pauses, then turns to* OSAWA.*)* How about you, Mother?

OSAWA: I'm fine. . . . Thanks. . . . Shall I pour for you? . . . *(Holds out her hand.)*

SENZŌ: No thanks. . . . *(Pours some into the cup in front of him. . . . Lays down the flask.)*

JŪKICHI: *(Takes out his pocket watch. Then, suddenly.)* Well, sorry to keep you up so late. *(Swigs down the rest of his sake.)*

SENZŌ: Here, have another.

JŪKICHI: I've had enough. . . . Thanks. *(Lays his cup down on the table.)* . . . Really, we've been keeping you up something awful. . . . *(Starts packing away his handkerchief and cigarettes, etc.)*

SENZŌ: Not at all. . . . You needn't be so concerned.

JŪKICHI: Well, now. . . . We've been terribly selfish.

SENZŌ: Have some tea. . . . Hey. . . . *(Insisting, makes to call* OYOSHI.*)*

JŪKICHI: *(Hesitating.)* Ah, no. I've had enough, thanks.

SENZŌ: But—

JŪKICHI: Really. Why, look at the time. . . .

SENZŌ: Are you sure?

JŪKICHI: In any case, I'll drop by again to see you in a couple of days.

SENZŌ: *(As if to interrupt.)* Not at all. . . . Next time, I'll come by to see you. . . . I'm always the one calling you over. . . .

JŪKICHI: Really, you needn't worry—

SENZŌ: Sorry to call you at such a busy time.

JŪKICHI: I'm afraid I've been no use whatsoever. . . . *(To* ISABURŌ.*)* Come along, then, Master Isaburō. We really must be going. . . . *(Begins to leave.* ISABURŌ *is silent.)* Isaburō-san. . . . *(*ISABURŌ *remains silent and doesn't even budge.)*

*(*SENZŌ *looks harshly at* ISABURŌ. . . . OSAWA *raises her head and steals a glance at him. Pause.)*

JŪKICHI: *(Ignoring them, repeats himself.)* Let's go. . . . We can't stay here forever, making a nuisance of ourselves. . . . *(*ISABURŌ *remains silent.)* . . . Come on. *(*JŪKICHI *Encourages him, but* ISABURŌ *remains silent. Pause.)*

SENZŌ: *(Forcing back his rising emotions.)* Have you understood nothing, Isaburō? . . . *(*ISABURŌ *remains silent.)* You still don't get it. Is that it? *(Reproachfully.* ISABURŌ *remains silent.)*

JŪKICHI: *(Intervening.)* Now, now, Master Isaburō. . . . *(Lowering his voice.)* . . . Right? You know it's for your own good. . . . *(*ISABURŌ *remains silent.)*

SENZŌ: *(Suddenly flying into a rage.)* You want me to yell at you again? . . . *(*OYOSHI *and* OSAWA *both look at* SENZŌ.*)*

JŪKICHI: *(To* ISABURŌ.*)* You mustn't. . . . No, you mustn't. . . . You can't be any more of a nuisance to these good people than you have already been. . . . You're too selfish. . . . Much too selfish. . . . You're only thinking of yourself. . . . I mean it. . . . *(*ISABURŌ *remains silent, hanging his head low. To* SENZŌ.*)* Well, then. . . . I'll apologize for him. . . . Please don't take offense.

SENZŌ: But you embarrass me saying such a thing. . . . I was the one who dumped this fellow on you, so I shouldn't meddle in this any more than I have to. . . . I shouldn't be giving *you* advice, but this fellow is more trouble than he's worth. . . . He's getting to be a real pest.

JŪKICHI: Yes, well, but. . . . It's not as if he doesn't understand because he does, I think. . . . He understands. . . . He has to. . . . But that's why—

SENZŌ: *(Cutting in.)* If you don't understand when we tell you what's right and wrong—

JŪKICHI: *(Intervening.)* Let's go home. I'll. . . . What I mean to say is, I'll hear what he has to say. . . . No doubt this wasn't the place for Master Isaburō to tell us everything what's on his mind. . . . Even if he'd wanted to, he probably couldn't. *(*SENZŌ *says nothing.* JŪKICHI *and* ISABURŌ *exchange words, whispering. There is a fairly long pause then again.)* Really, I've kept you up too late. . . . We've been a terrible nuisance. . . . *(To* OYOSHI.*)* Sorry to keep pestering you like this, ma'am.

OYOSHI: *(Leaving the brazier.)* You really mustn't worry. We've been the ones to bother you. . . . Please give your folks our regards.

JŪKICHI: Thank you.

OYOSHI: It's much too hot during the day, but in the evening when it cools down, if you're out paying respects to Kannon, please have your wife bring the little ones for a visit.[15] . . .

JŪKICHI: Thank you. . . . I'll tell them when I get home. . . . They've been meaning for ages to get out, but what with all the fuss. . . .

OYOSHI: There are so many of you, so I'm sure it isn't something you do every day. . . .

JŪKICHI: If ever you find yourself in the neighborhood, please do think of dropping by at our place. . . .

OYOSHI: I'll be sure to do that.

JŪKICHI: *(To* OSAWA.*)* Thanks for everything, ma'am.

OSAWA: Not at all. . . . *(She slips off her cushion to bow properly to him.)*

*(*JŪKICHI *makes* ISABURŌ *get up.* ISABURŌ *stands, looking blank and resigned to his fate. . . . They leave the room by way of the lattice door.* SENZŌ, OYOSHI, *and* OSAWA *see them out. Pause. The sound of the lattice door. . . . The calls back and forth of "good night" conjure up the sadness of the late hour. Pause. Outside, a dog barks for a while. . . .* OYOSHI *and* OSAWA, *led by* SENZŌ, *return to their original places. No one speaks. A listless mood, like a beach where the tide has gone out, lingers over the stage. Pause.)*

SENZŌ: *(To* OYOSHI.*)* What's the time now? . . .

OYOSHI: *(Scraping the leftovers off the plates.)* Last time the clock struck it was one.

SENZŌ: One o'clock?

OYOSHI: Yes.

SENZŌ: So late already?

OYOSHI: Yes.

SENZŌ: You put everybody to bed?

OYOSHI: Yes. . . . Only the kitchen staff is still up. . . .

SENZŌ: Tell them they'd better get to bed. . . .

OYOSHI: All right.

SENZŌ: *(Pulling together the collar on his kimono.)* It does get chilly when it's late like this.

OYOSHI: Yes, dear. . . . *(A* MAID *comes out to take away the dirty dishes.)* Before you take those away, go lock up the front. *(The* MAID *heads for the lattice door.)*

SENZŌ: *(Taking what's left of the* sake *in the flask.)* Heat this up, will you?

OYOSHI: *(Takes the flask and stands. . . . To* OSAWA.*)* Leave those be, Mother. . . . Okane can do that.

OSAWA: Right, then. . . . *(Eager to help out, she tidies up the table.)*

(OYOSHI goes over to the long brazier. Pause. The MAID returns, having locked up. . . . She takes the deep-sided tray out of OSAWA's hands and heads for the kitchen.)

OYOSHI: Just leave them in the sink. . . . You can do them tomorrow.

MAID: Yes, ma'am.

OYOSHI: Then go to bed.

MAID: Thank you, ma'am.

OYOSHI: *(To SENZŌ.)* What shall we do with Ofusa?

SENZŌ: Hm.

OYOSHI: *(To the MAID.)* When you retire, go tell her to come down. . . . *(The MAID leaves. OYOSHI brings the reheated sake.)* It might not be as hot as you'd like. . . .

(SENZŌ takes the sake. . . . He says nothing. . . . He pours a cup and immediately drinks it down.)

OSAWA: *(Kneels and bows.)* I can't begin to thank you for everything—

SENZŌ: *(Stopping her.)* Really, you needn't. . . . Look, Ofusa's coming. . . . *(OSAWA says nothing.)*

(OFUSA enters. . . . She sits down beside OSAWA.)

SENZŌ: *(To OFUSA.)* Well, girl, it all went as planned. . . . Isaburō's gone to live with Jūkichi. *(OFUSA says nothing.)* You and your mother both ought to feel relieved. . . . Everything's settled.

OSAWA: I'm really grateful. You've bent over backwards to help, really. . . .

SENZŌ: As for the letter of divorce. . . .

OSAWA: Yes.

SENZŌ: Jūkichi will make sure the man writes it. . . . He'll get it signed and bring it over. . . . So. . . .

OSAWA: I'm terribly grateful.

OYOSHI: *(From the other room. Concerned.)* But I wonder if he'll behave and do as Jūkichi tells him?

SENZŌ: *(Dismissively.)* No good will come of it if he refuses to. . . . If he digs in his heels now, after all that's happened, he's not going to get any sympathy out of us.

OYOSHI: But—

SENZŌ: He's always got away with things by acting up and drinking himself stupid. . . . But if he thinks all his griping is going to let him off the hook this time, he's got another thing coming. . . . This time, he's got me to contend with. Me! *(OYOSHI says nothing.)* I'm not going to put up with his nonsense anymore.

OYOSHI: *(Adding her own two cents' worth.)* Besides, now Jūkichi's wrapped up in this as well. . . .

OSAWA: Yes, we've caused him a lot of trouble too. . . .

OYOSHI: *(To* SENZŌ.*)* He's a good man, Jūkichi. *(*SENZŌ *says nothing.)* He's not forgotten his old debt. Still looks after the lad. . . . Still not fed up with him, despite all he's been dealt. . . . I don't think I could have done what he did.

OSAWA: That's for sure.

OYOSHI: The old master looked out for him, but the young one won't lift a finger. . . . Of course, if he came out and said that . . . it'd make him turn on the lad. And if he did, that would be the end of them. . . . But you can't say then he hasn't got a heart. . . .

OSAWA: I think so, too. . . .

OYOSHI: Anyone who's ever had to suffer will feel more kindly to others.

OSAWA: Someone who'd do as much as he did certainly has that much going for him.

OYOSHI: They say it's all up to fate, but I doubt that's all there is to it. . . . If a man doesn't have what it takes to hold up his end. . . .

OSAWA: That's for sure.

SENZŌ: *(Suddenly.)* I want to ask you something, just to set matters straight. *(*OFUSA *says nothing.* OYOSHI *and* OSAWA *stop talking and look at* SENZŌ.*)* . . . Let's say—for the sake of argument—that in two, three years from now, Isaburō sorts himself out, swears off the drink and stays out of trouble, sees to it that his kith and kin don't go hungry even if he has to sell nickel ice cream cones in the street. . . . What would you do then, Ofusa? *(*OFUSA *is silent.)* . . . What I mean is, would you take him back, or not? *(*OFUSA *is silent.)* I asked your mom what she thought the other day. . . . She said she wouldn't take him, no matter what happened. . . . She was very clear about that. *(*OFUSA *is silent.)* But she's not married to him; you are. . . . Anyway, I figured I'd better ask your opinion. . . . If I didn't, there's no telling what kind of mess there'd be. . . . If that came to pass, I for one wouldn't want people saying I wasted my life acting like a know-it-all. *(*OFUSA *is silent.)*

OSAWA: *(Pausing.)* Punching and kicking the girl *(pointing to* OFUSA*)*, saying he doesn't like her tone of voice, or taking off for a couple of days because he doesn't like the way she treats him? . . . Then, just when you thought he's back, he comes home roaring drunk. . . . Say anything and he snaps, "Shut up! Get out! . . . I don't need you people." . . . You couldn't get in two words edgewise before he'd scream at you, and at all hours of the night. . . . Are you ready for that again? . . .

SENZŌ: *(Cutting in.)* We've heard all that before, Mother. We're sick of hearing it. *(OSAWA says nothing.)* . . . That's why I'm asking . . . Say the man does sort himself out, quits drinking and getting into trouble, sees to it that his kith and kin don't go hungry even if he has to sell nickel ice cream cones in the street. . . . What then? . . . I'm asking you straight, what would you do then?

OSAWA: Actually—

SENZŌ: That's enough, Mother. You complain too much. *(OSAWA is silent. SENZŌ turns again to OFUSA.)* . . . Well, Ofusa? *(OFUSA is silent.)* . . . You sure you don't have any lingering feelings for the fellow? *(OFUSA is silent.)*

OYOSHI: *(Feeling sorry for her.)* Now, dear. . . . She couldn't.

SENZŌ: Why?

OYOSHI: Why? Because she couldn't. . . . *(To OFUSA.)* Could you, Ofusa? *(OFUSA is silent.)* That's all that needs to be said. . . . Till we get him to sign. . . .

SENZŌ: *(Even more derisively.)* Don't matter if it's a letter of divorce or a vow to the gods, it's all wastepaper if you tear it up. *(OYOSHI and OFUSA are silent. Pause. SENZŌ begins to raise his cup, then suddenly to OFUSA.)* How many years has it been, anyway? Since you two got together.

OFUSA: *(Barely audibly.)* Five.

SENZŌ: *(As if to himself.)* Where's the time gone? . . . *(Drinks.)*

OSAWA: After all you've done, too. . . . You were the one who introduced them. . . . *(SENZŌ is silent.)*

OYOSHI: Isa-san was so gentle, so timid then. . . . Back then, he wasn't hardly able to say half of what was on his mind. . . . How did he turn out like that, and in such a short time too?

OSAWA: It's a mystery to me too. . . . People said he changed, but I've never seen anybody change as much as he did. . . . He didn't use to drink so much, either. . . .

OYOSHI: Even if he did drink, he'd always make a point not to look drunk. . . . He was ashamed to show people how he looked when drunk. . . . So it seemed. . . . And now look at him! . . . *(To SENZŌ.)* Why do you think that is?

SENZŌ: It's obvious, ain't it? . . . He was turned out into the world before he knew anything about it. *(OYOSHI is silent.)* Fed with a silver spoon, he was the sort who'd think a cupboard was filled with snacks for him. . . . Didn't he know it had been cleaned out already?

OYOSHI: But—

SENZŌ: Know what I think? I don't think he's changed a bit. . . . The same old Isa he's always been. . . . Same old Isa, a coward, afraid to say even half of what's on his mind. *(OYOSHI is silent.)* He had a lot to be proud of back when. For one thing, he was Katsumi's kid. The young master of the Bizenya. . . . So things were good. . . . That's why he was able to get away with stuff. . . . But he's got nothing to be proud of now. . . . That's why he gets drunk and sulks. . . . If he didn't, he wouldn't have anywhere to turn. *(OYOSHI is silent. Then, with great feeling.)* When you consider that, you can't help but feel sorry for the poor sod.

OYOSHI: *(Led on.)* Well, maybe you're right. . . . Sweet-talked out of a roof over his head. His big brother told him what to do with his own inheritance and then up and died on him. . . . He's certainly had his share of misfortune. Plenty of cause to be in the dumps. That's what I think, anyway. *(SENZŌ is silent.)* . . . But . . . even so. . . . *(SENZŌ is silent.)* The way it is now, he's got to sort himself out. . . . Sort himself out, then think about rebuilding the legacy Katsumi left. . . . If Isa-san doesn't, who will? *(SENZŌ is silent. OYOSHI continues in this fashion, to OSAWA.)* He's got to look out for himself, right? For everybody's sake.

OSAWA: You know how people talk. Ever since what happened to the house, they've been blaming Isaburō for this and that. . . . Like, saying Isaburō turned out that way ever since he hooked up with Ofusa. . . . All sorts of stuff, without actually coming out and saying it. . . . I hate to talk about all this in front of you, madam, but folks have no idea just how awful I feel hearing such stories.

SENZŌ: No sense feeling sorry for yourself. . . . No matter what people say, surely you've got nothing to feel ashamed about.

OSAWA: I guess. . . .

SENZŌ: I'm sorry to hear about all the trouble he's caused, but damned if I know what to say. . . . It's nothing to be proud of, that's for sure. . . . You were dead set against him to begin with, Mother, saying this was a match that'd never work out. . . . But Ofusa just sat there and let me talk her into it. . . .

OSAWA: I never should have allowed it.

SENZŌ: *(Continuing.)* Be that as it may. . . . Whatever he was before, Isaburō's just a thorn in Ofusa's side now. . . . *He's* the one expecting *her* to put food on the table. . . . *(OSAWA is silent.)*

OYOSHI: *(To OSAWA.)* Ofusa's been a saint. If she hadn't buckled down and done what she did, Isaburō would never have—

OSAWA: Yes, but she's in no position to be teaching others. . . . Though I don't see what else she could have done. . . . *(OYOSHI nods.)* But luckily the master from Kuramae[16]—uh, you know who I mean, don't you?—

OYOSHI: Yes.

OSAWA: He's been most helpful, you know. . . . Setting her up with students, printing off new patterns for her. . . . This one *(gesturing toward* OFUSA*)* doesn't know, but he's been most kind.

OYOSHI: That's splendid, that is. . . .

OSAWA: That's what I say. . . . It's truly a load off my mind too. . . . Even if she's not very capable, we do hope she'll manage somehow to get by doing this.

OYOSHI: It'd be a damn shame if all Ofusa's been able to accomplish were left to go to waste. . . . I think what she's doing now is a good idea.

OSAWA: *(Thoroughly well meaning. . . . Seemingly even more at her wits' end than before.)* It wasn't like I'd trained her to be a businesswoman. . . . *(*OYOSHI *is silent. Pause.)*

SENZŌ: You can say all you like, but it ain't going to solve anything. . . . Let's go to bed.

OYOSHI: I suppose we should. . . . Let's clean up here. . . .

SENZŌ: You've got a place to sleep for Mother?

OYOSHI: Yes, I've had her bedding laid out upstairs, next to Ofusa's.

OSAWA: No, I . . . I don't have far to go. . . .

SENZŌ: Even if it's not far, it's not right for a woman to be out on the street at this hour. *(Suddenly, outside the sound of a dog barking fiercely. . . . Now far, now close by. . . . Pause. Violent rapping at the wooden rain shutters.)* Who is it?

JŪKICHI: *(Offstage, anxious and hurried, but of course not so clearly heard.)* It's me! . . . Please open up. . . . Please open the door. . . .

SENZŌ: It's Jūkichi.

OYOSHI: So it is!

*(*SENZŌ *gestures for* OYOSHI *to go open the door.* OYOSHI *stops putting away the table and stands.)*

SENZŌ: *(To* OFUSA*.)* Ofusa, you go hide. . . .

*(*OFUSA*, doing as she is told, hurries upstairs. Pause. A sound, first of the door being opened, and then a commotion, like that of someone bursting in.)*

OYOSHI: *(Offstage, her voice betraying her shock and consternation.)* Why, Jūkichi. . . . And Isa-san too! . . . *(Presently she returns.)* Dear, Jūkichi and Isa-san have both hurt themselves. . . .

SENZŌ: Hurt themselves?

OYOSHI: Mother, come here a sec. . . .

(Pause. OSAWA *hurriedly stands. . . . She and* OYOSHI *both exit. With* OYOSHI *leading,* JŪKICHI, ISABURŌ, *and* OSAWA *enter. . . . Both* JŪKICHI *and* ISABURŌ

look pale and their clothes are covered in mud. Something extraordinary appears to have happened. . . . OYOSHI *proceeds into the next room.)*

SENZŌ: *(To* JŪKICHI.*)* What happened?

JŪKICHI: Ye-e-e-s, well. *(A forced laugh.)*

SENZŌ: You hurt yourselves? How?

JŪKICHI: Ah, it's nothing. . . . Really. . . .

OYOSHI: Jū-san in the foot. . . . Isa-san in both the foot and the hand. . . . *(So saying, she runs to get medicine and bandages.)*

(Pause. OYOSHI *and* OSAWA *tend to* JŪKICHI *and* ISABURŌ's *wounds. Everyone goes strangely silent. The lamp casts a pale pall over the scene.)*

OYOSHI: *(Tying the bandage.)* Does it sting, the medicine?

JŪKICHI: No. . . .

OYOSHI: Hold it out. . . . Hold it out. . . . Your leg. . . .

JŪKICHI: Right. . . .

OYOSHI: Really! . . .

JŪKICHI: Right. . . .

SENZŌ: Don't get all formal on us, Jū-san. . . . Make yourself more comfortable, why don't you. . . . Make yourself comfortable.

JŪKICHI: Right. . . . With your permission, then. *(Stops kneeling and sits so that he can extend his leg.)*

SENZŌ: *(To* OYOSHI.*)* Bring some hot. . . . *(*OYOSHI *nods and stands.* OSAWA *has not yet finished tending to* ISABURŌ's *wounds.)* How the hell did you hurt yourselves?

JŪKICHI: *(Holding back his feelings.)* I'm embarrassed to say. . . . *(*SENZŌ *is silent.)* This is no time to come visiting you looking like this.

SENZŌ: But, you left my place, and then . . . ?

JŪKICHI: We'd left your place and had just made it as far as Umayabashi. . . . You can catch a rickshaw there. . . . So we thought, but hard luck for us—maybe 'cause it was so late—there weren't any. *(*SENZŌ *nods.)* . . . Maybe there'd be one if we crossed the bridge. . . . There's always a line of them at the corner where the hospital is. . . . And even if there weren't, if we went as far as Ishihara, we could figure something out. . . . So we started to cross the bridge. . . . That's when, suddenly, Isaburō-san saw his chance. . . .

*(*SENZŌ *glances at* ISABURŌ. . . . *Both* OSAWA, *who is by his side, and* OYOSHI, *who has left her spot by the long brazier, similarly look* ISABURŌ's *way. . . .* ISABURŌ *sits there, like a stone.)*

JŪKICHI: I can't let him bolt like that. . . . That's what I thought, and I latched onto him from behind.... He tried to shake me off.... But I wouldn't let him go.... And while we were struggling—

SENZŌ: You both tripped ...?

(OYOSHI *goes toward the table, carrying a freshly heated flask of sake.*)

JŪKICHI: Must've slipped on a stone, I think.... Went over like dominoes....

OYOSHI: Dear me! You poor things.... (SENZŌ *is silent.*) Here, have some....
(*Offers* JŪKICHI *a sake cup.*)

JŪKICHI: Ah, thank you. (*Takes it.*)

OYOSHI: Doesn't it hurt?

JŪKICHI: No, not really.... It's nothing special.... (OYOSHI *pours for him.*)

SENZŌ: (*Harshly.*) Isa-san!

JŪKICHI: (*Cutting in.*) Wait.... Please. (*Puts down his cup.* SENZŌ *looks at him questioningly.*) I've got something I want to say.

SENZŌ: To me?

JŪKICHI: Yes. (SENZŌ *nods, uncertainly.* JŪKICHI *forces the leg he had thrust out back under him and kneels formally, then politely bows.*) Once again, I'd like to beg your forgiveness.

SENZŌ: Jū-san, that's hardly—

JŪKICHI: (*Continuing.*) I know I'm clumsy, but you've all been good enough to let me be like part of your family—Master Isaburō's family. You even let me speak freely about all this.... I'm sure you must think I'm somebody who doesn't know his place.... I'm terribly sorry.... (SENZŌ *is silent.*) ... But, as you're all aware, I was lucky enough to be indebted—deeply so—to my former master, Katsumi-san.... I've been in their service since I was twelve, and if today I'm able to stand on my own two feet, it's all because of what the old master did for me.... I want to help Isaburō-san here, and in so doing hope to repay my debt to the master, even a ten-thousandth of what he did for me.... That's what I've wanted to do, if able. (SENZŌ *is silent.*) That's what I wanted, but tonight of all nights, I realized that somebody like me is really the odd man out here. (SENZŌ *is silent.*) Whatever I've tried to do, in fact, hasn't served Master Isaburō well at all. Indeed, I've realized that things haven't turned out anywhere the way I expected them to. (SENZŌ *is silent.*) I know you must be mocking me. You think I've got no right to speak.... But I can't help it.... Go ahead and scold me, but I'd rather you took him back. If you'd be so kind. So....

SENZŌ: (*Pausing.*) No, I understand.... (JŪKICHI *is silent.*) What can I say but agree with you? (JŪKICHI *is silent.*) That you, of all people, had to put up with all this for so long.... I'm sure it must've made your blood boil some-times.... *(JŪKICHI is silent.)* If anybody's going to apologize, let it be me.

JŪKICHI: But you mustn't.... *(SENZŌ is silent. Pause.)* I know it's terribly selfish of me to ask, but if you'd be so kind as to let me go now....

SENZŌ: As you wish.

JŪKICHI: *(To OYOSHI.)* You have my deepest apologies for all the trouble we've caused.

OYOSHI: *(Spare with her words.)* Thank you.

JŪKICHI: *(To OSAWA.)* ma'am, you've heard it all.... Please don't think ill of me....

OSAWA: *(Weakly.)* I'm really....

(JŪKICHI stands.... OYOSHI and OSAWA both stand too.)

SENZŌ: In that case, I'll—

JŪKICHI: Please.... *(He leaves, avoiding ISABURŌ's eyes.)*

(OYOSHI and OSAWA see him out. Pause. SENZŌ fills a teacup with sake.... He drinks.... ISABURŌ sits, still as a stone. The lamplight casts a pale pall.)

SENZŌ: Clean up here. *(He has OYOSHI and OSAWA put away the table when they return.... Doing as they are told, they take it into the next room. The dog barks for a while and then stops. Pause. To ISABURŌ.)* Come here. *(ISABURŌ is silent.)* We can't talk if you're going to sit over there.... Come closer. *(ISABURŌ is silent. SENZŌ's gorge rises.)* What nonsense was that you were trying to pull there? *(ISABURŌ is silent. SENZŌ speaks reproachfully.)* Well, what was it? Speak, you bloody fool. *(So saying, his glance happens to fix on ISABURŌ's face.... Witheringly.)* What is it now? Are you crying? You idiot. *(ISABURŌ is silent.)* What've you got to be sad about? ... So sad you have to cry? *(ISABURŌ is silent.)* Stop acting like an ass. *(Pause.)*

ISABURŌ: *(Suddenly looking up.)* I've got a favor to ask you, Uncle....

SENZŌ: What?

ISABURŌ: Please let me see Ofusa.... *(Holding back the tears.)*

SENZŌ: *(Coldly.)* What for?

ISABURŌ: You'll find out.... If you let me see her.... *(SENZŌ is silent.)* If you tell me to leave her, I will.... I'll leave her, but let me see her first.... Just once....

SENZŌ: What the hell were you doing? ... Just what the hell have you been doing? *(ISABURŌ is silent.)* Haven't you heard a word of what I told you? *(ISABURŌ is silent.)* Ofusa's had it up to here with you.... She's fed up and decided once and for all that she's through with you. *(ISABURŌ is silent.)* But you little bum! You won't let well enough alone.... You don't give a

damn about anybody else, getting drunk out of your mind. . . . And you're
the one to tell her to get out! . . . If you don't like what you see, you're the
one who ought to be leaving. . . . Whenever there's a problem, you're the
one who starts harping on about it, like you were the only one in the world
who was suffering. . . . Ofusa could see that coming; that's why she ran to
her sister's place in Kobe after you left. . . . I was very clear about that. Don't
you remember?

ISABURŌ: Please don't speak like that, Uncle. . . . I beg you. . . . All I'm asking
is to see her. . . . I beg you. . . . *(SENZŌ is silent.)* All I want is to see her and
ask her how she really feels. . . . That's all.

SENZŌ: You don't believe me then.

ISABURŌ: No, I believe you. . . . I really do, but *(with some difficulty)* there's no
way she could have gone to Kobe.

SENZŌ: And if she didn't go to Kobe, where did she go then? *(ISABURŌ is silent.)*
You saying I'm hiding her? . . . *(ISABURŌ is silent.)* If so, go ahead and look. . . .
Go see if she's here. *(ISABURŌ is silent.)* Who knows? She might be here
after all. . . . Go look. . . . Go ahead, search the whole house. See if I care.
(ISABURŌ is silent.) When you find her, ask her how she feels. . . . You don't
have a problem with that, do you? . . . I didn't think so. . . . But let's just say
she says no. . . . You might want to see her, but Ofusa might not want to see
you. And what are you going to do then? *(ISABURŌ is silent.)* Let's say she's
here now. . . . If it's true what you believe and Ofusa still loves you, then
you've only got to say the word and she'll pop out of the ceiling or the floor-
boards or wherever she's hiding and fly to you. . . . She'd have to. . . . 'Cause
if she heard you call and didn't come out, that'd mean she didn't have any
feelings left for you. . . . You're so bloody full of yourself. *(ISABURŌ is silent.*
There is a longish pause. ISABURŌ *stands, looking like a shadow. . . . He starts to*
leave.) Where are you going? Hey! *(Pause.)*

ISABURŌ: To look for her. *(SENZŌ looks at him inquisitively.)* I'm going to look
for Ofusa.

SENZŌ: Haven't you heard what I said? Idiot. *(ISABURŌ is silent.)* Why won't
you listen to me?

ISABURŌ: I am. If you tell me, I'll go back to Jū-san's place. . . . *(Clenches his*
teeth to stop the welling tears. Pause. He leaves.)
(A long pause. Again, a dog barks outside. . . . But this time, plaintively. . . .
OFUSA *slips downstairs without anyone's noticing and quietly sobs. . . .* OYOSHI
and OSAWA *begin to weep as well.)*

SENZŌ: *(Glancing at them.)* What the hell are you all crying about? . . . What have you got to cry about? Nothing, surely. *(OFUSA, OYOSHI, and OSAWA weep. SENZŌ, deliberately.)* At least Ofusa's got her reasons. . . . She's leaving her husband. But this isn't your place to cry, Mother. . . . Why are you crying? What are you so sad about? *(OSAWA weeps. To OYOSHI.)* And you, what are you trying to prove? *(OYOSHI weeps.)* The idiot dug his own hole; now he's got to lie in it. . . . Now settle down. . . . So long as he's with Jūkichi, nothing serious will happen to him. . . . Ah. If Jūkichi came back and asked us to reconsider this divorce, surely we couldn't refuse him. . . . For Ofusa and for Mother's sake, too, we have to make sure Jūkichi doesn't come to shame. *(To OFUSA and OSAWA.)* Ain't that so? *(OFUSA and OSAWA say nothing, but weep.)* But then that idiot acts up like the bloody fool he is. . . . Gets himself hurt wrestling with Jūkichi like that. A real lost cause. . . . *(OFUSA and OSAWA say nothing but weep.)* That's it. He's through with Jūkichi now. . . . No way he can go back. *(OFUSA and OSAWA say nothing but weep.)* Why aren't you laughing, Mother? . . . Why don't you say, "Serves him right"? . . . Why don't you say, "He's only got himself to blame"? . . .

OSAWA: But, Senzō, you can see he's so helpless. . . .

SENZŌ: So what? . . . It's his own business what the road holds in store for him. . . . It's a waste of breath our worrying. . . .

OYOSHI: But, dear—

SENZŌ: "But, dear," what? . . . You weren't any different. . . . You were behind me all the way, right up till now, saying stuff like, "He's not one of us," "He's being completely unreasonable," like Isa was your sworn enemy's offspring.

OYOSHI: But he's such a poor, wretched thing. . . .

SENZŌ: Wretched? . . . I'm the one who's wretched. *(OYOSHI is silent.)* If you all cry, what am I supposed to do? What've I got to be proud about? . . . *(OYOSHI is silent.)* Who was I doing this for? . . . Who? . . . Who do you think asked me to bust my ass doing what can't be done? *(OYOSHI is silent. Driving home his point.)* Wise up! Don't be such fools. . . .

(OFUSA, OYOSHI, and OSAWA weep.)

SENZŌ: *(Suddenly goes to the window. . . . He opens the shutter.)* . . . Thank heavens, the sky's getting lighter now. *(Moved to tears by the emotion welling up within him. . . .)*

(The three WOMEN continue to weep.)

—Curtain—

....

TWO MEN AT PLAY WITH LIFE

INTRODUCTION

More has been written in English on Kishida Kunio than on any other figure in modern Japanese theatre, and more of his works have been translated than those of any other prewar Japanese playwright. English criticism on Kishida nonetheless reflects the fierce debate his name stirs up in Japanese letters. For Thomas Rimer, author of a seminal study of Kishida and the *shingeki* movement, Kishida was "the first dramatist to succeed in putting into dramatic form the contemporary Japanese spirit."[1] David Goodman, in his trenchant introduction to a collection of Kishida's plays in English, reflects the more circumspect view taken by the majority of *shingeki* critics and practitioners when he claims that Kishida was "a major but tragically flawed Japanese dramatist whose work commands our attention because of its richly evocative language." Kishida's politics fatally compromised his artistic legacy, suggests Goodman.[2] Within months of the crackdown on *shingeki* companies and the arrest of hundreds on August 14, 1940, Kishida accepted the position of director of the cultural section of the Imperial Rule Assistance Association (Taisei Yoku-sankai), Japan's fascist wartime cabinet; the playwright's collaboration with

---

Photo of Kishida Kunio courtesy of the Tsubouchi Memorial Theatre Museum, Waseda University.

the militarists during the war earned him the undying enmity of most of his contemporaries in Japanese theatre. Critic Ōzasa Yoshio, whose assessment is more positive (he calls Kishida a "forgotten star"), points out that while the centenary of Chekhov's death in 2004 was commemorated in Japan with numerous publications and performances, the fiftieth anniversary that same year of Kishida's death went by largely unnoticed.[3] The issue is more complex than any claim that Kishida was a good artist but a poor judge of politics, and there seems little common ground between Rimer's and Goodman's assessments of the man beyond their acknowledgment that he was a superb stylist. Rimer calls Kishida a "moralist," where Goodman asserts that the writer's "lack of a comprehensible moral cosmology" precipitated his wartime collaboration. Indeed, Kishida's stance as an artist, Goodman claims, cannot be divorced from his politics. The playwright was a nihilist whose "dramaturgy provided no principles, no rationale, for resisting the war. Staunchly ahistorical and divorced from social reality, it provided no barricade against barbarism."[4]

At the heart of these two divergent opinions lies a debate on the meaning and purpose of dramatic art that goes back to the 1920s; in aesthetic terms at least, Kishida's differences with Osanai and other members of the Tsukiji Little Theatre revolved around the forms, uses, and limits of realism. (Kishida's debate with Osanai over whether to stage original Japanese plays and, if so, which ones, has been discussed in chapter 3.) Specifically, Kishida's and Osanai's positions represented two versions of realism, the former psychological, the latter sociological. A similar debate swept Japanese fiction at the time. The naturalism that had held Japanese theatre and letters in sway during the first decade of the twentieth century had spawned two antagonistic movements, one focused on confession and the exploration of the modern, privatized self, and the other increasingly devoted to the idea of art as an ideological tool to promote social action. Ultimately, this debate was about the limits of art itself: can art alone ever save anyone, either personally or politically?

Kishida defined his artistic differences with Osanai and the Tsukiji Little Theatre along the lines of "northern" and "southern" theatrical styles: Osanai and his followers represented the "northern" style of German, Scandinavian, and Russian theatre, whereas he ascribed to the "southern," French style of Jacques Copeau, whose student he had been from 1921 to 1923. The latter was, according to Kishida, a style that "valued fragrance over strength, nuance over depth; it does not deal directly with human suffering but uses all sorts of fantastic elements to turn suffering into comedy. Rather than portray 'society's cruelty,' it suggests (without any attempt at making sense of it) the self-contempt of humans who cannot bear such cruelty or who instead attempt to laugh off their indignation at their ill treatment."[5] Indeed, such a sensibility was opposed to that of Osanai and the Tsukiji Little Theatre's socially and increasingly politically motivated theatre. For his part, Osanai's view of Kishida's work could be summed up in a review he wrote of a performance of *Autumn in Tyrol* (*Chiroru no aki*, 1925). Osanai admired the younger writer's delicate style but warned: "To be sure, this work manages somehow to flourish within the confines of the so-called 'playhouse.' But if we were to take it outside, into the environment people like us live in today, it would wither just like a flower taken out of a hothouse.... Theatre's fundamental nature is to head for the outdoors."[6] For a socially committed theatre, words need to be weapons of resistance, not flowers of contemplation. Diametrically opposed to the leftist mainstream in *shingeki*, even Mishima Yukio found the intimacy of Kishida's world lacking, claiming that his plays were "chamber music for the theatre and fail[ed] completely to capture the orchestral grandeur of modern Japanese history."[7] But I think it is ultimately wrong to fault an artist for choosing one form or vision over another. We do not blame Beethoven for writing string quartets when he could have written nothing but symphonies, nor are Schubert or Chopin lesser artists for excelling in smaller forms.

Whereas the impulse for Osanai and his allies was outward (*soto e*), Kishida and others in his camp focused their steady gaze inward. For many, Kishida was the first Japanese dramatist to create truly individuated characters. Kishida's ideal is expressed in the following passages:

It is enough that we listen attentively to the subtle rhythms of the soul, transforming those rhythms into a natural concerto. The past, the future, dreams and reality, front and back, all phenomena of life are magnified immeasurably; we encounter the breath of each and every living moment and transcend both time and space. It is enough, then, that we surrender ourselves to the intoxication of what I call a "psychological lyricism."[8]

Human reality can be created in the theatre because the drama, through its artistic methods, is capable of poetic suggestion. The theatre is altogether suggestive, yet altogether direct. These elements are not in contradiction; to understand and make use of each is the secret of composing a fine play. Indeed a scene in which the author makes use of no indirect explanation but says directly all he wishes would not be accepted as real. For in real life there are no "explanations."[9]

We can see in these remarks that Kishida did not advocate any literal notion of realism; suggestion rather than representation, poetry rather than prose, and music rather than the photograph seem the appropriate analogues of his dramatic style.

Osanai's protégé Kubo Sakae, author of Japan's greatest work of socialist realist theatre, *Land of Volcanic Ash*, provided what is one of the most cogent critiques of Kishida's intimate ideal. Though not naming Kishida directly, he characterized the Tsukiji-za and *Playwriting* style as a "realism of manners" (*setaiteki riarizumu*) in an important 1934 essay called "Misguided Realism." Kubo showed no doctrinaire favoritism for the leftist camp, however; he launched his essay with a critique of the term "socialist realism" and the work of other leftist playwrights like Murayama Tomoyoshi and Miyoshi Jūrō, who, he claimed, took too schematic an approach to plot, theme, and characterization.[10] Their dramatic and rhetorical skills were insufficient to maintain the audience's interest over the course of a long work, like Murayama's adaptation of Shimazaki Tōson's novel *Before the Dawn*.[11] In contrast, he wrote, some felt that the plays the Tsukiji-za was staging at the Hikōkan Theatre "heralded the future of contemporary drama," but their focus on the small and inward limited their theatrical resources. Echoing Osanai, Kubo claimed the Tsukiji-za produced "hothouse flowers." He saw two possible courses that its "realism of manners" could take. One was Chekhov's: seek what is typical and universal about society as a whole in the small, personal, and domestic detail; the other course was a dangerous kind of mysticism: "Rather than producing an atmosphere of reality on stage, it creates an aura of the uncanny or blinds us to the realities of life with a smokescreen of lyricism. In so doing, it tries to escape the banality of portraying the world as it is. I give as ready examples of how this tendency makes art impotent the conclusions to [Kawaguchi Kazurō's] *Nijūrokubankan* and [Tanaka Chikao's] *Tachibana taisō onnajuku ura*."[12] Kubo's critique recalls that of another staunchly leftist realist, Györgi Lukacs, who, around the same time, decried the modernists' escape from social reality into hermetic worlds of pure aesthetic form.

Indeed, Kishida's subtle style naturally tended toward more symbolist and abstract forms; Ōzasa goes so far as to say that Kishida was an "anti-realist."[13] What, after all, could a realism of the spirit mean if the spirit cannot be seen or measured but only suggested? Other critics since have accused Kishida of being divorced from reality. Time in Kishida's plays, writes Saeki Ryūkō, "was at least idiosyncratic and, more to the point, obstructionist ... manifested solely in the here-and-now, where there is no history and where all that exists is language."[14] The one transcendental principle for a realist is history, and Kishida would seem to ignore it. Kishida's language, moreover, was of a particularly deracinated kind where, Saeki asserts, the very connection between words and things—essential for a realist—has been undermined. No doubt, Kishida's experience of being an expatriate and reluctant returnee to Japan created a sense of displacement and anomie that also affected his stance toward the Japanese language itself. Yuasa Masako notes that Kishida's Japanese was "purified" by his encounter with the French language; it became more rational, less sentimental.[15] Language is nonetheless the basis for Kishida's dramaturgy, whose elements—individual character, rhythm, structure, theme—all flow from the nuance of dialogue, notes Nagahira Kazuo.[16] It was not language's function of pointing to things per se that interested him, but its connotative nature: what mattered to him was the way a word could conjure a spirit or memory, sensation or sensibility.

And Kishida's sensibility was decidedly modern. He was a cosmopolitan, a bourgeois, and a skeptic at a time that demanded more conviction from its writers. His stance seems to point beyond the war and Japan's defeat, beyond even the leftist activism of 1950s *shingeki*, and anticipate the more radical dramatic experiments of the 1960s generation. Goodman notes how both Kishida and Betsuyaku Minoru used the empty stage as a symbol of the void.[17] Many others have remarked on the similarity of Kishida's work to that of Samuel Beckett and Betsuyaku. Yuasa Masako calls Kishida "a pioneer of Japanese absurdism,"[18] adding that "When absolute values are nonexistent, what needs to be communicated also loses its clarity; language thereby loses its fundamental function. Kishida's dramatic language itself is clear and pleasant to the ear, but in that respect his style is an absurdist one that no longer possesses the eloquence of modern drama's semantic universe."[19]

Nowhere is this tendency more obvious than in *Two Men at Play with Life*. The two men of the title are nameless, featureless sketches, identified only by what they wear: one wears glasses, the other, bandages that cover the face. They have run into each other at a level crossing where each plans to commit suicide, and the play consists of a debate between the two over the pros and cons of ending one's life or, more to the point, who has a better reason to die. In some respects it is one of the most rational of Kishida's works: here the dialogic form is used specifically to investigate certain philosophical questions—namely, What is the meaning of life? And under what circumstances does one have the right to end it? But as the title suggests, reason is played with here. His protagonists are romantics, but Kishida's gaze is wry, yet sympathetic and amused. He provides no easy answers. "Just what did I come here to do, anyway?" asks Bandages, to which Glasses replies, "You came to find out that your own life was worth more than somebody else's." The play's conclusion in an uneasy standoff, with neither one letting the other die, would seem to suggest that Kishida is no nihilist here. Yes, existence may be absurd, but it is our task as human beings to take responsibility for our lives and those of others. Before Sartre, before Beckett, Kishida was tackling many of the same existential problems and in a similar dramatic idiom; and here, at least, it would not be wrong to say that Kishida's proto-absurdist stance provides a moral.

This translation is based on the text in Kishida, *"Inochi o moteasobu otoko futari,"* in *Kishida Kunio zenshū,* 1:123–150.

Fukushima Hironori as Bandages and Taga Masaru as Glasses in *Two Men at Play with Life*, Kyoto Kaikan production, May 1977. Photo courtesy of the Tsubouchi Memorial Theatre Museum, Waseda University.

Kishida Kunio

TWO MEN AT PLAY WITH LIFE

FIRST PUBLISHED:

New Fiction, February 1925

FIRST PERFORMANCE:

Piccoloza, Imperial Hotel Theatre,
December 1925, dir. Takada Minoru

CHARACTERS

....

A man wearing GLASSES
A man in BANDAGES

PLACE: *A railway embankment. Below it, a spot used for storing lumber. Patches of muddy black earth and trampled down grasses. In the distance, a red signal lamp. The moon is out.*

(A man wearing GLASSES—*apparently in his mid-twenties—is perched on the lumber pile, deep in thought. He sighs, blows his nose, takes off his glasses and wipes them, yanks at his hair, crosses his arms, smoothes out the wrinkles in his clothes, sticks out his tongue.*

Enter a man in BANDAGES. *That is, his face is swathed in bandages but for gaps for his eyes, nose, and mouth. He walks back and forth in front of the man in* GLASSES, *apparently unaware that there is anyone there. He climbs up the embankment, then immediately descends.)*

GLASSES: Hey, you. The crossing—it's further on.

BANDAGES: *(Seemingly unsurprised.)* That so? The crossing's further on, is it? *(As if to himself.)* The crossing's further on ... he says. *(Sits down beside* GLASSES.)*

GLASSES: Going someplace?

BANDAGES: That's the plan. What about you? You going someplace?

GLASSES: To go or not—I'm still undecided.

BANDAGES: I see. Not a bad idea, but what do you think? Is it so easy to do away with yourself?

GLASSES: I'll just have to try and find out, won't I?

(A long silence.)

BANDAGES: How about this place? This sure looks like the spot.

GLASSES: I suppose it is.

BANDAGES: My mind's made up, but still, one hesitates.

GLASSES: That's 'cause one gets to thinking. After all, this is a kind of last resort, isn't it?

BANDAGES: You know, I'm a man who hates the sentimental. I haven't left a note or anything. I mean, it's clear why I'm doing it. Besides, the reasons are entirely prosaic.

GLASSES: Ah, in that respect, I'm just like you. I mean, we all choose our own paths in this life, but all said and done, some wounds just won't heal, eh?

BANDAGES: I'm not sure I quite understand you. What I meant was not that I wanted to kill myself to solve all my troubles, but rather, seeing as how I'm as good as dead already, I prefer to finish off the job myself. Ergo, I've got no need whatsoever, out of some kind of heroic resignation or unrealistic flight of fancy, to concoct some sort of tragic tale out of this moment. Not at this stage of the game.

GLASSES: Why, I'd say the same myself. I'm a coward, you see. Defeated by Life. Sacrificed on the altar of Fate. Having thus considered the matter....

BANDAGES: Uh uh, I don't think you understand. That's all as it should be. But it's only the circumstances of the moment that have pushed you into thinking that way. Like being dumped by your girlfriend or embezzling the company funds or killing somebody by mistake....

GLASSES: Hah, hah, hah, hah! Do I really look that way? I'll say no more then. Writing off a person's suffering, the suffering of one man, like that ... why, I won't let you get away with that.

BANDAGES: Was I wrong? Well, be that as it may. One thing's for sure—we've both picked the very same time and place to die. There's no sense denying the fact that fortune has thrown us together, you and me. Please, don't mind me....

GLASSES: No, please, the offense is all mine.... But the fact is, I'm still very much alive. It'd be an awful nuisance if you were to go off and do something stupid right in front of me. The crossing's not that far away. How about it? Shall I call somebody?

BANDAGES: Call somebody? . . . What would be the point of that? *(Pause.)* Wouldn't that be causing trouble for the both of us?

GLASSES: You know, I'm what you might call a deep thinker. I can't tell you how disagreeable it is to be told I'm rash or reckless.

BANDAGES: Well, then, all the more reason. So tell me, why are you doing it? What happened to you?

GLASSES: I don't mind telling my story, but what about you? It hardly seems that there was anything profound in your case. . . .

BANDAGES: Is that how it looks? Why, it's no skin off my nose if you think that way. Hah, hah, hah, hah! Have you any idea why I wear this bandage?

GLASSES: Were you burned in a fire perhaps?

BANDAGES: That's putting it a bit too lightly, that is. . . . Well, I'll let that pass.

GLASSES: There's really good medicine for burns now.

BANDAGES: Let's say it was a burn then. And what if it healed?

GLASSES: That'd be wonderful, wouldn't it?

BANDAGES: Even if I had scars all over my face? . . . So bad you couldn't tell if I had two eyes or three?

GLASSES: What line of business are you in?

BANDAGES: I'm not in any line of business. I'm engaged in research in applied chemistry. Which is to say, I'm a scientist. There I was, I was wracking my brains trying to discover how to make artificial diamonds—this close to finding the answer I was—when something went wrong and the whole thing blew up in my face.

GLASSES: If you were that close, all the more reason, surely, to keep at it! You're bound to finish what you started. As for your face, don't be so vain. Gentlemen engaged in such work as yourself aren't, generally speaking—

BANDAGES: Now hang on there. As a matter of fact, I'm still single.

GLASSES: Good for you, surely.

BANDAGES: I have a fiancée.

GLASSES: And what does she say?

BANDAGES: She says she doesn't mind.

GLASSES: So what are you complaining about? Sheesh! I mean, look. . . .

BANDAGES: I mean, she's in love with me.

GLASSES: No kidding!

BANDAGES: One time, I made up my mind and took off the bandages and showed her my face.

GLASSES: And she said she liked you just the way you are, right?

BANDAGES: *(Nods.)* And she put her head on my chest and cried. She said she wasn't sad, but she cried.

GLASSES: I know how she felt.

BANDAGES: I don't.

(A longish pause.)

GLASSES: Don't you?

BANDAGES: If I did, it'd mean she was lying to me. *(A longish pause.)* I made up my mind. Or rather, I've resigned myself. That's it—I've resigned myself.

GLASSES: That's right—we've resigned ourselves.

BANDAGES: Ain't that so? Nothing could be simpler. *(Pause.)* You know, I'm a man who hates the sentimental.

GLASSES: And I'm what you might call a deep thinker, don't you know. I'm an actor—if I told you my name, you might know it, so I won't—anyway, I'm an actor, somebody well known in *shingeki* circles. When I was eight, I lost my parents and the man who was my uncle—if I mentioned his name, you might know it, so I'd rather not—anyway, I was adopted into my uncle's family. He had a daughter.

BANDAGES: Say no more—I've got a pretty good idea what happened next. Just another love story, eh?

GLASSES: What d'you mean by "just another"? And what about you? You think people are going to pack it in out of some sort of banal sense of duty?

BANDAGES: It's not a matter of packing it in or not. So what happened?

GLASSES: You said you had a pretty good idea, so what's the point of my telling you?

BANDAGES: Now, don't get cross.

GLASSES: Who ever heard of somebody asking a guy, "So what happened next?" before he'd even had a chance to start talking? It's not like we were trying to score points on each other or anything.

BANDAGES: You're quite right—we aren't trying to score any points. We can hardly be proud of this, can we? So anyway, you and the girl didn't end up happily ever after, after all. So it would seem it has to end in tragedy.

GLASSES: What d'you mean, "it would seem"? No! No! No! It's not like that at all! Hah, hah, hah! You simply don't understand other people, do you? The girl got sick and died. *(Sobbing.)* I did something I'll forever regret. You see, I planted the seeds of her sickness. There was a rumor that some actress and I had been carrying on. Nothing of the sort happened. The poor girl took it badly—I mean, she believed it, she fretted over it night

and day. It broke her poor heart. The actress married the head of my theatre troupe—if I mentioned his name, you might know it, so I'd rather not.
The girl wouldn't believe a word I said till she read it in the papers. But by
the time we cleared that little misunderstanding up, it was too late. She lay,
worn and wasted, in her hospital bed. *(Wipes his tears, blows his nose.)* I was
a fool, a coward. I think to myself, why didn't I quit acting and say to her, "I
told you so!" Instead, I frittered my time away trying to learn some dumb
lines, my head full of half-baked dreams about Art. . . . It makes me mad,
mad and sad, to think I was like that. . . . And so, too late as it is, I've made
up my mind—I'm going to take the girl's feelings to heart and go keep her
company in the next world.

BANDAGES: Now, that's really banal. What do you think is going to happen
if you die? Do you think you'll go join her for eternity? Hardly. . . . I see.
I understand your suffering perfectly. But your suffering's not something
that's bound to last forever, you know. You're sure you'll never forget her
now. That's what's so beautiful about you. How old are you, anyway?

GLASSES: How old do I look?

BANDAGES: *(Pause.)* It doesn't matter, really. You're still young. The flower of
life still awaits you, don't you see?

GLASSES: How old are you?

BANDAGES: Me? Guess. . . . Er, I suppose that'd be difficult, wouldn't it? I'm
thirty-five. But in my case, age isn't the problem.

(A longish pause.)

GLASSES: There's somebody coming. They'd better not find us here. *(Gets up.)*

BANDAGES: It's the railway watchman. Quick, let's hide.

(The TWO *hide themselves. A* MAN *passes by up on the embankment. The light
of his safety lamp skips across the stage. A train whistle blows. The sound of an
approaching train.)*

GLASSES: *(Showing himself.)* The coast is clear.

BANDAGES: *(Also coming out.)* The outbound, isn't it?

GLASSES: The express for Kobe.

BANDAGES: *(Sitting.)* You of all people ought to give up this idea. You really
shouldn't do anything rash.

(The train passes on the embankment above. The TWO *gaze up at it.)*

GLASSES: Looks packed.

BANDAGES: Was it? There's something depressing about a night train, ain't there?

GLASSES: *(Pause.)* Look at you—you've got this terrific job. That alone is reason to live, isn't it?

BANDAGES: Reason to live? Who gives a damn? Work's one thing, life is another. You've got your own life ahead of you—any number of jobs you can do, and any number of women you can still fall in love with. Besides, for an artist, work itself is your lover. Or that's what they say, anyway, don't they? Folks like me have a hard time grasping it, you know, the—what do they call it?—a kind of voluptuist? Isn't that the word for it? You know. I mean, can't you forget it all and throw yourself into pleasure, just for the sheer thrill of it?

GLASSES: But surely you must feel your line of work is like a lover too. I mean, you get so wrapped up in your job that you forget all about eating and sleeping. . . . Don't you hear all the time about these guys who turn their back on the world, on their families even?

BANDAGES: There's where you're wrong. Well, I see what you mean—scientists can be that way. But you won't get the complete picture unless you see the other side as well. It's a human problem, in other words. It's got nothing to do with logic. Don't you see? Go ask some other young guy who's in the same boat as you. He's got the same sorrows, the same troubles. Why, he might even decide to deal with them the same way. But no, it's more normal not to. Not to do so is the correct way.

GLASSES: Not to do so isn't necessarily correct.

BANDAGES: Whatever, I'm against it. *(Pause.)* So how about it? Shall I hand you over to the cops?

GLASSES: The police? . . . What do you mean to achieve by that? *(Pause.)* Didn't we agree we weren't going to get in each other's hair? You're really out of line there.

BANDAGES: Forget it—why don't you just go home? I won't say anything. Take it from somebody who's older than you.
(The sound of a train whistle.)

GLASSES: *(Gets up.)* That's enough. Say no more. *(Makes to run up the embankment.)*

BANDAGES: *(Grabbing his sleeve.)* Stop! It won't do you any good, you know.

GLASSES: *(Twisting to free himself.)* Let me go! It's my body and I can die if I want to!

BANDAGES: Yeah, it's your body. That's very true. That's why I say you shouldn't do anything stupid. You know, I'm a man who hates the sentimental. Of course, I'd let somebody die—that is, if it made any sense. *(Suddenly speaking roughly.)* You idiot! Pull yourself together!
(Drags GLASSES down.)

GLASSES: *(The force of* BANDAGES*'s words making him lose heart.)* So what're you going to do?

BANDAGES: *(Knocking* GLASSES *away.)* This! *(Dashes up the embankment.)*

GLASSES: Ah! He's done it! He's gone and done it, the bastard. *(No sooner has he said this than* BANDAGES *slinks back down the embankment.)* Huh? You didn't do it?

BANDAGES: *(Out of breath.)* I did! I did it, but I was too fast. Or to be more precise, I put too much force into it. Jumped clean over to the other side of the tracks. I blew it. Oh well, next time. . . .

GLASSES: That's why you should've let me go first.

BANDAGES: Oh, I couldn't do that. If I'd done that, I could never respect my-self. There's no way I could stand by and watch you commit suicide. I'm against it. If I don't give a damn about myself, then at least I've got a duty to see you get home safely or hand you over to the cops, whatever. But I can't. If you're not prepared to listen to me, if you want to do something, then go off and do it someplace else where I can't see you. It's not like this is the only place in the world, buster.

GLASSES: Hey, I was the one who got here first.

BANDAGES: I'm not talking about who got here first. I just want you to know that so long as I'm alive, I'm not going to let you die.

GLASSES: So how 'bout this—to keep me alive, you'll have to survive too. Oth-erwise, you're not making any sense.

BANDAGES: I get it—you never really planned to die after all. Did you? Well, if that's how it is, there's no point hanging around here forever. You missed your chance. That's the ten o'clock now, bound for Hamamatsu.

GLASSES: You're the one who doesn't want to die. Botching a suicide on the train tracks—you're not exactly going to start a trend there, are you?

(A whistle blows; then the sound of a train approaching.)

BANDAGES: Okay, then watch this! *(Bolts up the embankment.)*

GLASSES: It's my turn! *(Drags* BANDAGES *down.)*

BANDAGES: What are you doing?

(GLASSES takes the opportunity to dash up the embankment. The train passes. He disappears.)

BANDAGES: He's gone and done it. He's really done it now, the bastard. This is very awkward for me, having to be second. *(As he mutters this to himself, he gazes up and sees* GLASSES, *rubbing his eyes and tramping down the embank-ment.)* Don't tell me you missed too?

GLASSES: No good—it was a freight train.

BANDAGES: A freight train?

GLASSES: Ouch! *(Rubs his eyes.)* Got some soot in my eye. This is bad. Ouch! That smarts.... *(Pause.)* Sorry, but could you have a look?

BANDAGES: *(Checking his eyes.)* Sure, but in this light.... Hey, raise your head a bit. And don't squint like that.

GLASSES: *(Holding open his eyelids with both hands.)* Have you found it? It was the right.

BANDAGES: You think I can see anything in this light? *(A whistle. The sound of a train.)* Here comes another. Do it yourself! *(Makes to climb the embankment.)*

GLASSES: Ouch! Ouch! *(Clings onto* BANDAGES.*)* For heaven's sake, not before you remove it!

BANDAGES: But look here.... *(Resumes his attempt to find the piece of soot in* GLASSES's *eye.)* How the hell can I remove something I can't see? *(The train is approaching.)* Why, if it hurts so much, come on, here's your chance. Finish off the job!

GLASSES: Be sensible and do something. I'm in no shape to fool around like this.

(The train passes overhead. An empty lunch box is tossed down and lands beside the TWO.*)*

BANDAGES: *(Picking it up.)* Polished that off, didn't he?

GLASSES: Ouch! Ouch! Ouch! ... Hurry up!

BANDAGES: *(Tosses the lunchbox.)* You are a pest, aren't you? Pull out a hankie or something.

GLASSES: It's in my pocket—please get it for me.

BANDAGES: *(Pulls out the handkerchief from* GLASSES's *pocket.)* This the one? *(As he pulls it out, a photograph falls to the ground.)* Something fell out. *(Looks around. Picks up the photograph.)* Hey, it's a photo.... *(Holding it up to the light.)* I see. She was the one, was she? Nice hairdo. Ain't she a beauty? Hm? Look at that smile....

GLASSES: Please, later....

BANDAGES: Wait. First things first here. But what lovely eyes she's got! There aren't that many around with eyes like these, my boy.

GLASSES: You think so? *(Pause.)* Those eyes ... are now shut, in eternal sleep.

BANDAGES: These eyes—damn shame what they've done. And look at her lips! Unusually bewitching for her age.

GLASSES: "Forgive me!" those lips said to me. *(His voice chokes with tears.)* Those were her last words.

BANDAGES: These lips, eh?

GLASSES: That's what she said.

BANDAGES: Why, look at these hands! So innocent. Like they were made to hold a beanbag.

GLASSES: No, they held my hand. *(Moans.)* Crying, "F-f-forgive me, please!" she clutched m-m-my hands in h-h-hers. Th-th-then. . . . Th-th-then, they went l-l-limp. *(Collapses in tears.)*

BANDAGES: These hands, eh? *(Thinking to himself, "Is that what she said?" he dabs at his eyes with* GLASSES's *handkerchief.)* Bugger. What are these? Tears?

GLASSES: *(Pause.)* You know, I'm what you might call a deep thinker. She's the only reason why I made up my mind to do what I plan to do.

BANDAGES: I see. I get your point. For you, it's meaningless to go on living. You can say what you like, but, well, my problems are ahead of me, after all. What I guess I'm saying is, I've taken too pessimistic a view of my own situation. That's how things turned out. Even if I was right about how my fiancée felt, still, I could at least try to be a bit more optimistic, more honest. I could try to look at the bright side of things. To think my own existence was standing in the way of somebody else's happiness—there's no sense in that. She might not think so, even if I did. In point of fact, there's this letter. *(Pulls a letter from his pocket.)* Here, read it for yourself. *(*GLASSES *takes the letter, opens and tries to read it, but cannot make it out very well.)* Can't read it? *(Not looking at the letter.)* This is what it says: "I have read your letter. You are mistaken. On the occasion in question, the tears simply flowed unbidden. But I should be offended were you to think that crying was a simpleminded reaction on my part. Rather, just knowing that your eyes could see just as well as ever made me so happy that I wept. I was worried most about your eyes, you see. As for the burns to your face—the only physical thing important to me was the fact it showed you still had a heart.

"In the five years we have been separated, from the spring of my twentieth year to the fall of my twenty-fifth, I have never once looked at your photograph. I can tell you this now. It is because I had realized how meaningless that mute image, that insensible form, was. You are, of course, in Germany. You are slaving away in your laboratory at Berlin University. Just knowing that is enough to comfort me. Sometimes, I can hear your voice, the words of your love, in those messages you send to me, those little notes like telegrams. The person you are is a mystery to me. That face, always lost in thought about something or other—it isn't the sort of face a woman could easily fall in love with. That's why I always made it a point to go watch you from behind, as you were working away at some project or other in your study. The way your back looked as you sat there, head in your hands, reading a book—from the line of your neck to your shoulders and from your shoulders down to your waist, I could sense how calm your breathing was— you mustn't laugh at me—this alone, I felt, was mine. . . . That, and that voice of yours, that voice, which even now is still unchanged, the voice that used to call 'Miichan, tea!' . . . That was mine, too." *(His voice increasingly emotional.)* Here, she ends her sentence with that little word "too."

GLASSES: Truly an impressive person. But I have to wonder. Surely it's asking too much to take that at face value. Just listening to that letter breaks my heart. You can tell how she poured her sorrow into each and every phrase. It seems you've got a duty after all, to set that person free. That much I can figure out. You have to die.

BANDAGES: *(Walking back and forth.)* Why aren't women more cold-blooded? They're too warm. What tortures us is those warm hearts of theirs. Or at least our memories of them.

GLASSES: You can't say all of them are like that. Some women can be really cold-hearted.

BANDAGES: Those aren't the type to give men trouble. Men aren't bothered by that kind. A man's slave to a woman's warm heart, no matter how cruel she is. Women are too kind, in other words. They were born with such warm hearts. That's what really floored me. And, of all women, my fiancée was special. Go ahead, read this letter through to the end.

GLASSES: I've pretty much got the gist of it.

BANDAGES: You understand, right? You'd be lying if you didn't. What did she write? "Dearest, if you believe you look so ugly, I will do all I can to make myself look ugly too. I will do anything for the sake of others. I'll go out with my face smeared with charcoal. But I am a woman. To care for how I look, to make myself more beautiful, even just a little, is the least I can do for you. Not to be beautiful is something as much to be feared for me as for you not having any talent. These are dreadful things for the both of us. Anything else is simply a matter of how we feel for each other. You do not scorn my empty little head. So how could I speak of beauty or ugliness if I did not at least pay homage to your face, your form?" What do you think? What could I say to say to that? Nothing. So why am I unhappy? Why am I in such pain? Why do I have to die?

GLASSES: It's your male pride. Sometimes we can't take what's offered us.

You're not an egoist, like most men out there. Nor should you be. It's because you have such convictions that you could make up your mind to do something like this. That's really impressive.

BANDAGES: But I'm not pure-hearted like you. That's why I'm so dissatisfied with myself. "Forgive me," said the girl with that fetching hairdo as she laid her head on the bosom of her lover, waiting for death—a man's life can't pay for words like those. I don't know how long ago it was she said that, but it's a mystery to me you've managed to survive so long. In pursuit of a fantasy, a man can see neither hill nor dale . . . much less a train.

GLASSES: I have to disagree with you. Put it that way, somebody like me is free. If it's a fantasy, so be it—just picturing it in my head gives me reason to live. Aside from what I told you, the two of us had nothing but good memories. Our last month together was our happiest, filled with quiet memories of our first love. I gave her strawberries, strawberries shaped like little hearts, in milk. I fed those lips with a spoon and as I did, she'd narrow those eyes of hers and say to me, "Merci!" "Merci, merci, merci!" Ah, no matter how often I hear those words, I never tire of them. A single little strawberry would fill her mouth. Sometimes that "merci" would sound like "mushy," sometimes like "mercy!" And, oh, the mouth, those lips that spoke so! I couldn't bear it, truly I couldn't. How many strawberries did I stuff her face with, just to hear those words again?

BANDAGES: *(As if to himself.)* Strawberries?

(A long silence.)

GLASSES: I guess I'm free, after all. But only in my feelings. In your case, though, the decision you have to make is completely different from my own: will you make your woman happy or sad? The sooner you make up your mind the better.

BANDAGES: I can do it any time I choose.

(Another fairly long silence.)

GLASSES: But I had to ask.

BANDAGES: By the way, how's your eye?

GLASSES: All those tears just now seem to have flushed it out.

BANDAGES: Anyway, meeting you here tonight, having this conversation has made me realize you don't really need a reason to die. Even if we do wait for the next train, we'll just get into another fight over who goes first. So how about it? Why don't we have ourselves a drink, then go off and do it on our own someplace?

GLASSES: On our own, eh? *(Pause.)* You do it tonight, and I'll be your witness.

BANDAGES: A witness, eh? Not a bad idea. How 'bout this?—You go first.

(Pause. The TWO *laugh.)*

GLASSES: This is hardly a laughing matter, though.

(A long silence. The TWO *laugh again.)*

BANDAGES: To do this sort of thing, it's best not to have an audience, don't you think? I know it's what you do for a living, but still. . . .

GLASSES: It's all nonsense, eh?

BANDAGES: Life—whose is it, anyway? You've got to wonder, don't you?

GLASSES: One thing's for sure—it doesn't belong to anybody else.

BANDAGES: You sure about that?

GLASSES: *(Pause.)* Let me give that some thought. *(Pause.)* Just what did I come here to do, anyway?

BANDAGES: You came to find out that your own life was worth more than somebody else's.

GLASSES: I really can't believe my life is worth more than somebody else's.

BANDAGES: But for you, there's somebody here whose life is worth less, much less, than your own.

GLASSES: You really think so? But I'd made up my mind and all.

(A whistle. The sound of a train.)

BANDAGES: If you've made up your mind, here's your chance to do it. If I'm in the way, I'll leave. Or do you want me here to give you some encouragement?

(The train is slowly getting closer.)

GLASSES: *(Rising dejectedly.)* Give me that photo. *(Takes the photograph and studies it with great feeling.)* Right. Can't be a coward any longer! *(Suddenly grabs* BANDAGES*'s hand.)* Come with me! Let's die together!

BANDAGES: *(Being pulled.)* No, really, after you. I'm in no rush. I've got plans, you know. . . .

GLASSES: *(Dragging* BANDAGES *against his will.)* What? Chickening out now?

BANDAGES: You're the one who's chickening out. *(Wresting his hand away, starts to push* GLASSES *up the embankment from behind.)* Go on, quit complaining!

GLASSES: *(Resisting with his arms and legs from being pushed up.)* Just what the hell do you think you're doing? *(Paying him no mind,* BANDAGES *continues shoving him up the slope.)* Th-this is . . . preposterous! Watch it there! That hurts! Ouch! Hey! You listening to me?

(The sound of the train bearing down on them.)

BANDAGES: *(Letting go.)* It's now or never!

GLASSES: *(Dashes down the embankment as if falling.)* Don't get violent on me!

BANDAGES: *(Plunks himself down on the woodpile.)* Sorry about that.
(The train passes by on the embankment. Saying nothing, his head down, GLASSES also sits down on the woodpile.)

BANDAGES: That's enough, my boy, surely. *(Stands up. As if encouraging him.)* So shall we call it a night?
(GLASSES rises mechanically and staggers away.)

BANDAGES: *(Clinging to GLASSES in an effort to keep up with him.)* You know, I'm a man who hates the sentimental. *(Sadly.)* But how shall I put it? If I had to let you die, then I'd rather I died first. And that's a fact.

—Curtain—

HASEGAWA SHIGURE

RAIN OF ICE

INTRODUCTION

Only seven years younger than Higuchi Ichiyō, Hasegawa Shigure (1879–1941) was Japan's first woman playwright and an indefatigable supporter of women writers. As editor of the magazines *Women's Art* (1923) and its successor, *Shine* (*Kagayaku,* 1934), she helped launch the careers of Okamoto Kanoko (1889–1939), Hirabayashi Taiko (1905–1972), Ozaki Midori (1896–1971), and Sata Ineko (1904–1998), to name just a few. *Women's Art* was the venue for Ueda (Enchi) Fumiko's debut work, a play, as well as Hayashi Fumiko (1904–1951)'s *Diary of a Vagabond* (*Hōrōki*). Shigure may even lay claim to being Japan's first "new woman." Back in 1911, at the first Japanese production of *A Doll House,* critic Ihara Seiseien coined the term when he saw Shigure weeping in the audience.[1]

If Shigure was a "new woman," however, there was much of the old with which she had to contend. The eldest child of Japan's first licensed solicitor, Shigure demonstrated a love of reading and the *kabuki* theatre, to which her father often took her, but her mother thought such bookishness was unbecoming in a woman and arranged for her to go into domestic service after completing

Photo of Hasegawa Shigure courtesy of the Museum of Modern Japanese Literature, Tokyo.

elementary school. (It was common for young women, even those who were well born, to serve as maids in mansions of high-ranking samurai—and by Meiji, the peerage—as a kind of finishing school.) Illness sent her back home, where for a while she studied classical literature under the eminent scholar Sasaki Nobutsuna, but in 1897, at the age of nineteen, a marriage was arranged for her with a wealthy ne'er-do-well whose profligate ways soon ensured his disownment but not, unfortunately, Shigure's divorce from him. It was during this loveless marriage that she wrote her first work, a short story entitled "Embers" (Uzumibi, 1901). Her views on marriage were captured in a later story, "Pale Gray" (Usuzumiiro), published in Hiratsuka Raichō's magazine *The Blue Stocking:* "My bedroom is a jail that enslaves me, locked up by a man with a golden key, with the fine words that 'it's for your protection.' Under the name of 'wife' I am gagged like a monkey so I cannot cry out. Bound hand and foot with invisible chains, I'm forced to endure this unspeakable humiliation."[2] Shigure would eventually leave her husband, but it was some years before she was able to secure a formal divorce from him.

Shigure's literary breakthrough came with a prize-winning play, *Tidal Soundings* (*Kaichōon*, 1905), which also won her recognition from Tsubouchi Shōyō. She would remain associated with Shōyō and his efforts at theatre reform for several years. The *shinpa* theatre staged *Tidal Soundings,* starring Ii Yōhō and Kitamura Rokurō at the Shintomi-za in 1908, but it was the *kabuki* theatre, and Kikugorō VI particularly, who would champion Shigure in the coming decade. A historical play, *The Flower King* (*Hanaōmaru*), was also staged in 1908 at the Kabuki-za, which also staged her *Chastity* (*Misao,* 1910) for a twenty-two-day run in December 1911. As many as forty thousand people came to see this play. Shigure's name was displayed prominently on the billboards, and the theatre sold her photograph along with those of the *kabuki* actors who starred in her play.[3] Toward the end of the Meiji era, Shigure threw herself into writing and publishing about the theatre, founding a society with Kikugorō VI to foster the creation of new dance plays (*buyōgeki*) and the revival of classical dance pieces. She would continue to write dance plays for the *kabuki* until just before her death in 1941.[4] In 1912, she founded the magazine *Play* (*Shibai*), which published translations of Strindberg's *Miss Julie* and Chekhov's *The Cherry Orchard.* Two years later, she (with Kikugorō VI and several others) established the Kyōgen-za production company (Mori Ōgai, Tsubouchi Shōyō, and Natsume Sōseki were on the board of directors), which premiered Ōgai's *Soga Brothers,* Shōyō's *Urashima Tarō: A New Lyric,* Kinoshita Mokutarō's *At the Gate of the Barbarians' Temple* (*Nanbanji monzen*),

Yoshii Isamu's *The Death of Haikaitei Kuraku* (*Haikaitei Kuraku no shi*), and Shigure's dance play *A Kabuki Picture Book* (*Kabuki zōshi*).

For much of the Taishō era, Shigure went into semi-retirement, helping out her parents' business and promoting the career of her new husband, the popular novelist Mikami Otokichi (1891–1944). During this time she published a series of profiles of famous Japanese women, including Higuchi Ichiyō, Kawakami Sadayakko (1871–1946), and Matsui Sumako, which would later be republished in the collection *Lives of Modern Beauties* (*Kindai bijinden*, 1927). As indicated above, in 1923, together with her friend Okada Yachiyo, she founded *Women's Art*, which, together with *Shine*, would publish drama, essays, and fiction by the leading women writers of the day. Enchi Fumiko claimed that *Women's Art* was a woman writer's only support at this time.[5] One of Shigure's last major works, *Old News of Nihonbashi* (*Kyūbun Nihonbashi*, 1935), was a memoir of her native Tokyo neighborhood; it ranks with Osanai Kaoru's *By the Banks of the Great River* (*Okawabata*) for its evocation of Meiji Tokyo.

Born Hasegawa Yasuko, the pen name Shigure came to her when writing her debut work as she watched a cold, late autumn rain (*shigure*) fall.[6] A similar image is conveyed in the title of the play translated here, *Rain of Ice*. The work is dark and starkly naturalistic, a far cry from the colorful *kabuki* historical and dance plays for which she had made a reputation.[7] Shigure claimed that she had grown somewhat frustrated with trying to "put new wine into the old bottle" that was *kabuki*. Indeed, the search for what was a more realistic stage art in the Taishō and early Shōwa eras is reflected in a number of plays by Shigure with contemporary settings, including *One Afternoon* (*Aru hi no gogo*, 1912) and *The Dog* (*Inu*, 1923). These works are written in a modern (albeit Tokyo-inflected) colloquial language. Shigure's involvement with *The Blue Stocking* (which published *One Afternoon*) no doubt was the impetus for creating more realistic drama that addressed issues important to women. Tayo, the heroine of *One Afternoon*, is a young woman who can speak her mind and is not easily fooled by the sweet talk of men. Here, Shigure is able to transcend the social and dramatic conventions that confined her in the historical plays. Inoue Yoshie even credits Shigure for creating modern realism in Japanese drama before writers like Kikuchi Kan, Kume Masao, and Yamamoto Yūzō took up the form.[8]

The focus on society's dregs in both *Rain of Ice* and *The Dog* may reflect a rising interest in the 1920s in proletarian fiction and drama, but the tendency was already seen in *One Afternoon*, which, Inoue Yoshie notes, portrays a lower level of society than that typically addressed in the pages of *The Blue Stocking*, whose readers were generally upper-middle-class women (Tayo and her father,

Senzō, eke out a living repairing wooden clogs on the edge of a farming village).[9] *Rain of Ice* concerns the final hours of an old prostitute, Tamayo, who slips in and out of consciousness. The setting—Shigure makes no attempt to sugarcoat Tamayo's depressing fate—provides an economical dramatic structure for examining her wretched life and her tortured relationships with her only friend, Otoku, and her daughter, Toyoko, who appears to be unwittingly having an affair with a man who may in fact be her own father. Toyoko considers her mother a foul-smelling nuisance—her line, "It stinks in here," opens the play—and she soon leaves her mother to meet her lover. For her part, Otoku may have ulterior motives for her sickbed visit. Two other women, an old servant and a nurse, apparently have their eyes on grabbing what little is left of Tamayo's possessions when she dies. The only trace of sentimentality in the play lies in Tamayo's raving reminiscences of her foreign lover, the "Capitaine." Otherwise, the play is a cold and even cynical, but masterful, portrait of a woman in extremis.

This translation is based on the texts of Hasegawa, *"Kōri no ame,"* in *Nihon gikyoku zenshū,* 36: 451–461, and in *Shigure kyakuhonshū* 1: *Kindai josei sakka seisenshū* 14: 183–207.

Tadokoro Keiko as Tamayo in the Azanai production of *Rain of Ice*, December 2001, Art Space, Osaka. Dir. Yoshizaki Yōko. Photo courtesy of Kuroda Yukiko, Azanai.

Hasegawa Shigure

RAIN OF ICE

FIRST PUBLISHED:
Women's Art, 1926

FIRST PERFORMANCE:
Geijutsu Sōzōkan, Osaka,
December 2001, dir. Yoshizaki Yōko

CHARACTERS
....

TAMAYO, a *woman who, when young*
made a living selling her body but is
now terminally ill
TOYOKO, TAMAYO's *daughter, twenty years old*
OKEI, *a nurse*
OTOKU, TAMAYO's *friend, a café proprietress*
GRANNY, *sixty years old*

(A sick room. At stage center, over a small cupboard next to the tokonoma *are altars to the household gods and buddhas.*[10] *Beside it, an arched doorway. On the right, a round window opening onto a withered garden. To the left, a corridor on the house's perimeter, and beyond the shoji door,* TOYOKO's *room. The shoji for this room is shut. Suspended from the ceiling over the place where* TAMAYO *is lying is a Western-style model sailing ship, about two feet in length. Although rather old and battered, it is well crafted.*

It is some time past eight o'clock in the evening. OKEI *is writing in her log by* TAMAYO's *bedside. The sound of rain.)*

TOYOKO: *(Entering from her room and gazing into the sickroom.)* It stinks in here. The smell is really unbearable! How can you stand staying indoors like this?

OKEI: *(Quietly standing.)* Hush! Madam's just fallen asleep.

TOYOKO: Perfect! Come on, then. Let's go.

OKEI: But it wouldn't be right.

TOYOKO: I've been keeping them waiting.

OKEI: But she's your own mother.

TOYOKO: Oh, yeah. Somebody showed up calling herself my mother.

OKEI: There you go again. You're hopeless! The doctor did warn us, after all.

TOYOKO: *(Somewhat concerned.)* But surely it won't be tonight.

OKEI: Well, with her disease, probably not so soon.

TOYOKO: Really! You're the one who really wanted to come with me! And even if you say you're keeping her company, all you do is sit here. I can't bear another minute breathing in this putrid air. It'll make us all sick. What's the point?

OKEI: It's my job.

TOYOKO: Let Granny take care of her. This isn't anything for a young woman.

OKEI: It can't be helped—I take my job seriously. You shouldn't be saying such things.... To tell the truth, that is an awful smell, though.

TOYOKO: See what I mean? Come on.

OKEI: Shall I, just for a bit? I won't be in the way?

TOYOKO: Oh, please! Don't worry—I'm not going to take you anywhere I don't want you to be.

OKEI: Well, well! *(Rolling her eyes.)* Fine, then! Actually, your mother was in good spirits, saying that old Otoku was coming to see her.

TOYOKO: That's not good. *(Frowning exaggeratedly.)* She's a pest. They'll be saying bad things about me.

OKEI: Don't tell me you're worried about something like that too.

TOYOKO: Forget about it. We shouldn't talk too much. It wouldn't do if she woke up.

OKEI: That's right. *(Tucking in her neck, she follows* TOYOKO, *then stops in front of* TOYOKO's *room.)* Miss Toyoko, shall I get some pocket money? She's stashed it under the quilt.

TOYOKO: That won't be necessary—I've still got some left.

OKEI: But she'll never know now. No matter how often she counts it.... It'd be a waste if Granny got her hands on any of it.

TOYOKO: So you've been dipping into it yourself, have you!

OKEI: Why, of course not! Never! I may not look it, but I'm pure as the driven snow.... Goodness! The smell's got to me as well. Lend me some of your perfume. No sense trying to get too dolled up, but.... Mind if I borrow a jacket? *(Enters* TOYOKO's *room and takes a* haori *from the rack.)* Such flashy tastes you have! A fine daughter, you are. Say something—tell me I look good!

TOYOKO: What a racket you're making! *(Sits at the mirror, trying on a hat, a Western dress.)*

OKEI: Tell me, Toyoko. Your mother's mad about that sailboat of hers. What's all that about, then?

(TOYOKO glances at her.)

OKEI: *(With curiosity mixed with greed.)* I bet there's something inside it.

TOYOKO: How should I know? *(Looks into her eyes as if to try to read her mind.)* Like what? She's stingy with me, but the old woman's got her wrapped around her little finger. That boat is nothing but rubbish. She babbles on about it, saying her first love's sailing on it. When she dies, she says, it'll be a wedding carriage taking her to the spirit world. Nonsense like that.

OKEI: Is that all?

TOYOKO: Yeah! That's all!

OKEI: Strange.

TOYOKO: What's so strange about it? Come on, let's go.

OKEI: Oh, what'll I do? Maybe I'll forget it, after all. It's turned terribly cold—it'd be a real nuisance if it started to snow.

TOYOKO: You greedy witch! That boat's empty. Come when I tell you to come! I'll let you drink all you want. I'll even listen to you tell me all about your lover boy.

OKEI: But he'll be there, too, listening to everything I say—no fun for me sticking around. No way I'm getting drunk. *(Meaningfully.)* Besides, I've got someone very ill to look after.

TOYOKO: Suit yourself, you raccoon.

OKEI: Some daughter you are. I'm impressed.

(TOYOKO pays her no attention but leaves by the door at the end of the corridor at left.)

OKEI: *(Muttering to herself.)* Who cares if she says she doesn't think she's her mother. She's going too far! Even a stranger would feel more love than she does. *(So saying, she gazes at TAMAYO, then goes into TOYOKO's bedroom, turns off the light, then hurriedly follows her out.)*

(GRANNY enters from the door at right and begins to pick up the newspapers and magazines OKEI has left lying around.)

GRANNY: *(Holding her sleeve to her nose and looking at TAMAYO.)* Hasn't she lost a lot of weight, though! I wonder—is it really all right to go off and leave someone at death's door like this? It doesn't seem right. . . . My, but it's gloomy in here! I wish Madam would get here. . . . Could this be a forty-watt bulb? It's awful dark! *(Turns inside. Then, pricking up her ears hopefully.)*

Why, you were here all along? *(Hurriedly goes inside.)*

(The light goes out. In the darkness, one can hear TAMAYO *prattling on deliriously.)*

TAMAYO: Why, don't be silly, young man. Telling me to die and all—committing suicide isn't as easy as you think it is. Forgive me, please.... Now, now! You mustn't go around threatening a girl like me with knives. Now, stop that, I say! *(Silence. Then, changing the tone of her voice and sounding coquettish.)* Stop that, Capitaine! Don't you go pretending it's poison—that's some fine wine, surely. You really are sweet, you know? I know I can rely on you. You're always bringing me the most wonderful presents. Darling? Are you listening to me? You do love me, don't you? Of course, you say. But why did you have to die, then? Even if you did leave me some money, there isn't a penny left now. Capitaine! Capitaine, I'm talking to you! Come make love to me.... Who is that? Whose clammy hand is that? It's you, isn't it? Don't take me with you! Who'd want to die with you, huh?

GRANNY: *(Coming in with* OTOKU *from the door off the corridor.)* Why, the light's gone out. What happened?

OTOKU: The light bulb must have blown. Mind you don't step on her.

GRANNY: I'll go turn on the light in Toyoko's room. *(Fumbling in the dark, goes to open the shoji.)*

TAMAYO: *(Screaming.)* Murderer!

(Shocked, GRANNY *falls to her haunches.* OTOKU *clutches onto the shoji, trembling.)*

OTOKU: Hurry, Granny! The light, the light—

TAMAYO: Ah! Help! Help me, somebody.

OTOKU: Tamayo-san, Tamayo-san. *(Holding onto* GRANNY, *she backs away as she speaks.)*

(The light goes on. TAMAYO *stares at the two.)*

OTOKU: *(Trembling.)* Tamayo-san, you were having a nightmare. *(*TAMAYO's *eyes dart around the room.)* Hurry up, Granny, and turn on the light over there too.

GRANNY: But, ma'am, I'm scared....

OTOKU: Some help you are. As soon as the young ones get back, the place'll feel brighter. It's not like anything really happened. She was just having a bad dream with the lights out—gave us a bit of a shock, that's all.... *(Laughing artificially.)* But I can't say I care for that dirty old sailing ship hanging there. It's filthy. Why did you have to hang up that ugly old thing?

GRANNY: Nobody knew we had it. She made me bring it out when she fell ill.

OTOKU: It's very old, that's for sure. A ship's captain filled it up with presents and gave it to her one Christmas.

GRANNY: Was that the gentleman, I wonder? The one so kind to the missus. Was he her patron?

OTOKU: It used to have blue sails and red sails, didn't it? . . . Was it after the captain died that the sails were changed to white ones?

GRANNY: What are you saying? The sails are black.

OTOKU: Black sails? Don't scare me, Granny! Why, look! They're white, surely!

GRANNY: What? I see. . . . Oh, I hate the thing. It's just like a ghost or something there, floating overhead like that.

OTOKU: Hush! She's waking up. We don't want to worry her. . . . Hello, dear! How are you feeling? A bit better?

TAMAYO: *(Fully awake.)* Why, when did you get here? I had no idea.

OTOKU: *(Prevaricating.)* Well, just now. Of course.

TAMAYO: And you're so busy too. I'm sorry to put you out.

OTOKU: Not at all. Business is slow on a night like this. . . . I heard you wanted to see me for some reason?

TAMAYO: Yes, I've been waiting for you! There's something I want to talk about. *(*GRANNY *gazes at* OTOKU *meaningfully.)* Granny, go get something nice to eat and drink for her. This lady likes to enjoy herself, so I'm afraid it's not much fun for her to sit beside somebody as sick as me.

OTOKU: You're always saying that, aren't you.

TAMAYO: You and I go back a long way, don't we?

OTOKU: You needn't be so formal with me. *(Heavily spraying the air with perfume.)* You don't have to bother, Granny. It's cold tonight, so I had a stiff shot of whisky before I left the house.

TAMAYO: Granny, have a look in the cupboard over there—in the back. I should have a few bottles left. Take them out.

GRANNY: Why, I haven't seen these in ages! There's so many.

TAMAYO: I had them brought out figuring I was really done for this time. *(To* OTOKU.*)* The Capitaine brought them.

OTOKU: You were keeping these old things?

TAMAYO: *(Laughs without replying. Then, nostalgically.)* The Capitaine was so kind to me. I want to go be with him.

OTOKU: *(Dismissively.)* What are you talking about? *(Spelling out the letters on the bottle.)* Vermouth. . . . I bet this is smooth. *(Uncorks the bottle.)*

TAMAYO: He was especially fond of that. Used to hold me tight and give me little sips of it.

OTOKU: Well, well! That's all very lovey-dovey, ain't it? Old's good for wine, but lovers' stories are best when fresh. Tell me about one of your more recent conquests.

TAMAYO: There ain't nobody.

OTOKU: You're not fooling me. I know there's somebody. No sense getting sick.

TAMAYO: But I couldn't help it. I was lonely. I didn't see no point in living.

OTOKU: That's true for us both. Were you lonely 'cause you let Toyoko's father get away? *(TAMAYO shakes her head.)* No? So it was the Capitaine, was it? Give me a break! It's been twenty-five years since he was your patron, and a bloody barbarian he was too. What would the man who knocked you up think if he found out?

TAMAYO: *(Coldly.)* How the hell am I supposed to know whose child Toyoko is?

OTOKU: You're the mother.

TAMAYO: Of course. But you know I didn't want the child.

OTOKU: *(Sighing faintly.)* So much for the girl being good to her mother, I guess.

TAMAYO: You say that, but the fact is, I do love her. She's the only one I care about now. . . . *(Unable to continue, sobs.)* Oh, I've been such a sinful woman!

OTOKU: *(Curtly.)* True enough, neither of us has been innocent, exactly. But we've not been all that bad.

TAMAYO: *(Belying her illness, sharply.)* I know all about how she carries on, but I'm too ashamed of myself to scold the girl. If there's one thing that won't let me go to my grave in peace, it's that I don't know who her father is. It's tearing me up inside. When I think that's the reason she's such a sullen child, my heart feels like it'll burst. If ever she asked me, I don't know what I'd tell her. Just looking at her scares me.

OTOKU: Now settle down. You'll only make yourself sicker getting yourself all upset like that. Settle down. Toyo-chan's a smart girl; she'll never ask you that. She's all too aware of how you made your living, so she'd never say anything to hurt you intentionally.

TAMAYO: That's not true. She's sure to ask me when it's my time. . . . And when she does, . . . when she does, what on earth am I going to tell her?

OTOKU: *(Looking slightly malicious.)* To tell you the truth, I don't know why, but it's been bothering me too. Time and again I've been on the verge of asking you, but I just couldn't bring myself to do it. The one you're worried about is that Yasuda-san, right? (TAMAYO's *eyes bore into* OTOKU, *who is startled.*) Isn't that so?

(TAMAYO's *face blanches. She stares at* OTOKU *with vacant eyes and trembles.*)

OTOKU: *(Sighing.)* Is that so? You know, he hasn't the faintest idea? He's gone all sweet on the girl, saying stuff like Toyo-chan looks just like Tamayo-san did when she was in her prime. You got to be kidding, I thought. . . . Toyo-chan won't tell him her mother's name—you know how she looks like a fine young lady from an upstanding family—he's got no idea you're her mother. But it's all very innocent, you know. So don't fret, you needn't worry at all. Toyo-chan would never do anything stupid, no matter how besotted the man was. . . .

TAMAYO: *(Groaning.)* I'll go see him.

OTOKU: Don't be silly. I tell you what, though. What say I tell the two myself? Don't you worry, now.

TAMAYO: *(Clutching tightly to* OTOKU's *hand.)* This is dreadful.

OTOKU: Are you telling me you're sure of this? (TAMAYO *doesn't respond.*) If this is all a tempest in a teapot, you'll be the fool. If she knew he was an old "friend" of yours, she'd think you'd get jealous, and then her going out with him would be like pouring oil on the fire. If that was the case, she might even fall for a guy she doesn't like just for spite. Toyo-chan's not the only one—lots of girls her age are full of cheek and act stronger than they really are.

TAMAYO: You don't know. Her character's just like his in that respect. What'll I do? If that happened, she'd go straight to hell.

OTOKU: Now, stop that! You really mustn't get yourself so worked up! If you start worrying about stuff like that, there'll be no end to it. You've gone soft. You'd never have been able to do what we did for a living if you'd started out like that. Our customers too—nobody ever gave a damn if we got knocked up and got rid of the kid. They all knew from the get-go how we dealt with it.

TAMAYO: *(Covering her ears.)* The Capitaine's making me pay for all this. I should've gone to my grave without ever giving birth to the girl.

OTOKU: *(Laughing bitterly.)* Suit yourself! First you become a whore, then you want to be a good mother, so it's no wonder you're suffering. Besides, you weren't exactly nice to that captain either, were you?

TAMAYO: You know, he was so strong he could hold me in his arms and carry me.

OTOKU: *(Sarcastically.)* As if he was the only man who ever held you in his arms.

TAMAYO: If only I'd sailed away with him on that steamship. It wouldn't have sunk, and he'd never have drowned.

OTOKU: *(Stretching.)* Say what you like, then. I put up listening to you 'cause I thought you were sick, but this is the limit. I'll say one thing, though—you never loved the captain. I was the one who was really crazy about him.

TAMAYO: You always had a nasty habit of wanting to grab what belonged to somebody else, with those eyes you make and your sexy walk. And not only men. You even fooled me. Took my money, even my telephone away. . . .

OTOKU: After all these years, you're still jealous? That's an old grudge. . . . Are you all right?

TAMAYO: You'd show up and trick anybody that had anything to do with me. Finally I figured it out. When I asked you if I should go with the Capitaine, you were the one who stopped me. You were the one who turned Mr. Yasuda off me. And it was your idea to set up Toyo-chan with Yasuda. You've had it in for me since way back.

OTOKU: I'm asking you, are you all right, Tamayo?

TAMAYO: And I told you everything, thinking you were my only friend. It's all because of you my life has gone to hell.

OTOKU: *(Holding back her rage.)* Really, it won't do you any good talking like that. If your life has gone to the dogs, you've got only your own bloody-mindedness to blame. Who enjoys being hated? I don't like saying this, but nobody would come visit a stink-hole like this if they didn't have to. I can stand it because I'm your friend, so wise up. If you're going to hate me and say the most spiteful things to my face like this, I've had enough.

TAMAYO: I might have known it. I can see through that kindness of yours. You thought I might leave you something, didn't you? When you realized all I was worth was what's here, well, you started regretting you'd ever been nice to me at all.

OTOKU: You really amaze me. I'd never have taken you for such a bitch. I was a fool to think anything else. You can beg me all you like now 'cause I'm never going to come bother you again.

TAMAYO: Please don't. It was your meddling that screwed up my life in the first place.

OTOKU: Say what you like. You're too pigheaded and greedy to die.

TAMAYO: That's right! I won't die! I'll turn myself into a demon and get you! *(Terrified by her own babbling.)*

OTOKU: *(Sits there, horrified, then bursts into tears.)* I've never met a woman with a tongue as sharp as yours. I'm willing to put up with it because you're ill, but you've really gone too far. When we were young, we were so close sometimes we hated each other, but there ain't that many been friends as long as we have. I didn't have any family dear to me, and who did you have to look after you? So I thought I was doing you a favor by coming here to tend to you at death's door like this, and that's something, coming from a tough old coot like me! But you've gone too far this time.

TAMAYO: What are you going on about? You're still trying to pull one over on me with that glib tongue of yours. *(But then becoming weak.)* It's nothing I didn't know already. . . . You know you're the only one in this world I can rely on, but even so, you're just mocking me, making an old friend on her deathbed mad. . . .

OTOKU: Mocking you? . . . Hardly. I'll be frank with you—neither of us knows when we'll part. . . . So let's be friends, eh? Don't leave any hard feelings behind. *(TAMAYO says nothing.)* You didn't used to be so cold. Did you, Tamayo? *(TAMAYO stares at her and laughs weakly.)* Do you really think I tried to take your man away from you? That's not so. It's just I hated the idea there was somebody you loved more than me. *(TAMAYO laughs again; her voice is weak.)* If you don't want me here, I'll go. *(Begins to leave.)*

TAMAYO: *(Calling after her.)* Hey! You're leaving me? Bitch. Didn't I say I had something to ask you? Why the hell did you come, anyway?

OTOKU: I'll go look for Toyo-chan. I won't be long.

TAMAYO: Don't throw a fit—I'm not going to die just yet, and I'm not going to read you my last will and testament either. I just want to wipe my face. Go get me some hot water.

OTOKU: *(Relieved.)* Was that all? I'll bring some in a sec. *(She goes out by the arched doorway.)*

TAMAYO: *(Slips into a delirium and begins babbling again.)* What a fine day it is! The sky's so bright I bet the sea's nice and calm. . . . Look! There, on the horizon, between the blue of the sky and the sea's deep indigo, you can see white sails. That's my ship! He's come for me. I'd better go wash my hair.

OTOKU: *(Helped by* GRANNY, *brings in a washbasin filled with hot water. To* GRANNY.) Look at her! Why, aren't you in fine form today!

TAMAYO: *(Babbling.)* Otoku-san, go look out the window. Can you see a ship with white sails? It's come for me.

OTOKU: Huh?

TAMAYO: What a fine day it is! See how clear it is to the west.

OTOKU: *(To* GRANNY, *under her breath.)* What's she talking about? It's freezing rain outside.

GRANNY: *(Also keeping her voice down.)* She's not acting right this evening, is she?

OTOKU: *(Speaking up.)* Tamayo-san, we brought some hot water for you.

TAMAYO: *(Reviving.)* Ah, thanks. The weather was so fine, I felt so good, I thought I'd wash my hair.

OTOKU: Silly, let me wipe your face.

TAMAYO: Let me wash just my hands, then. Add a bit of alcohol. And a sprinkle of perfume as well. . . . I should clip my nails, at least. Look how long they've got! . . . Let me apply some nail polish.

GRANNY: *(To* OTOKU.*)* Shall I get a brighter lamp, ma'am?

OTOKU: *(Clipping her nails.)* If you have one.

*(*GRANNY *turns on a lamp with a green shade.)*

TAMAYO: Cancer of the womb—maybe I got what I deserved. Still, I don't think it's that. . . . The weather's so fine today.

OTOKU: *(Looking away sadly.)* You'll be better in no time.

TAMAYO: Granny, bring my mirror stand. Before I go aboard, I want to go see Yasuda. *(To* OTOKU.*)* I'm going to deal with that smug bastard myself. I couldn't bear it if he ever wronged Toyoko. I just hope he isn't. . . .

OTOKU: *(Darkly.)* Bad news all round, if you ask me.

TAMAYO: *(Beside herself with despair.)* Otoku-san, the girl's all right, isn't she?

OTOKU: *(Stony-faced.)* Sure.

TAMAYO: You're certain.

OTOKU: *(Says nothing.)*

TAMAYO: *(Pause. Then holds out her hand.)* My face paint. *(Applies her makeup.)* *(*OTOKU *stands up, no longer able to bear it.)*

GRANNY: Where are you going? If it's Toyoko you want, I'll go find her.

OTOKU: *(To herself.)* Once it's done, you can't take it back.

GRANNY: But I can't stay here by myself.

OTOKU: I'll be right back. It's even getting to me. I won't be long. *(Leaves.)*

TAMAYO: *(To* GRANNY, *who is following* OTOKU *out.)* Granny, show me the mirror.

GRANNY: *(A long pause.)* Why, aren't you all dolled up now.

TAMAYO: It's been a while, hasn't it? Go open the window there, Granny.

GRANNY: But, ma'am! It's freezing rain and sleet.

TAMAYO: Surely not. The weather's beautiful. Go open the window and show me. . . . Not that black hole; open the brighter one.

GRANNY: *(On the verge of tears.)* This is the window. It's night out now and pitch dark.

TAMAYO: Don't lie to me. *(Slipping off the cushions on which she was resting and addressing the ship overhead.)* Why, it's a fine day, isn't it? Such calm seas! . . . Granny, I'm sailing away today, you know.

*(*GRANNY *covers* TAMAYO *up; then, unable to take any more, backs away and flees inside. The light goes out. Only the green lamp is still on.)*

TAMAYO: *(Delirious.)* Why, Capitaine, come in! It's so good to see you! All that money you left me—gone for my sickness. That's why I thought I'd go to you. You know, I'm all alone, and you're the only one I remember. I want you. . . . No! Yasuda was just a little mistake. . . . I'm worried about Toyoko, though. . . . Oh, what'll I do? Toyoko knows nothing. What if she has his child? That'd be the same as giving birth to her own brother! You men are all sex fiends. We aren't mothers or daughters to you—just women. . . . What? Don't stop me. I'll go see for myself. I couldn't bear it if that bastard had his way with her. Toyoko's my child! She's my kid, not his. Nobody can blame her. Still, I worry 'cause she doesn't have a father. . . . Haven't you made my life hell enough already? Is that Yasuda there? If Toyoko's your child, what do you want with her? Give Toyoko back to me! Give her back!

*(*GRANNY *looks in, roused by* TAMAYO's *screams. Seeing that all is calm again, she retreats back inside. The sound of sleet falling.* OTOKU *and* OKEI *return, followed by* GRANNY *on their heels.)*

GRANNY: *(Coming down the corridor.)* Didn't Miss Toyoko come back with you?

OTOKU: She left Okei behind. . . . Why, the light's gone out again! I'll go turn on the one in the other room. *(Followed by* GRANNY, *she goes into* TOYOKO's *room.)*

OKEI: *(Brings the lamp closer to* TAMAYO, *then cries out.)* Come quick! *(Still groping for the light,* OTOKU *and* GRANNY *stand petrified.)* Call a doctor, quick! Hurry! *(Frantically feeling* TAMAYO's *body.)* It's too late. Too late.

GRANNY: *(Trembling, she clasps her hands in prayer and whispers to* OTOKU.) Keep your wits about you, ma'am. That nurse has her eye on the sailing ship.

*(*OTOKU, *weeping, nods.)*

—Curtain—

TANAKA CHIKAO

················

MAMA

INTRODUCTION

Known best for his postwar dramas, Tanaka Chikao's (1905–1995) debut play, *Mama*, is a remarkably accomplished work.[1] The playwright Tsujimura Sumiko—she would marry Tanaka in 1934—saw the premiere and recalled: "What impressed me was how the Japanese language could be conveyed so vividly. Each and every line was thrillingly dramatic. There was no plot to speak of, but I discovered what I had never encountered before: that the love of a mother and child could be so intensely portrayed, almost exclusively through their dialogue. And all who saw the play felt the same."[2]

Tanaka was a protégé of Kishida Kunio, and, like Kishida, he was a brilliant student of French dialogue and dramaturgy. In 1927, while still a student of French literature at Keiō University, he joined the New Theatre Research Institute (Shingeki Kenkyūsho), which had been established by Kishida, Iwata Toyoo, and others. In 1931, he became a staff writer for *Playwriting*, serializing a translation of Léon Brémont's *L'Art de Dire*. *Mama* was Tanaka's first play. The strong cast included Tamura Akiko, who played the title role; Nakamura Nobuo as the son (1908–1991; like Sugimura, he was a fixture

---

Photo of Tanaka Chikao courtesy of the Tsubouchi Memorial Theatre Museum, Waseda University.

206

in Ozu films and was later to become Betsuyaku Minoru's favorite actor); Horikoshi Setsuko as the daughter, Mineko; and Sugimura Haruko as Mrs. Munakata. Senda Koreya's brother, Itō Kisaku (1899–1967), designed the set. The Tsukiji-za practice was to stage a new production once every month for a run of three to five days. *Mama* played only three days, but it was a hit. The Tsukiji-za revived it the following year. It then toured the Osaka region; NHK (then Japan's only radio network) broadcast a studio recording of the play. The play was a perfect collaboration between a magazine devoted to new drama and a theatre company whose express purpose, like its precursor, the Tsukiji Little Theatre, was the creation of modern theatre in Japan.

The story is deceptively simple: Ogura Saka, a widow from Shimabara in Kyushu, has had to struggle to raise her two children, Eiichirō and Mineko, on her own in Tokyo. Eiichirō is in his final year at university, and it is the night before his second job interview with a newspaper company. His little sister, Mineko, is a high school student. Saka is concerned about her son's prospects, but Eiichirō seems strangely indifferent. In fact, he has already accepted a position in a bank in Nagoya, something Saka learns only later when a boy and his mother, Mrs. Munakata, arrive unexpectedly at their door to thank Eiichirō for teaching her son for the past four years. Saka is shocked that her son has told these strangers but kept the truth from her. She decides to follow him to Nagoya and leave her daughter in lodgings in Tokyo.

The work, which many critics have called the original "home drama" (domestic soap opera, a popular genre on Japanese television), is a remarkably deft portrayal of an overprotective mother and a resentful son eager to strike off on his own—a theme that still resonates, and not just with Japanese audiences. At the same time, however, the play's balanced portrayal of each character and its wry humor avoid any trace of melodrama or sentimentalism so characteristic of this genre. In both theme and style, the play is as fresh today as when it was first written. Tanaka's skill in writing dialogue and character is remarkable in such an early work. Oyama Isao notes the following:

> The charm of Tanaka Chikao's works during this [prewar] period lies chiefly in their dialogue. His language is lively, witty, and well articulated; every twist and turn of his characters' psychology is brilliantly portrayed with penetrating insight. *Mama* is a classic example of this, and in dramatizing so skillfully an ordinary day in the life of the most ordinary sort of people, it displays a fresh appeal that the more schematic and ideologically oriented proletarian plays of that time were incapable of portraying.[3]

In such postwar works as *Education* (*Kyōiku*, 1954) and *The Head of Mary* (*Maria no kubi*, 1959), Tanaka would use highly figurative and poetic language to tackle difficult philosophical and metaphysical problems.[4] Here, however, his gaze is level and quotidian, his language resolutely realistic. The only trace of the author's Christianity is a portrait of Christ on the wall, but this is juxtaposed with the banal, a photograph of an actress and a rugby poster. The image of Christ no doubt refers to the mother's birthplace, Shimabara, and Saka's conflicted feelings toward this historically Christian region of Japan are an important element in the play, but she is more inclined to pray for her son's success at a Shinto shrine than in a church. If the sacred is being juxtaposed with the profane here, it is the latter that is dominant. It is enough, however, that Tanaka portrays with the skill he does the dynamics of family relationships—the bond (sometimes in this play it seems forged in iron) between mother and son is at the heart of this play—but he is equally good at limning the affectionate rivalry between brother and sister, as well as Saka's nastier jealousy toward her daughter. This is, after all, the fodder of Freud's family romance, the sort of material that makes us who we are.

Just as the family is a master trope for examining issues of modern selfhood, it is also a synecdoche of society itself; it is the lens through which we are able to project ourselves upon the world. There are problems here, Tanaka tells us, and inasmuch as the family is a metaphor, perhaps metaphysics are at work here as well. Tanaka himself admitted that women represented for him both a spiritual stumbling block and a challenge. In an interview he confessed that "man's ego is for him the absolute. He thinks that he alone is absolute. Yet there are obstacles to this belief. One is woman."[5] Tanaka thus regarded women as either the object of spirituality (the Virgin Mary) or agents of an ego-erasing sexuality. He admitted that his prewar plays had oscillated between "woman-hating" works and "woman-worshipping" works. Critic Abe Itaru has noted that for Tanaka, "Women both exist in time and eternally transcend its influence. . . . It is as if Tanaka wished to say that women possess no subjectivity."[6] At center in this play is the primal relationship between a man and a woman, and it is essentially the mother's lack of subjectivity that is the problem.

Kikuchi Kan's play *Father Returns* focused on how the prodigal father's return stirred up the elder son's resentment. Here, the father is long dead, and Saka has assumed what feminist Ueno Chizuko has called a "transvestite patriarchy": she is a woman with no identity of her own.[7] She lives vicariously through her son; her daughter stands in the way of her almost sexual connection with Eiichirō. The play focuses on a time of peak anxiety for her: her elder brother from back home has just left after a stay with them that stirred up uncomfortable feelings of how far she and her children have come down in the world. At the same time, Eiichirō is preparing to graduate from college and join the workforce, becoming the head of the family—that is, assuming the family will stay together—but he is eager to escape the maternal embrace. Mineko mentions to her mother that Eiichirō had expressed an interest in moving out—most of his friends live on their own—and she herself betrays a naïve and romantic notion of the pleasures of independence. When Saka asks her who would wash her socks, cook her dinner, and do her dishes, Mineko quickly loses interest in this fantasy—for the time being, the comforts of family life make the responsibility of independence seem too burdensome—but her mother turns the tables on her by proposing at the end of the play to abandon her in order to set up a cozier domestic arrangement with her brother in Nagoya, something neither of the children want. The play thus builds on the tension created by Saka's anxiety and ignorance of her son's plans, and when this tension is released by the revelation that her son means to go to Nagoya, the play concludes with a new cycle of tension created by her decision to accompany him.[8] Saka masks her selfishness in the form of maternal self-sacrifice; her treatment of her son is suffocating and that of her daughter, callous. Yet she is no monster; Tanaka portrays her with considerable wit and affection. We may not completely sympathize with her, but we can understand her.

The Japanese text can be found in Tanaka, *"Ofukuro,"* in *Tanaka Chikao gikyoku zenshū* 1:7–55.

Horigoshi Setsuko as Mineko, Tamura Akiko as Mother, and Narumi Shirō as Eiichirō (left to right) in *Mama*, Mitsukoshi Theatre production, Tokyo, February 1951. Photo courtesy of the Tsubouchi Memorial Theatre Museum, Waseda University.

TANAKA CHIKAO

MAMA

FIRST PUBLISHED:
Playwriting, March 1933

FIRST PERFORMANCE:
Tsukiji-za, June 1933,
dir. Kawaguchi Kazurō.

CHARACTERS

· · · · · · · · · · · · · · · ·

SAKA (Mrs. Ogura), *the mother*
EIICHIRŌ, *her son*
MINEKO, *her daughter*
TEIKO, *a girl next door*
MRS. MUNAKATA
RYŌ, *her son*
A MAN

(A six-mat living room at stage left and, at stage right, a four-and-a-half-mat sitting room. There is a low shoji window upstage center in the living room; to its left is a table and to its right a desk. On the wall over the desk is a portrait of Christ on the Mount and a bromide of an actress. The lamp on the table is lit, and there EIICHIRŌ *is studying, his back to the audience. On the wall on this side hangs a rugby poster. In the center of the room is a* kotatsu.⁹ *Wearing back to front a jacket instead of the tunic of her school uniform,* MINEKO *has dozed off, lying half buried in the* kotatsu, *face up, with an English reader under her nose.* SAKA *sits in the sitting room, absorbed in her sewing. The sliding door dividing the sitting room from the living room is half open but completely prevents one from seeing into the next room. The entranceway is off to the left of the living room; to the right of the sitting room, there is a kitchen. It is a winter night. Far off are heard the wooden clappers of the night watchman.)*

TEIKO: *(Offstage.)* Mine-chan!
MAN: *(Offstage.)* Hello?
TEIKO: Huh?
MAN: Can I cut through this way?
TEIKO: No.

MAN: Really? *(His voice trails off.)*

TEIKO: Mine-chan!

EIICHIRŌ: *(Looking over.)* Hey, Teiko's calling you. *(There is no reply. He gets up and opens the shoji. A view of a little shrine on the other side of a small garden; the moonlight casts its roof in silhouette.* TEIKO *is standing in the alleyway that divides the garden from the shrine, but we cannot see her.)* She's asleep. Dead to the world.

*(*MINEKO *sleepily opens her eyes, then falls asleep again.)*

TEIKO: Why, it's you, Eiichi.

EIICHIRŌ: What's up?

TEIKO: Uh, there's something I don't quite get. *(She sounds bashful.)*

EIICHIRŌ: What? English?

SAKA: Why don't you teach her?

EIICHIRŌ: *(Turning toward the next room.)* I'm busy right now.

SAKA: No, you're not.

TEIKO: In that case, I'll drop by first thing tomorrow.

EIICHIRŌ: That so?

SAKA: First thing tomorrow? She'll be asleep, Teiko. *(So she says, but can* TEIKO *hear her?)*

TEIKO: Uh, your exam's tomorrow, isn't it, Eiichi?

EIICHIRŌ: I'm gonna fail.

TEIKO: No, you're not. You'll pass, I'm sure. And then, finally, you'll become a "journalist." That's swell.

EIICHIRŌ: You must be cold. Say hi to your mother. G'night. . . . *(He closes the shoji and goes back to his seat.)*

TEIKO: Good night. *(Her voice trails off.)*

SAKA: Do you have to be so rude to her, Eiichi? *(Pause.)* Mine-chan. *(No reply.)* Mine-chan.

MINEKO: Uh?

SAKA: You fell asleep. Again.

MINEKO: *(Surprisingly clearly.)* No, I didn't. I was studying.

(Pause. EIICHIRŌ *flops back in his chair, as if to show how tired he is.)*

SAKA: Mine-chan. . . . *(No reply, as usual.)* Mine-chan!

MINEKO: Mhn.

SAKA: You fell asleep again.

MINEKO: I told you I was studying. Leave me alone! *(Pulls the quilt up over her chest. A long pause.)*

SAKA: Mi . . . ne . . . chan! . . . Mi . . . ne . . . ko. Wake her up, Eiichi. . . . Eiichi.

EIICHIRŌ: She'll get up. If you leave her be.

SAKA: When it's twelve, you mean.

EIICHIRŌ: Yeah.

SAKA: I'll be asleep by then. She's a strange kid. She eats, then crawls into the *kotatsu* and dozes off. When she wakes, it's the middle of the night. Then she's up reading again.

EIICHIRŌ: She can't help it if she's sleepy. She's going full throttle all day, playing.

SAKA: She's got exams to prepare for. What to do with the girl? But I hate to wake her when I see her fast asleep like that. . . . What're you up to, anyway?

EIICHIRŌ: Can't I smoke if I like? It's not me who's sleeping, Ma.

SAKA: Well, I should hope not. *(Pause.)* You know, Eiichi. For her sake, you'd better get tougher on her. *(EIICHIRŌ doesn't reply.)* If we let her do as she pleases, who knows how she'll turn out? *(EIICHIRŌ doesn't reply.)* And you should behave more like a big brother. *(EIICHIRŌ grunts in a noncommittal fashion.)* Why, this morning too, she slept in till 8:35. Then she got in a big huff, saying I was to blame. Dashed out leaving her bowl and chopsticks on the table for me to wash. I don't care how fast she can run—of course she was going to be exhausted. And the same all over again, every night. Won't wash even her own dishes but makes her mother do everything. Dumps her school sewing on me too. And then she gets all uppity. . . .

EIICHIRŌ: You don't have to get so worked up about it.

SAKA: She made me so mad, just now I wanted to bawl her out. *(Suddenly lowering her voice.)* You know, the other day when I got mad, the woman next door laughed and said I was a real witch. . . . Is my voice so loud, I wonder?

EIICHIRŌ: Loud enough to curdle the milk. When you're mad, Ma.

SAKA: Sometimes I think it'd be so much better if I could get mad at you. *(EIICHIRŌ says nothing.)* When I think how much better that'd make me feel. . . .

EIICHIRŌ: So, why don't you? Give it a try.

SAKA: *(Laughing.)* Why. . . . All I said was, if I could get mad. . . .

EIICHIRŌ: You'd really like to, wouldn't you? Really let me have it. It's bugging you something awful, isn't it? I know.

SAKA: You're a good boy, you are. *(Silence.)* The weirdest hats are in fashion these days. Mineko has started to bug me again.

EIICHIRŌ: Can you be quiet for a second?

SAKA: Mineko keeps saying, buy me that hat! Buy that one!

EIICHIRŌ: You bought her one just a while back, didn't you? The felt one.

SAKA: Wanted another, she said. Or something like it. You know, the kind with a string sticking out the top?

EIICHIRŌ: You mean a beret.

SAKA: Yes. And not a cheap one neither, she said.

EIICHIRŌ: I really detest those hats. Hunters in Europe used to wear them. Don't buy her one.

SAKA: That's why I told her to wait till April. Your brother will get himself a job for a newspaper and be drawing a salary. . . .

EIICHIRŌ: Don't joke around, Ma. It isn't as easy as all that. She sure is trouble, that girl.

SAKA: Okay, okay. I'll buy her one. Tomorrow if she likes.

EIICHIRŌ: In that case, you can buy me something too. How 'bout an overcoat?

SAKA: No way! Buy your own.

EIICHIRŌ: So did something happen with the hat you bought her, then?

SAKA: That's right. Said she wanted to alter it, so she cut it all up. Just bought it for her, too.

EIICHIRŌ: Just like Balzac's Cousin Bette, that girl. I got it—she figured a beret wouldn't take much to make.

SAKA: If her friends are wearing one, she wants one too. Wasn't it Mr. Seki's little sister who started wearing them?

EIICHIRŌ: Mr. Seki's little sister—she's turned into a real looker, hasn't she? Finally mastered makeup, it seems. Mineko will want to do the same pretty soon.

SAKA: Well, her mother won't let her. I don't care what she says, she's still a schoolgirl. She ought be like the girl next door. But, you know, Eiichi. I couldn't help notice, but the girl's got a lot of facial hair. Teiko. And her eyebrows grow into each other like a Neanderthal's. She really ought to pluck them.

EIICHIRŌ: It's because Seki's mother is so fashionable.

SAKA: Indeed, quite the clotheshorse. I. . . .

EIICHIRŌ: You've met her?

SAKA: *(Flustered.)* No . . . er, that's what I heard. From Mineko. She said you'd think she was only thirty-four or -five.

EIICHIRŌ: You gotta be joking.

SAKA: And what about Mr. Seki? When he gets out of school?

EIICHIRŌ: He'll probably stay put. In school, that is.

SAKA: His house is right by Meiji Shrine, isn't it.

EIICHIRŌ: Yeah, not three blocks away.

SAKA: It's further than that, surely.

EIICHIRŌ: No, it isn't.

SAKA: It is.

EIICHIRŌ: You've been there, then, have you, Ma?

SAKA: No, but that's what Mineko said. And what about Mr. Inoue? The tall fellow?

EIICHIRŌ: Mitsui Bank. His dad's on the board.

SAKA: Ain't it nice coming from a good family? How come your friends are all rich kids? You're the only one who isn't. . . . What I can't figure out is, they all seem to get along with you just fine, even if you are so gruff and grumpy all the time.

EIICHIRŌ: Give me a break!

SAKA: Who's the one going to be adopted?[10]

EIICHIRŌ: Kanbara. You've asked a thousand times already.

SAKA: Ah! They're all getting set up. The only one left is . . . you. Hope things go well for you tomorrow. . . . They will, won't they, Ei-san? I got a feeling I won't be able to sleep tonight. (EIICHIRŌ *makes a point of turning around to reply, then stops.*) I put in a good word for you this morning, I did, Eiichi.

EIICHIRŌ: What?

SAKA: I said a prayer at Meiji Shrine. Took the long way there. Was it ever cold!

EIICHIRŌ: What! Why?

SAKA: Why? For you, silly. So's you'll pass your exam. "Please, God, give my boy a good job," I prayed.

EIICHIRŌ: A paragon of motherhood, saying a prayer for her son!

SAKA: Of course. I got up first thing, before you two knew anything about it, and when the light of the sun flooded in from the east, I clasped my hands and bowed my head.

EIICHIRŌ: You've been doing that ever since you were little, I bet.

SAKA: A day hasn't passed I haven't prayed above all for you and Mineko.

EIICHIRŌ: I know already.

SAKA: And then, at nighttime . . . what I mean is, at night . . . I go to bed and my mind gets to thinking, "What if? What if something was to happen?" I've done all I can but still feel in my bones I haven't done enough. I wear myself out, my mind goes blank, and then. . . .

EIICHIRŌ: And then you fall asleep?

SAKA: Uh uh. . . . *(Sighs.)* Your mother's nowhere near as strong as she used to be.

EIICHIRŌ: Ah. Time then for you to devote yourself to the gods and buddhas, I guess. Like everybody else.

SAKA: Are you trying to make your mother an old woman before her time?

EIICHIRŌ: Not exactly. But it might be a comfort for you.

SAKA: Your mother hates what you call "comfort."

EIICHIRŌ: You mean to say, then, that you enjoy worrying about us kids. No thanks, Ma. When I see you worrying, it makes me feel like I'm doing something to make you worry about me, even when I'm not. I'd rather you didn't.

(SAKA takes a small talisman out of her wallet, walks over to where EIICHIRŌ is seated, and, without saying anything, throws it down in front of him.)

EIICHIRŌ: Whoa! What's this? Ma!

SAKA: See for yourself. Stick it on the wall. There. *(Returns to her spot.)* You'll find out.

EIICHIRŌ: *(Looking at the talisman.)* You can't fool me, Ma. This is from the Hikawa Shrine.[11] I thought you were acting strange. Now I know.

SAKA: What?

EIICHIRŌ: You went to see Mr. Seki today, didn't you. *(SAKA says nothing.)* Didn't you? After all I told you.

SAKA: What else could I do? I didn't have a choice, did I?

EIICHIRŌ: That's all right. I'll forgive you. You can't tell a lie, can you, Ma? You always do something to give it away. How can I get mad at you?

SAKA: Mr. Seki's father's still young, isn't he? He was just on his way out but was good enough to invite me in for a while. I asked him to be nice tomorrow. I told him, Eiichi told me not to ask him, but I came anyway without telling you 'cause I was worried, came to ask him to be good to you, and he said, "Well, I'm sure there won't be any problem." . . . Then he invited me in, offered me lunch, but if they served some fancy Western stuff, I wouldn't know how to eat it, so I made excuses and fled. His wife makes herself look so young, too. Then, just when I was at the front door, ready to make a break for it, suddenly behind me I hear Mrs. Seki calling me, "Mrs. Ogura, Mrs. Ogura." Put me on my toes, let me tell you. Says, you mustn't call him "Eiichi" all the time in front of others. Call him "my boy." You're my own son, so I can call you what I like, can't I? As if I needed her advice. But folks is always like that, I guess.

EIICHIRŌ: Especially when you go traipsing off to places you've got no business going.

SAKA: Well, I happen to think it's perfectly reasonable asking a close friend's father for a favor.

EIICHIRŌ: It's because he's a close friend you can't.

SAKA: Surely it's the other way 'round. . . . You're not—what?—embarrassed, are you?

EIICHIRŌ: Enough already.

SAKA: You are.

EIICHIRŌ: *(Getting angry.)* I said enough already! *(Pause.)* Ma.

SAKA: Yes?

EIICHIRŌ: I'm not going to the interview tomorrow.

SAKA: There you go again, doing it just to spite me.

EIICHIRŌ: In any case, it'd be no use my going. . . . I don't want them to think I haven't got what it takes. I know it'd be no use; that's why it's a waste of my time.

SAKA: You know? How do you know?

EIICHIRŌ: 'Cause that's the way it is. Favoritism or money buys you a job. All said and done.

SAKA: That's the way it used to be. But nowadays. . . .

EIICHIRŌ: That's what everybody says. Especially with that company. You say there's no favoritism, but look at you, you go off crying to Mr. Seki. . . .

SAKA: *(Offended.)* Who said I did any crying?

EIICHIRŌ: Maybe you didn't literally cry, but still, you're relying on connections, aren't you? Besides, Ma, Mr. Seki may be a section chief, but he's the section chief of the advertising department. He's the last person you'd want to go to for help in getting a job in that company.

SAKA: Well, he's better than nothing. You think too much. Why not give it a try? Can't hurt.

EIICHIRŌ: Since I know from the start it's no use, what'd be the point of my wasting my time and train fare going there? They ask all sorts of ridiculous questions, like how many steps did you climb to get to the office that morning. The long and short of it is I'd gag on their stupid mind games and be driven off, tail between my legs.

SAKA: And what's the matter with that? A little fun won't hurt you. Nothing ventured, nothing gained.

EIICHIRŌ: So you say, and you can say it all you like, but I've got nothing to gain by going.

SAKA: Nothing to gain, nothing to gain—you'll gain nothing by not going. Anyways, please try and go. Listen to your mother.

EIICHIRŌ: Haven't I told you? I'm not going.

SAKA: You're a stubborn boy. If you'd gone and then failed, maybe you could say what you said. . . .

EIICHIRŌ: You don't get it, do you? Just consider—for the seven who are going to be picked, close to six hundred have already shown up. Hm? Do you think they're going to make their decisions based on what somebody's really worth, Ma? People's brains aren't that different, you know. It's all about how good the company is at fooling you.

SAKA: Saying such a thing's a crying shame, surely. Of the whole lot you mentioned, maybe eighty people will be left, right? So, for you, there's still some. . . .

EIICHIRŌ: That's what I hate about all this! Forget the "maybe there's still some. . . ."—I want people to recognize my real worth. Otherwise. . . .

SAKA: You don't want to be hired. That's the stuff! So you'll wait till they come to you, bowing and scraping? Hah! You think anybody these days is going to be so nice? *(EIICHIRŌ says nothing.)* So how come you took the exam in the first place? Spending all that time and train fare. *(EIICHIRŌ says nothing.)* You're nuts, you know that?

EIICHIRŌ: I went 'cause you were badgering me about it so much, Ma. I put down any old answer that came into my head, so how was I to think I'd pass the first screening?

SAKA: You amaze me. How on earth are you ever going to get a job with that attitude?

EIICHIRŌ: I won't.

SAKA: You wo—. . . ? Heavens! *(Suddenly more seriously.)* Eiichi—do you really want a job? . . . Huh? Huh? Answer your mother.

EIICHIRŌ: Yeah.

SAKA: If so, then try a little. . . .

EIICHIRŌ: Can you stop pestering me, please? I go to school, and at school all anybody can ever talk about is jobs. Please, can't you let me relax a little in my own home?

SAKA: It's because you don't know anything about the world you can say that. You can't expect to get what your friends have. If you're really serious about getting a job, you'll have to show a bit more initiative. And even if they don't tell you to come, then it stands to reason that you go, don't it? As many times as you got.

EIICHIRŌ: I can't do that.

SAKA: "Can't do that." You got a lot of nerve talking like that. . . . You're just trying to dodge your mother, aren't you?

EIICHIRŌ: That's why I told you, you needn't go there, right? It wasn't clear how sincere that job prospect was. As for going today to Mr. Seki's place— I didn't say you needn't go; I said you can't.

SAKA: That minister's wife comes from back home, so I figured maybe. . . . The five yen I spent on fruit for them was a waste. A waste. But rather than wait till now to make such a big fuss, I should've done as Madam Minister said and asked them a year ago.

EIICHIRŌ: In any case, it's no use trying to push things. I'll figure something out. So would you please not go traipsing off like that?

SAKA: But how can I feel good about leaving things to you? It's times like this I wish I had family here. Most times we're better off without them because they can't bother us. Your father's friends have passed away, most of them. . . . Please consider this—if you don't get a job, you're going to leave the whole family stranded.

EIICHIRŌ: (Slamming his book shut.) "Stranded," she says! Really! I'm popping out for some smokes.

SAKA: It's cold outside. Here I thought you'd stay put at home for a while and you're going out again. Why don't you wait till morning. (Not replying, EIICHIRŌ turns off the lamp and stands up.) I told you, save it for the morning. . . . Nobody in this house listens to a word I'm saying. Oh, Mr. Kanbara—no, Mr. Inoue. Did you write back to him?

EIICHIRŌ: Not yet. (Pokes MINEKO with his foot.) Hey, get up.

SAKA: You don't have to pick on Mineko.

EIICHIRŌ: Get up. You can't sleep your life away.

MINEKO: Ouch. Stoppit, Eiichi.

EIICHIRŌ: Get up and buy me some Bats.[12]

MINEKO: Uh uh.

EIICHIRŌ: If you buy me some, I'll take you to the Hōgaku-za.[13] I'll take you mini-golfing. Saturday. What'ya say?

MINEKO: (Rising sluggishly.) And you'll buy me a beret too?

EIICHIRŌ: Yeah, yeah. (As if to mock her.) What'ya say?

MINEKO: No way. (Lies down again.) You're not going to pull that rug on me. . . .

EIICHIRŌ: (Quickly.) Rug?

MINEKO: That's not it.

SAKA: (Laughing.) You mean pull the wool over your eyes.

MINEKO: Th-that's it—pull the wool.

EIICHIRŌ: Sheesh. Schoolgirls these days—what happened to their brains?

MINEKO: You're mean! Aren't you? That's because somebody trained me so well. You keep saying, "I'll take you, I'll take you," but you never have, have you? Not once.

EIICHIRŌ: That's why I'm saying this time I will.

MINEKO: And I'd just got nice and warm.

EIICHIRŌ: So I'm off the hook. You were snoring, don't you know. Kept farting too. You think I could go out with a little sister like that?

MINEKO: *(Springs up again.)* Was I, Ma? Really?

SAKA: Just like Uncle.

MINEKO: What, both?

SAKA: You put us to shame.

MINEKO: There must be something wrong with my nose. *(Makes sniffing noises.)*

EIICHIRŌ: You're fooling us.

MINEKO: Must have been the burdock I ate yesterday. *(Clutches her belly.)*

EIICHIRŌ: You eat 'em year 'round.

MINEKO: *(Suddenly.)* Eiichi. Where are you going?

EIICHIRŌ: For some smokes. *(Heads for the front door.)*

MINEKO: He's lying, Ma. He's going to shoot pool.

SAKA: Ei-san, Ei-san!

EIICHIRŌ: Wha-at?

SAKA: Write to Mr. Inoue.

EIICHIRŌ: I'll do it later.

SAKA: "Later, later." So you say, and a week's gone by already. He was good enough to speak for you. They're all waiting for you, aren't they?

MINEKO: I bet they're mad at you.

SAKA: Write it now.

EIICHIRŌ: *(Offstage.)* Uh uh.

SAKA: An offer like Yokohama even we'd be happy to accept. But Nagoya. Why? Why? I don't care how good the wage is, you think I'd leave you all alone stuck in a place like that? Pool—you can play that anytime.

MINEKO: Hey. The drugstore's next door.

SAKA: Drugstore?

MINEKO: To the Red Ball.

SAKA: Oh.

MINEKO: Or maybe it's mahjong he's off to.

*(*EIICHIRŌ *returns and takes his cape off the hook. Unbeknownst to him, a hand towel drops to the floor.)*

MINEKO: One or the other.

EIICHIRŌ: I'll write it when I get back.

SAKA: Is it okay to be going out on the town all the time? Yesterday it was the Shiba Garden Theatre.

MINEKO: No kidding!

EIICHIRŌ: You've been digging in my wastepaper basket again, haven't you?

SAKA: And you haven't finished your thesis either.

MINEKO: That's right, you haven't. And it's been more than ten days since the deadline passed. We'll all be in trouble if you don't wise up, Eiichi. If you don't pass, I won't have anything to do with you, ever again. *(*EIICHIRŌ *raps her on her head with his knuckles, and she raps him back.)* He's hitting me again. On the head. *(*EIICHIRŌ *raps her again. She punches him back.)* That must be why my brain's not working properly.

EIICHIRŌ: Gotcha. *(Twists* MINEKO's *arm behind her back.)*

MINEKO: Ouch! You're breaking my arm. You're going twist it right off! . . . Ow! . . . Ma! . . .

SAKA: Ah! It's a match. Go on, tackle your big brother. Give him what for. . . .

EIICHIRŌ: How 'bout it?

MINEKO: You always beat up on me. . . . Ouch! . . . Ow! . . . Ma! . . .

SAKA: Eiichi! Why do you have to be so childish? . . . Don't make your little sister cry. She'll kick up a fuss if you do. . . . *(To* MINEKO.*)* You don't have to shout.

EIICHIRŌ: See ya later. *(Starts to leave.)*

MINEKO: A man of twenty-four pitted against a poor little seventeen-year-old maiden like me! Pervert.

EIICHIRŌ: *(Gently.)* Excuse me?

MINEKO: Whoa! *(Laughing, flees into the sitting room.)*

SAKA: Pipe down!

MINEKO: But. . . .

EIICHIRŌ: *(Picking up the fallen hand towel.)* Whose is this?

MINEKO: Oh, that's Uncle's. Where was it?

SAKA: He got all flustered, saying, "Can't find my towel." When he was leaving.

EIICHIRŌ: Is he home yet, I wonder?

SAKA: He'll be home by now, all right.

EIICHIRŌ: *(Reading the lettering on the towel.)* "Sea as far as the eye can see,

sails both full and trimmed. Splendid prospects. Bring a companion."
What the hell is this? Says "Brightwater Lodge."

MINEKO: Show me. *(EIICHIRŌ throws her the towel.)*

SAKA: It's that new restaurant. It didn't exist when I was little.

MINEKO: "Bring a companion." I'd sure like to go. To where Ma was born.

EIICHIRŌ: All you gotta do is hop on a train. Surely you can manage that.
(Heads for the front door.)

MINEKO: But I've never been there. They say you can see Amakusa from
there.[14]

EIICHIRŌ: *(Off.)* No, you can't!

MINEKO: Yes, you can. What do you know anyway? Don't you want to go back,
Ma? Uncle said, "Don't it make you lonely for home seeing the likes of
me?" *(Imitating him.)* Don't it. . . . Ain't it. . . .

SAKA: *(Laughing.)* When your brother. . . . What're you doing there, Eiichi?

EIICHIRŌ: *(Off.)* Checking how much cash I've got.

SAKA: Really!

MINEKO: Don't you ever want to go back, Ma?

SAKA: Not till your brother gets settled.

MINEKO: Go home and shower them in brocade, eh?

SAKA: Rags, more like it.

MINEKO: Besides, we'll have to go back once Eiichi graduates. Uncle said
they'd find him a bride.

SAKA: Hardly.

MINEKO: Eiichi will never get a girl to fall in love with him. He goes beet red
every time he meets one.

EIICHIRŌ: *(Off.)* Shut up!

MINEKO: He's listening. What're you waiting for there? Hurry up and leave.
But with a mother-in-law like Ma in the house, I bet the poor bride
wouldn't last three days before taking off.

SAKA: Now, don't you start. . . .

MINEKO: *(Cutting in.)* She would.

SAKA: I'm too old to change. . . .

EIICHIRŌ: *(Off.)* Ma.

SAKA: What is it? I don't have any cash for the pool hall!

EIICHIRŌ: *(Off.)* I don't have to answer Mr. Inoue just yet, do I?

SAKA: What? *(EIICHIRŌ doesn't answer.)* So you mean you want to go to Nagoya after all?

EIICHIRŌ: *(Off.)* If there weren't anything here, I'd go anywhere. I don't care.

SAKA: You think you could just go anywhere and survive on your own? Go ahead and refuse them. Politely, mind you.

EIICHIRŌ: *(Off. Repeating himself.)* I'd go anywhere. I don't care.

SAKA: What do you want me to say?

EIICHIRŌ: *(Off.)* So what am I supposed to do, Ma? Get a job, you tell me. Fat chance of that in Tokyo. But if there was something in Nagoya . . . say, or someplace else, I'd take it. And you tell me I can't. All the while you're standing in the way of my finding anything, you're blaming me for not even getting off my ass and trying. . . .

SAKA: What're you fretting about there? You'll be fine, just fine.

EIICHIRŌ: I'll be fine? Just fine? So what am I supposed to do then? What'll happen to me? Ma, you haven't got *(his voice trembling)* the faintest idea how I feel.

SAKA: Eiichi. . . .

EIICHIRŌ: How can you have any idea? . . . I'm going to hop a freighter for South America. I'll get there and then I'll cough up blood and quietly croak.

(He leaves. The two who are left behind look at each other, struggling to avoid making too much of the eerie silence.)

SAKA: Is your brother serious about going to Nagoya?

MINEKO: *(Laughing.)* 'Course not. He's gonna work for a newspaper.

SAKA: But he said he's not going tomorrow. . . . Just now.

MINEKO: Really? He was joking.

SAKA: I really don't understand what goes on in that boy's mind. Not these days. Did he say anything to you?

MINEKO: No. . . . Oh, yeah. He asked me if I thought I could live with you, just the two of us. Four, five days ago.

SAKA: Hm. . . . Maybe he's been reading too many novels. *(Pause.)* I wish that boy could try to be a better provider. . . . How? How can we just send him off to any old place in the provinces?

MINEKO: *(Suddenly.)* Maybe he wants to move out on his own.

SAKA: Move out? Why, he's got a perfectly good home right here.

MINEKO: He's got a home, that's why he wants to move out. I mean, if you ask his friends, they're all living on their own.

SAKA: What? You're kidding!

MINEKO: And you know what? People from the boonies who come to Tokyo to live on their own all say how nice it is to have a home here. It's completely the opposite. Isn't that strange? . . .

SAKA: Of course they think that way. But it's weird for folks who've got their homes here to want to move out. Why on earth would they want to go out of their way to make life difficult for themselves?

MINEKO: But it's freer living that way. On your own. . . . Me too, if I could. . . .

SAKA: Do you really think, girl, when you got home there'd always be a snack waiting for you? If you was living on your own?

MINEKO: Uh uh.

SAKA: Right! Or always have a fresh change of socks for your feet?

MINEKO: I guess not.

SAKA: 'Course not. And when you caught a cold, who'd be there to take care of you? *(MINEKO is silent.)* Hm? So what is it these Tokyo people don't like? What mother or father would do something to make their own child hate them? . . . They're all just selfish.

MINEKO: But I don't think he's really going to move out. He's just talking, that's all.

SAKA: And your mother doesn't think he means it neither. . . .

MINEKO: Right.

SAKA: Let's leave it at that, shall we? . . . Your uncle even said to me he'd do anything for us if I decided to go home, but—I didn't tell your brother—I refused. I've never, ever been a thorn in my family's side, and I ain't going to be one now. There's no way I'm going back there, bowing and scraping. All they'd do is tell me "I told you so."

MINEKO: You don't get along with the folks back home, Ma?

SAKA: They don't care for your mother trying to make her own way in the world, see? If only I'd gone back then, when I could. . . . It's taken me all these years to figure that out.

MINEKO: Best to stay put in Tokyo. No way I want to go to the boonies.

SAKA: Let's go home. Nobody listens to me here! *(MINEKO grimaces uncomfortably.)* If only we'd gone back to Shimabara when your dad died, we'd be living easy now, I can tell you. Just think how much better it'd be than living here, being laughed at all the time and called a yokel? And 'cause I was too stubborn to go back, we left your father's inheritance behind. . . . Ah! Mine-chan!

MINEKO: *(Earnestly.)* Are you regretting what you did, Ma?

SAKA: Regret? No, not over my dead body. . . . But, still. . . . These days, I just can't seem to get worked up about anything. I was just joking.

MINEKO: It's okay, Ma. Don't fret. I'll become a typist or something and support you. *(SAKA, still sewing, giggles.)* You sure it's okay to make it so short here?

SAKA: 'Course it is.

MINEKO: But I could swear the teacher said you mustn't do it that way.

SAKA: Miss Shimura? Surely not.

MINEKO: But that's what she said.

SAKA: Then your teacher's wrong.

MINEKO: But....

SAKA: You tell Miss Shimura your mother said so. And what your mother says can't be wrong.

MINEKO: Oh, Ma.... *(Pause. She looks around.)* I guess we'll be able to sleep easy now.

SAKA: I'm sure your uncle was shocked to see how we lived. I bet you never in his dreams did he ever imagine we'd come down so far in the world.

MINEKO: And of all times he had to come when he did. Surely not for sight-seeing in Tokyo; Eiichi's writing his thesis, and I've got my exams starting this week. He knows he's in the way, and still he keeps hanging around. For one thing, no way three can sleep in a little room like this. Sawing logs and getting up to pee all night, and every time he got up, he had to go through your room, Ma. I bet he was spying on you as you slept.

SAKA: That's why every time I heard footsteps, I pulled the covers over my head. It ain't easy having guests, is it? Why, we haven't had a man sleep here since your father passed away.

MINEKO: You should've told him no from the start. There's nothing shameful in being poor.

SAKA: But I was sure our place would seem so grubby to him he'd want to get out as fast as he could. I kept waiting for him to go, but he settled himself right in.

MINEKO: Well, you were the one who kept serving *sake* to him.

SAKA: Your uncle always liked his drink, you know, and I thought to myself, the man needed company, so.... And there, I'd made up my mind I wasn't going to serve any drinks to anybody, not even if it was New Year. Till your brother got a job.

MINEKO: He could sure hold his liquor.

SAKA: Yes, he liked his fun in the old days. Why, when your mother was a girl, he used to mock me all the time. He was quite the character.

MINEKO: He made fun of you, Ma? I bet you were cute when you were a girl. How'd you do your hair then? Did you wear that pasty white makeup? How'd he mock you?

SAKA: *(Chuckling.)* Pass me the scissors. Look at you, girl! Put that jacket on properly. You're a disgrace.

MINEKO: *(Passing the scissors.)* It's warmer this way. You're almost done.

SAKA: A fine thing you ask your mother to do. You were supposed to do it yourself, but there you were, fast asleep in the *kotatsu*.

MINEKO: But there isn't anybody who does it by herself, Ma.

SAKA: What're you going to do when you've got a husband?

MINEKO: I'll have him wear Western clothes.

SAKA: What, all day?

MINEKO: Sure. And we'll go dancing.

SAKA: *(Clicks her tongue.)* They should never have taught you how to dance at school. What was it you did? At the last field day. The four of you, with the band.

MINEKO: The quadrille? Not like that. Here, like this—just two. . . .

SAKA: What's so fun about that sort of thing? Why, just watching them, it don't seem like any of the girls are enjoying themselves. All they do is twirl around, staring off blankly with their mouths open, like it was some kind of mental arithmetic competition. . . .

MINEKO: That's 'cause you have to keep in step to the music. . . .

SAKA: Why is it your school didn't stick to doing more ladylike stuff, the way it used to, like the tea ceremony and flower arranging and *koto*? Ever since your school got that new principal, things there have gone to the dogs. Move. . . . Your foot's filthy! Don't you ever wash? . . . Hey, what happened there?

MINEKO: It was at relay practice. Today, with Oiwa. We were running. I was trying to turn and Oiwa was trying to go straight ahead, and our legs got tangled up and we both tripped. We'll be practicing every day after we finish exams. If you don't keep in practice, even when it's cold, you'll never improve your record. Running keeps you warm.

SAKA: Filthy. You're all bloody. Why, it's grotesque.

MINEKO: Please, Mother, I wish you wouldn't try using words when you don't know what they mean. Just because there's a little blood doesn't make it "grotesque." I can't take you anywhere—you'd embarrass me too much.

SAKA: I wouldn't go, even if you invited me. No thank you. Why do you like those rough sports, like racing and dancing? I know at the field day even your mother felt her heart flutter to see you shooting off like a bolt in the blue, but when I thought of your future, I couldn't help but think I'd failed your father by raising a daughter like a man. And what girl would take on her own brother like that? Ignore him if he mocks you like that. . . .

MINEKO: But he made me mad. . . .

SAKA: You know your mother's never wrong. Look at Teiko next door. So obedient! Always listens and says yes.

MINEKO: Yeah, but. . . .

SAKA: She'd never leave her dishes all over the shop after dinner, then dive into the *kotatsu* and read the paper. Not like you. Why can't you do the dishes first before you read? Nobody'd have cause to complain then. When she's got a moment to spare, Teiko's at her desk practicing her calligraphy. Always makes sure when she goes to bed she puts out the bedding for her mum and dad and her little brother too. And then, when she gets up in the morning. . . .

MINEKO: *(Losing her patience.)* But Teiko's different, Ma.

SAKA: How nice it'd be to be that girl's parents! Just think what they've got to look forward to!

MINEKO: But, Ma, what if I broke the ten-second record for the hundred meters? I'd make the Olympics, just like Miss Hitomi.[15]

SAKA: *(Clicks her tongue.)* You? Dream on.

MINEKO: You don't have to make fun of me, Ma! If there's something you don't care for, Ma, you sure rub it in, you know.

SAKA: Of course I do! Who wouldn't?

MINEKO: I'm not like that. I'm ready to try anything. I'm not picky like you.

SAKA: Well, picky's better than being shallow. Folks have what they call their own nature, and women have a woman's nature. Your mother fails to understand why any girl would want to turn her nose up at what a woman does best.

MINEKO: Yeah, yeah. I want to be just like Teiko too. I really do. . . . But, right now, I want to have some fun.

SAKA: Four years already, and still you can't sew a thing like this? Look at Teiko—why, she can sew silk even. Anyways, I figured I'd shut up and let you do as you pleased, at least till you finished school, so I guess I can't complain. . . . But let me tell you, once you leave school, I'm not going to let you get away with it. I'll boss you around from morn till night, just like a servant.

MINEKO: Yikes! *(Flees into the* kotatsu.*)* The old guard versus the avant-garde.

SAKA: The *kotatsu* again? You and your brother—lazybones, the both of you. A real pair. Why, if your father was still alive. . . .

MINEKO: Even if he was, I'm sure I'd be the same.

SAKA: You wouldn't get so smart with me, girl.

MINEKO: I'm not getting smart. . . .

SAKA: Yes, you are. The both of you just make fun of your mother.

MINEKO: How can I help the way I am? It's not like somebody else gave birth to me. You did, Ma.

SAKA: That's the living end, that is. You blame your mother, do you?

MINEKO: In any case, this is an age of free respect.

SAKA: *(Laughs.)* You mean self-respect, I think. . . .

MINEKO: *(Raps her head with her knuckles.)* Oh yeah, oh yeah. *(Takes up the reader lying there and flicks through the pages.)* Er, Lincoln were . . . ah, Lincoln was. . . . *(Reads in a comical accent.)* "One day Lincoln and a party of his friends were traveling through a thicket of wild plum trees. It was a warm day, and they stopped to water their horses. Soon. . . ." Ma.

SAKA: Mhn?

MINEKO: I hadn't any idea. Was I that bad?

SAKA: What? . . . *(Laughs.)* Why, you were like this. *(Mimics her snoring.)*

MINEKO: Nah. I don't snort like Uncle.

SAKA: Yes, you do. Honest. *(Snores some more.)*

MINEKO: You're mean. "Soon the party was ready to start again, but Linc. . . ." *(distracted by the sound of the bell ringing in the shrine.)* I'd like to take down that bell and tie it 'round a cat's neck.

SAKA: Shut up and study.

MINEKO: "But Lincoln was not to be found. 'Where is Lincoln?'"

SAKA: Oh, while you were sleeping, Teiko called for you. Some homework she wanted to ask you about. . . .

MINEKO: Shut up and work. "Everyone asked. . . ." Asparagus. Ma. Ma!

SAKA: What is it?

MINEKO: Do you know what happens if you eat asparagus?

SAKA: What happens. . . . Well, it's good for you, folks say.

MINEKO: That's not what I meant.

SAKA: Who'd want to eat such a thing?

MINEKO: Forget it. "'I saw him.' . . . Everyone asked, looking around, 'I saw him a few minutes ago,' answered one of the party. He had found. . . ."

SAKA: Is that how you're supposed to read English?

MINEKO: *(Affecting an accent.)* But of course, my dear mother. Ah! I think I'll doze off again. *(Turns over.)*

SAKA: If you're going to sleep, go to bed properly. Your mother hates you acting so slovenly.

MINEKO: Do you have to say "hate" all the time like that? *(Yawns.)* What a nuisance. Make my bed, Ma. I promise I'll make yours tomorrow night.

SAKA: I doubt it. There's no way I'm going to let myself be taken care of by an ungrateful child like you. Enough. Time to take a break. *(Turns off the light and enters the living room.)* I really hate that, I do. Mineko, you're going to catch cold. . . . *(Grumbling, she gets into the* kotatsu.*)* Don't pull the covers like that! I'm all exposed here. Look. . . . *(Yanks at the quilt.)*

MINEKO: It's c-o-o-l-d.

SAKA: You are a pest. *(Stands and gets a quilted coat from the cupboard and covers* MINEKO.*)*

MINEKO: Poke the coals a bit, would you?

SAKA: He's taking his time, your brother. *(Sticks her head under the covers to check the heater.)*

MINEKO: The Red Ball, I told you. Notice how he's got a lot of their matches these days?

SAKA: How could he play pool at a time like this! This the evening edition? *(Takes the paper and starts reading.)* Still not caught that murderer. . . . The one got killed yesterday had four kids. Poor mother. . . . *(Pause.)* Teiko's reading next door. You know, I've got this feeling your uncle's going to come back tonight. Can't shake it.

MINEKO: That's 'cause he's suddenly gone, after being here all this time. You got used to him being around.

SAKA: Still, something bothers me.

MINEKO: What?

SAKA: I think we should've been nicer to him. We should've offered him more to drink. . . . Day before yesterday, he kept staring at me, like he wanted some more. And there was I, pretending I didn't notice, though I knew all the time. Must've thought I was a real shrew. Well, he can think what he likes, I can't help it. Hey, don't fall asleep here. Come on.

MINEKO: *(Sleepily.)* I'm not sleeping.

SAKA: *(Pause.)* Tell me, Mineko. If your dad was still alive, which of us do you think you'd love more?

MINEKO: *(Vaguely.)* Uh uh.

SAKA: Your dad, I bet. *(*MINEKO *doesn't reply.)* I'm right, aren't I? *(*MINEKO *doesn't reply.)* That so? I thought as much. But your mother can't help the way she is. *(Pause. She picks up the paper again.)* Who is this actress? We'll give a gold ring to the one who knows. Who is she, I wonder. . . . Must be nice, being an actress. . . . Hey, that's cheap, this phonograph. . . . Maybe we oughta get one for the house. What d'you say, Mineko? Look. *(*MINEKO *doesn't reply.)* Fallen asleep. *(Stares at* MINEKO'*s sleeping face. Begins to nod off herself.)*

(Pause. A confusion of footsteps, then the front door opens. SAKA *doesn't notice.)*

MRS. MUNAKATA: *(Offstage.)* Hello? . . . Uh, anyone home?

SAKA: Yes?

MRS. MUNAKATA: *(Offstage.)* Sorry to disturb you at this hour, but is this the home of Mr. Ogura? Mr. Eiichirō Ogura?

SAKA: Yes. . . .

MRS. MUNAKATA: *(Off.)* Would you be Mrs. Ogura, I presume?

SAKA: Er, yes. *(Shakes* MINEKO *and hurriedly goes to the door.)*

MINEKO: *(Sleepily.)* What?

MRS. MUNAKATA: *(Off.)* You come in too. . . . Pleased to meet you. I'm Mrs. Munakata, the mother of this boy Mr. Ogura's been so kind to. I know it's frightfully late, but this boy wanted to make sure we came tonight and thanked him for all he's done.

SAKA: *(Off.)* Yes. Um. . . .

MRS. MUNAKATA: *(Off.)* The fact is, the reports came out at two this afternoon, and I should have come straight over, but, well, I was late. . . . *(Laughs.)*

SAKA: *(Off.)* Yes. Um, what. . . ?

MRS. MUNAKATA: *(Off.)* Huh? . . . Why, the boy's teacher deserves to be properly thanked, don't you see. I was really worried because he's so inept at arithmetic, but, well, hah, hah, hah. . . . *(To* RYŌ.*)* Weren't you lucky, though? *(To* SAKA.*)* There was the boy's name, on the list of those who passed. Of course, the fact I can say that is entirely thanks to Mr. Ogura. I mean it. . . . Here, I've been rattling on. . . . Why, I suppose you must be Mr. Ogura's mother?

SAKA: *(Off.)* Yes, I'm Eiichi's mother. Er, please do come in.

MRS. MUNAKATA: *(Off.)* I've heard a lot about you. Would the teacher be in, then?

SAKA: *(Off.)* Yes, well, he's just popped out for a minute. . . . But he'll be back anytime now. Please.

MRS. MUNAKATA: *(Off. To her son.)* What shall we do? Shall we wait? The boy passed, you see, so he wants to show off to everybody. Hah, hah. . . .

SAKA: *(Off.)* Why, what a clever-looking boy he is, too. Mineko, run and get your brother.

MINEKO: *(Aware that strange guests have dropped in on them, she quickly puts on her jacket the proper way.)* What, to the Red Ball? *(Claps her hand over her mouth.)*

MRS. MUNAKATA: *(Off.)* Please, don't bother.

SAKA: *(Off.)* It's right over there. Hurry and get him. Please, come in.

MRS. MUNAKATA: *(Off.)* Well, if you insist. Shall we, then?

(MINEKO *stands up and flutters around.*)

SAKA: *(Entering.)* What's the matter with your head?

(*Enter* MRS. MUNAKATA, *followed by her son* RYŌ. SAKA *offers them cushions and the brazier to warm them, then starts to make tea.*)

SAKA: I'm afraid it's rather messy.

MRS. MUNAKATA: Was that Mr. Ogura's little sister just now? My, what a strapping young thing she is!

SAKA: Yes, well, she's such a tomboy. . . .

MRS. MUNAKATA: Not at all. Why, when I compare her to my own girls. . . . I heard the other day she'd bobbed her hair. . . . Please don't fuss. Forgive me, but this is a mere token—nothing, really, but, you see, the teacher's so fond of *yōkan.*[16]

SAKA: Why, you really shouldn't have. . . .

MRS. MUNAKATA: Every time he comes to our place, he gobbles up a piece this big. *(Laughs.)* It's black *yōkan.*

SAKA: Oh, that boy. . . . *(Laughs.)*

MRS. MUNAKATA: Not to worry, he's become such a fixture around our place. So much so the girls call him Mr. Black. . . . *(Laughs some more.)*

SAKA: Well, thank you very much. *(Silence.)*

MRS. MUNAKATA: Why, such a quiet neighborhood here! Where we live, it's nothing but poor folk like us, all cheek to jowl.

SAKA: Not at all. I'm sure it's very cheerful. Uh, where would that be?

MRS. MUNAKATA: Huh? Oh, you know, over by Tsukiji.

SAKA: Why, you've come all this way. . . .

MRS. MUNAKATA: Not at all. The boy's really fond of Mr. Ogura, you see— we've enjoyed his company for going on three years now. This one's my youngest, and he's a real handful, I can tell you, but he always does what the teacher tells him. Don't you, boy? Honestly, it makes his own mother jealous.

SAKA: So you mean to tell me Eiichi—my boy, that is—goes to your place and—how shall I say?—looks after your son?

MRS. MUNAKATA: Yes, indeed he does, ma'am. He covers all the core subjects.

SAKA: Yes, but I find that hard to believe. . . .

MRS. MUNAKATA: You mean that he hasn't told you anything about us at all?

SAKA: No, this is the first time I've heard.

MRS. MUNAKATA: Well, now! . . . Come to think of it, judging by your reaction

... My, my. I was wondering whether we'd got the wrong house. Hah, hah, hah.

SAKA: Not at all, please forgive me. What you're telling me, then, is my son is your boy's tutor?

MRS. MUNAKATA: Rather, you might say he's more like one of the family. *(SAKA says nothing.)* That my boy managed to get into the prefectural school is all thanks to Mr. Ogura. The boy's so inept at arithmetic, you see, I was a bit worried. Hah, hah, hah. . . . His father should have come in person himself to thank you, but. . . .

SAKA: Not at all, you're most kind. Now, where is that boy? He never even so much as mentioned it. Mind you, it wasn't as if I was probing him. . . . Really, had I known, I would've had to go thank you. What's with that boy, now? When he gets home, I'll really give him a piece of my mind.

MRS. MUNAKATA: Thank me? Not at all.

SAKA: He's always acting like that. He might go and tell others what he's thinking and doing but doesn't say a word to his own mother. Why, ask him, and he wouldn't even give me the time of day, so I've kind of left him to his own devices, you might say. Uh huh, he's quite the character.

MRS. MUNAKATA: Not at all. He's so earnest, but for all that, there's something gentle about him. A fine young man. Isn't he, Ryō?

RYŌ: Yes, very.

SAKA: Thank you. But I still can't get over the fact that everybody's saying such fine things and fawning all over him. What on earth is it about the boy that folks find so appealing?

MRS. MUNAKATA: It's because you're his mother you can say that. It's the way a parent shows her pride. I hear that you've managed everything, a woman all on your own. It can't have been easy.

SAKA: No, not such that folks can say so.

MRS. MUNAKATA: If you can say that, you're strong.

SAKA: Not as strong as some folks say. *(Silence.)* But, you know, sometimes I think, what's the point of being a parent? Ain't done much for me, let me tell you.

MRS. MUNAKATA: I know exactly how you feel.

SAKA: When I think how much it hurt to give birth to them, and then they can be such a pain in the neck. . . . *(Suddenly self-conscious about her accent.)*

MRS. MUNAKATA: But for someone like me with eight kids of my own, ma'am—mind you, three passed away—it seems the most natural thing to do is, well, not just love them all, but deal with them each according to how they turn out, you might say. All in all, it's best you think of them as somebody else's kids, ma'am.

SAKA: Doesn't that make you feel sad?

MRS. MUNAKATA: True enough, as you say. It makes me sad. But it can't be helped. . . . They've sure made me cry in my time—this one's big brother, for example. For all the love you shower on them, they don't return a tenth of it. It's a crying shame, isn't it? Honest. But I guess it's just a parent being selfish. . . .

SAKA: *(Putting herself down.)* But I . . . I don't think I could ever feel the way you do.

MRS. MUNAKATA: *(Feeling she has touched a tender nerve.)* Well, yes, of course not.

(Silence.)

SAKA: Here, boy, have some treats. Go on. *(Silence.)* Honestly, what am I to do? If you hadn't shown up, I could have died and still never found out. Why, I could have run into you on the street—it wouldn't have been impossible—and walked right by you like you was nobody.

MRS. MUNAKATA: Now, really, that's. . . .

MINEKO: *(Returns, out of breath.)* He's not there. Then it occurred to me, maybe he's. . . .

SAKA: Don't just stand there. Greet our guests properly.

MINEKO: Thanks for coming.

MRS. MUNAKATA: Forgive us for disturbing you so late.

SAKA: He wasn't there? Where did he get to, then? . . . Not to that coffee shop, surely.

MINEKO: Venice, you mean. I went there, but he wasn't there either.

MRS. MUNAKATA: That's fine, really. All I wanted to do was let him know this boy passed his exam. So, Ryō-chan, shall we say goodbye? . . . Has your foot gone to sleep?

SAKA: Dear me. Poor boy. Please, wait just a bit longer.

MINEKO: He's just gone for a walk. He'll be back in a moment.

MRS. MUNAKATA: Thank you, but, really. . . . Oh, yes, I hear he's found himself a job. I must congratulate you. Joining a bank in Nagoya. So he says. . . .

SAKA: Huh? Who will?

MRS. MUNAKATA: *(Dubiously.)* Or perhaps he's decided to take some other position? What was it, Ryō-chan? Four, five days ago he visited. Told us then, "I'm going to Nagoya, to work in a bank. It's been decided." . . . Seems his friend Mr. Inoue helped him land the job. We said we'd throw a farewell party before he left, so my girls and this one are all in a tizzy about it now. I've really overstayed my welcome. Your daughter must come too. Well, then. . . .

SAKA: Please, it's no trouble at all. Come back soon.

(Led by MRS. MUNAKATA, *the four move toward the front door.)*

MRS. MUNAKATA: *(Off.)* Sorry to have troubled you. You really must come to our party, young lady. Well, please give the teacher our regards.

SAKA: *(Off.)* No trouble at all. Goodbye, boy.

RYŌ: *(Off.)* Goodbye.

(After a while, SAKA *and* MINEKO *return and each go to their places in the kotatsu.)*

MINEKO: What was all that about?

SAKA: He's been that boy's tutor. For the past four years.

MINEKO: Eiichi?

SAKA: I don't know what line of business they're in, but they've been very kind to him. *(Lost in thought.)*

MINEKO: A very well-spoken lady, wasn't she? Quite stylish, too. *(*SAKA *says nothing.)* Mind if I open this? *(Without waiting for an answer, goes to get a knife. Pause.)*

SAKA: *(As if muttering to herself.)* Just like one of the family. . . . For four years. . . .

MINEKO: Eiichi's not all bad. That's why they treat him so well.

SAKA: Everybody says so, but it's only to his mother that. . . .

MINEKO: Aren't you happy for him? Still, he's going to Nagoya after all. Wasn't he sneaky, though? Getting Mr. Inoue's help. But, you know, I think if he wants to go to Nagoya, then you oughta let him. . . . I mean, what else can you do? . . . And if we could live, just the three of us, together there, you couldn't ask for more. Given the way things turned out. . . .

SAKA: I don't want to hear no more about it.

MINEKO: What I really hate about you, Ma, is the way you always let things get you down so quick. You start whining and then. . . .

SAKA: How can I go on living without that boy?

MINEKO: Ahem! So I mean nothing to you, do I? Ah!!

(Pause. The front door quietly opens and EIICHIRŌ's *voice calls, "I'm home."* MINEKO *dashes to the front door. In an attempt to compose herself,* SAKA *makes a pretense of being absorbed in the newspaper.)*

MINEKO: *(Off.)* Where'd you go? I was looking all over for you.

EIICHIRŌ: *(Off.)* So I heard. What's up?

(The two appear.)

MINEKO: They say you're going to Nagoya. This Murataka woman dropped by and. . . .

EIICHIRŌ: Munakata. Yeah, I ran into her. At the postbox.

MINEKO: You saw her then?

EIICHIRŌ: That *yōkan*'s from her, right?

MINEKO: It's delicious.

EIICHIRŌ: I know. *(Takes a bite.)* Said you looked all over the place. . . . There's a frost. In the alley in front of the shrine.

MINEKO: You taught that boy, Eiichi?

EIICHIRŌ: Mhn? Uh huh.

MINEKO: A big place? Where?

EIICHIRŌ: Uh huh.

MINEKO: Is it fun? I've been invited. . . .

EIICHIRŌ: Uh huh. Hey, stop eating so much.

MINEKO: How much they pay you?

EIICHIRŌ: None of your business.

MINEKO: You spend it all by yourself?

EIICHIRŌ: Yeah. All by myself. You got a problem with that?

MINEKO: Wow. Go ahead, spend it all. See if I care. Hey, Ma.

(Saying nothing, SAKA doesn't avert her eyes from the newspaper.)

EIICHIRŌ: Is it 'cause I wouldn't take you to the pictures? I told you I wouldn't, didn't I?

MINEKO: But that. . . .

EIICHIRŌ: No go. *(So that SAKA may not be aware, gestures to MINEKO, "What's with Ma?")*

MINEKO: *(In a whisper.)* She's mad. *(Louder.)* Hey. You're being sneaky.

EIICHIRŌ: Gotta write that thesis. *(Gets up.)* Hey, bring some tea.

MINEKO: Get some yourself.

EIICHIRŌ: I've never seen you say yes and jump for anyone.

MINEKO: You're the one who's standing, so you can go help yourself, can't you? You've got legs.

EIICHIRŌ: You've always got to have the last word.

MINEKO: You wanna make something out of it? Come on.

(The two tussle. SAKA doesn't so much as glance their way. Even though MINEKO flees to her, she shows no interest. MINEKO clings to SAKA.)

SAKA: *(Suddenly slaps MINEKO's cheek with the palm of her hand.)* I told you, stoppit! *(At first MINEKO just looks at her, shocked. Then, she stands up, goes to the next room, and sits down by the long brazier, sniffling quietly.)*

EIICHIRŌ: Look.

SAKA: *(Looks up at him as he goes to sit down on the chair.)* Ei-san.... *(Smiles in an attempt to hide her sadness.)* Is it true, dear, you're going to Nagoya? ... I guess it can't be helped. Go. Go on. It's all right with me. Your mother's made up her mind.

(MINEKO edges over to the partition dividing the two rooms.)

SAKA: *(Almost bashfully.)* I'll come live with you in Nagoya. And Mineko.... I'll put her in boarding school.

—Curtain—

Notes

Preface

Epigraph. Osanai Kaoru, "Enshutsu nōto: *En no gyōja* no daiichiya wo oete" (A director's notes: Completing the first night of *En no gyōja*), in Osanai, *Osanai Kaoru zenshū* 6 (Kyoto: Rinsen shobō, 1975), 460.

1. See Ōyama Isao, *Kindai Nihon gikyokushi,* 4 vols. (Yamagata: Kindai Nihon gikyokushi kankōkai, 1968).

2. A recent exception is Tsuno Kaitarō's biography, *Kokkei na kyojin: Tsubouchi Shōyō no yume* (Heibonsha, 2002).

3. Two recent books—Ayano Kano's *Acting like a Woman in Modern Japan: Theater, Gender, and Nationalism* (New York: Palgrave, 2001) and Brian Powell's *Japan's Modern Theatre: A Century of Continuity and Change* (London: Routledge Curzon, 2002)—have focused on acting and the establishment of theatre companies. J. Thomas Rimer's *Toward a Modern Japanese Theatre: Kishida Kunio* (Princeton, NJ: Princeton University Press, 1974); Brian Powell's *Kabuki in Modern Japan: Mayama Seika and His Plays* (Houndmills, Basingstoke, Hampshire: Macmillan in association with St. Antony's College, Oxford, 1990); and my own *Spirits of Another Sort: The Plays of Izumi Kyōka* (Ann Arbor: Center of Japanese Studies, University of Michigan Press, 2001) are devoted to individual playwrights.

4. Suwa Haruo dates the influence of *kabuki* dramaturgy on fiction to the Hōei and Kyōhō periods (ca. 1703–1736). Ejima Kiseki (1666–1735) was one of the first authors to adopt *kabuki* techniques of plotting and scenic structure. See Suwa

Haruo, *Edo: Sono geinō to bungaku* (Mainichi shinbunsha, 1976), 187–192. *Kōdan* was the term used in the Meiji era for *kōshaku*, a popular genre of storytelling that specialized in military narratives like the *Taiheiki*, vendettas and tales of knights-errant. *Rakugo* (comic monologue) had its start in the Edo era (1600–1868) and remains a most popular art.

5. Kishida Kunio, "Engeki yori bungaku wo haijo subeki ka" (Should theatre be rid of literature?), in Kishida, *Kishida Kunio zenshū* 21 (Iwanami shoten, 1989), 210. Kishida borrows the phrase "beggar's art" from the French dramatist Jules Amedée Barbey d'Aurevilly.

6. Kobayashi Hideo, "Yakusha," in *Kangaeru hinto;* cited in Miyashita Nobuo, "Gikyoku," in Suwa Haruo and Sugai Yukio, eds., *Kōza Nihon no engeki* 1: *Nihon engekishi no shiten* (Benseisha, 1992), 109.

7. Cited in Gioia Ottaviani, "'Difference' and 'Reflexivity': Osanai Kaoru and the *Shingeki* Movement." *Asian Theatre Journal* 11, no. 2 (Fall 1994): 220.

8. "Gekijō no setsubi ni taisuru kibō" (My hopes in regard to the theatre, 1913), in Tanizaki, *Tanizaki Jun'ichirō zenshū* (Chūō kōronsha, 1982), 22:10, 11.

9. Nihon kindai engekishi kenkyūkai, ed., *Nihon no kindai gikyoku* (Kanrin shobō, 1997).

Chapter 1: Meiji Drama Theory before Ibsen

1. The first so-called command performance, or *tenrangeki*, before Emperor Meiji of *nō* was in 1878. Iwakura Tomomi, who had led the 1871–1873 mission to Europe and the United States, was instrumental in establishing a public *nō* theatre where Hōshō Kurō (1837–1913), Umewaka Minoru (1828–1909), and other lead actors were able to ensure *nō*'s revival.

2. Cited in Fujiki Hiroyuki, "Gikyokushi 3," in *Gikyokuron* (*Engekiron kōza* 5), edited by Tsugami Tadashi, Sugai Yukio, and Kagawa Yoshinari (Shōbunsha, 1977), 127.

3. Ibid.

4. For a discussion of the effect of censorship on the development of *shingeki* in the late Meiji era, see Ayako Kano, *Acting like a Woman in Modern Japan: Theater, Gender, and Nationalism* (New York: Palgrave, 2001), 154–156ff.

5. See the account in Komiya Toyotaka, *Japanese Music and Drama in the Meiji Era*, translated and adapted by Donald Keene (Tōyō bunko, 1969), 191. Kan'ya's Morita-za was the first theatre to move from its original location in Saruwaka-chō, next to the Yoshiwara licensed quarters, to the more central Shintomi-chō. It burned down in 1876, and the Shintomi-za that replaced it was

touted as Japan's first "modern" theatre. See Yuichirō Takahashi, "*Kabuki* Goes Official: The 1878 Opening of the Shintomi-za," in *A Kabuki Reader*, edited by Samuel L. Leiter (Armonk, NY: M. E. Sharpe, 2002), 123–151.

6. Toyama Masakazu, for one, pushed for the eradication of *kabuki*'s traditional stage conventions. See "Engeki kairyōron shikō" (Personal thoughts on theatre reform), in *Meiji bungaku zenshū* 79: *Meiji geijutsu, bungaku ronshū*, edited by Hijikata Teiichi (Chikuma shobō, 1975), 139–148.

7. Suematsu Kenchō, "Engeki kairyō iken," in *Kindai bungaku hyōron taikei* 9: *Engekiron*, edited by Nomura Takashi and Fujiki Hiroyuki (Kadokawa shoten, 1985), 18–19.

8. Ibid., 20.

9. Ibid., 22.

10. Tsubouchi Shōyō, "Suematsu-kun no engeki kairyōron o yomu" (Reading Suematsu's theory on theatre reform), in Nomura and Fujiki, *Kindai bungaku hyōron taikei*, 26. Shōyō's rebuttal was first published in the *Yomiuri shinbun*, October 20–21, 1886.

11. Cited in William Lee, "Chikamatsu and Dramatic Literature in the Meiji Period," in *Inventing the Classics*, edited by Haruo Shirane and Tomi Suzuki (New York: Columbia University Press, 2000), 187.

12. See the discussion by Mōri Mitsuya in "Ipusen izen: Meijiki no engeki kindaika o meguru mondai (1)," *Bigaku/bijutsushi ronshū* (July 1987), 6:3–10. *Engeki*'s first entry in the Japanese lexicon was in *Saikoku risshi hen*, the 1870 translation of Samuel Smile's *Self Help*, where it served as a rendition of "opera."

13. See Wolfgang Schamoni, "The Rise of 'Literature' in Early Meiji," in *Canon and Identity: Japanese Modernization Reconsidered: Trans-cultural Perspectives*, edited by Irmela Hijiya-Kirschnereit (Munich: Iudicium, 2000), 55.

14. See Earl Miner, *Comparative Poetics: An Intercultural Essay on Theories of Literature* (Princeton, NJ: Princeton University Press, 1990), 22–23, and Lee, "Chikamatsu," 192.

15. Cited in Tsugami, Sugai, and Kagawa, *Gikyokuron*, 138.

16. Shōyō used the term *shingeki* in Tsubouchi, "Suematsu-kun no engeki kairyōron o yomu." Other related terms at this time include *shin-engeki* or *shin-engei*.

17. See Kano, *Acting like a Woman*, 151–153ff. The expression "interpretive slaves" is taken from Jacques Derrida's discussion of Antonin Artaud's critique of Western drama theory in "The Theatre of Cruelty and the Closure of Representation," in *Writing and Difference*, translated by Alan Bass (Chicago: University of Chicago press, 1978), 232–250.

18. Maeda Ai, "From Communal Performance to Solitary Reading: The Rise

of the Modern Japanese Reader," translated by James Fujii, in Maeda Ai, *Text and the City: Essays on Japanese Modernity*, edited with an introduction by James Fujii (Durham, NC: Duke University Press, 2004), 223.

19. Ibid., 227, 228.

20. "Kōshō bungei to wa nani ka," in Yanagita Kunio, *Yanagita Kunio zenshū* (Chikuma bunko, 1990), 8:14–82.

21. Tsubouchi Shōyō, "Dokusho o okosan to suru shui" (A prospectus for the encouragement of reading); cited in Maeda, *Text and the City*, 234.

22. For a detailed discussion of *genbun itchi*, see Karatani Kōjin, *Origins of Modern Japanese Literature* (Durham, NC: Duke University Press, 1993), 39–40, 45–75.

23. Maeda, *Text and the City*, 245. See also Malcolm Andrews, *Charles Dickens and His Performing Selves: Dickens and the Public Readings* (Oxford: Oxford University Press, 2006).

24. Cited in Tsugami, Sugai, and Kagawa, *Gikyokuron*, 141. For further discussion of the introduction of European drama theory to Japan, see ibid., 137–142.

25. Mori Ōgai, "Surprised by the Prejudice of Theatre Reformers" (Engeki kairyō ronja no henken ni odoroku), translated by Keiko McDonald, in Mori Ōgai, *Not a Song Like Any Other: An Anthology of Writings by Mori Ōgai*, edited by J. Thomas Rimer (Honolulu: University of Hawai'i Press, 2004), 145. The Japanese text can be found in Nomura and Fujiki, *Kindai bungaku hyōron taikei*, 46–49. Ōgai's essay originally appeared in *Shigarami zōshi*, October 1889.

26. Mori Ōgai, "Surprised," 147.

27. Ibid., 148.

28. Ibid., 149; Nomura and Fujiki, *Kindai bungaku hyōron taikei*, 48.

29. See Mori Ōgai, "Gekijō-ura no shijin," in Nomura and Fujiki, *Kindai bungaku hyōron taikei*, 302–312 (the essay first appeared in *Shigarami zōshi*, February 1889), and *"Tamakushige futari Urashima* no kōgyō ni tsuite" (On the production of *The Jeweled Comb Box and the Two Urashimas*, 1902); cited in Ochi Haruo, *Meiji Taishō no gekibungaku* (Hanawa shobō, 1971), 12.

30. Ishibashi Ningetsu, *Gikyokuron*, in Nomura and Fujiki, *Kindai bungaku hyōron taikei*, 312–316. Ningetsu's essay first appeared in *Kokkai*, December 12, 1893.

31. Ibid., 315.

32. Ibid., 316.

33. Ibid., 315.

34. See Donald Keene, *Four Major Plays of Chikamatsu* (New York: Columbia University Press, 1961), 5.

35. See Lee, "Chikamatsu," 182ff.

36. Tsubouchi Shōyō, "Wagakuni no shigeki," in Nomura and Fujiki,

Kindai bungaku hyōron, 49. Shōyō's essay was serialized in *Waseda bungaku*, October 1893–March 1894, with related criticism subsequently published in *Waseda bungaku*, *Taiyō*, and other journals. Donald Keene discusses Shōyō's essay in *Dawn to the West: Japanese Literature of the Modern Era* (New York: Holt, Rinehart and Winston, 1984), 2:410–411.

37. Tsubouchi, "Wagakuni no shigeki," 51.

38. Ibid.

39. This is a device not strange to Hollywood. It is lampooned in "Luxury Lounge," episode 72, season 6, of *The Sopranos*, in which the character Christopher Moltisanti attempts to pedal an idea for a screenplay on Ben Kingsley, describing it as *"The Ring* meets *Texas Chainsaw Massacre."*

40. See Megumi Inoue, "Why Did *Sewamono* Not Grow into Modern Realist Theatre?" in *Modern Japanese Theatre and Performance*, edited by David Jortner, Keiko McDonald, and Kevin J. Wetmore Jr. (Lanham, MD: Lexington Books, 2006), 3–15, which discusses how *naimaze* and the tastes of Edo audiences resisted the development of realism. James Brandon and Samuel L. Leiter discuss the impact of *midori* programming on *kabuki* dramaturgy in their introduction to *Kabuki Plays on Stage*, vol. 4: *Restoration and Reform, 1872–1905* (Honolulu: University of Hawai'i Press, 2003), 32–36.

41. Tsubouchi, "Wagakuni no shigeki," 57.

42. This idea is developed further in his "Bijiron-kō" (*Waseda bungaku*, May–June 1892). See Ochi, *Meiji Taishō no gekibungaku*, 23, 28, passim.

43. Kitamura Tōkoku, "Gekishi no zento ikaga," in Kitamura, *Tōkoku zenshū*, edited by Katsumoto Sei'ichirō (Iwanami shoten, 1964), 2:335, 336. Note that the term Tōkoku uses for "drama" is not *gikyoku* but *gekishi*, which means something like "dramatic poetry."

44. Ibid., 337.

45. Ibid., 338–339, 340–341.

46. Matsumoto Shinko, *Meiji engekiron shi* (Engeki shuppan-sha, 1980), 236.

47. In Tōson's autobiographical novel *Haru* (Spring), Tōkoku—who is given the name Aoki—is described as devoting his energies to work he hopes may one day be staged. See Akiba Tarō, *Nihon shingekishi* (Risō-sha, 1971 [1956]), 1:233.

48. For further discussion of this play, see Poulton, *Spirits of Another Sort*, 89–90.

49. Akiba, *Nihon shingekishi*, 1:236.

50. "I came to feel that research into Shakespeare might be the most useful means of improving the Japanese drama," wrote Shōyō. Cited in Donald Keene, *Dawn to the West*, 2:413. Keene discusses Shōyō's plays on pages 2:410–417.

51. Tsubouchi, "*A Sinking Moon over the Lonely Castle Where the Cuckoo Cries*," in Brandon and Leiter, *Kabuki Plays on Stage*, 4:368.

52. Kano, *Acting like a Woman*, 70. Kano stresses that, in any case, "direct speech, in the strictest sense does not exist, since pure direct speech would deny the materiality of the body that must produce the speech." Her analysis continues to page 73.

53. Ibid., 170.

54. See Sakai Shinnosuke, "Kindai gikyoku no tenkai—sono kokoromi: Ōgai made," *Nihon kindai bungaku* 6 (May 1967): 17.

55. Hirata Oriza, *Engeki nyūmon* (Kōdansha gendai shinsho, 1998), 121.

56. Chief exponent of the so-called "quiet theatre" (*shizuka na geki*) of the 1990s, Hirata calls his own style "contemporary colloquial theatre"(*gendai kōgo engeki*). He has advanced his ideas on the development of modern colloquial stage dialogue in a number of books, including *Gendai kōgo engeki no tame ni* (Benseisha, 1995) and *Engeki no kotoba* (Iwanami shoten, 2004).

57. Kinoshita Junji, *Nihongo no sekai* 12: *Gikyoku no Nihongo* (Chūō kōronsha, 1982), 39–42, 146.

58. See my discussion of this play in Poulton, *Spirits of Another Sort*, 91–100.

59. Hirata, *Engeki no kotoba*, 51–52.

60. See Kinoshita's analysis in *Nihongo no sekai*, 143–157.

61. For a detailed study of new *kabuki*, see Nakamura Tetsurō, *Kabuki no kindaika: Sakka to sakuhin* (Kabuki's modernization: Writers and their work) (Iwanami shoten, 2006). Modern playwrights continue to write *kabuki* drama. Mishima Yukio (1925–1970) wrote several successful *kabuki* plays, and actor Nakamura Kanzaburō XVIII (b. 1955) has commissioned works by Noda Hideki (b. 1955) and Watanabe Eriko (b. 1955). Despite their popularity, however, the settings of these plays are typically pre-Meiji.

62. Okamoto Kidō, "Shirōto no kyakuhon," in *Shin-engei* (January 1918); cited in Akiba, *Nihon shingekishi*, 1:224. In Mishima's time, apparently, this situation had not changed substantially. See "Onnagata" (1957), translated in Mishima, *Death in Midsummer and Other Stories* (Harmondsworth: Penguin Books, 1971), which describes how the traditional *kabuki* world intimidates a modern *shingeki* playwright.

63. Brandon and Leiter, *Kabuki Plays on Stage*, 4:30–31.

64. Ibid., 31.

65. More complete accounts of *shinpa* are given in Kano, *Acting like a Woman*, 57–119, and Poulton, *Spirits of Another Sort*, 17–51.

66. Sakata Tōjūrō, "Dust in the Ears," in Hachimonjiya Jishō, *The Actors' Analects*, edited and translated by Charles Dunn and Bunzō Torigoe (New

York: Columbia University Press, 1969). On Edo constructs of realism, see Kamiyama Akira, "'Shizenshugi' no naka no 'Edo': Hōgetsu, Ryūgai shinpa no hitobito," *Engekigaku ronshū* 37 (1999): *Tokushū: Nihon no kindai engeki,* 281–307, and Kamiyama Akira, Saitō Tomoko, Seto Hiroshi, Nagata Yasushi, and Mori Mitsuya, "Hyōgenshi ni okeru riarizumu" (panel discussion), *Engekigaku ronshū* 38 (October 2002): 45–78.

67. Mōri Mitsuya, in "Thinking and Feeling: Characteristics of Intercultural Theatre," in *Japanese Theatre and the International Stage,* edited by Stanca Scholz-Cionca and Samuel L. Leiter (Leiden: Brill, 2001), 357–365, describes how shocked many nineteenth-century Europeans were by the almost carnal realism of *kabuki* acting. I deal in greater detail with the issue of realism in Japanese theatre, past and present, in "The Rhetoric of the Real," in Jortner, McDonald, and Wetmore, *Modern Japanese Theatre and Performance,* 17–32.

68. See the "cluster definition" of melodrama provided by Ben Singer, *Melodrama and Modernity: Early Sensational Cinema and Its Contexts* (New York: Columbia University Press, 2001), 50. The classic guide on melodrama is Peter Brooks's *The Melodramatic Imagination: Balzac, Henry James, and the Mode of Excess* (New Haven, CT: Yale University Press, 1976). See also my discussion of melodrama and *kabuki* in Poulton, *Spirits of Another Sort,* 17–51 passim.

69. See Singer, *Melodrama and Modernity,* 57.

70. Ibid., 176.

71. Nicholas Vardac, *Stage to Screen: Theatrical Method from Garrick to Griffith* (Cambridge, MA: Harvard University Press, 1949).

72. Singer, *Melodrama and Modernity,* 168.

73. For Ayako Kano, "straight" drama especially marks the emergence of a heterosexual theatre, in contrast to the "queer" theatre of *kabuki* (a term that originally meant something like "bent," "kinky" or "twisted"). See Kano, *Acting like a Woman,* 57–84.

74. Hanayagi Shōtarō, *Yakusha baka;* cited in Hagii Kōzō, *Shinpa no gei* (Tōkyō shoseki, 1984), 211, 213. Kano, *Acting like a Woman,* is the definitive analysis of performing femininity in modern Japanese theatre.

75. See Poulton, *Spirits of Another Sort,* 17–54, for further discussion of *shinpa* adaptations of Kyōka's fiction; the appendix, 320–323, lists stage performances since 1986.

76. "Bunshō no onritsu," in Izumi Kyōka, *Kyōka zenshū* (Iwanami shoten, 1988), 28:718. Many writers have remarked on how inherently "theatrical" Kyōka's prose is. A dramatic reading of his novel *Nihonbashi,* directed by the *nō* actor Kanze Hideo at Theatre X in Tokyo, March 2003, underscored the performative qualities

of this writer's work. Much of the story is told through dialogue, and though the characters are not individualistic in the modern sense, their language is vividly distinguished along class, gender, and personality lines.

77. Saeki Junko, *Izumi Kyōka* (Chikuma shobō, 2000), 76.

78. *Nihonbashi*, act 1. In Izumi, *Kyōka zenshū*, 26:279.

79. Cited in Imamura Tadazumi, "Serifu kara mita kindaigeki," *Higeki kigeki* 43, no. 8 (August 1990): 13.

80. See Kano's account of the Kawakamis' adaptation of Shakespeare's *Othello* in *Acting like a Woman*, 105–109. Ink Stone writer Emi Suiin (1869–1934), who was commissioned by Kawakami to write the adaptation, was offered at the time the unprecedented sum of ¥1,000 but was never paid more than half what had been promised. See Poulton, *Spirits of Another Sort*, 32. On the adaptations phenomenon, see also J. Scott Miller, *Adaptations of Western Literature in Meiji Japan* (New York and Basingstoke: Palgrave, 2001).

81. Cited in Kinoshita, *Nihongo no sekai*, 129–130; see also Kinoshita's appraisal of Kōyō's drama on p. 125.

Chapter 2: The Rise of Modern Drama, 1909–1924

1. Tanizaki Jun'ichirō, *Seishun monogatari* (1932); in Tanizaki, *Tanizaki Jun'ichirō zenshū*, 13:386. At the time, Osanai was only twenty-eight years old and Tanizaki twenty-three.

2. Kikuchi Kan, "Osanai-san to bokura"; Kume Masao, "Haiku kara geki, shōsetsu"; both cited in Endō Tasuke, "Kindai ni okeru gikyoku jidai: Sono seiritsu no ichimen," *Nihon kindai bungaku* 6 (May 1967): 28.

3. Mori Ōgai, *Youth*, translated by Shōichi Ono and Sanford Goldstein, in *Youth and Other Stories*, edited by J. Thomas Rimer (Honolulu: University of Hawai'i Press, 1994), 412.

4. Tsubouchi Shōyō, "Shaōgeki wo okosan to suru riyū" (1910); cited in Mōri Mitsuya, "Ipusen shoen zengo (2): Meijiki no engeki kindaika wo meguru mondai (4)," *Bigaku/bijutsushi ronshū* 12 (March 1999): 138.

5. See Kano (*Acting like a Woman*, 184–199) for an account of the Literary Society's production of *A Doll House* and the debate on the "new woman" that it inspired. I follow Ayako Kano in using *A Doll House* as the English title for Ibsen's play.

6. A friend of Tanizaki's, actor and director Kamiyama Sōjin (1884–1954) was a fascinating individual who deserves more study. Instrumental in the early Taishō years in the introduction of Western drama to Japan, he later went to Hollywood, where, like Hayakawa Sessue, he played exotic heroes and villains in

a slew of silent films, including the Mongol prince in Douglas Fairbanks's *Thief of Baghdad* (1924) and Charlie Chan in *The Bombay Parrot* (1927). Talkies, which revealed a foreign accent not appreciated by American audiences, led to his demise as a Hollywood star, and he returned to theatre and cinema in Japan. One of his last roles was as the blind minstrel in Kurosawa's *The Seven Samurai* (1954).

7. Endō Tasuke, "Kindai ni okeru gikyoku jidai," 30.

8. See, for example, Kaneko Sachiyo, "Nora no yukue: Mori Ōgai to Ipusen no gikyoku," in *Mori Ōgai kenkyū* (Izumi shoin, 1989), 3:117. Novelist and playwright Masamune Hakuchō (1879–1962) was one of the first to take issue with a play about old age being the catalyst for the New Theatre movement.

9. Kano (*Acting like a Woman*, 186–187) notes that the first German production of *A Doll House* in 1880 changed the ending of the play so that Nora does not leave her husband and children. This "happy" ending, enforcing conventional notions of a woman's marital and maternal duties, remained the dominant one for German productions throughout the 1880s, and Shimamura Hōgetsu's first translation of this play in 1906 reflected this bowdlerized version.

10. Mori Ōgai, "Gendai shoka no shōsetsuron wo yomu," *Shigarami zōshi* 2 (November 1889); Tsubouchi Shōyō, "Kaigai bungaku ni tsuite," *Waseda bungaku* (October 15, 1892); both cited in Mōri Mitsuya, "Ipusen shoen zengo (1): Meijiki no engeki kindaika wo meguru mondai (3)," *Bigaku/bijutsushi ronshū* 10 (September 1995): 181.

11. Partial translations of *An Enemy of the People*, *The Master Builder*, and *A Doll House* appeared in 1892; complete translations of *The Master Builder* and *John Gabriel Borkman* were published in 1897.

12. Nakamura Kichizō, "Ōshū bungaku no torai no eikyō," *Waseda bungaku* (April 1926); cited in Kaneko, "Nora no yukue," 114.

13. Mōri Mitsuya, "Ipusen shoen zengo (1)," 189.

14. Yanagita Kunio, "Ipusen zakkan," *Waseda bungaku* (July 1906): 99; cited in Mōri Mitsuya, "Ipusen shoen zengo (2)," 133.

15. Mōri Mitsuya suggests that Hōgetsu's notable absence from this roster is due to the fact that he and Osanai never got along; Mōri Mitsuya, "Ipusen shoen zengo (2)," 134.

16. Ibid., 132.

17. Györgi Lukacs, "The Sociology of Modern Drama" (1914), translated by Lee Baxandall, in *The Theory of the Modern Stage*, edited by Eric Bentley (Harmondsworth: Penguin Books, 1968), 429.

18. Ibid., 445.

19. Ibid., 426.

20. Ibid., 439–440.

21. Ibid., 429

22. Ibid., 433.

23. Peter Szondi, *Theory of the Modern Drama*, translated and edited by Michael Hays (Minneapolis: University of Minnesota Press, 1987).

24. Cited in ibid., 22.

25. August Strindberg, "The One-Act Play" (1889); cited in ibid., 55.

26. Kikuchi Kan, "Ichimakumono ni tsuite," *Engeki shinchō* 1, no. 2 (February 1924): 2–3.

27. Szondi, *Theory of the Modern Drama*, 55–56.

28. Ōgai translated as many as fifty plays between 1908 and 1918, amounting to more than ten volumes of his complete works. Some twenty-two of these were published in *Kabuki*, and all but seven of them were staged between 1910 and 1916. See Kaneko Sachiyo, "Ōgai to *Kabuki*," in *Mori Ōgai kenkyū* (Izumi shoin, 1995), 6:226–227. For a list of Ōgai's translations, see the appendix to Richard Bowring, *Mori Ōgai and the Modernization of Japanese Culture* (Cambridge: Cambridge University Press, 1979), 259–269.

29. Cited in Kaneko, "Ōgai to *Kabuki*," 225, 230.

30. See Poulton, *Spirits of Another Sort*, 91–94, for a discussion of *The Jeweled Comb Box*. Four of Ōgai's plays have been translated: *Masks* (*Kamen*, 1909) has been translated by James M. Vardaman Jr., in Mori Ōgai, *Youth and Other Stories*, 291–311, and three have been translated by Andrew Hall: *Shizuka, The Ikuta River*, and *Without Introductions* (*Nanoriso*, 1911), in Mori Ōgai, *Not a Song Like Any Other*, 150–184.

31. Mori Ōgai, "Kyakuhon *Purumura* no yurai" (1909); cited in Kinoshita, *Nihongo no sekai*, 173.

32. See the analysis of Ōgai's style in Kinoshita, *Nihongo no sekai*, 169–177.

33. Kano, *Acting like a Woman*, 158.

34. Mori Ōgai, *Youth and Other Stories*, 412–413.

35. Ibid., 406–407.

36. Critics of modern Japanese drama are in agreement on this. See Rimer, *Toward a Modern Japanese Theatre*, and Akemi Horie-Webber, "Modernization of the Japanese Theatre: The *Shingeki* Movement," in *Modern Japan: Aspects of History, Literature and Society*, edited by William G. Beasley (Berkeley: University of California Press, 1975), 147–165. This point is further elaborated by Gioia Ottaviani in two essays: "'Difference' and 'Reflexivity,'" and "The *Shingeki* Movement until 1930," in *Rethinking Japan*, vol. 1: *Literature*, edited by Adriana Boscaro, Franco Gatti, and Massimo Raveni (Sandgate, Folkstone, Kent: Japan Library, 1990), 178–183.

37. Ottaviani, " 'Difference" and 'Reflexivity,'" 226.

38. Cited in Rimer, *Toward a Modern Japanese Theatre*, 83.

39. "Kyakuhon no hon'yaku ni tsuite," in Osanai, *Osanai Kaoru zenshū*, 6: 11. Osanai's essay was first published in the February 11 and 14, 1909, issues of the *Yomiuri shinbun*.

40. Osanai, "Haiyū D-kun e," *Engei gahō* (January 1909); cited in Brian W. F. Powell, "A Parable of Modern Theatre in Japan: The Debate between Osanai Kaoru and Mayama Seika, 1909," in *Themes and Theories in Modern Japanese History: Essays in Memory of Richard Storry* (London: Athlone Press, 1988), 150.

41. Cited in Powell, "A Parable of the Modern Theatre in Japan," 150.

42. Mayama Seika, "Atarashiki shushi wo make," *Engei gahō* (February 1909); cited in ibid., 156.

43. Cited in Powell, "A Parable of the Modern Theatre in Japan," 159.

44. Hasegawa Tenkei, "Meishin gekijō," and "Nihon no gekijō wa hon'yakugeki wo suteyo," *Taishō engei* (May 1913); cited in Sugai Yukio, *Kindai Nihon engeki ronsōshi* (Miraisha, 1979), 109–117.

45. Masumoto Kiyoshi, "Shingeki no chōraku"; cited in Fujiki Hiroyuki, "Taishōki no gikyoku 1: 1910-nendai no gekisakka," *Higeki kigeki* 29, no. 11 (November 1976): 39.

46. Cited in Sugai, *Kindai Nihon engeki ronsōshi*, 118.

47. "*Gendai gikyoku zenshū* jobun" (1925), in Tanizaki, *Tanizaki Jun'ichirō zenshū*, 23:85.

48. Tanizaki was not entirely ignorant of stagecraft, directing his own *Okuni to Gohei* in 1922 at the Imperial Theatre, but Osanai did not think highly of Tanizaki's skills; see Ōzasa Yoshio, *Nihon gendai engekishi* (Hakusuisha, 1987), 1:408.

49. Osanai Kaoru, "Gikyokuka toshite no Tanizaki Jun'ichirō-kun ga aruita michi" (The road Tanizaki has walked as a dramatist, 1923); reprinted in *Kanshō Nihon gendai bungaku: Tanizaki Jun'ichirō*, edited by Chiba Shunji (Kadokawa shoten, 1982), 345. Tanizaki's *Okuni and Gohei* (1922) has been translated by John Gillespie in *The Columbia Anthology of Modern Japanese Literature*, vol. 1: *From Restoration to Occupation, 1868–1945*, edited by J. Thomas Rimer and Van C. Gessel (New York: Columbia University Press, 2005), 627–639.

50. Kishida Kunio, "Taiwa saseru jutsu" (The art of making dialogue); cited in Saitō Yasuhide, "Gikyokuron kara mita kindaigeki," *Higeki kigeki* 43, no. 8 (August 1990): 30.

51. Horie-Webber, "Modernization of the Japanese Theatre," 284n67.

52. See Hirata, *Engeki no kotoba*, 50–52.

The Boxwood Comb

1. Cited in Wakashiro Kiiko, "Watakushi gikyoku *Tsuge no kushi:* Okada Yachiyo no jiga" (*The Boxwood Comb*, an I-drama: Okada Yachiyo's ego). *Higeki kigeki* 35, no. 1 (January 1982): *Tokushū: Joryū sakka*, 11–13. The playwright Wakashiro was one of Okada's disciples.

2. The text can be found in Akiba Tarō, ed., *Meiji bungaku zenshū 86: Meiji kindaigekishū* (Chikuma shobō, 1969), 166–181. See Rimer and Gessel, eds., *Columbia Anthology*, 275–292, for a translation by David O. Mills of an excerpt of Roka's original story.

3. Akiba, *Nihon shingekishi*, 2:29–30.

4. According to Wakashiro. Other sources say it was Ōgai who proposed the match.

5. Akiba, *Nihon shingekishi*, 2:31.

6. Cited by Inagaki Tatsurō, "Okada Yachiyo joshi no sakuhin" (Madam Okada Yachiyo's work, 1943); reprinted in *Meiji bungaku zenshū 82: Meiji joryū bungakushū 2*, edited by Senuma Natsuba (Chikuma shobō, 1965), 397.

7. Inoue Yoshie, "Okada Yachiyo *Tsuge no kushi*," in *20-seiki no gikyoku*, edited by Nihon kindai engekishi kenkyūkai (Shakai hyōronsha, 1998), 1:126.

8. Ōe Ryōtarō, "Komon no niatta Serikage joshi: Okada Yachiyo sensei o shinobu," *Bungaku sanpo* (June 1962); cited by Hayashi Hirochika, "Okada Yachiyo *Tsuge no kushi* o yomu," *Engekigaku ronshū* 43 (October 2005): *Nihon engekigakkai kiyō*, 147–164.

9. Inoue Yoshie, "Okada Yoshie *Tsuge no kushi*," 125.

10. Mori Ōgai, "Half a Day," translated by Darcy Murray, in Mori Ōgai, *Youth and Other Stories*, 86–87.

11. *Kiyomoto* is a form of ballad sung to the accompaniment of the *shamisen*, sung in teahouses and often used as incidental music in *kabuki*.

12. *Shimada:* a traditional hairstyle commonly worn by unmarried women. *Furoshiki:* a large kerchief used to carry things.

13. Osode is referring to the *shinpa onnagata* Kawai Takeo. In contrast to *kabuki*, where actors are customarily called by their personal names, *shinpa* actors were referred to by their family names. Kawai incidentally starred in a production of this play at the Shōchiku-za in 1927.

14. "Gingko leaf" style (*ichōgaeshi*): a hairstyle commonly worn by married women.

15. Floats (*taru mikoshi*): *sake* barrels that are paraded through the streets like portable shrines.

16. Memorial tablet (*ihai*): a tablet with the posthumous name of a person, enshrined in the family Buddhist altar kept at home.

The Ruby

1. Quoted in Iwasa Shin'ichi, "Kyōka-mono no jōen," *Kokubungaku: kaishaku to kanshō* 14, no. 5 (May 1949): 38.

2. Sangu Makoto, "Inoue-kai no yagaigeki o mite" (Seeing the open-air performance by the Inoue Company), *Teikoku bungaku* (December 1913); cited in Muramatsu Sadataka, *Izumi Kyōka jiten* (Yūseidō, 1982), 162.

3. See the excellent review by Saeki Junko, "Izumi Kyōka to shichōkaku geijutsu" (Izumi Kyōka and audiovisual arts), *Uryū tsūshin* 26 (April 2003): 28–31. Kitamoto Masaya directed the Yūgekitai production in December 2002 at the Osaka Geijutsu Sōzōkan. Saeki and another Kyōka scholar, Tanaka Reigi, both happened to be in the audience when I went to see the play, and I wish to express my thanks to them, and to Charles Inouye, for their advice on the interpretation of some passages.

4. In an essay entitled "Swirling Flowers and Falling Leaves" (Hika rakuyō, 1898; Izumi, *Kyōka zenshū* 28:298–299). Kyōka describes—in much the way that it is portrayed here—a game in which a group of children dance in a circle, singing this riddling song until they fall into a trance. Mt. Haguro (Black Feather) is a holy mountain in Yamagata Prefecture, a site for mountain austerities. The crow is the "servant" or avatar of the mountain.

5. The Chambermaid calls the table a *kokkuri-san*, which is a table made of three sticks tied together with a platter laid on top. Three people would sit around such a table; one would act as the medium, and when the medium was possessed by a spirit, the table would begin to pitch around.

6. There are a number of untranslatable allusions here. "Gates of hell" (*jigoku no mon*): possibly an allusion to the Yoshiwara brothel district. A "crow" (*karasu*) is slang for a prostitute (*kurōto*, literally a "black person" or professional).

7. The bluffs over Kobe: Hiodorigoe, a reference to Minamoto no Yoshitsune's surprise assault on the Taira forces at Ichinotani (part of present-day Kobe) in 1183.

8. According to Buddhist scripture, the *udumbara* (a type of fig native to the Himalayas) blossoms only once in three thousand years. Here the crow is comparing the mistress to an exotic flower.

9. *Suzugamori:* A forest along the Tōkaidō from Shinagawa and a major execution ground during the Edo era.

Father Returns

1. Kikuchi Kan "*Chichi Kaeru* no koto," in Kikuchi, *Kikuchi Kan zenshū* 14 (Chūō kōronsha, 1938), 389. The essay originally appeared in *Bungei shunjū*, March 1923.

2. Cited in Kōno Toshirō, "Kikuchi Kan, Kume Masao no gikyoku no ichizuke," in *Higeki kigeki* 39, no. 2 (February 1986): *Tokushū: Kikuchi Kan to Kume Masao,* 13.

3. Kobayashi Hideo, "Kikuchi Kan ron," *Chūō kōron* (January 1937); cited in Nagahira Kazuo, "*Chichi kaeru* no doramaturugii," in *Kindai bungaku* 4: *Taishō bungaku no shōsō,* edited by Miyoshi Yukio and Takemori Ten'yū (Yūhikaku, 1977), 136.

4. Kikuchi Kan, "Engeki zuihitsu"; cited in Oyama, *Kindai Nihon gikyokushi,* 2:514.

5. Oyama, *Kindai Nihon gikyokushi,* 2:518; Yashiro cited in Nagahira, "*Chichi kaeru* no doramaturugii," 139.

6. Cited in Inoue Yoshie, "Kazoku no zanshō: Kikuchi Kan *Chichi kaeru,*" in Inoue Yoshie, *Kindai engeki no tobira o akeru* (Shakai hyōronsha, 1999), 77.

7. Ibid., 78.

8. See ibid., 74.

9. But as Inoue notes, Eguchi wrote this in 1943, at a time when his memory may have been playing tricks on him; ibid., 76.

10. Kishida Kunio, "Shunjū-za no *Chichi kaeru,*" *Engeki shinchō* (Spring 1924); cited in Inoue Yoshie, *Kindai engeki no tobira o akeru,* 81–82.

11. Takechi Tetsuji, "*Chichi kaeru* ni tsuite"; cited in Inoue Yoshie, *Kindai engeki no tobira o akeru,* 83.

12. Lit. "a small city on the Nankaidō coast" (*Nankaidō no kaigan ni aru shō tokai*). Nankaidō refers to the old provinces adjoining the eastern region of the In-land Sea—that is, from modern Wakayama Prefecture to Hyōgo Prefecture along the Honshū coast and including the islands of Awaji and Shikoku. Kikuchi is no doubt alluding to his birthplace, Takamatsu in Kagawa Prefecture. The dialect spoken in the play is that of this region.

13. Otaka is referring here to the Sino-Japanese War of 1895–1896.

14. "Family studies" (*ie no gakumon*) refers to the Confucian learning that would have been a tradition in a samurai family such as theirs.

The Valley Deep

1. Suzuki's collected works, the one-volume *Suzuki Senzaburō zenshū,* edited by his friend Kagayama Naozō (Osaka: Puratonsha, 1925), contains only fourteen

of his twenty-two extant plays and none of his essays, reviews, or diary materials. Volume 11 of the seventeen-volume series *Gendai kyakuhon sōsho* (Shinchōsha, 1923) contains five earlier plays: *Tanizoko* (The valley deep, 1921), *Hiaburi* (Auto da fé, 1921), *Futari no mibōjin* (Two widows, 1922), *Aru jidai* (A certain age, 1922), and *Jirōkichi zange* (Confessions of Jirōkichi, 1923).

2. Cited in Nishimura Hiroko, "Suzuki Senzaburō kenkyū—Suzuki Mariko-shi shozō no mihappyō shiryō to *Ikiteiru Koheiji*," *Engekigaku* 21 (1980), edited by Waseda Daigaku Engeki Gakkai, 48. This essay has been republished in revised form in Nishimura Hiroko, *Sanjō no senshi: Nihon kindaigeki no doramaturugii* (Kanrin shobō, 2002), 1:511–566.

3. See Nishimura, "Suzuki Senzaburō kenkyū," 48, for examples.

4. It is not included in his complete works, and Nishimura, ibid., claims no copy of it exists.

5. A translation into English of this play is available: "Burning Her Alive," in *New Plays from Japan*, edited and translated by Yozan Iwasaki and Glenn Hughes (London: Ernest Benn, 1930).

6. Kōno Toshirō, "Suzuki Senzaburō—*Gendai kyakuhon sōsho Jirokichi zange* o megutte," *Higeki kigeki* 43, no. 8 (August 1980): 20.

7. Nishimura, "Suzuki Senzaburō kenkyū," 51.

8. Suzuki Senzaburō, "Wakai dōshi e okuru kotoba," *Shin-engei* (February 1913); cited in Ochi Haruo, "Taishōki no tamensei—Suzuki Senzaburō no baai," in Ochi, *Kyōka to gikyoku* (Sunago shobō, 1987), 189. Ochi's essay first appeared in Takada Mizuho, ed., *Taishō bungakuron* (Yūseidō, 1981).

9. Ihara Seiseien, in a review published in the *Miyako shinbun*; cited by Nishimura, "Suzuki Senzaburō kenkyū," 48.

10. Suzuki, "Shinpageki no ichi tenki," *Yomiuri shinbun* September 12, 1920; cited in Nishimura, "Suzuki Senzaburō kenkyū," 46.

11. Suzuki, "Wakai dōshi e okuru kotoba," in Ochi, *Kyōka to gikyoku*, 188.

12. Hanibuchi Yasuko, "Suzuki Senzaburō *Tanizoko*," in Nihon kindai engekishi kenkyūkai, *20-seiki no gikyoku*, 1:192. See also Nishimura Hiroko, "Suzuki Senzaburō *Tanizoko*: Ai suru koto o shiranakatta josei no jiko shobatsu," in Nishimura, *Sanjō no senshi*, 567–581.

13. Emery grass (*tokusa*): a grass with an abrasive surface that could be used for polishing nails.

Chapter 3: After the Quake

1. Information on the earthquake is drawn from a variety of sources, one being the National Information Service for Earthquake Engineering: http://nisee .berkeley.edu/kanto/yokohama.html (accessed August 12, 2005).

2. Nakajima Kenzō, *Shōwa jidai* (Iwanami shoten, 1957); cited in Sofue Shōji, "Kantō daishinsai to engeki," *Shakai bungaku* 8 (July 1994): 26. A disquieting reminder of this suspension was made by Tokyo governor Ishihara Shintarō on April 9, 2000, when he offered the city's support to the Japanese Self-Defense Forces to crush any uprising by so-called *sangokujin* (resident Korean and Taiwanese minorities but also apparently intended to include any illegal immigrants) after a disaster like an earthquake. His remarks raised a storm of protest but no retraction from Ishihara.

3. Brian W. F. Powell, "Japan's First Modern Stage: The Tsukiji Shōgekijō and Its Company, 1924–26," *Monumenta Nipponica* 30, no. 1 (Spring 1975): 69–85.

4. Osanai Kaoru, "Tsukiji Shōgekijō to watakushi," in Osanai, *Osanai Kaoru engekiron zenshū*, edited by Sugai Yukio (Miraisha, 1965), 2:43. Osanai's lecture was first published in *Mita shinbun*, May 30, 1924.

5. Ibid.

6. Osanai himself wrote several plays, such as *Dai'ichi no sekai* (The first world, 1921) and *Musuko* (The son, 1922), which he or others staged.

7. Osanai, lecture in *Osanai Kaoru engekiron zenshū*, 2:44.

8. See Fujiki Hiroyuki, "Tsukiji Shōgkijō no sōsakugeki," *Higeki kigeki* 30, no. 9 (September 1977): 9–10. Inoue Yoshie (*Kindai engeki no tobira o akeru*, 240n3) cites Hijikata's wife as recalling her husband's shock at Osanai's pronouncement.

9. Osanai was a member of the editorial board, which included Kikuchi Kan, Yamamoto Yūzō, Kume Masao, Ihara Seiseien, Ikeda Daigo, Tanizaki Jun'ichirō, and many other luminaries of the Taishō literary and theatre worlds.

10. "*Engeki shinchō* kaiwadan 6," *Engeki shinchō* 1, no. 7 (July 1924): 30–31.

11. Cited in Ōzasa *Nihon gendai engekishi*, 2:397.

12. Cited in Fujiki "Gikyokushi 3," 9.

13. Cited, with alterations, in Powell ("Japan's First Modern Stage," 75), who translates the whole address. Powell uses the word "drama" for *engeki,* but I have rendered it as "theatre" to distinguish it from the word commonly used to translate *gikyoku.* Indeed, since the Meiji era, *gikyoku* was the accepted rendering for "drama."

14. "*Engeki shinchō* kaiwadan 7," *Engeki shinchō* 1, no. 8 (August 1924): 24–27ff.

15. Ibid., 39.

16. Ibid., 40.

17. Ibid., 27.

18. There is considerable debate in the secondary literature over what actually happened. In his biography of Osanai, the playwright Kubo Sakae implies that Kishida could have alerted Osanai but chose not to; cf. Inoue Yoshie, *Kindai engeki no tobira o akeru*, 226. The fullest account I have read is Abe Kōichi, *Dorama no gendai: Engeki/eiga/bungaku ronshū* (Kindai bungei-sha, 1993), 100–110; it is based on various accounts and suggests that Kishida managed to read the original only after it had been lent to Osanai, who had decided it was too late to make any changes.

19. *Old Toys* was a revised version of a play, *Un sourire jaune* (A wan smile), which Kishida had originally written in Paris for the Russian actor Georges Pitoëff, who had asked him to recommend some contemporary Japanese drama for him to read. See Kishida's account in Rimer, *Toward a Modern Japanese Theatre*, 146.

20. Cited in Fujiki Hiroyuki, "Taishōki no gikyoku 2: 1920-nendai no gekisakka," *Higeki kigeki* 29, no. 12 (December 1976): *Tokushū: Taishō no gikyoku*, 2, 44.

21. Kishida Kunio, *Kishida Kunio zenshū* (Iwanami shoten, 1989), 19:83. For another account of Kishida's views, see Rimer, *Toward a Modern Japanese Theatre*, 68–69.

22. Osanai, "Shōgekijō to daigekijō"; cited in Ōzasa, *Nihon gendai engekishi*, 2:400.

23. Powell, "Japan's First Modern Stage," 85. Powell implies that this first Japanese play, *En the Ascetic*, opened in June 1926, but in fact it opened on March 21 and ran until April 11, 1926.

24. Fujii would later become an ultra-nationalist.

25. Akita Ujaku in *Engei gahō* 20, no. 5 (1926): 34; cited in Linda Klepinger Keenan, "*En no gyōja:* The Legend of a Holy Man in Twelve Centuries of Japanese Literature" (PhD dissertation, University of Wisconsin–Madison, 1989), 299.

26. Osanai, "*En no gyōja* no daiichiya o oete," in Osanai, *Osanai Kaoru zenshū*, 6:460.

27. Kubo Sakae wrote that the theatre moved up the date for productions of Japanese plays because it was losing its audience. Cited in Fujiki, "Tsukiji Shōgekijō no sōsakugeki," 12.

28. Keenan, "*En no gyōja*," 299.

29. Cited in ibid., 300.

30. Cited in ibid., 284–285, 298.

31. Complete charts of the Tsukiji Little Theatre's productions can be found in *Engekijin* 4 (January 2000): 17–21, and Kurahashi Sei'ichirō, *Shingeki nendaiki: Senzen hen* (Hakusuisha, 1966).

32. Fujiki, "Gikyokushi 3," 13.

33. See Powell, *Japan's Modern Theatre*, 75–76 for a discussion of this play.

34. Fujiki, "Gikyokushi 3," 14. It was at the opening party for Ueda (Enchi) Fumiko's (1905–1986) play that Osanai collapsed and died. For an account of Enchi Fumiko's dramatic work, see Ayako Kano, "Enchi Fumiko's *Stormy Days: Arashi* and the Drama of Childbirth," *Monumenta Nipponica* 61, no. 1 (Spring 2006): 59–91.

35. See Powell, *Japan's Modern Theatre*, 83–113, and Jean-Jacques Tschudin, *La Ligue du Théâtre Prolétarien Japonais* (Paris: L'Harmattan, 1989), for a more complete account of *shingeki* in the 1930s.

36. Sugai, *Kindai Nihon engeki ronsōshi*, 155.

37. Rimer, *Toward a Modern Japanese Theatre*, 96.

The Skeletons' Dance

1. Ujaku had learned Esperanto from a charismatic blind Russian, Vasilij Eroshenko, whom he first met in February 1915. Like many idealists in the early twentieth century, he believed that Esperanto would help bring about world peace.

2. Cited in Fujiki Hiroyuki, *"Gaikotsu no buchō,"* in Nihon kindai engekishi kenkyūkai, *20-seiki no gikyoku*, 209.

3. Cited in Fujiki, *"Gaikotsu no buchō,"* 210.

4. Ujaku, "Shukan kaihō no geijutsu e," *Engeki shinchō* (March 1924); cited in Inoue Yoshie, "Akita Ujaku *Gaikotsu no buchō* tōjō no igi," *Shakai bungaku* 8 (July 1994): 61.

5. Ōzasa (*Nihon gendai engekishi*, 2:162) lists a number of plays inspired by the earthquake, including those by Kikuchi Kan, Nakamura Kichizō, Osanai Kaoru, and others, but the consensus is that Ujaku's work is the most accomplished.

6. Neither I nor my source for this information has been able to locate a copy of the Esperanto version. See Nakazawa Hiroshi, "Shi no butō o odoru hitobito—Akita Ujaku to hyōgenshugi," *Shōnan kokusai joshi tanki daigaku kiyō* 10 (2002): 23.

7. Ujaku wrote in his diary entry for December 27, 1922, that he was impressed by a screening of the film in a theatre at Waseda; cited in ibid., 31n4.

8. The offshoot of the Futurist Art Association (Miraiha Bijutsu Kyōkai), Mavo held its first exhibition at Denpōin Temple in Asakusa, Tokyo, July 28–August 3, 1923. Gennifer S. Weisenfeld, *Mavo: Japanese Artists and the Avant-Garde* (Berkeley: University of California Press, 2002), 217–245, gives a detailed account of Murayama Tomoyoshi's early career as theatre artist and set designer with Mavo, Sanka (Third Section Plastic Arts Association [Sanka Zōkei Bijutsu Kyōkai]), and the Tsukiji Little Theatre.

9. Inoue Yoshie, "Akita Ujaku," 64.

10. A trick question to catch out a foreigner: a Japanese would readily answer the reign year (*nengō*) in which he was born—in this case, Meiji 32 (1899).

Brief Night

1. Nagahira Kazuo, *Kindai gikyoku no sekai* (Tokyo daigaku shuppankai, 1972), 134.

2. Cited in ibid., 133.

3. Although seven of Kubota's plays were staged in the Taishō era, some critics, like Komiya Toyotaka, thought that his work was best suited for the "ideal stage" that a reader creates inside his head; Komiya Toyotaka, "Pari taizaiki"; cited in Kawasaki Akira, "Kubota Mantarō ni okeru gikyoku no hōhō—shoki no sakuhin ni tsuite," *Bungei kenkyū* 34 (April 1960): 31. Kubota would prove a skillful director of his own plays, and a good case can be made that they are best appreciated in live production and not *lesedrama*.

4. Kikuchi Kan, "Gikyoku geppō," *Engeki shinchō,* June 1924; cited in Takada Mizuo, "Kubota Mantarō Ōdera gakkō no seikaku," *Kokubungaku kaishaku to kyōzai no kenkyū* 11, no. 11 (October 1966): 95. Italicized words are in English in the original.

5. Tanaka Chikao, *Gekiteki buntairon josetsu* (Hakusuisha, 1977), 1:295.

6. Kubota Mantarō, "Shi to geki to no kōryū," *Higeki kigeki,* no. 3 (May 1948); cited in Kawasaki, "Kubota Mantarō," 31ff.

7. Kawasaki, "Kubota Mantarō," 37.

8. Cited in Dōmoto Masaki, "Kubota Mantarō ron: Yuki nareya Mantarō," in Dōmoto, *Dentō to gendai* (San'ichi shobō, 1971), 283. Dōmoto's essay first appeared in *Mita bungaku,* June 1967.

9. Ibid., 271.

10. Ibid., 273.

11. Ibid., 274.

12. George Steiner, *Language and Silence: Essays on Language, Literature and the Inhuman* (New York: Atheneum, 1967).

13. Tanaka Chikao, *Gekiteki buntairon josetsu,* 1:299.

14. *Charamela:* a reed instrument like an oboe, introduced by the Portuguese and customarily used in Japan by itinerant noodle vendors.

15. Kannon (Kannonsama): The bodhisattva of mercy. Oyoshi is referring specifically to Asakusa's center of worship, Sensōji Temple.

16. A district near Asakusa on the west bank of the Sumida.

Two Men at Play with Life

1. Rimer, *Toward a Modern Japanese Theatre*, 275.

2. David G. Goodman, ed., *Five Plays by Kishida Kunio* (Ithaca, NY: Cornell East Asia Series, 1989), 24.

3. Ōzasa Yoshio, "Godoku no naka ni shōritsu shita Kishida Kunio zō," *Chūō kōron* 119, no. 10 (October 2004): 254.

4. See Rimer, *Toward a Modern Japanese Theatre*, 254–256; Goodman, *Five Plays*, 22.

5. Kishida Kunio, "Shingeki-kai no bunya"; cited in Ōta Shōgo, "Heya-saki no hana: Kishida Kunio ni okeru geki kōzō ni tsuite," *Shingeki* 23, no. 9 (September, 1976): *Tokushū: Kishida Kunio*, 140.

6. Osanai Kaoru, "Engeki ni taisuru kōsatsu"; cited in Ōta, "Heya-saki no hana," 140. Despite certain fundamental differences in Osanai's and Kishida's ideas of theatre, many scholars suggest that had Osanai lived longer, the Tsukiji Little Theatre would have staged one of Kishida's plays.

7. Cited in Goodman, *Five Plays*, 11.

8. Kishida, "Kindai engeki ron"; cited in Yuasa Masako, "Gendai Nihon ni okeru junsui engeki kara fujōrigeki e no nagare no kōsatsu: Kishida Kunio, Betsuyaku Minoru, Iwamatsu Ryō," *Engekigaku ronshū* (*Nihon engeki gakkai kiyō*) 34 (1996): 25.

9. Kishida, cited in Rimer, *Toward a Modern Japanese Theatre*, 139.

10. Kubo Sakae, "Mayoeru rearizumu," in Kubo, *Kubo Sakae zenshū*, 6:117–125. Kubo preferred the terms "revolutionary realism" or "anti-capitalist realism" since, unlike Soviet Russia, socialism had not yet been established in Japan.

11. Ibid., 123.

12. Ibid., 125. Kawaguchi's *Nijūrokubankan* (House number twenty-six) is set in a community of expatriate Japanese in New York City. Tanaka's *Tachibana taisō onnajuku ura* (Behind Tachibana women's gymnasium) is considered to be a sequel to *Ofukuro*, translated here as *Mama*.

13. Ōzasa, "Godoku no naka ni shōritsu shita Kishida Kunio zō," 261.

14. Saeki Ryūkō, cited in Goodman, *Five Plays*, 16.

15. Yuasa, "Gendai Nihon ni okeru junsui engeki kara fujōrigeki e no nagare no kōsatsu," 34.

16. Nagahira, *Kindai gikyoku no sekai*, 152.

17. Goodman, *Five Plays*, 22.

18. Yuasa, "Gendai Nihon ni okeru junsui engeki kara fujōrigeki e no nagare no kōsatsu," 23.

19. Ibid., 35.

Rain of Ice

1. See Carole Cavanaugh's preface to her translation of Shigure's *Wavering Traces* (*Chōji midare*, 1911), in *Modern Drama by Women 1880s–1930s: An International Anthology*, edited by Katherine E. Kelly (London and New York: Routledge, 1996), 256.

2. Cited in Ogata Akiko, "Watarikiranu hashi—Hasegawa Shigure, sono sei to sakuhin," in *Feminizumi hihyō e no shōtai: Kindai josei bungaku o yomu*, edited by Ogata Akiko et al. (Gakugei shorin, 1995), 101.

3. The title was changed to *A Blizzard of Cherry Blossoms* (*Sakura-fubuki*) for the stage production.

4. The Kabuki-za staged one of these dance plays, *Izumo no Okuni*, about the founder of *kabuki*, in December 2004. Though starring the celebrated *onnagata* Bandō Tamasaburō V, nowhere in any of the posters or other literature about the play was the author's name mentioned.

5. Cited in Ogata, "Watarikiranu hashi," 114.

6. Ibid., 103.

7. Noted *kabuki* critic Watanabe Tamotsu has expressed his shock at how dark Shigure's modern plays were: Watanabe Tamotsu, "Kaisetsu: kannō to zetsubō," in Hasegawa Shigure, *Jōnetsu no onna: Kindai josei sakka senshū* (Yumani shobō, 2000), 28:6. Another one-act play, the lyrical, romantic *Tegona* (1914) is more typical of Shigure's *kabuki* plays. Based on the same legend that is the source for Mori Ōgai's *The Ikuta River*, the play concerns a woman who chooses death over two men who seek to marry her.

8. Inoue Yoshie, "Hasegawa Shigure *Aru hi no gogo*," in *Nihon kindai engeki-shi kenkyūkai, 20-seiki no gikyoku*, 1:121–122. *One Afternoon* had its first production in 1995, in a double bill with Okada Yachio's *The Boxwood Comb*, at Theatre X in Tokyo.

9. Inoue Yoshie, "Hasegawa Shigure *Aru hi no gogo*," 121.

10. *Tokonoma:* altars to the household gods and buddhas. The *tokonoma* is an alcove typically used to hang a painting or display an artwork or flower arrangement; the altars include a small Shinto shrine for worshiping spirits that bring good luck and prosperity to a house or business and a Buddhist altar for worshiping the ancestors.

Mama

1. For a discussion in English focusing on Tanaka's postwar career, see J. Thomas Rimer, "Four Plays by Tanaka Chikao," *Monumenta Nipponica* 31, no. 3 (1976): 275–298.

2. Tanaka Sumiko, "*Ofukuro* kaisetsu"; cited in Abe Itaru, "Tanaka Chikao no shoki gikyoku: *Ofukuro* kara *Hi no Yama* made," *Engekigaku* 22 (1981): 20.

3. Oyama, *Kindai Nihon gikyokushi*, 3:468.

4. David G. Goodman has translated *Maria no kubi* as *The Head of Mary* in *After Apocalypse: Four Japanese Plays of Hiroshima and Nagasaki* (Ithaca, NY: Cornell East Asia Series 71, 1994), 107–181.

5. "Gekisakka no isu 17," *Higeki kigeki* 23, no. 11 (November 1970): 34; cited in Rimer, "Four Plays by Tanaka Chikao," 277. Tanaka goes on, however, to confess his faith in a transcendent being but notes that in Japan, such a faith had taken the dangerous form of emperor worship.

6. Abe Itaru, "Tanaka Chikao no shoki gikyoku," 29.

7. Ueno, *Ueno Chizuko ga bungaku o shakaigaku suru* (Asahi bunkō shinkan, 2007), passim.

8. See Betsuyaku Minoru, "Taiwa buntai no ronri: Tanaka Chikao *Ofukuro* yori." Part 1 of this essay was published in *Shingeki* 23, no. 2 (February 1976): 66–75, and part 2 in *Shingeki* 23, no. 4 (April 1976): 70–82.

9. A low table with quilted skirts, under which is a small heater for keeping warm in winter.

10. Families at this time often considered it a good investment to adopt a promising boy, and it was a useful way of avoiding conscription since first-born or only sons were exempt.

11. Hikawa-sama, also called Hikawa Daimyōjin. Located in Ōmiya, in Saitama Prefecture, the shrine—the largest in the old Musashi Province—was especially favored by the samurai class.

12. Bats: Golden Bat was a popular brand of cigarette.

13. A theatre that specialized in musicals.

14. Amakusa: a chain of islands off the coast of Kyushu in Nagasaki Prefecture.

15. Hitomi Kinue won Japan's first women's track and field medal—a silver—for the 800 meters at the 1928 Olympics in Amsterdam. Credited for helping to make women's sports respectable in Japan, she was criticized by some for her unladylike behavior of flashing her thighs.

16. A jellied confection made of sweet beans, chestnuts, and other such things.

Bibliography

Unless otherwise noted, all works in Japanese were published in Tokyo.

Plays in Japanese

Akiba Tarō, ed. *Meiji bungaku zenshū 86: Meiji kindaigekishū.* Chikuma shobō, 1969.

Akita Ujaku. *"Gaikotsu no buchō."* *Engeki shinchō* 1, no. 4 (April 1924): 28–49.

———. *"Gaikotsu no buchō."* In *Akita Ujaku gikyokushū,* 1–33. Hirosaki: Ujakukai, 1975.

———. *"Gaikotsu no buchō."* In Nihon kindai engekishi kenkyūkai, *Nihon no kindai gikyoku,* 148–159.

Gendai gikyoku zenshū. 20 vols. Kokumin tosho, 1925–1926.

Gendai kyakuhon sōsho. 17 vols. Shinchōsha, 1921–1925.

Hasegawa Shigure. *"Kōri no ame."* In *Nihon gikyoku zenshū* 36, 451–461. Shun'yōdō, 1929.

———. *"Kōri no ame."* In *Shigure kyakuhonshū 1: Kindai josei sakka seisenshū* 14, 183–207. Yumani shobō, 1999.

Itō Sei et al., eds. *Gendai Nihon gikyoku senshū,* 12 vols. Hakusuisha, 1955–1956.

Izumi Kyōka. *"Kōgyoku."* In *Kyōka zenshū* 26, 1–27. Iwanami shoten, 1988.

Kikuchi Kan. *"Chichi kaeru."* In Sofue and Asada, *Nihon kindai bungaku taikei,* vol. 49, 127–141.

Kishida Kunio. *"Inochi wo moteasobu otoko futari."* In *Kishida Kunio zenshū* 1, 123–150. Iwanami shoten, 1989.

Kubota Mantaro. *"Mijikayo."* In *Kubota Mantarō zenshū* 5, 375–392. Chūō kōronsha, 1967.

Nihon engeki kyōkai, ed. *Shōwa Taishō gekishū.* Engeki shuppansha, 1989.

Nihon gekisakka kyōkai, ed. *Gendai gikyoku taikan.* Shinchōsha, 1922.

Nihon kindai engekishi kenkyūkai, ed. *Nihon no kindai gikyoku.* Kanrin shobō, 1997.

Okada Yachiyo. *"Tsuge no kushi."* In *Nihon gikyoku zenshū* 36, 480–496. Shun'yōdō, 1929.

———. *"Tsuge no kushi."* In Nihon kindai engekishi kenkyūkai, *Nihon no kindai gikyoku,* 63–77.

Senuma Natsuba, ed. *Meiji bungaku zenshū* 82: *Meiji joryū bungakushū* 2. Chikuma shobō, 1965.

Sofue Shōji and Asada Shōjirō, eds. *Nihon kindai bungaku taikei,* vol. 49: *Kindai gikyokushū.* Kadokawa shoten, 1974.

Suzuki Senzaburō. *"Tanizoko."* In *Jirōkichi zange hoka 4-hen: Gendai kyakuhon sōsho* 11, 69–106. Shinchōsha, 1923.

———. *"Tanizoko."* In Nihon kindai engekishi kenkyūkai, *Nihon no kindai gikyoku,* 105–118.

———. *Suzuki Senzaburō zenshū.* Edited by Kagayama Naozō. Osaka: Puratonsha, 1925.

Tanaka Chikao. "Ofukuro." In *Tanaka Chikao gikyoku zenshū* 1, 7–55. Hakusuisha, 1976.

Toita Yasuji, ed. *Meiji bungaku zenshū* 85: *Meiji shigekishū.* Chikuma shoten, 1966.

Tsubouchi Shōyō et al., eds. *Nihon gikyoku zenshū,* vols. 33–54: *Gendai hen.* Shun'yōdō, 1928–1930.

Drama in English Translation

The following is a selected bibliography of mostly prewar Japanese plays in translation. For a more comprehensive bibliography of works translated into English, see Kevin J. Wetmore, "Modern Japanese Drama in English" (bibliography), Asian Theatre Journal 23, no. 1 (Spring 2006): 177–205.

Bell, Eric S., and Eiji Ukai, eds. *Eminent Authors of Contemporary Japan: One-Act Plays and Short Stories.* 2 vols. Tokyo: Kaitaku-sha, 1930.

Clark, Barrett Harper, ed. *World Drama: An Anthology.* New York: Dover Publications, 1960.

Goodman, David G. *After Apocalypse: Four Japanese Plays of Hiroshima and Nagasaki.* Ithaca, NY: Cornell East Asia Series 71, 1994.

Hasegawa Shigure. *Wavering Traces* (*Chōji midare*, 1911). Translated by Carole Cavanaugh. In Kelly, *Modern Drama by Women 1880s–1930s*.

Iwasaki Yozan and Glenn Hughes, eds. and trans. *New Plays from Japan*. London: Ernest Benn, 1930.

———. *Three Modern Japanese Plays*. New York: Core Collection Books, 1976.

Kelly, Katherine E., ed. *Modern Drama by Women 1880s–1930s: An International Anthology*. London and New York: Routledge, 1996.

Kikuchi Kan. "The Saviour of the Moment." In *The Passion by S. Mushakoji and Three Other Plays*, translated by Noboru Hidaka with an introduction by Gregg M. Sinclair. Honolulu: Oriental Literature Society, 1933.

———. *Tojuro's Love and Four Other Plays by Kikuchi Kwan*. Translated by Glenn W. Shaw. Tokyo: Hokuseidō, 1925. [Translations of *Katakiuchi ijō, Chichi kaeru, Okujō no kyōjin, Kiseki,* and *Tōjūrō no koi*.]

Kishida Kunio. *Five Plays by Kishida Kunio*. Edited and translated by David G. Goodman. Ithaca, NY: Cornell East Asia Series, 1989. [Translations of *Nyonin katsugō, Shūu, Ochiba nikki, Kami fūsen,* and *Sawa-shi no futari musume*.]

———. "It Will Be Fine Tomorrow" (Ashita wa tenki). In *Eminent Authors of Contemporary Japan*, vol. 2, translated by Eiji Ukai and Eric Bell. Tokyo: Kaitakusha, 1931.

———. "Roof Garden" (Okujō no teien). In *The Passion by S. Mushakoji and Three Other Plays*, translated by Noboru Hidaka with an introduction by Gregg M. Sinclair. Honolulu: Oriental Literature Society, 1933.

———. "The Swing" (Buranko). Translated by David G. Goodman. In *The New Columbia Anthology of Modern Japanese Literature*, edited by J. Thomas Rimer and Van Gessel. New York: Columbia University Press, 2004.

Kōri Torahiko. *The Complete Works of Torahiko Kōri: The English Works with a Memoir by Hester Sainsbury*. Tokyo: Sōgensha, 1936.

Kubo Sakae. *The Land of Volcanic Ash* (*Kazan baichi*). Translated by David G. Goodman. Ithaca, NY: Cornell East Asia Series, 1986.

Kurata Hyakuzō. *The Priest and His Disciples* (*Shukke to sono deshi*). Translated by Glenn W. Shaw. Tokyo: Hokuseidō, Foreign Division Kyobunkan, 1922.

Mayama Seika. "Genboku and Chōei" (Genboku to Chōei). Translated by Brian Powell. *Nissan Occasional Papers Series*, no. 26, 1996.

———. "Yoritomo's Death: A *Shin Kabuki* Play" (Yoritomo no shi). Translated by Brian Powell. *Asian Theatre Journal* 17, no. 1 (Spring 2000): 1–33.

Mori Ōgai. *The Ikuta River* (*Ikutagawa*, 1910). Translated by Andrew Hall. In Mori, *Not a Song Like Any Other: An Anthology of Writings by Mori Ōgai*, edited by J. Thomas Rimer. Honolulu: University of Hawai'i Press, 2004, 150–161.

———. *Masks* (*Kamen*, 1909). Translated by James Vardaman. In Mori, *Youth and Other Stories*, edited by J. Thomas Rimer, 291–311. Honolulu: University of Hawai'i Press, 1994.

———. *Shizuka* (1910). Translated by Andrew Hall. In Mori, *Not a Song Like Any Other*, 162–171.

———. *Without Introductions* (*Nanoriso*, 1911). Translated by Andrew Hall. In Mori, *Not a Song Like Any Other*, 172–184.

Mushakōji Saneatsu. "Bodhidharma" (Bōdidaruma), "I Don't Know Either" (Watashi mo shiranai), and "Monk Ikkyū" (Aru hi no Ikkyū oshō). Translated by Hirano Umeyo. In *Buddhist Plays from Japanese Literature*, translated and edited by Hirano Umeyo. Tokyo: CIIB, 1962.

———. *"The Passion"* (Aiyoku). In *The Passion by S. Mushakoji and Three Other Plays*, translated by Noboru Hidaka with an introduction by Gregg M. Sinclair. Honolulu: Oriental Literature Society, 1933. [Repr. Westport, Conn.: Greenwood Press, 1971.]

Nakamura Kichizō. *The Death of Ii Tairo* (*Ii Tairō no shi*). Translated by Mock Joya. Tokyo: Japan Times, 1927.

———. "The Razor" (Kamisori). Translated by Yozan Iwasaki and Glenn Hughes. In *Three Modern Japanese Plays*, edited and translated by Yozan Iwasaki and Glenn Hughes. New York: Core Collection Books, 1976.

Shay, Frank, ed. *Fifty More Contemporary One-Act Plays*. New York: D. Appleton, 1928.

Suzuki Senzaburō. "Burning Her Alive" (Hiaburi). Translated by Yozan Iwasaki and Glenn Hughes. In *New Plays from Japan*. London: Ernest Benn, 1930.

———. "Living Koheiji" (Ikiteiru Koheiji). In *The Passion by S. Mushakoji and Three Other Plays*, translated by Noboru Hidaka with an introduction by Gregg M. Sinclair. Honolulu: Oriental Literature Society, 1933.

Tanizaki Jun'ichirō. "The Man with the Mandolin" (Mandorin o hiku otoko). Translated by Donald Keene. *New Directions*, no. 24. New York: New Directions, 1972.

———. "Okuni and Gohei" (Okuni to Gohei). Translated by John K. Gillespie. In *The New Columbia Anthology of Modern Japanese Literature*, edited by J. Thomas Rimer and Van Gessel. New York: Columbia University Press, 2004.

Tsubouchi Shōyō. "En the Ascetic." Translated in Keenan, *"En no gyōja."*

———. *A Sinking Moon over the Lonely Castle Where the Cuckoo Cries*. Translated by J. Thomas Rimer. In Brandon and Leiter, *Kabuki Plays on Stage*.

———. *Urashima: A Drama of the New Style* (*Shinkyoku urashima*). Translated by Furusawa Kwanshō. Urawa: Furusawa, 1936.

Yamamoto Yūzō. "A Case of Child Murder" (Eiji-goroshi). Translated by Eric S. Bell and TadaYoshinobu. In *Eminent Authors of Contemporary Japan: One-Act Plays and Short Stories*, vol. 1, edited by Eric S. Bell and Eiji Ukai. Tokyo: Kaitaku-sha, 1930.

―――. *Three Plays*. Translated by Glenn W. Shaw. Tokyo: Hokuseidō, 1935. [Translations of *Tōjin Okichi, Seimei no kanmuri*, and *Sakazaki dewa no kami*.]

General Criticism and History

Abe Itaru. *Kindaigeki bungaku no kenkyū*. Ōfū-sha, 1980.

―――. "Tanaka Chikao no shoki gikyoku: *Ofukuro* kara *Hi no Yama* made." *Engeki-gaku* 22 (1981): 20–34.

Abe Kōichi. *Dorama no gendai: Engeki/eiga/bungaku ronshū* Kindai bungei-sha 1993.

Akiba Tarō. *Nihon shingekishi*. 2 vols. Risō-sha, 1971 [1956].

Andrews, Malcolm. *Charles Dickens and His Performing Selves: Dickens and the Public Readings*. Oxford: Oxford University Press, 2006.

Betsuyaku Minoru. "Taiwa buntai no ronri: Tanaka Chikao *Ofukuro* yori" (1). *Shingeki* 23, no. 2 (February 1976): 66–75.

―――. "Taiwa buntai no ronri: Tanaka Chikao *Ofukuro* yori" (2). *Shingeki* 23, no. 4 (April 1976): 70–82.

Boscaro, Adriana, Franco Gatti, and Massimo Raveni, eds. *Rethinking Japan*, vol. 1: *Literature*. Sandgate, Folkstone, Kent: Japan Library, 1990.

Bowring, Richard. *Mori Ōgai and the Modernization of Japanese Culture*. Cambridge: Cambridge University Press, 1979.

Brandon, James R., and Samuel L. Leiter, eds. *Kabuki Plays on Stage*, vol. 4: *Restoration and Reform, 1872–1905*. Honolulu: University of Hawai'i Press, 2003.

Brooks, Peter. *The Melodramatic Imagination: Balzac, Henry James, and the Mode of Excess*. New Haven, CT: Yale University Press, 1976.

Chiba Shunji, ed. *Kanshō Nihon gendai bungaku: Tanizaki Jun'ichirō*. Kadokawa shoten, 1982.

Chikamatsu, Monzaemon. *Four Major Plays of Chikamatsu*. Translated and edited by Donald Keene. New York: Columbia University Press, 1964.

Derrida, Jacques. "The Theatre of Cruelty and the Closure of Representation." In *Writing and Difference*, translated by Alan Bass, 232–250. Chicago: University of Chicago Press, 1978.

Dōmoto Masaki. *Dentō to gendai*. San'ichi shobō, 1971.

Endō Tasuke. "Kindai ni okeru gikyoku jidai: Sono seiritsu no ichimen." *Nihon kindai bungaku* 6 (May 1967): 27–39.

Engekijin kaigi, ed. *Engekijin* 1 (Spring 1998).

——. *Engekijin* 4 (January 2000).

"*Engeki shinchō* kaiwadan 6." *Engeki shinchō* 1, no. 7 (July 1924): 27–46.

"*Engeki shinchō* kaiwadan 7." *Engeki shinchō* 1, no. 8 (August 1924): 23–45.

Fujiki Hiroyuki. "Gaikotsu no buchō." In Nihon kindai engekishi kenkyūkai, *20-seiki no gikyoku*, 1:208–214.

——. "Gikyokushi 3." In Tsugami, Sugai, and Kagawa, *Gikyokuron (Engekiron kōza* 5).

——. "Shingeki no seiiritsu ni tsuite no ichikōsatsu." *Engekigaku ronshū (Nihon engekigakkai kiyō)* 4 (March 1961).

——. "Taishōki no gikyoku 1: 1910-nendai no gekisakka." *Higeki kigeki* 29, no. 11 (November 1976): 37–45.

——. "Taishōki no gikyoku 2: 1920-nendai no gekisakka." *Higeki kigeki* 29, no. 12 (December 1976): *Tokushū: Taishō no gikyoku*, 2, 40–46.

——. "Tsukiji Shōgkijō no sōsakugeki." *Higeki kigeki* 30, no. 9 (September 1977): 8–15.

Goodman, David G., ed. *Five Plays by Kishida Kunio*. Ithaca, NY: Cornell East Asia Series, 1989.

Hachimonjiya Jishō, ed. *The Actors' Analects (Yakusha rongo)*. Edited and translated by Charles Dunn and Bunzō Torigoe. New York: Columbia University Press, 1969.

Hagii Kōzō. *Shinpa no gei*. Tōkyō shoseki, 1984.

Hanibuchi Yasuko. "Suzuki Senzaburō *Tanizoko*." In Nihon kindai engekishi kenkyūkai, *20-seiki no gikyoku*, 1:192–195.

Hasegawa Shigure. *Jōnetsu no onna: Kindai josei sakka senshū* 28. Yumani shobō, 2000.

Hayashi Hirochika. "Engeki no kindai o meguru shiteki oboegaki." *Kokugo to kokubungaku* 74, no. 5 (May 1997): 31–44.

——. "Gikyoku." *Bungaku/Gogaku* 175 (February 2003): *Tokushū: Heisei 13nen kokugo kokubungakkukai no dōkō: Kindai*, 118–122.

——. "Okada Yachiyo *Tsuge no kushi* o yomu." *Engekigaku ronshū* 43 (October 2005): *Nihon engekigakkai kiyō*, 147–164.

Henny, Sue, and Jean-Pierre Lehmann, eds. *Themes and Theories in Modern Japanese History: Essays in Memory of Richard Storry*. London: Athlone Press, 1988.

Hijikata Teiichi, ed. *Meiji bungaku zenshū*, vol. 79: *Meiji geijutsu/bungaku ronshū*. Chikuma shobō, 1975.

——, ed. "Mori Ōgai to Meiji Bigakushi." In Hijikata, *Meiji bungaku zenshū*, vol. 79.

Hijiya-Kirschnereit, Irmela, ed. *Canon and Identity: Japanese Modernization Reconsidered: Trans-cultural Perspectives*. Munich: Iudicium, 2000.

Hirata Oriza. *Engeki no kotoba.* Iwanami shoten, 2004.

———. *Engeki nyūmon.* Kōdansha gendai shinsho, 1998.

———. *Gendai kōgo engeki no tame ni.* Benseisha, 1995.

Horie-Webber, Akemi. "Modernization of the Japanese Theatre: The S*hingeki* Movement." In *Modern Japan: Aspects of History, Literature and Society,* edited by William G. Beasley, 147–165. Berkeley: University of California Press, 1975.

Hoshō Masao. "Kishida Kunio made." *Higeki kigeki* 43, no. 8: *Tokushū: Nihon no kindaigeki o kangaeru* (August 1990): 22–28.

Ihara Seiseien [Toshirō]. *Meiji engekishi.* Ōtori shuppan, 1975 (reprint).

Imamura Tadazumi, ed. *Sakka no jiden* 48: *Yamamoto Yūzō.* Nihon tosho sentā, 1997.

———. "Serifu kara mita kindaigeki." *Higeki kigeki* 43, no. 8 (August 1990): 8–14.

Inoue, Megumi. "Why Did *Sewamono* Not Grow into Modern Realist Theatre?" In Jortner, McDonald, and Wetmore, *Modern Japanese Theatre and Performance,* 3–15.

Inoue Yoshie. "Akita Ujaku *Gaikotsu no buchō* tōjō no igi." *Shakai bungaku* 8 (July 1994): 60–65.

———. "Bunkakai/Nihon kindai engekishi kenkyūkai." In *Nihon engeki gakkai kiyō* 18: *Tokushū: Nihon no kindai engeki* (1979), 107–110.

———. "Hasegawa Shigure *Aru hi no gogo.*" In Nihon kindai engekishi kenkyūkai, *20-seiki no gikyoku,* 1:119–122.

———. *Kindai engeki no tobira o akeru.* Shakai hyōronsha, 1999.

———. "Okada Yachiyo *Tsuge no kushi.*" In Nihon kindai engekishi kenkyūkai, *20-seiki no gikyoku,* 1:123–126.

Ishibashi Ningetsu, *Gikyokuron.* In Nomura and Fujiki, *Kindai bungaku hyōron taikei,* 312–316.

Iwasa Shin'ichi. "Kyōka-mono no jōen." *Kokubungaku: Kaishaku to kanshō* 14, no. 5 (May 1949): 37–45.

Izumi Kyōka. *Kyōka zenshū.* 29 vols. Iwanami shoten, 1988–1990.

Jortner, David, Keiko McDonald, and Kevin J. Wetmore Jr., eds. *Modern Japanese Theatre and Performance.* Lanham, MD: Lexington Books, 2006.

Kamiyama Akira. "'Shizenshugi' no naka no 'Edo': Hōgetsu, Ryūgai shinpa no hitobito." In *Engekigaku ronshū* (*Nihon engeki gakkai kiyō*) 37 (1999): *Tokushū: Nihon no kindai engeki,* 281–307.

Kamiyama Akira, Saitō Tomoko, Seto Hiroshi, Nagata Yasushi, and Mōri Mitsuya. "Hyōgenshi ni okeru riarizumu" (panel discussion). *Engekigaku ronshū* (*Nihon engeki gakkai kiyō*) 38 (October 2002): 45–78.

Kanbayashi Gorō. "Kikuchi, Kume, Yamamoto." *Higeki kigeki* 39, no. 2 (February 1986): *Tokushū: Kikuchi Kan to Kume Masao,* 30–31.

Kaneko Sachiyo. "Nora no yukue: Mori Ōgai to Ipusen no gikyoku." In *Mori Ōgai kenkyū* 3, 112–136. Izumi shoin, 1989.

———. "Ōgai to *Kabuki.*" In *Mori Ōgai kenkyū* 6, 215–233. Izumi shoin, 1995.

Kano, Ayako. *Acting like a Woman in Modern Japan: Theater, Gender, and Nationalism.* New York: Palgrave, 2001.

———. "Enchi Fumiko's *Stormy Days: Arashi* and the Drama of Childbirth." *Monumenta Nipponica* 61, no. 1 (Spring 2006): 59–91.

Karatani Kōjin. *Origins of Modern Japanese Literature.* Translation edited by Brett de Bary. Durham, NC: Duke University Press, 1993.

Kataoka Teppei, Okamoto Kanoko, Ueda Fumiko et al. "*Kōri no ame* gappyō." *Nyonin geijutsu* 2, no. 12 (December 1928): 120–131.

Katō Mamoru, ed. *Nihon gikyoku sōmokuroku: 1880–1980.* Yokohama: Yokohama engeki kenkyūjo, 1985.

Kawasaki Akira. "Kubota Mantarō ni okeru gikyoku no hōhō—shoki no sakuhin ni tsuite." *Bungei kenkyū* 34 (April 1960): 30–38.

Keenan, Linda Klepinger. "*En no gyōja:* The Legend of a Holy Man in Twelve Centuries of Japanese Literature." PhD dissertation, University of Wisconsin–Madison, 1989.

Keene, Donald. *Dawn to the West: Japanese Literature of the Modern Era.* 2 vols. New York: Holt, Rinehart and Winston, 1984.

———, ed. and trans. *Four Major Plays of Chikamatsu.* New York: Columbia University Press, 1961.

Kikuchi Kan. "*Chichi Kaeru* no koto." In *Kikuchi Kan zenshū* 14, 387–391. Chūō kōronsha, 1938.

———. "Ichimakumono ni tsuite." *Engeki shinchō* 1, no. 2 (February 1924): 2–5.

Kinoshita Junji. *Nihongo no sekai* 12: *Gikyoku no Nihongo.* Chūō kōronsha, 1982.

Kishida Kunio. *Kishida Kunio zenshū.* 28 vols. Iwanami shoten, 1989–1992.

Kitamura Tōkoku. "Gekishi no zento ikaga" (What lies ahead for drama?). In *Tōkoku zenshū*, vol. 2, edited by Katsumoto Sei'ichirō, 333–341. Iwanami shoten, 1964.

Komiya Toyotaka. *Japanese Music and Drama in the Meiji Era.* Translated and adapted by Donald Keene. Tokyo: Tōyō bunko, 1969.

Kōno Toshirō. "Kikuchi Kan, Kume Masao no gikyoku no ichizuke." In *Higeki kigeki* 39, no. 2 (February 1986): *Tokushū: Kikuchi Kan to Kume Masao,* 8–13.

———. "Suzuki Senzaburō—*Gendai kyakuhon sōsho Jirokichi zange* o megutte." *Higeki kigeki* 43, no. 8 (August 1980): 15–21.

Kubo Sakae. "Mayoeru rearizumu." In *Kubo Sakae zenshū* 6 (San'ichi shobō, 1962), 117–125.

Kurahashi Sei'ichirō. *Shingeki nendaiki: Senzen hen.* Hakusuisha, 1966.

Kurata Yoshihiro. *Nihon kindai shisō taikei* 18: *Geinō*. Iwanami shoten, 1988.

Lee, William. "Chikamatsu and Dramatic Literature in the Meiji Period." In *Inventing the Classics*, edited by Haruo Shirane and Tomi Suzuki, 179–198. New York: Columbia University Press, 2000.

Leiter, Samuel L. *Frozen Moments: Writings on Kabuki, 1966–2001*. Ithaca, NY: Cornell East Asia Series, 2002.

———, ed. *A Kabuki Reader: History and Performance*. Armonk, NY: M. E. Sharpe, 2001.

Lukacs, Györgi. "The Sociology of Modern Drama" (1914). Translated by Lee Baxandall. In *The Theory of the Modern Stage*, edited by Eric Bentley, 425–450. Harmondsworth: Penguin Books, 1968.

Maeda Ai. *Text and the City: Essays on Japanese Modernity*. Edited with an introduction by James Fujii. Durham, NC: Duke University Press, 2004.

Matsumoto Shinko. *Meiji engekiron shi*. Engeki shuppan-sha, 1980.

Miller, J. Scott. *Adaptations of Western Literature in Meiji Japan*. New York and Basingstoke: Palgrave, 2001.

Miner, Earl. *Comparative Poetics: An Intercultural Essay on Theories of Literature*. Princeton, NJ: Princeton University Press, 1990.

Mishima, Yukio. *Death in Midsummer and Other Stories*. Harmondsworth: Penguin Books, 1971.

Miyoshi Yukio and Takemori Tenyū, eds. *Taishō bungaku no shosō* (*Kindai bungaku* 4). Yūhikaku, 1977.

Mōri Mitsuya. "Ipusen izen: Meijiki no engeki kindaika o meguru mondai (1)." *Bigaku/bijutsushi ronshū* 6 (July 1987): *Seijō daigaku daigakuin bungaku kenkyūkai*, 3–39.

———. "Ipusen izen: Meijiki no engeki kindaika o meguru mondai (2)." *Bigaku/bijutsushi ronshū* 7 (November 1988): 3–37.

———. "Ipusen shoen zengo (1): Meijiki no engeki kindaika o meguru mondai (3)." *Bigaku/bijutsushi ronshū* 10 (September 1995): 171–198.

———. "Ipusen shoen zengo (2): Meijiki no engeki kindaika o meguru mondai (4)." *Bigaku/bijutsushi ronshū* 12 (March 1999): 119–144.

———. "Thinking and Feeling: Characteristics of Intercultural Theatre." In Scholz-Cionca and Leiter, *Japanese Theatre and the International Stage*, 357–365.

Mori Ōgai. *Not a Song Like Any Other: An Anthology of Writings by Mori Ōgai*, edited by J. Thomas Rimer. Honolulu: University of Hawai'i Press, 2004.

———. "Surprised by the Prejudice of Theatre Reformers" (Engeki kairyō ronja no henken ni odoroku). Translated by Keiko McDonald. In Mori, *Not a Song Like Any Other*, 145–149.

————. *Youth and Other Stories.* Edited by J. Thomas Rimer. Honolulu: University of Hawai'i Press, 1994.

Muramatsu Sadataka. *Izumi Kyōka jiten.* Yūseidō, 1982.

Nagahira Kazuo. "*Chichi kaeru* no doramaturugii." In *Kindai bungaku 4: Taishō bungaku no shōsō,* edited by Miyoshi Yukio and Takemori Ten'yū, 133–140. Yūhikaku, 1977.

————. *Engeki kairyō ronshū.* Kuresu shuppan, 1998.

————. *Kindai gikyoku no sekai.* Tokyo daigaku shuppankai, 1972.

Nakamura Tetsurō. *Kabuki no kindaika: Sakka to sakuhin.* Iwanami shoten, 2006.

Nakazawa Hiroshi. "Shi no butō o odoru hitobito—Akita Ujaku to hyōgenshugi." *Shōnan kokusai joshi tanki daigaku kiyō* 10 (2002): 146–136 [21–31].

National Information Service for Earthquake Engineering. http://nisee.berkeley.edu/kanto/yokohama.html (accessed August 12, 2005).

Nihon engeki kyōkai, ed. *Shōwa Taishō gekishū.* Engeki shuppansha, 1989.

Nihon kindai engekishi kenkyūkai. *20-seiki no gikyoku 1: Nihon kindai gikyoku no sekai.* Shakai hyōronsha, 1998.

————. *20-seiki no gikyoku 2: Gendai gikyoku no tenkai.* Shakai hyōronsha, 2002.

Nishimura Hiroko. "Kindaigeki ryaku nenpyō." *Kokubungaku kaishaiku to kanshō* 27, no. 3, 173–181.

————. *Sanjō no senshi: Nihon kindaigeki no doramaturugii.* Kanrin shobō, 2002.

————. "Suzuki Senzaburō kenkyū—Suzuki Mariko-shi shozō no mihappyō shiryō to *Ikiteiru Koheiji.*" *Engekigaku* 21 (1980): 40–70.

Nomura Takashi. *Gikyoku to butai.* Libroport, 1995.

Nomura Takashi and Fujiki Hiroyuki, eds. *Kindai Nihon bungaku hyōron taikei,* vol. 9: *Engekiron.* Kadokawa shoten, 1985.

Ochi Haruo. *Kyōka to gikyoku.* Sunago shobō, 1987.

————. *Meiji Taishō no gekibungaku.* Hanawa shobō, 1971.

Ogata Akiko. "Watarikiranu hashi—Hasegawa Shigure, sono sei to sakuhin." In *Feminizumi hihyō e no shōtai: Kindai josei bungaku o yomu,* edited by Ogata Akiko et al. Gakugei shorin, 1995.

Osanai Kaoru. *Osanai Kaoru engekiron zenshū,* edited by Sugai Yukio. 5 vols. Miraisha, 1964–1968.

————. *Osanai Kaoru zenshū.* Kyoto: Rinsen shobō, 1975.

Ōsone Shōsuke. *Gekibungaku: Kenkyū shiryō sōsho (Nihon koten bungaku 10).* Meiji shoin, 1983.

Ōta Shōgo. "Heya-saki no hana: Kishida Kunio ni okeru geki kōzō ni tsuite." *Shingeki* 23, no. 9 (September 1976): *Tokushū: Kishida Kunio,* 139–144.

Ottaviani, Gioia. "'Difference' and 'Reflexivity': Osanai Kaoru and the *Shingeki* Movement." *Asian Theater Journal* 11, no. 2 (Fall 1994): 213–230.

———. "The *Shingeki* Movement until 1930." In Boscaro, Gatti, and Raveni, *Rethinking Japan*, 178–183.

Ōyama Isao. *Kindai Nihon gikyokushi*. 4 vols. Yamagata: Kindai Nihon gikyokushi kankōkai, 1968.

Ōzasa Yoshio. "Godoku no naka ni shōritsu shita Kishida Kunio zō." *Chūō kōron* 119, no. 10 (October 2004): 254–263.

———. *Nihon gendai engekishi*. 8 vols. Hakusuisha, 1987.

Poulton, M. Cody. "The Rhetoric of the Real." In Jortner, McDonald, and Wetmore, *Modern Japanese Theatre and Performance*, 17–32.

———. *Spirits of Another Sort: The Plays of Izumi Kyōka*. Ann Arbor: Center for Japanese Studies, University of Michigan Press, 2001.

Powell, Brian W. F. "Japan's First Modern Stage: The Tsukiji Shōgekijō and Its Company, 1924–26." *Monumenta Nipponica* 30, no. 1 (Spring 1975): 69–85.

———. *Japan's Modern Theatre: A Century of Continuity and Change*. London: Routledge Curzon, 2002.

———. *Kabuki in Modern Japan: Mayama Seika and His Plays*. Houndmills, Basingstoke, Hampshire: Macmillan in association with St. Antony's College, Oxford, 1990.

———. "A Parable of the Modern Theatre in Japan: The Debate between Osanai Kaoru and Mayama Seika, 1909." In Henny and Lehmann, *Themes and Theories in Modern Japanese History*.

Rimer, J. Thomas. "Four Plays by Tanaka Chikao." *Monumenta Nipponica* 31, no. 3 (1976): 275–298.

———. *Toward a Modern Japanese Theatre: Kishida Kunio*. Princeton, NJ: Princeton University Press, 1974.

Rimer, J. Thomas, and Van C. Gessel, eds. *The Columbia Anthology of Modern Japanese Literature*, vol. 1: *From Restoration to Occupation, 1868–1945*. New York: Columbia University Press, 2005.

Saeki Junko. *Izumi Kyōka*. Chikuma shobō, 2000.

———. "Izumi Kyōka to shichōkaku geijutsu." *Uryū tsūshin* 26 (April 2003): 28–31.

Saeki Ryūkō. *Gendai engeki no kigen*. Renga shobō shinsha, 1999.

Saitō Yasuhide. "Gikyokuron kara mita kindaigeki." *Higeki kigeki* 43, no. 8 (August 1990): *Tokushū: Nihon no kindaigeki o kangaeru*, 29–35.

Sakai Shinnosuke. "Kindai gikyoku no tenkai—sono kokoromi: Ōgai made." *Nihon kindai bungaku* 6 (May 1967): *Tokushū: Kindai gikyoku*, 14–26.

Schamoni, Wolfgang. "The Rise of 'Literature' in Early Meiji." In Hijiya-Kirschnereit, *Canon and Identity*.

Scholz-Cionca, Stanca, and Samuel L. Leiter, eds. *Japanese Theatre and the International Stage*. Leiden: Brill, 2001.

Seki Minoru. "Kindaigikyoku no jōen o tōshite: Enshutsuka sengen 2003." *Engekijin*, no. 13 (2003): *Tokushū: Enshutsuka sengen*, 42–45.

Senuma Natsuba, ed. *Meiji bungaku zenshū 82: Meiji joryū bungakushū 2*. Chikuma shobō, 1965.

Seto, Hiroshi, ed. *Engekigaku ronshū (Nihon engeki gakkai kiyō)* 38: *Tokushū riarizumu no engeki*. October 2000.

Shillony, Ben-Ami. *Politics and Culture in Wartime Japan*. New York: Oxford University Press, 1981.

Shōyō kyōkai, ed. *Shōyō senshū*. 17 vols. Daiichi shobō, 1977–1978.

Singer, Ben. *Melodrama and Modernity: Early Sensational Cinema and Its Contexts*. New York: Columbia University Press, 2001.

Sofue Shōji. "Kantō daishinsai to engeki." *Shakai bungaku* 8 (July 1994): 25–37.

———. "Kindaigeki shuyō sankō bunken annai." *Kokubungaku kaishaku to kanshō* 27, no. 3 (March 1962): *Tokushū: Kindaigeki no rikai no tame ni*, 170–172.

———. *Kindai Nihon bungaku e no tansaku: Sono hōhō to shisō to*. Miraisha, 1990.

———. "Shōwa jūnendai to shingeki: Sono ichimen ni tsuite no mitorizu." *Kokubungaku kaishaku to kanshō* 27, no. 3 (March 1962): 41–47.

Steiner, George. *Language and Silence: Essays on Language, Literature and the Inhuman*. New York: Atheneum, 1967.

Suematsu Kenchō. "Engeki kairyō iken." In Nomura and Fujiki, *Kindai bungaku hyōron taikei*, 18–19.

Sugai Yukio. "Engeki sōzō no keifu." In *Nihon kindai engekishi kenkyū*. Aoki shoten, 1983.

———. *Kindai Nihon engeki ronsōshi*. Miraisha, 1979.

———. "Nihon kindai engekishi kenkyū e no shikaku." In *Engekigaku ronshū (Nihon engeki gakkai kiyō)* 18 (1979): 1–14.

———. "Osanai Kaoru ron." In Osanai, *Osanai Kaoru engekiron zenshū 5*.

———. "Osanai Kaoru ron 1, 2, 3." In *Engeki no dentō to gendai*. Miraisha, 1969.

———. "Osanai Kaoru to Tsukiji Shōgekijō." *Kokubungaku kaishaku to kanshō* 27, no. 3 (March 1962): 34–40.

Suwa Haruo. *Edo: Sono geinō to bungaku*. Mainichi shinbunsha, 1976.

Suwa Haruo and Sugai Yukio, eds. *Kōza Nihon no engeki*. 8 vols. Benseisha, 1992–1998.

Szondi, Peter. *Theory of the Modern Drama*. Translated and edited by Michael Hays. Minneapolis: University of Minnesota Press, 1987.

Takada Mizuho. "Kubota Mantarō *Ōdera gakkō* no seikaku." *Kokubungaku kaishaku to kyōzai no kenkyū* 11, no. 11 (October 1966): 91–95.

Takahashi, Yuichirō. "*Kabuki* Goes Official: The 1878 Opening of the Shintomi-za." In *A Kabuki Reader,* edited by Samuel L. Leiter, 123–151. Armonk, NY: M. E. Sharpe, 2002.

Tanaka Chikao. *Gekibungaku.* Kadokawa shoten, 1959.

———. *Gekiteki buntairon josetsu.* 2 vols. Hakusuisha, 1977.

Tanaka Eizō. *Meiji Taishō shingekishi shiryō.* Engeki shuppansha, 1964.

Tanaka Hajime. *Kindaigeki (Nihon bungaku kyōyō kōza* 12). Shibundō, 1951.

Tanizaki Jun'ichirō. *Tanizaki Jun'ichirō zenshū.* 30 vols. Chūō kōron, 1982–1983.

Toyama Masakazu. *Engeki kairyōron shikō.* In *Meiji bungaku zenshū* 79: *Meiji geijutsu, bungaku ronshū,* edited by Hijikata Teiichi, 138–148. Chikuma shobō, 1975.

Tschudin, Jean-Jacques. *La Ligue du Théâtre Prolétarien Japonais.* Paris: L'Harmattan, 1989.

Tsubouchi Shōyō. "Suematsu-kun no engeki kairyōron o yomu" (Reading Suematsu's theory of theatre reform). In Nomura and Fujiki, *Kindai bungaku hyōron taikei,* 24–26.

———. "Wagakuni no shigeki." In Nomura and Fujiki, *Kindai bungaku hyōron,* 49–60.

———. "Wagakuni no shigeki." In *Tsubouchi Shōyō-shū: Meiji bungaku zenshū* 16, edited by Inagaki Tatsurō, 287–315. Chikuma shobō, 1969.

Tsugami Tadashi, Sugai Yukio, and Kagawa Yoshinari, eds. *Gikyokuron (Engekiron kōza* 5). Shōbunsha, 1977.

Tsuno Kaitarō. *Kokkei na kyojin: Tsubouchi Shōyō no yume.* Heibonsha, 2002.

Uchimura Naoya. "*Ofukuro* hoka." *Higeki kigeki* 38, no. 5 (May 1985): *Tanaka Chikao tokushū,* 20–21.

Uchiyama Jun. "Kinen kōen o enshutsu shite—*Suishagoya* to *Gaikotsu no buchō.*" *Higeki kigeki* 39, no. 6 (June 1986): 24–26.

Ueno Chizuko. *Ueno Chizuko ga bungaku o shakaigaku suru.* Asahi bunko shinkan, 2007.

Vardac, Nicholas. *Stage to Screen: Theatrical Method from Garrick to Griffith.* Cambridge, MA: Harvard University Press, 1949.

Wakashiro Kiiko. "Watakushi gikyoku *Tsuge no kushi:* Okada Yachiyo no jiga." *Higeki kigeki* 35, no. 1 (January 1982): *Tokushū: joryū sakka,* 11–13.

Waseda daigaku gikyoku kenkyūkai, ed. *Genkyoku ni yoru Nihon gikyokushi.* Awaji shobō, 1956.

———, ed. *Genten Nihon gikyokushi.* Harima shobō, 1954.

Watanabe Kazutami. "Kishida Kunio to Osanai Kaoru." *Bungaku* 48, no. 7 (1980): 1–18, 55–56.

Watanabe Tamotsu. "Kaisetsu: Kannō to zetsubō." In Hasegawa, *Jōnetsu no onna.*

Weisenfeld, Gennifer S. *Mavo: Japanese Artists and the Avant-Garde.* Berkeley: University of California Press, 2002.

Wetmore, Kevin J. "Modern Japanese Drama in English" (bibliography). *Asian Theatre Journal* 23, no. 1 (Spring 2006): 177–205.

Yamada Hajime. *Kindaigeki* (*Nihon bungaku kyōyō kōza* 12). Shibundō, 1951.

Yamamoto Yūzō. "Chichi kaeru o mite." In *Yamamoto Yūzō* (*Sakka no jiden* 48), edited by Imamura Tadazumi, 20–24. Nihon tosho sentā, 1997.

Yanagita Kunio. "Kōshō bungei to wa nani ka." In *Yanagita Kunio zenshū* 8, 14–82. Chikuma bunko, 1990.

Yuasa Masako. "Gendai Nihon ni okeru junsui engeki kara fujōrigeki e no nagare no kōsatsu: Kishida Kunio, Betsuyaku Minoru, Iwamatsu Ryō." *Engekigaku ronshū* (*Nihon engeki gakkai kiyō*) 34 (1996): 23–37.

Index

absurdist, absurdism, xiv, 176–177
acting, actor: Japanese playing Europeans, 4, 20, 29, 40–42, 124; *kabuki*, viii, 1, 3, 4, 5, 7, 10, 11, 13, 15–16, 19, 30–31, 101, 192, 248n.13; modern drama, ix, 18, 20, 22, 23, 25, 30, 101, 132, 154–155, 206–207, 244n.6; *onnagata*, 4, 21–22, 23, 248n.13; *shingeki*, ix, 7, 31, 43, 130, 135, 154–155; *shin-kabuki*, 18, 20, 23, 31; *shinpa*, viii, x, xii, 1, 22, 23, 24, 31, 69, 101, 248n.13; status of, xii, 8, 10, 15–16, 20, 43, 86, 253n.19; women, 4, 21–22, 30
adaptation (*hon'an*): of classical Japanese drama, 18, 42; of Japanese novels, 131, 175; *shinpa*, 19–25, 48, 153; of Western drama, 4, 17, 18, 24, 30, 40, 244n.80. *See also* Shakespeare
adultery, viii, xiv, 69, 100. *See also* marriage
Akiba Tarō, 14, 48, 49
Akita Ujaku, vii, xiii, 33–34, 42, 129, 130, 134–138, 254n.1, 254n.7; plays, 130, 136–138
anarchism, anarchists, 122
angura theatre, 68
anthologies, 14, 31, 38–39
anti-dramatic, 37–38, 128
anti-theatrical, xi–xii, 154

Aoyama Sugisaku, 30, 131, 156
Arishima Takeo, vii, 31, 34, 129
Art Theatre (Geijutsu-za), 30, 129, 135
atarashii onna. *See* new woman
author. *See* fiction; playwrights
Auto da fé (*Hiaburi*), 100–101
avant-garde, 68, 137

Before the Dawn (*Yoake-mae*, fp. 1934), 131, 175
Betsuyaku Minoru, 9, 176, 207
Blue Stocking, The (*Seitō*), 47, 48, 192, 193
Boxwood Comb, The (*Tsuge no kushi*), xiv, 48–50, 257n.8
Brief Night (*Mijikayo*), xiv, 154–157
Bungaku-za. *See* Literary Theatre
Bungei Kyōkai. *See* Literary Society
bunmei kaika. *See* civilization and enlightenment
buyōgeki. *See* dance

censorship, 1–3, 136, 238n.4
Central Review, The (*Chūō Kōron*), 31, 86, 158
Chekhov, ix, 36, 42, 124, 125, 156, 173, 175, 192
Chichi Kaeru. *See* Father Returns
Chikamatsu Monzaemon, ix, 4, 10, 42